D1012813

"Fascinating and eminently enjoyable from the first page to the last, this skillfully written book is populated with unique characters who never bore. *Night Huntress* rocks! Don't miss it!"
—*Romance Reviews Today*

DRAGON WYTCH

"Action and sexy sensuality make this book hot to the touch."
—*Romantic Times* (★★★★)

"Ms. Galenorn has a great gift for spinning a compelling story. The supernatural action is a great blend of both fresh and familiar, the characters are each charming in their own way, the heroine's love life is scorching, and the worlds they all live in are well-defined." —*Darque Reviews*

"This is the kind of series that even those who do not care for the supernatural will find a very good read." —*Affaire de Coeur*

"If you're looking for an out-of-this-world, enchanting tale of magic and passion, *Dragon Wytch* is the story for you. I will be recommending this wickedly bewitching tale to everyone I know!" —*Dark Angel Reviews*

DARKLING

"The most fulfilling journey of self-discovery to date in the Otherworld series . . . An eclectic blend that works well." —*Booklist*

"Galenorn does a remarkable job of delving into the psyches and fears of her characters. As this series matures, so do her heroines. The sex sizzles and the danger fascinates." —*Romantic Times*

"The story is nonstop action and has deep, dark plots that kept me up reading long past my bedtime. Here be Dark Fantasy with a unique twist. YES!" —*Huntress Book Reviews*

"Pure fantasy enjoyment from start to finish. I adored the world that Yasmine Galenorn has crafted within the pages of this adventurous urban fantasy story. The characters come alive off the pages of the story with so many unique personalities . . . Yasmine Galenorn is a new author on my list of favorite authors."
—*Night Owl Romance*

continued . . .

CHANGELING

"The second in Galenorn's D'Artigo Sisters series ratchets up the danger and romantic entanglements. Along with the quirky humor and characters readers have come to expect is a moving tale of a woman more comfortable in her cat skin than in her human form, looking to find her place in the world." —*Booklist*

"Galenorn's thrilling supernatural series is gritty and dangerous, but it's the tumultuous relationships between all the various characters that give it depth and heart. Vivid, sexy, and mesmerizing, Galenorn's novel hits the paranormal sweet spot."
—*Romantic Times*

"I absolutely loved it!" —*Fresh Fiction*

"Yasmine Galenorn has created another winner . . . *Changeling* is a can't-miss read destined to hold a special place on your keeper shelf." —*Romance Reviews Today*

WITCHLING

"Reminiscent of Laurell K. Hamilton with a lighter touch . . . a delightful new series that simmers with fun and magic."
—Mary Jo Putney, *New York Times* bestselling author

"The first in an engrossing new series . . . a whimsical reminder of fantasy's importance in everyday life." —*Publishers Weekly*

"*Witchling* is pure delight . . . a great heroine, designer gear, dead guys, and Seattle precipitation!"
—MaryJanice Davidson, *New York Times* bestselling author

"Galenorn's kick-butt Fae ramp up the action in a wyrd world gone awry . . . I loved it!"
—Patricia Rice, *New York Times* bestselling author

"A fun read, filled with surprise and enchantment."
—Linda Winstead Jones

"*Witchling* is one sexy, fantastic paranormal-mystery-romantic read." —Terese Ramin

NIGHT VEIL

An Indigo Court Novel

YASMINE GALENORN

BERKLEY BOOKS, NEW YORK

THE BERKLEY PUBLISHING GROUP
Published by the Penguin Group
Penguin Group (USA) Inc.
375 Hudson Street, New York, New York 10014, USA
Penguin Group (Canada), 90 Eglinton Avenue East, Suite 700, Toronto, Ontario M4P 2Y3, Canada
(a division of Pearson Penguin Canada Inc.)
Penguin Books Ltd., 80 Strand, London WC2R 0RL, England
Penguin Group Ireland, 25 St. Stephen's Green, Dublin 2, Ireland (a division of Penguin Books Ltd.)
Penguin Group (Australia), 250 Camberwell Road, Camberwell, Victoria 3124, Australia
(a division of Pearson Australia Group Pty. Ltd.)
Penguin Books India Pvt. Ltd., 11 Community Centre, Panchsheel Park, New Delhi—110 017, India
Penguin Group (NZ), 67 Apollo Drive, Rosedale, Auckland 0632, New Zealand
(a division of Pearson New Zealand Ltd.)
Penguin Books (South Africa) (Pty.) Ltd., 24 Sturdee Avenue, Rosebank, Johannesburg 2196,
South Africa

Penguin Books Ltd., Registered Offices: 80 Strand, London WC2R 0RL, England

This is a work of fiction. Names, characters, places, and incidents either are the product of the author's imagination or are used fictitiously, and any resemblance to actual persons, living or dead, business establishments, events, or locales is entirely coincidental. The publisher does not have any control over and does not assume any responsibility for author or third-party websites or their content.

NIGHT VEIL

A Berkley Book / published by arrangement with the author

PRINTING HISTORY
Berkley mass-market edition / July 2011

Copyright © 2011 by Yasmine Galenorn.
Excerpt from *Courting Darkness* by Yasmine Galenorn copyright © by Yasmine Galenorn.
Cover art by Tony Mauro. Cover design by Rita Frangie.
Interior text design by Laura K. Corless.

ISBN: 978-0-425-24204-9

BERKLEY®
Berkley Books are published by The Berkley Publishing Group,
a division of Penguin Group (USA) Inc.,
375 Hudson Street, New York, New York 10014.
BERKLEY® is a registered trademark of Penguin Group (USA) Inc.
The "B" design is a trademark of Penguin Group (USA) Inc.

PRINTED IN THE UNITED STATES OF AMERICA

10 9 8 7 6 5 4 3 2 1

Dedicated to

Molly the Owl
for all she has taught me,
even though she doesn't know I exist.

ACKNOWLEDGMENTS

Thank you to my beloved Samwise. You make life a joy, always and forever. And to my agent, Meredith Bernstein, and to my editor, Kate Seaver: Thank you both for helping me stretch my wings and soar. To Tony Mauro, an incredible cover artist. To my assistant who helps me keep track of everything. To my "Galenorn Gurlz," those still with me, those who have come into my life the past year, and those who crossed over the Bridge the past years—I will always love you, even through the veil.

Most reverent devotion to Ukko, who rules over the wind and sky; Rauni, queen of the harvest; Tapio, lord of the woodlands; and Mielikki, goddess of the Woodlands and Fae Queen in her own right. All, my spiritual guardians. And to the Fae—both dark and light—who walk this world beside us.

And the biggest thank-you of all: *To my readers*. Your support helps me continue to write the books you love to read! You can find me on the Net at Galenorn En/Visions: www.galenorn.com. If you write to me snail mail (see website for address or write via the publisher), please enclose a stamped, self-addressed envelope if you would like a reply. Promo goodies are available—see my site for info.

The Painted Panther
Yasmine Galenorn
November 2010

I heard the owl scream and the crickets cry.
Did not you speak?

—WILLIAM SHAKESPEARE, *MACBETH*

You can only come to the morning through the shadows.

—J.R.R. TOLKIEN

The Beginning

Myst led her people into the shadows and ice, and there they hid, sheltered in the depths of lore. The Vampiric Fae were pariah, kept a dirty secret, shamefully debasing the entire realm of Faerie. And so in furtive silence, the Host fed and drank deep and did rend the flesh of its victims and feast. But their thirst was unquenchable, and it was then that Myst discovered one of their newfound powers: Members of the Indigo Court could drink from the souls of the magic-born . . . With this discovery, a vision for the future began to evolve, and the foundation of terror began . . .

—From *The Rise of the Indigo Court*

The Beginning

Chapter 1

The great horned owl sat in the oak.

I could see the bird from my window as it huddled in the sparse branches, trying to protect itself from the snow. I longed to join it, to strip off my clothes and turn into my owl self, to fly free under the haunting winter moon, but the weather was harsh and cold. And Myst was out there, hiding in the forest with her people, waiting.

And somewhere, hidden in her mists and shadows, Grieve is there, captive, caught in Myst's web. Can he still possibly love me? Can he still be saved from the blood that flows through his veins? How can I let him go, now that we've found each other again?

I opened the window and leaned out, glancing down at the yard below. The snow gleamed under the nearly full moon, a crystal blanket of white flooding the lawn. The Golden Wood—or Spider's Wood, as I called it—was aglow as usual, with a sickly green light that I'd seen every night since returning home to New Forest. A thousand miles and years seemed to separate me from my former existence, although it had been only a couple of weeks since I arrived back in town. But in that short time, my life had turned upside down, in every possible way.

The wind called to me to come and play and I closed my eyes, reveling in the feel of the breezes lashing against my skin. My owls shifted, urging me to fly. The tattoos—a pair of blackwork owls flying over a silver moon impaled on a dagger—banded both arms.

Slipping on my leather jacket and gloves, I cautiously climbed out on the shingles, making sure that the snow that had built up didn't slip, sending me sliding to the ground, but it had turned to ice. I scooted until my back rested against the window, then brought my knees up, circling them with my arms, and nestled as best as I could against the cold.

As I stared up into the oak, the great horned owl let out a soft hoot, stirring my blood. Over the past month, he'd taught me to shake off the fear of falling, to soar through the unending night turning on a wing, catching mice in the yard, while always, *always*, keeping an eye on the forest.

You are Uwilahsidhe. You are magic-born. You must keep watch for Myst, he constantly reminded me. *The Queen of the Indigo Court seeks to destroy you.*

I raised one hand in salute, the snowflakes softly kissing my skin, and he hooted again, a warning in his tone.

"What is it?" I whispered. "What are you trying to tell me?"

Ulean, my Wind Elemental, swept around me like a cloak, answering for him. *He fears for you. There are ghosts riding the wind tonight, and the Shadow Hunters are out and about. There will be death before the morning.*

More death. More blood. My stomach churned as I thought about the four killings reported over the past two days. One had been a child. All had been torn to bits, eaten to the bone.

I gazed at the forest. What were Myst and her people up to tonight? Who were they hunting? The bitch-queen was ravenous and without mercy.

There has been so much death over the past few days. They are terrorizing the town and now everyone fears them, even though they don't know from whom they run. I leaned against the gentle current that signaled Ulean was embracing me. She had been my guardian since I was six years old, bonded to me through ritual, a gift from Lainule, the Fae Queen of Rivers and Rushes.

And they should fear. Myst won't just go away. She is here to make her mark and conquer. She is here to destroy. Ulean caught up a skiff of snow and sent it into the air, spiraling around me.

I glanced back inside at the clock. Seven P.M. Another two hours before we were to meet with Geoffrey. Finally, after five days of silence, the Northwest Regent of the Vampire Nation had summoned us. Five days after we had rescued our friend Peyton from Myst. Five days after I'd lost Grieve. Five days during which the Indigo Court had rained hell on the town, killing eight people.

The owl hooted again and as I glanced in his direction, a shadow of movement caught my eye from below, over near the herb gardens.

Crap—something was rooting around down there. Not an animal, so what was it? Another glance over at the Spider's Wood showed nothing amiss, but we couldn't take any chances.

Ulean, do you know what that thing is?

A moment passed and then she drifted gently around me again. *Not one of the Shadow Hunters, but I have no doubt it belongs to the Indigo Court. Myst is attracting the sinister Fae.*

I leaned forward, trying to keep it within my sight.

I need to know what it is. We can't take a chance on letting it prowl around our land.

Scrambling back through the window, I paused just long enough to slip on my wrist sheath and make sure my switchblade was firmly affixed. Grabbing my fan from the dresser, I slipped back out on the roof and edged my way to the overhang.

The two-story drop was problematic, but a couple of days ago I'd installed a roll-up ladder. I'd been out flying and landed back on the roof, only to discover that somebody in the house had thought I was off shopping and had shut my window and locked it. I'd been stuck out in the snow, naked, too tired to change back into owl form to fly down to the ground and come through the front door. Now, I had the option of climbing down, which was a whole lot easier than shapeshifting when I was exhausted.

I rolled the ladder over the edge and was about to swing onto the rungs when Kaylin stuck his head through the window.

"What are you doing?"

"Goblin dog or something of the sort in the backyard. I was going to check it out."

"Give me ten secs and I'll come with you." He ducked back through the window as I headed down to the ground. A moment later, Kaylin was shimmying down the ladder to land next to me. The dreamwalker was far older than his looks belied, and he was far more skilled in fighting than I was. Having him at my back made me feel much more secure.

"Where are the others?" I hadn't seen my cousin Rhiannon all day.

"Rhiannon is out shopping, and Leo is on a last-minute run for Geoffrey."

Leo was a day-runner for the vampires. More specifically, he worked for the Regent, running errands that Geoffrey and his wife couldn't do during the daylight hours.

"What about Chatter?"

"He's in the basement, working on charms against the Indigo Court."

"I thought the house seemed quiet." I moved forward, cautiously.

The backyard of the Veil House was more like the back forty. Filled with herb gardens, stone circles, and fruit trees, it lay blanketed in a thick layer of snow, and the rising moon set off a bluish tinge to everything around. We stopped, listening to the owl as he hooted again, his warnings echoing through the yard.

We were as quiet as possible, but at one point I stepped

on a fallen branch, buried by the snow. It snapped in two. The creature, which had apparently been working its way toward the house, heard us and froze.

This way, Kaylin mouthed, circling around it.

I followed his lead, edging closer to whatever it was. We managed to slip behind a nearby bush before it could back away. There didn't appear to be more than one, and we were able to get a good look at it.

The creature was about four feet tall, with a bloated stomach and long bony arms that dragged along the ground. Its head was distorted, elongated and elliptical, with longish ears. The eyes were wide-set and cunning. As it drew back its lips into a grimace, drool dripped from between its needle-sharp teeth.

"Have any idea what it is?" I whispered to Kaylin, wishing he could talk on the slipstream. It was much easier to avoid being overheard when sending messages along with the currents of air.

Kaylin cocked his head, his ponytail shifting slightly. "Goblin. One of Myst's toadies, no doubt. If we let it live, I guarantee it will bring others. The dark Fae can get through our wards where Myst's Shadow Hunters can't, so she's probably testing how far she can push into our land using her allies."

"Kill or wound as a message?"

"Go in for the kill. If we just wound it, we'll have yet another nasty enemy on our hands."

I gave him a short nod, saving my breath as we burst out of the bushes and poured on the speed. As we caught up to the thing—the goblin was terribly quick—I pulled out my fan, whispered *"Strong Gust,"* and snapped the fan open, waving it twice.

A quick blast of air slammed against us—and the goblin. Startled, the creature skidded to a halt at the edge of the forest, looking confused. Kaylin dove forward, rolling to come up in fighting stance. He kicked it in the chin. As the goblin lurched back, I slipped through on the left side and brought my switchblade down on its arm, stabbing it deeply.

Kaylin fumbled for his shurikens as an icy gust of wind came whistling from the direction of the forest, and a shadow figure loomed at the border dividing the woods from the magical barrier we'd constructed. A glimpse of pale skin with a cerulean cast to it told us all we needed to know. One of the Vampiric Fae. *A Shadow Hunter.*

"Shit," I muttered, steeling myself as the goblin launched itself at me.

The Shadow Hunter raised a bow, his sight intent on Kaylin. He might not be able to set foot on our land, but his weaponry could. I shouted a warning to Kaylin and waved my fan in the direction of the Vampiric Fae, whispering, *"Strong Gust."* The arrow came zinging our way, but missed by inches.

The goblin landed on me and we both went down, rolling into the snow. I couldn't use my fan in such close quarters, so I struggled to catch the creature by the throat. I was bigger than the goblin, but not as tough. After thrashing against his leathery skin, I finally managed to get one hand on his neck.

Gnashing his teeth, the goblin lashed at my hand and I pulled away just in time. Even if I didn't lose any fingers, chances were good he had some nasty bacteria in that mouth and I wanted no part of any infection he might be carrying. We wrestled, me trying to force back his hands as he scrabbled to reach my face. One swipe of those claw-like nails could take out an eye. The stench of the creature was putrid, like a combination of gas and vomit, and his eyes were round and lidless.

I sucked in a deep breath and heaved, pushing with both hands and feet, and managed to roll on top, trapping him between my knees. I squeezed my thighs together, trying to keep the goblin from slipping away from me. At that moment, Kaylin let out a shout and I jerked around. A muscle pulled in my neck.

"Fuck!" The Shadow Hunter's second arrow had grazed his arm.

The bolt had penetrated the heavy leather he was wear-

ing but looked like it hadn't gone too deep. Kaylin yanked
the arrow out, tossing it to the ground, and dashed over the
boundary line. The Shadow Hunter hadn't been prepared
for him to go on the offensive and went down, Kaylin atop
him in the snow, a flurry of fists flying.

I turned my attention back to the goblin. If I let this thing
get away, he'd be back, with reinforcements. I flipped the
blade on my switchblade and paused. Killing creatures—
even our enemies—was still new and did not come easy to
me. I sucked in a deep breath.

*You can do it. Steady. Aim for the forehead. Goblins are
vulnerable in the third eye area.* Ulean flurried around me,
trying to keep the snow from blinding my vision.

With a surge in the pit of my stomach, I brought the blade
down, wincing as it slid through the goblin's head. New Forest had become a town of *kill or be killed*. We no longer had
the luxury of allowing our enemies to live in peace.

I drove the blade in to the hilt. The goblin screeched,
loud and jagged through the twilight, and then fell limp as
a fountain of blood stained the snow red, diluting into petal
pink. The scent of the creature lingered, joined by that of
blood. I withdrew my blade, yanking when it resisted.

Another shout. I looked up to realize that—in my
fight—I'd also passed the boundary line and the Shadow
Hunter was on the run, aiming directly for me. I froze, but
he merely shoved me aside and fell to the side of the goblin's body, his face pressed against the creature's wound.

As I backed away, horrified, he lapped at the blood, and
then began to transform, his mouth unhinging like that of
a snake as he shifted into a doglike monster, his jaws lined
with spiny teeth. With ravenous fury, he bit off the head,
chewing it, spattering bits of brain matter every which way.

Kaylin brushed his fingers to his lips and slowly edged
up on the Shadow Hunter. He brought out a short dagger,
serrated and coated in a magical oil. As he plunged the
knife into the side of the Vampiric Fae, aiming for the
heart, the oil encouraged the blood to flow and the crimson
liquid stained the snow still further.

The Shadow Hunter turned, but I was quicker, stabbing his haunch with my blade and dragging it through his tough hide. Then Kaylin and I lightly danced backward, out of reach of those deadly teeth.

A voice echoed from behind us and I turned to see my cousin Rhiannon, panting as she stretched out her hands, a small red charm in the palm of her right. She whispered, just loud enough for us to hear, *"Flame to flame, bolt to bolt, fire to fire, jolt to jolt. Lightning, let me be thy rod."*

All hell broke loose as a bolt of snow lightning came forking out of the gathering clouds, ripping to the ground to shatter the Shadow Hunter into a thousand pieces, as if he were a glass dish smashed on concrete.

As soon as the spell sang out of her body, Rhiannon collapsed and Kaylin raced over to catch her. I stared at the remains of the Shadow Hunter and the goblin. Not much left. Nothing to take home with us, except two more notches on our belt, and the hope that we'd be able to sleep soundly, knowing there was one less member of Myst's court in the world. One less toady of hers to slip onto our land.

Kaylin shivered. He was bleeding through the rent in his jacket from the arrow. At that moment, I noticed a trickle running down my own shoulder. I glanced down. A puncture wound had penetrated my jacket. I slipped it off to see blood saturating my top. The goblin must have stabbed me with its claw. I hadn't even noticed.

"We're growing numb to our pain," I said as we turned away from the carnage we'd just inflicted.

"We have to," Kaylin said. "We have to learn to weather the battles because there will be far more to come before things get back to normal. If there even *is* such a thing as 'normal' anymore."

I nodded and looked at Rhiannon. "You saved the day." The *thank you* was implied.

She slipped her arm around my waist and leaned down to kiss my forehead. "I just got home and saw the commotion from the car. Leo's still in town and I don't know where Chatter is."

"In the basement, working with the charms."

"Ah. Good. We'll need them."

"I guess we'd better get back on our land, before anything else comes out of the woods. We need to tend to our wounds and make sure they don't get infected." I wearily turned back to the house.

As we crossed the demarcation line that magically divided the Golden Wood from the Veil House, I couldn't help but shudder. Like it or not, we were pawns in a war between two powerful enemies—Geoffrey and Myst—and we were doing our best just to stay alive.

Chapter 2

"Cicely? Are you ready? It's time." Leo's voice echoed up the stairs. My cousin's fiancé, and a day-runner for the vampires, he'd gotten home shortly after our encounter with the goblin.

After a long shower to wash away my aches and pains, I'd dressed in a cobalt sweater and black jeans, making sure I was neat and tidy. Geoffrey and Regina owned my services—quite literally—and they demanded that their employees appear before them nicely dressed.

My wolf growled as I ran my hand over the tattoo of the beautiful silverish beast that spread across my body, over my stomach.

"Sshh . . . " I whispered. "Hush. I know, I know you're out there hurting, but I can't do anything about it right now."

The wolf growled again and I pressed my lips tight, my heart sore. The memory of Grieve's face, of his hands on my body, his needle-sharp teeth nipping at my skin, swept over me and I dashed my hand across my eyes, careful not to mar the mascara and liner I'd put on. Grieve was lost to the enemy. Myst had claimed him for her own. I was determined to win him back, but in the depths of my heart I was afraid that none of us would come out of this alive.

"Cicely! Get a move on!"

"Yeah, yeah, I'm coming." I hurried into my favorite boots—a pair of Icon Bombshells—and slung my purse over my shoulder. Polishing a smudge off my left boot, I decided that I was as good as I was going to get, especially after a tussle with a goblin and a Shadow Hunter.

My hair hung free, smooth and ink-black to my shoulders, and I pulled it back into a sleek ponytail, then slipped on a pair of driving gloves and my leather jacket. I slid my moonstone pendant over my neck and secreted it beneath my sweater, then clattered down the stairs.

"Let's get this show on the road," I said.

Rhiannon was waiting, freshly showered herself, in a pair of khakis she'd paired with a plaid button-down shirt, and a camel wool coat.

My cousin was as bright as I was dark. Heather, her mother, used to call us Amber and Jet—fire and ice. Her hair was flame red, my own jet-black. We were both twenty-six, both born on the summer solstice—she in the waxing hours, me in the waning. I was short and sturdy, Rhiannon tall and willowy. Opposites, yet we had referred to ourselves as twins when we were little.

Leo looked snazzy as usual. Geoffrey insisted he dress well for work, and most day-runners had extensive—and expensive—wardrobes. Leo was lucky. In his case, Geoffrey financed his expenses. Leo's tawny hair was a mass of curls barely skimming his neck and he towered over me, more lean than gangly.

"Be careful," Kaylin said, looking up from his spot on the sofa, where he was reading while petting a half dozen cats who sprawled around him, including Bart, Leo's Maine Coon familiar. "You go off half-cocked and try to stake Lannan and you'll be in a world of hurt."

Lannan. My face flushed and I let out a low growl. Lannan Altos was near the top of my *wish-you-were-dead* list, only slightly lower than Myst. He was a vampire—one of the Vein Lords—and I was bound to him by an ironclad contract. He'd mind-fucked me once already while drinking the monthly blood tithe I owed him. Next time it would be worse.

Lannan wants to break you, Ulean whispered on a light current of air.

I know, trust me. I know. He can try all he likes, he won't do it.

Ulean brushed me with her impatience. *Don't be too cocky. Lannan has thousands of years of experience. He is a master of head games. Just be careful.*

I will. Have no fear. I've already made too many mistakes. I'll watch my back.

"Cicely? Promise us you won't go off on Lannan? We can't afford to alienate him." Kaylin caught my gaze and would not let go.

"Because he's helped us *so much* already?" I shot him a nasty look. "Lannan *knew* he was infecting me and that I'd infect Grieve, and now look at the whole mess. The Indigo Court is far more dangerous than they were, even if they can no longer walk under the sun. They were bad enough before; now they're like a pack of rabid dogs. With nasty big teeth and soul-sucking abilities."

Geoffrey and Regina, agents for the Crimson Queen—the queen of true vampires—had come up with a hunkydory plan to stop the Vampiric Fae. Only it hadn't worked right. It prevented the Indigo Court Fae from walking abroad during the day all right, but now light sent them into a feeding frenzy—a rage from which they could not extricate themselves until the darkness once again hit. I'd been the weapon, unknowingly passing a plague to them when I'd kissed Grieve, thanks to Lannan's infecting me with his bite, and I'd never forgive them for that.

"He was doing his job," Leo said, grimly. "Remember, when Regina and Geoffrey decide something, everybody jumps. Even Lannan."

"Right. Doing his job, just like the SS during World War Two. Goddamn, I'd like to dust that pervert. He hurt

Grieve! And he . . ." I stopped, not wanting to think about what he'd done to me. "You just know Lannan's going to sit there, looking so smug and self-satisfied—"

At Kaylin's raised eyebrows, I stopped, catching my breath. My fury surprised even me. I knew I wanted to dust Lannan, but I didn't expect to be quite so explosive about it. After a moment, I added, "Okay, okay. I promise. I'll keep my mouth shut. But I don't have to like it."

The phone rang and Rhiannon answered while we went on talking.

"Actually, I doubt Lannan had much to do with producing the virus," Leo said, sliding on his gloves. "And he's one of the true vampires—why *would* he care about Grieve? He cares about no one except his sister and himself. Lannan's not interested in politics, and my bet is he'd rather ignore Myst and her Court. He's too self-centered to really give a fuck about whether the Shadow Hunters take over the town, as long as they leave him and his stable alone."

That was the longest speech I'd heard out of Leo and I wasn't sure I wanted to hear another. He seemed too willing to take Lannan's side. But I had to admit, he was probably right. Lannan wouldn't have been the engineer on this plan. He wasn't that ambitious. It was probably all Regina could do to force him to play his part in carrying it out.

"If Myst gains control of New Forest, his stable will end up as mangled as that goblin did," I muttered.

"Crap, that was Anadey. There's been another attack," Rhiannon said as she replaced the receiver on the cradle. She paled, shaking her head.

"Another? Where? Who?" The past five days had been hell. The attack on a movie theater the other night pretty much outed the fact that a pack of hunters was on the loose. The majority of people didn't know exactly *who* was behind the attacks, but they knew that anybody was fair game and that people were dying.

"Two. A mother and a child. Eaten down to the bone. Cops found them two hours ago and are circulating the rumor that there are wild dogs in the area."

"That makes *ten* victims, including two children." I stopped, giving her a bewildered look. "Did you say *wild dogs*? They really expect people to believe that?"

Kaylin bookmarked his novel and put it on the table. He frowned. "It's amazing what people will accept when they don't want to believe something worse."

"Oh, I don't think people are that dense. They know something's out there. They also must realize by now that the cops aren't going to protect them. I can understand why the magic-born aren't all leaving—we're connected to this land by the energy. But why aren't the yummanii leaving?"

Yummanii was the term the magic-born used among themselves for those born fully human. The yummanii possessed their own kind of magic—not as obvious or flamboyant as the magic-born, but a psychic energy . . . call it instinct, if you will, and the power had grown more noticeable among the yummanii children of the past few generations. Whether the yummanii realized they were growing strong, we did not know. But it wasn't our place to tell them or we risked altering their natural evolution.

As for the yummanii, they had always known about the magic-born, and they accepted us. Just like they knew about the Weres and the vampires and Fae.

"Perhaps they can't leave. It costs money to pull up stakes, to head out of town and start a new life. And if you have a good job, or children, then it's that much harder. Unemployment is low here in New Forest and—until Myst came—life was relatively safe. Geoffrey keeps a watch on the vampires and doesn't allow many rogues. All sound reasons to stay put." Kaylin shrugged. "It's easier to take a few precautions and hope for the best."

I nodded. The dreamwalker made a lot of sense.

"We need to get moving. Geoffrey will have us by the neck if we're late." Leo shuffled, glancing at the door as if it might burst open to reveal the Regent.

I shook my head. "If he's so all fired up to talk to me, why the hell has he kept me waiting this long?"

"Calm down, Cicely." Chatter's voice whispered softly

from behind me. I whirled to see the Fae leaning against the arch leading into the dining room and kitchen. "You cannot help Grieve if you lose the support of the vampires. Myst cannot be defeated without them and you know it."

"I know. Trust me, I know. I can't get away from them no matter how much I might want to. They own me for the rest of my life. How can I *ever* forget that?" With a snort, I added, "Let's get this show on the road."

Leo, Rhiannon, and I headed out, leaving Chatter and Kaylin to watch over the house. As we stepped into the icy night, a lazy shower of snow drifted down. Myst had brought with her a long winter to blanket the town, a cold and chill premonition of what life under her rule would be like.

The Queen of Winter, a tainted Fae Queen whom the vampires had once tried to turn as if she were human, Myst had risen from her deathbed before she could die, fully alive and far more dangerous than the vampires ever dreamed possible, and from her descended the Vampiric Fae. They could breed, and they were ruthless killing machines who lived to feed and spread across the land.

And now she had traced down her maker and looked to wipe out Geoffrey and his people. She aspired to take over the land, one town at a time.

I climbed into the driver's seat of Favonis, my Pontiac GTO, and, making sure our doors were locked, we headed over to Geoffrey's to plan out a war.

❧

Geoffrey's mansion sat on two acres, and it was truly a manor, three stories high. Who knew how far it extended underground? As it glittered white with gold trim, a dizzying array of lights sparkled from inside the building and armed guards—all vampires since we were into the night— wandered the grounds.

Last time I'd been here, I'd unwittingly signed away my freedom, but there was nothing I could do about it, so I decided to let it go and move on. We drove up to the valet, who took one look at Leo and nodded us toward the entrance.

At the door, a tall, broad-shouldered guard stopped us. Like all of the true vampires, his eyes were jet-black, gleaming like obsidian with no patches of white or other color marring their surface. That alone spooked me about the Vein Lords: How could they see through those inky orbs?

He searched all of us, including Leo, and then opened the door. A maid—a bloodwhore by the look of her outfit and the fact that she wasn't a vampire—motioned for us to follow her.

I'd thought we might be heading into Geoffrey's office, but instead she led us to a room to the right of the grand staircase and opened the door, all without a word. Peering in, I saw Geoffrey—he motioned for us to enter, and the maid closed the door behind us.

A glance around the room told me that the parlor was really a royal hall in disguise. The room was geared for an audience, and the chair in which Geoffrey sat might as well be a throne, with its crimson velvet and placement.

The Vein Lord wasn't very tall, but the power he wielded hit me over the head like a brick. He reeked of authority. He wore his long black hair smoothed back in a French braid; a royal purple jacket with ruffled sleeves, open to show his bare chest; and leather pants.

As he leaned back in his chair, crossing his legs, a faint smile flickered across his lips. One thing I had to say about Geoffrey: Of all the vampires we'd met, he was the most polite and deliberate of action. Sure, he could rip your head off in a second, but he'd think it through first and say "Pardon me" afterward.

"Please, sit and be comfortable." He motioned to the semicircle of chairs, all facing his own. "Welcome. Our other guests should be here shortly."

Now that I thought about it, Geoffrey reminded me of a vampire version of Kaylin, only more seductive and dangerous. According to history, he'd been some sort of warlord during the Xiongnu period, in a region that would later become Mongolia.

I nodded and slipped into the seat opposite him. Leo

and Rhiannon sat on my right. Just then, the door opened again and Regina and Lannan Altos sauntered in. Well, Lannan sauntered. Regina's heels clipped on the hardwood floor at a quick, steady pace. Twins and lovers, they were dangerous and both of them were freakshows, though Regina had more restraint than her brother. Regina was the Emissary to the Crimson Court, and she was top dog around here.

I opened my mouth to speak, but Geoffrey held up one hand and I quickly shut up. When the Vein Lords order silence, obey.

"We are waiting on Lainule; save your words for when she arrives."

And so we sat in silence for another moment until the door opened again and the Queen of Summer came gliding in. Even in the dim light, her brilliance shone against the others. Without thinking, I rose and knelt before her.

Lainule smiled down at me, then leaned down and cupped my chin in her hand. "Take your seat, Cicely."

I silently obeyed.

Geoffrey cleared his throat. "Welcome, Your Majesty. My home is graced by the presence of the Queen of Rivers and Rushes—"

She waved his words away. The three of us stared. Nobody *ever* cut off Geoffrey, unless it was Regina. Or the Crimson Queen herself.

"Save your chatter, Regent. We have no time for pleasantries, nor am I in the mood for small talk." She grew taller in her impatience. "Have you figured out whether the Consortium knows what's going on?"

He nodded. "I have, Your Majesty. They know nothing, as far as we can tell. And my sources are reliable."

Considering his words, she finally shrugged. "Very good. We *must* keep it that way. I cannot imagine what they would do should they find out about the Shadow Hunters. Especially considering what our plan unleashed." Turning to me, she asked, "Have you ever heard of the Consortium, Cicely?"

I blinked. "The Consortium? Of course, hasn't everybody?"

With a low chuckle, Geoffrey leaned back in his chair and stared at me, those glowing obsidian eyes following every movement I made. "Oh, Cicely, you can be amusing."

"*Our* Cicely is delightful, in so many ways." Lannan's voice slid warm and rich over my name, making me shiver as if he'd just stroked my body with those ice-cold hands of his. "She's also quite the vixen."

He leaned back against his seat, his legs outstretched and crossed at the ankles, his hand lightly resting on his crotch. Another moment and he'd be wanking off right there.

Regina laughed, rich and throaty, but she gave me a speculative look, which I did not return. Best not to let a vampire catch your gaze—especially one who might consider you set to woo away her lover. Even when you'd rather stake him.

Geoffrey gave Lannan a long, slow shake of the head, then turned back to me, ignoring him. "Not everyone has heard of the Consortium, and many who have wisely stay a good distance from them."

I pressed my lips together and clenched my fists. I refused to allow Lannan to get a rise out of me. I would *not* let him goad me. After taking a long, deep breath and exhaling slowly, I nodded. "The Consortium is a volatile and dangerous agency. I have no interest in making their acquaintance."

A worldwide organization to oversee the magic-born, the Consortium pulled strings behind the scenes and, together with the Vein Lords and the top yummanii officials, were the real power running most of the world. And as in most powerful organizations, corruption was rife, with magic used to remove those who opposed them.

Geoffrey nodded. "Lainule speaks wisely. If they find out about Myst, they may take it upon themselves to fight her. As powerful as they are, they are no match for the Queen of the Indigo Court. She is Vampiric Fae, and as much as I am loath to admit it, we have no clue how far her powers extend."

"Nobody ever kept track . . ." I shook my head. "What about their history—*The Rise of the Indigo Court*?"

He shrugged. "A scratch on the surface. Add to that, the members of the Consortium have an arrogance matching that of the Vein Lords. Only they would not admit they need aid. So keep your mouth shut. This is the reason I instructed the police to issue the statement about wild dogs causing the current spate of attacks." Geoffrey gave me a long look, as if challenging me to argue his decision.

The Regent fascinated me. He was terribly intelligent, and he ran things aboveboard, for the most part. As we held each other's gaze, it occurred to me that all of this was his fault. He'd been the vampire who decided to try to conquer the Unseelie Court by turning the dark Fae, so many eons ago. But now, as I searched his face, I realized that playing the blame game would be stupid. We had to deal with the present.

Geoffrey's lips curled at the edges, and all of a sudden we were sitting together, alone in a small room surrounded by mist. He leaned forward and took my hands. "You are curious about me, Cicely. Know that I do not share Lannan's tastes for games of humiliation. If you should ever want a sire, I would be more than willing to take you into the fold, to turn you, to teach you our ways. My wife is a lovely woman who does not object to sharing our bed with others."

His hands were as cold as Lannan's had been, but his lips were full and promised the sting of ecstasy. His tongue flickered out, for just a second, and I wondered if it would be different, having someone drink from me who wasn't out to crush my spirit.

"Think about it," he said, and sat back, and suddenly we were in the parlor again, and nothing had changed. No one seemed to notice what had gone on between us but for Lannan, who slowly turned his head toward Geoffrey, then toward me. An angry possessive look stole over his face.

I quickly averted my eyes, but I could feel the Vein Lord staring at me long after I glanced away.

"We have been working on an antidote," Lainule said. "A way to shift the plague we sent into the Shadow Hunters that will minimize their rage. We had no idea that the light-rage would happen, and to be honest, we have no idea what the counteragent will do to them. We might make things worse. At least we have managed to keep them from wandering abroad during the daylight but . . ."

"How do you intend to get this 'antidote' to them? Will it be spread like the first plague?" I asked, ignoring Lannan, who was still staring in my direction. Let him look. We had another couple of weeks until my next blood tithe and by then, who knew? I could be dead. So could he—and *that* idea, I rather liked.

She shook her head. "First, we have more testing to do. Then we worry about spreading it through the colony. That's what they are, you know—a colony that's breeding and spreading. A swarm of destruction, a brilliant and beautiful deadly disease. And we have to eradicate every member we find. Myst and her people aren't the only off-shoots of the Indigo Court—too many years have passed since the *first* infection for there not to be others." She looked pointedly at Geoffrey, who said nothing.

I delicately skirted her allusion. No need to get in the middle of a war between vampire and Fae. "What about Grieve?"

Her eyes were limpid, pools of clear water in the middle of a desert. She shook her head. "You cannot save your lover, Cicely. I know that you have been together in more than one life. I know that you love him more than you love anything or anyone else. And I know you are angry at us for using you, but you must understand: You were the easiest weapon we could employ to spread the infection through the colony."

Weapon. I was a weapon to her. Her calm, collected words made me want to scream, but I knew that wouldn't help matters any. But I wasn't going down without a fight.

"Grieve and I are meant to be together, and there's nothing on this earth that will make me give him up unless he tells me to go. I can't just leave him in Myst's arms. She'll destroy everything that was ever good about him."

Leo cleared his throat and tugged on my arm. "Cicely—"

"No!" I shook him off. "I'm going to have my say."

Lannan laughed in the background, and I ignored him.

Lainule frowned. "Leave her to speak. She may say what she likes to me without fear of retribution, unlike with *some* of her compatriots." Here, she shot a quick, steely gaze at Lannan, who winked at her.

I brushed Leo's hand away. "Oh, I *will* have my say, Your Majesty. I respect you. I truly do, and I'm one of your people—at least on my father's side—so I will listen to you. But I won't necessarily obey you on this. Grieve is my soul mate. He's a prince in your realm. How can you just leave him in her web?"

Lainule stood and faced me, taking me by the shoulders. Her smile was a fading glimpse of summer. "Cicely, I'm telling you this one time and one time only, and I expect you to obey: Walk away. Leave Grieve behind. He was lost to us the day Myst drank from his throat and turned him. The prince of my court is dead, and in his place, a pale Shadow Hunter now follows the hem of Winter. There is no place for him should he return to my realm. I would reject him. *Or kill him.*"

And with that, she turned away. Stunned, I could only stare at her back as she motioned to Geoffrey. "Vampire, we must talk in private. We have much to discuss." Over her shoulder, she said, "Cicely, go home. Work your magic and tend your business for the townsfolk. They need the help. Do as Geoffrey and Regina command you, since you've seen fit to indenture yourself to them. And leave Grieve in the dust. We will conclude matters later."

In silence, she passed out of the room. Geoffrey motioned to his servant. "Ensure that Her Majesty is comfortable and tell her I'll be there shortly."

He turned to me. "Lainule is right. You will only come to despair if you seek out Grieve. Meanwhile, you will continue to report anything you notice. Lannan will see you out. Good evening." Opening the door, he escorted Regina out.

I didn't want them to leave. Even with Leo and Rhiannon in the room, I didn't feel safe around Lannan. And

I was right to be nervous. As soon as Geoffrey and Regina disappeared down the hall, Lannan turned to Leo.

"Cicely will meet you in a few moments. Go and wait for her at the front door." He waved them off. Though I could see by their faces that they wanted to protest, they were smart enough to keep quiet.

As they passed out of the room, I closed my eyes, steeling myself. Knowing Lannan, anything could be coming my way. He closed the door softly and turned toward me. The golden man, Apollo incarnate, with shimmering hair and obsidian eyes, and oh-so-breathtaking looks. But looks were deceptive.

He circled me.

I stood still, silent. *Stifle the feelings, turn on the numbness, barricade the emotions. Let him do what he wants and then get on with life.*

He stopped by my side. "Cicely?" He reached out and cupped my chin. His voice was so soft I could barely catch what he was saying. "My lovely, beautiful, breathing woman. Your face is so warm, so vibrant. You're blushing." A smile, feral and predatory, crept into the corners of his lips. He held my chin so I couldn't look away and leaned forward, mere inches from my lips.

I swallowed my fear, forcing myself to remain steady. Lannan had the bite to back up his actions, and he was all about humiliating others.

With breathless lips close to mine, he slid his hand from my chin down my throat, his fingers trailing around the side of my neck, making me shiver despite myself.

"Cicely, listen to me," he whispered. "You do not belong to Geoffrey. You will *never* belong to Geoffrey, even if I have to kill you and turn you myself, so don't bother considering his offer. If I find out he's touched you, I'll drain you dry. You're *my* toy, and I don't share my favorites."

I thought of protesting but stopped. I'd seen this side of Lannan, and I knew what he was capable of when he flew into a rage.

His lips almost on mine, he said, "And Lainule is right. Forget your Fae Prince. You've lost him. Join my stable. While Regina is my Queen, you will be the first among my bloodwhores."

"I am no bloodwhore." I didn't try to break free—that would spur him on—but slowly, I tried to ease my head away.

But Lannan had other ideas. His arm was suddenly around my waist and his lips were on mine. I could feel him rigid and hard against me. He slid his tongue inside my mouth.

A warm sensation began to rise through my body as the euphoria of his kiss filtered through every cell. I realized that I had melted; I was pressing against him, wet and warm and aching for release. Furious, I pulled back, pushed his mouth away from mine.

Lannan arched his eyebrows. Grabbing my wrist, he twisted until I was gritting my teeth. "Don't ever push me away again, girl. Not if you value what life you have left." Once again, he fastened his lips on mine and ravished me with his tongue, his hands gripping my butt, wandering over my body, stirring heat. I let out a moan, angry and fearful, as my hunger for him grew.

As he broke away, holding me by the back of the head, forcing me to look him in the eye, my cheeks grew hot as I tried to stanch the tears aching to flow.

"Damn you . . . damn you. I hate you. I hate your touch and your icy hands. If I could, I'd stake you right here." I knew I was playing on dangerous ground, but I couldn't help it.

But Lannan merely laughed. "I like it when you resist. I want you even more when you try to squirm away. It thrills me to know you've creamed your panties when you don't want to come. Anticipation is *so good* for the soul. I promise you this, Cicely: Next bloodletting, I'm going to fuck you so hard and long with my fangs that you'll beg for my cock. I'm going to have you down on your knees begging me to ream your wet little pussy."

And then, he shoved me back. I stumbled against the

sofa as he turned away. "You can go now. Sleep well, and have sweet dreams, my *pet*."

I ran out of the house to find Rhia and Leo waiting for me. They took one look at my face and led me back to the car where Leo climbed behind the wheel. Rhia held me in the backseat as I cried all the way back home.

Chapter 3

I was standing in the pale light of twilight, at the edge of the Golden Wood, naked, but I couldn't seem to feel the cold. I ran my fingers lightly over my wolf, closing my eyes. The tattoo was complex: a vine that wound itself up my left thigh, then crossed my lower stomach, ending near my ribs beneath my right arm. Silver roses and violet skulls dappled the vine, and right above my navel, a wolf gazed into the world through brilliant emerald eyes. Grieve . . . my wolf was connected to Grieve, and through it, I could feel my Fae Prince, when he was hurting or angry.

"Where are you? What are you thinking? Are you missing me?" I whispered, closing my eyes. I didn't consciously send the message down the slipstream, but the words swept out of my mouth and caught themselves lightly on a hook of wind, gusting along the currents of air playing past me.

As I slowly brought my left hand up, my fingers lightly brushing my breast, I caught my breath. And then, I felt hands on me and gasped, but as my eyes flew open, it was not Lannan touching me—but my perilous Grieve.

His gleaming black eyes sparkled with stars, stark against

the platinum shag that fell to his shoulders. He gazed into my soul, the scents of cinnamon and freshly turned earth enveloping him. His white kimono with delicate indigo patterns embroidered on the silken material rustled as he touched me.

"Grieve, is it really you?" I whispered, pressing against him.

He said nothing but pulled me in, his lips touching my own. I breathed in his scent, reveling in the feeling of being in his arms again, wanting to stay here forever. Grieve, regardless of his nature, was my other half—my soul mate. My love. He murmured softly as he fisted my hair and slid his hands over my body.

"Cicely." His voice was sultry and I melted into his embrace. "My own Cicely." One hand rose to stroke my breast and I bared my neck, aching for the needle-sharp sting of his teeth. It was so different than when Lannan bit me—this I enjoyed, reveled in.

As he lowered his lips to my neck and gently slid through the flesh, I gasped again, sliding into the dream-filled ecstasy that his bloodletting brought to me. My body raced with heat, the blood pumping through my veins as he gently licked it from the wound on my throat. He circled my waist with his left hand as his right slid down, across my stomach to between my thighs.

My wolf whimpered and I let out a long sob as he gently circled my clit with a feather-light touch, claiming me as he stoked my fires. All thoughts of Lannan and his perverted whims faded into the background, becoming white noise, as my hands sought out Grieve's chest and I slid down that olive skin. Grieve claimed me with his kiss, stoking my fires, sliding between my legs to carry me away from fear and pain. Another few inches and I held Grieve in hand, his rigid desire throbbing against my palm. He slid both hands under my butt and lifted me up, pressing me back against a mossy tree as he thrust himself inside me, so deep that he touched my core.

The moss on the tree itched against my back, but it protected me from the bark as Grieve drove himself into me. I wrapped my legs around his waist, and he freed one hand to stroke me again, his flesh soft and warm and living against me.

"I missed you so much," I whispered. "I love you so much."

"I miss you, too. I can't stand that Myst holds my chain. Every time she demands my attendance, I want to attack her, to destroy her, but I can't. She is too powerful. I don't even think the gods themselves can strike her down."

"Myst can't have you—you're mine. We belong together. We've always belonged together. I won't lose you again."

"I'll never give in, never give her the satisfaction of thinking she can let down her guard near me. You're mine, Cicely Waters . . . I will be with you forever, or die in the attempt."

And then, a gust of wind swept past, chilling me to the bone.

"*Cicely . . .*" His voice sounded distant, as if he were speaking through a long tunnel, and his touch began to fade as I came, sharp and with a sting of pain.

"Grieve—what's happening?" I found myself standing by the tree, and he was reaching for me but now we were separate, divided by some invisible chasm.

"*Cicely . . . I love you . . .*"

I realized that I was now frozen and cold, and the snow hurt against my bare feet. I looked around frantically as Grieve began to fade, still reaching for me. "No, you can't go. Don't leave me—"

But a tall woman clad in a gossamer gown woven from the silk of her ice spiders glided up behind him. She was as glorious as a midwinter day, with hair as black as the night and her eyes spun with starlight. Her skin held a cerulean cast to it. Her breasts were firm and her belly slightly rounded, just enough to give her curves. She put her hand on Grieve's shoulder and he languidly turned to her, opening his arms to her embrace. Her hair fell against his, jet against his platinum strands, and as she bent to kiss him and his lips touched hers, I let out a long, single cry.

No . . . can you still hear me? Can you feel me? You have to fight her. Please. Fight Myst with everything you have.

Myst turned to look at me, laughing. "You've lost, Uwilahsidhe. You traitorous bitch. I warned you long ago that I would destroy you for what you did. I've only just begun. Geoffrey's not my only target. Know that, Cicely Waters, Wind Witch. I will systematically take everything you hold dear and taint it. I will destroy everything and everyone you love. You will be broken and alone at the end, with no one left to care. Then, and only then, I will come for you, and teach you what it means to betray me."

She swept Grieve into her arms and kissed him deep, and his gaze slid away from me as he lost himself to her, and they faded from sight.

With a sharp cry, I shot up in bed, covered in a cold sweat. I jumped out of bed. Was it just a dream? A nightmare brought on by Lannan's threat? But as I turned back to the sheets, I saw loose moss scattered in the bed, and a few leaves, moldy from the snow and weather.

I glanced in the mirror at my back. The imprint of bark ran down my skin, and moss clung to me. I realized that I'd had an orgasm. My body no longer ached, but my heart felt like it was breaking.

No . . . it was real. Grieve is out there and he was thinking of me, and somehow I went to him. But Myst . . .

The reality of what we were facing hit home then. With tears flowing fast and thick, I climbed in the shower and quickly rinsed off, and then changed my sheets. But the memory of Myst's words rang in my head, and it was a long time before I was able to get to sleep again.

❄

The next morning, I woke, feeling hungover from emotion and adrenaline. As I stared out of the window, squinting in vain for any sign of Grieve, Ulean swept around me.

He is not there. He is sleeping now; the pain of the light eats them into madness otherwise. Try to focus on something other than vampires and the Indigo Court. That is all you can do for the moment.

As much as I didn't want to admit it, I knew she was right. *I can work on Wind Charms . . . we're almost ready to open and Peyton is coming over this morning to help me put the finishing touches on the storefront.*

Ulean made sounds of approval. *Good. Cicely . . . do not give up hope. Myst is a fierce and terrifying adversary, but Grieve is not totally lost to you. Not yet. I would know if he were. He is torn, conflicted, but there is still a faint hope.*

I knew about torn and conflicted. I'd been that way every day of my life, it seemed. But with Grieve . . . one time stood out. A time I wished I'd never had to experience.

I headed for another quick shower, the bracing water waking me up as my mind turned in a million different directions.

I'd never expected to go into business for myself, but when Marta, Crone-Priestess of the now defunct Thirteen Moons Society, had left me her magical shop—or rather the inventory and clientele—in her will, it seemed the most natural thing in the world to take her place.

Most of my life I'd lived on the road. When I was six years old, Krystal—my junkie, bloodwhore mother—had dragged me away from my aunt Heather and the Veil House and Grieve, and everything that was familiar. Even then, I knew nothing would ever be the same.

I sniffed my vanilla body wash. The scent was warm and inviting, and it comforted me gently as I lathered up. It reminded me of the visits home. Aunt Heather always had plenty of vanilla and lavender bath wash waiting for me. Every year or so, Krystal would put me on a bus and send me, alone, back to New Forest for a week. And when it was time for me to go back to life on the road, Heather would cry as she returned me to the bus. If she'd tried to keep me, Krystal would have taken me away forever.

In my early teens, I'd fallen in love with Grieve. At

seventeen, he'd asked me to stay with him. And I . . . I'd
walked away.

❧

Grieve and I sprawled under the cedar, lolling around on
one of my rare visits back to the Veil House. My mother let
me return once a year for a couple of weeks, and I took full
advantage of it. I missed living here, missed being off the
streets. My mother had snatched me away when I was six
from all I'd ever known—my aunt Heather, cousin Rhiannon . . . the Veil House . . . and Grieve and Chatter. I'd
been on the run ever since, learning to steal, to bluff my
way through potentially dangerous situations. At seventeen, I felt old—older than any teenager has any right to be.

Before my mother ran away with me, Grieve had helped
me bond with Ulean and sent her with me as a protector.

I'd tried to forget. Even at six, I knew that if I held on to
the past, I'd never be able to face the present. But Grieve . . .
I couldn't forget him. My child's memories of his kindness,
of his otherworldly nature, remained safely tucked in my
heart. With each year, as I visited, he grew out of being a
child's crush and I realized I was falling in love with the
Fae Prince.

When I was fifteen, he began to kiss my hand. To walk
with me in the ravine. To talk to me like an adult. At six-
teen, I handed him my heart, made the first move and
kissed him on the lips as we ran through the glades, laughing and dancing in the sunlight.

Grieve never pushed, never made a step over the line.
But with that first kiss, his lips crushing mine, a longing so
deep it nearly tore me apart rose up and I broke down
weeping, wanting only to stay with him. To be with him.
To love him. To never leave his side.

And now . . . at seventeen, I was home again. I whispered to him gently, tickled his ear, and opened my heart
and body to him.

"You cannot leave me," he said, toying with my fingers,

kissing their tips slowly. "I love you. I've been waiting for you to remember."

I stared at him, afraid to say those three words for fear of what they'd bind me to. But I couldn't help wondering what it would be like to be a princess in his realm. What would it be like to be with my love forever?

"Remember . . . what am I supposed to remember?"

He swept his gaze to my face, his lashes long and lazy. "Oh, my sweet. If you have to ask . . . never mind. It's no matter. But stay with me? I must protect you. Take you away from the life you lead. You long to be here; I can feel it. The Golden Wood is your home. Your cousin and aunt are here. You belong by my side." Stretching out on his back, he folded his arms behind his head as the sunlight broke through the clouds and splashed across his face.

He was gorgeous, my prince. With eyes so blue they mirrored the morning sky, and hair as silky as spun platinum. His skin was a deep olive and he barely looked human. But his energy was that of summer apples and warm hay, of long nights under the stars with the scent of roses heavy on the breeze. I caught my breath, wondering again at the connection that I felt with this man. This Fae Prince. For it ran like a river beneath the surface, wide and vast and deep, rolling thunder as it moved along and took me with it.

I leaned down, slowly, brushing my lips to his. "You are the most incredible man I've ever met."

He slid his arms out from beneath his head and ran his hands lightly up my shoulders. "Cicely . . ." His voice was hoarse. "Cicely, you are like wild honey wine. I can't get enough of you. You were adorable when you were a child, but now . . . now you are grown and you are my passion and dream. I wish you could remember . . ."

"What is it, my love?" I sprawled in his arms and he rolled me over, looming above me.

"I cannot tell you . . . I cannot interfere. But one day, you will know the truth of our bond, and you will be mine forever." A shadow brushed across his face and he whispered, "Or perhaps you will forsake me."

"Never! I will never let you go. I love you, Grieve." I sprang up, blurting out the words that I'd wanted to say for the past three years, but I'd been too young. Too afraid. Even now, I knew it was too early—that I couldn't back up my feelings. My mother still controlled my life and I was at her beck and call.

But to Grieve, they were the magic key. He pulled me to him, his gaze searching my face. "You love me . . . how much do you love me? Enough to stay? Enough to marry me now?"

My breath caught in my throat. Marry him? The promise loomed lovely and brilliant and my heart skipped a beat. And yet . . . the image of my mother sprang up in my mind.

Krystal, strung out on heroin. On crack. On whatever she could get her hands on. Krystal, her dark eyes wide with fear, with the desire to forget who she was. It was me who kept us alive, ever since I was little. I'd learned how to survive. I'd kept myself off the dope and out of the bars. I'd learned how to pick pockets, to steal, to beg if need be. Together with Ulean, my Wind Elemental, I managed to keep us one step away from the cops and the pimps and the gangs.

If I left my mother . . . she'd die. She wasn't prepared for the life into which she'd slid. I was the only thing standing between her and death.

I slowly turned to Grieve, torn. Wanting to say yes. Wanting to stay and live my own life. Wanting to come in from the cold. But . . . my mother was my mother. And she'd never come back to New Forest. She'd let me go, and then die cold and alone in some alley. How many times had she said, "Without you, I'd be dead. Cicely, never leave me. I can't do it on my own. I need you."

"I . . . I can't. Not yet."

He stared at me, a flash of pain shooting through his eyes. "Cicely . . . I need you. I need you to be with me. We complete one another. You are my soul mate. My only love."

I stood, slowly. "My mother . . . she needs me."

"You would choose your mother—she who has done nothing for you, who's made your life a living hell? You would choose her over me?" He jumped up, cheeks flushing, voice bitter. "Are you toying with me? I wait for every summer, just to see you return home. The past few years, you've led me to hope for the future."

His love was overwhelming, and even though it felt so right, I was afraid of how dark his eyes had clouded. "Grieve, I'm still young."

"You are magic-born, not yummanii. You are older than your age. Cicely, I've waited all my life for you. I've waited a lifetime and more for you to find your way back to me, and now that you have, you turn me away?"

Shivering, I slowly backed away. "Just for a while . . . just till my mother gets herself settled—"

"And when will that be? She's had you on the run eleven years. Is she showing any signs of getting better? Of finding her way in the world? She'll keep you with her, a crutch, as long as she can."

I choked up and waved my hands in the air, trying to make him realize how unreasonable he was being. But even as the words, "You're talking about my mother!" came out of my mouth, I knew that he was right.

"I can't promise when, but I will return to you," I whispered low on the slipstream, and he heard me loud and clear.

"I need to know that I'm not waiting for a promise written on the wind. For a hope that will never come. I'd rather leave the Golden Wood than wait here, knowing I'll never have you by my side." He was angry now, and the hurt filled his face, making me feel horrible.

I turned, shaking my head, wanting nothing more but to forget my mother. Forget the streets. My wolf tattoo on my stomach was snarling and I reached down, trying to soothe it. Grieve paused, holding his breath.

I finally shook my head. "I promise I will return to you. But I don't know when. I have to look out for my mother. I'm all she has."

"Then go to her. Go to her now. Leave me with my

pain." He tossed the flowers he'd picked for me on the ground at my feet. "Go. Just go."

"Grieve . . ." My words drifted off as he turned and slowly, head down, walked away from me, not looking back.

As a shadow passed over the wood, I turned and ran.

I should have gone back, talked it through with him, but I was young and afraid to fully trust anyone. I'd learned how dangerous it was, in my short years on this planet. And even though Grieve was standing there, heart on his sleeve, and I wanted to be with him, I knew that now wasn't the time. I'd never trust him fully at this point—or myself.

Run, but never forget. Never forget him, Cicely. At the right time, you will return and your love for him will be fully grown, mature, ready to make promises.

I hope so, Ulean. I shivered as I left the Golden Wood, my tears so dark they could not fall. It would be nine long years until I saw Grieve again, but I thought of him every day, and grew to understand just what I'd given up.

❧

I closed my eyes and leaned against the shower stall. If only I'd stayed—could I have prevented the massacre out at the barrow? Could I have saved the Court of Rivers and Rushes? Could I have made a difference?

No. Ulean was firm. *You could not have stopped Myst, and she might have destroyed you if you had tried. You were not so strong back then. You knew it wasn't the right time. You did what you needed to.*

I shook my head. She was right. In the two years I wandered around alone after Krystal died, I'd grown even stronger, more independent.

Stepping out of the shower, I reached for the towel. When I thought about it, Krystal had, in her own fucked-up way, prepared me for this. She'd taught me to trust only myself, to stand on my own two feet.

I toweled off, wandering around my room. A picture of Heather and Krystal on my desk caught my attention. Doomed sisters, my aunt and my mother. Were Rhiannon and I doomed as well? Were we fated to unhappy ends, to lose our loves, perhaps even our lives?

You are at war. War is never easy, and seldom pretty. Ulean swept around me. *Try to stay in the present. Looking forward can do more harm than good, and looking into the past will merely make you melancholy.*

You're right. I will be strong. I won't let you—or my cousin or Grieve—down . . .

※

When I finally went downstairs, Rhiannon had left my breakfast on the counter. I could see her outside, sweeping the snow off the back steps.

Kaylin wandered into the room, dressed in camo cargo pants and a black wifebeater. His muscles were tight and defined, and he gave me a long look. "What have you been up to?"

I didn't feel like talking. For one thing, I wasn't sure what the hell had happened during my so-called dream. For another, even if I did, Kaylin would tell me what everybody else had: Forget Grieve, let him go and accept that Myst had won. And I couldn't do that.

"Looks like Rhiannon made breakfast." I slapped some toast and bacon on a plate, then added a hard-cooked egg and moved to the table.

Kaylin made an egg-and-cheese sandwich and joined me. "I heard about last night."

Jumpy, I jerked my head up. "Last night?" Had I been making noise?

"Yeah, Lannan and everything. You need to talk?"

"Oh, Lannan. Right." I was never sure what to think about Kaylin. He was 101 years old, a martial arts expert and computer geek, and he was also a dreamwalker. A night-veil demon had embedded itself into him, body and soul, while he was in the womb and had altered his very DNA. I thought he might be attracted to me, but I wasn't sure if that was just him trying to be friendly or what. When Kaylin wanted to help, he could ferret out extremely private information.

I swallowed a bite of toast and licked the melted butter off my fingers, then told him about Geoffrey's offer, and Lannan's reaction. "I don't know what to do. I don't want to be a vampire, so I'm not interested in Geoffrey's proposition. Nor do I want Lannan thinking he has some proprietary claim over me. I am indentured to the Crimson Court, not to *him*."

"You are walking a thin line. Lannan is not your master, but he holds the key to punishing you if you disobey Regina or Geoffrey. And he's very good about creating infractions where there are none. Hindsight is twenty-twenty, but I sure wish you'd insisted on Geoffrey overseeing you."

"Me, too." I played with the bread, then shrugged. "Nothing I can do except deal with him the best I can. One day, though, I'll stake him through the heart and that will be the end of Lannan Altos. But putting Perv Boy aside, I can't imagine how badly they are going to fuck this up. They already screwed things over once trying to infect the Indigo Court. Look at how their plan backfired. Now . . . another attempt?"

"Stupid, really. Fool me once, shame on you. Fool me twice, shame on me. And this antidote is definitely in the 'fool me twice' category. But we can't do anything to stop them. Talk down a group of vampires and a Fae Queen? I don't think so. We need them. And though Myst routed Lainule from her forest, the Queen of Rivers and Rushes is not to be trifled with."

"No, but neither is Myst. Chatter still has nightmares, he told me. The blood from Myst's routing of Lainule's people stained the barrow red. And remember, he's always been Grieve's best friend, and he had to leave him behind. The Shadow Hunters have unleashed a horror on New Forest, even if the town doesn't realize how much. Yet."

"Eat." Kaylin pointed to my dish. "We need all our strength because while they argue and plan in their mansions, we're the ones sitting on the edge of hell. Is Peyton coming over today?"

I nodded, finishing off my toast. "We're setting up the

back parlor as my shop and her headquarters. We decided
we might as well combine the two, especially since she's
only going to be working a couple evenings a week for a
while. She still needs to help Anadey in the diner."

"I think it's a great idea to join forces." He finished his
breakfast and took my plate with his to the sink, where he
ran a sudsy sponge over them. "So what's next?"

"Lainule and Geoffrey told me to go about my business
as usual and to stay away from Grieve. I guess . . . we figure
it out as we go along, since they don't seem interested in
entertaining our suggestions. Mostly, we try to stay alive."

The doorbell rang and I hopped up to go answer. It was
Peyton.

Half werepuma and half magic-born, she took a lot of
crap from the lycanthropes around town. Werewolves
hated the magic-born and heckled us whenever possible.
Peyton's lineage was cause for ridicule in their circles, and
she had endured a lifetime of it.

Peyton was half Native American; her father had run off
years ago, leaving Anadey—a shamanic witch who used
all four elements—and Peyton alone to fend for themselves. Peyton had grown up strong. Though soft-spoken,
she was an expert in martial arts and she wanted to open a
magical investigations agency.

"Hey, lady," I said, inviting her in.

She was carrying a box, and I took it from her and set it
on the floor. "I come bearing gifts from Mother. Ready to
get the office in order?"

"As ready as I'll ever be." I motioned to her and we
headed back to our headquarters.

The room we were using for our joint operations was the
back parlor. It was papered with pale roses and old coiling
ivy vines; the floors were hardwood and the ceilings vaulted.
A bay window faced the side of the house away from the
Golden Wood, and built-in shelves covered one wall.

With room for two desks, as well as several display
cases, both Peyton and I would have plenty of space. We'd
managed to wheedle a good price on the display cases

from a shop going out of business, and we'd each provided our own desk—Peyton had taken one of her grandmother's antiques, and I'd confiscated one I found in the attic at the Veil House.

"How's your mom?" I asked. Anadey had become intricately involved in our fight against the Shadow Hunters.

"Tired. The diner is running her ragged. She doesn't say anything, but I know she's afraid that I'll quit before she can find someone to take my place. She shouldn't worry, but she does." Peyton paused for a moment, then quietly asked, "But how are you? You've been through a lot in a short time."

"Yeah." I blinked. Returning to New Forest had been like being tossed in a pot of boiling water. Learn to handle the heat or die. "I'm taking it day by day. I have no idea where this is all going and I'm in too deep to consider taking off again."

"Have you been flying lately?"

I smiled shyly. "Yeah . . . every night that I can. Finding out I'm part Uwilahsidhe has been the only saving grace. It's the only thing helping me keep it together. When I'm out there on the wing, nothing else matters. Lannan, Grieve, Heather, Myst . . . nada. In my owl form, I can find a little taste of freedom. There are times I never want to turn back. It would be so much easier to just fly off to a different forest and live in my owl shape." I paused, lifting my gaze to meet hers. "But I always come back."

"I can understand that. When I was a little girl and being teased by the Lupa Clan, all I wanted to do was turn into my puma and race off into the forest. I tried a couple times and my mother would come out, hunting for me. Of course, by then I'd be so scared that I'd run for her and she'd see this cougar cub bouncing over and know it was me. Once a female puma—full grown—found me, and after figuring out what was going on, she carried me home by the scruff of the neck and dropped me on the doorstep."

Nodding, I laughed. Animals and Weres and shifters understood one another in ways that needed no language. Or rather, we had a language but it just wasn't the one two-leggeds used. Even though I was new to the life, I caught on quick, especially since I could already listen to the wind.

"Think we'll be ready to open on Monday?" Peyton arranged a bouquet of roses she'd bought on my desk.

We'd scheduled the opening of both Wind Charms and Mystical Eye Investigations for two days from now and were scrambling to finish last-minute preparations.

"All I have left to do is create a few more premade charms and to arrange all the candles and spell components that Marta left to me." Marta had been Peyton's grandmother, but there hadn't been a lot of love lost between them. Nor between Anadey and Marta—the two had always been at odds.

We got back to work and within half an hour, the room was ready for clients. I squeezed a card table into the corner and snapped a black tablecloth over it—Peyton was good with the cards and she could schedule readings. As we were setting up a display of charms to ward trouble away, I looked up to see Kaylin in the doorway, looking strange.

"What's wrong? You okay?"

"I don't know," he said, his voice husky. "I feel . . . strange. It started just a few minutes ago. I'm . . . it's hard to think—the room—" And then he let out a low groan and slumped against the door.

Peyton and I rushed over to his side just in time to catch him and keep him from sliding to the floor. His eyes were open, but he was unresponsive.

"Crap, help me get him onto the sofa in the living room. Then go call Rhiannon and ask her where Leo is—he's the healer."

As Peyton helped me carry Kaylin to the sofa, I stared at his open eyes, rolled back in his head, and wondered if he was dead. We got him onto the couch and knelt by his side, feeling for his heartbeat. There it was, slow and steady. I shook him by the shoulder but nothing, no response.

"I'll get Rhiannon," Peyton said, springing to her feet.

"She's out back, clearing the sidewalks." I turned back

to Kaylin as she raced off. "Kaylin, Kaylin? Can you hear me? Dude, wake up!"

Frustrated and scared, I felt for his pulse again. It was slow and even, and he didn't seem to be clammy or showing any other sign of a heart attack. I grabbed an afghan off the back of the rocking chair and spread it over him, not wanting to take a chance on shock. If he'd had an allergic reaction, he wouldn't be breathing—I knew that much from experience. I carried an EpiPen wherever I went.

Rhiannon came on the run, shedding her jacket and gloves along the way. She pulled off her boots, then nimbly raced over to my side and slid down beside me.

"What happened?"

"I don't know. He just came into the parlor and said he didn't feel good and then collapsed. No sign of shock, no clammy skin, his heartbeat sounds good. I have no clue as to what's going on."

"We need Leo. I called him on his cell. He's out doing errands for Geoffrey, but he's just finishing up at the post office and will be here as soon as he can. Peyton, can you go into the herb room and find the smelling salts? My mother kept them around 'just in case,' as she used to say."

"Sure." Peyton headed out of the room.

"Good idea. If they don't bring him around, then I don't know what will." Medicine was a tricky subject with Supernaturals—the magic-born, Weres, the Fae; some meds that worked wonders on the yummanii would kill us, and herbs that would barely touch one of their illnesses might be a miracle cure in our systems. We didn't dare give Kaylin anything until we knew more about what was going on. Because he was part demon, it could react badly on him.

But the smelling salts had no effect and so the three of us sat beside him, waiting for ten minutes until Leo came bounding through the door.

"How is he? Has his condition changed any?" Leo motioned for us to move and began to examine Kaylin. Besides his job working as a day-runner for Geoffrey, Leo was a healer and skilled with herbcraft. He asked Peyton to bring him the first-aid kit and slid the thermometer under Kaylin's tongue, then glanced at it, shaking his head.

After a few moments, he sat back, looking puzzled. "I haven't a clue as to what's wrong with him. This is weird. There's no sign of any problem other than the fact that he's comatose. His temperature is normal. I don't know—should we take him to the hospital?"

"I suppose we could, but . . . I have a feeling that what we're dealing with isn't medical—at least not in the traditional sense. I'm going to fetch Lainule. She can come help us for once." I put on my leather jacket and slid my keys in my pocket. "I'll be back soon. I have my cell—keep an eye on him and call me if there's any change."

"How are you going to find the Queen of Rivers and Rushes? She keeps out of sight, you know." Rhiannon frowned. "I don't think I like her much."

"Don't worry. I know where she is." With that, I slammed out of the door and jumped into Favonis, heading for Dovetail Lake, where Lainule kept her displaced Court.

※

The drive down was uneventful, even if I did pour on the speed. Fuck the cops. If they tried to stop me, they could face Geoffrey's wrath. He ruled the town, anyway, and I had a feeling that the vampire would be willing to do a lot of minor favors for me as long as I asked with respect.

But nobody bothered me and I swung into Dovetail Lake and skidded to a stop in the parking lot. Jumping out of the car, I caught my balance as I nearly fell on my butt, sliding on the slick snow that covered chunky ice below.

"Lainule! I know you're out here. I know you can hear me. I need to talk to you *now*! We need your help and I'll keep shouting so everybody and their brother can hear me until you show yourself."

The Summer Queen didn't like people knowing where she hid out. It was dangerous, and I knew I could get a rise out of her that way. Of course, she'd be pissed at me but right now, I didn't care.

Sure enough, within a moment there was a shimmer in the tattered remains of summer's rushes next to the lake, and one of her guards stepped out of the decrepit vegetation.

"What do you need?" He gave me an icy stare, but I ignored it.

"I need the Queen's help. It's an emergency." I wasn't going to tell him anything that might lead him to decide I really didn't need to see Lainule.

He paused, studying my face, then nodded for me to follow him. As I slipped through the portal in the dying reeds, a soft breeze swept around me and I found myself staring at a clear sky, pale blue with faint tendrils of sunlight breaking through a haze of distant clouds. The reeds disappeared and I was on the shores of a gorgeous lake, while a meadow spread out to the side. The grass was dry and soft, and butterflies wisped by on thin wings.

Lainule was sitting on a patchwork blanket by the water, staring silently into the gentle ripples. She looked up as I knelt beside her.

"Cicely—I did not summon you."

No pleasantries, but I didn't expect them. She was as far removed from the Cambyra Fae over which she ruled as were the vampires.

"Kaylin is . . . there's something wrong and we can't figure out what it is. I thought you might be able to help." I gazed up at her eyes and she smiled then, softly, and the world brightened.

"You come for your friend, not for yourself. Bless you for that, child. I cannot come to your house—it is too close to my woodland and Myst. But wait—there may be a way I can help." She snapped her fingers, and one of her serving girls knelt beside her. "Bring me Astralis."

The girl silently jogged off. As we sat there, I longed to beg Lainule to reconsider, to find a way to save Grieve from Myst's clutches, but I knew that might endanger her willingness to help us with Kaylin.

"Lady, may I ask you something?" I might not be able to

ask about Grieve, but there was something I could venture to discuss.

"What, child?"

"My father. I'd like to meet him." I only knew that his name was Wrath, and that he was one of the Uwilahsidhe.

Lainule frowned. "It is not the time, but soon—soon, I think. There are so many things that could tip the scales of fate, Cicely. And I hold many of their threads in my hands. If you meet him, if you find out your parentage, how will it affect the war? And make no mistake: War is upon us."

I considered her words. Begging wouldn't work, nor would whining, so I shelved the thought for the time being. "Then tell me, how can I keep out of Lannan's clutches?"

This brought a cloud across her face. "Oh, my child, I wish I'd talked to you before you made your deal; I could have warned you about how to proceed. But we were worried it might change your mind. And we needed you to take the contract. These are dark days, and darker still to come. The world is clouded with pain, and Myst's people are not confined to the Golden Wood."

"You mean there really are others?"

"While the Queen herself makes her home in my lands, her people have spread throughout the world. But if we can strike the heart of the hive, then we have a chance to break all of the swarms. For there is only one Queen; there is only one mother of the race. And make no mistake: Myst would conquer the world if she could, cloak it in an eternal winter, and keep both the magic-born and the yummanii as cattle—one for soul drinking, the other for blood and flesh."

"What about Lannan?"

She hung her head and for once, she was no longer Lainule the tattered Queen of Summer, but a woman, like me. She reached out and took my hands. "I wish I could help, but oh my dear, there is nothing I can do to stop him. Regina favors him, and if I were to step in, she might break the pact and the vampires need the Summer Fae, even if

they don't realize it. They would not win alone against
Myst and her people."

"So I'm sacrifice to his whims." I stared at her hands as
they held mine. "I made the bargain, I didn't think. I just
was hoping . . ."

"I'm sorry, so sorry."

At that moment, the girl returned with a silver bowl.
Lainule motioned for her to leave, then dipped it into the
silent lake, filling it full with the warm water of summer.
She waved her hand over it, whispering something, and
leaned close. As I watched, she breathed on the water and
then closed her eyes.

Her eyes flew open and she looked up at me. "Cicely,
Kaylin is in danger. He's evolving on his path. His demon
is trying to wake. Unless he receives the help he needs, he
will slide forever into a dark hole in his mind and never
regain consciousness. There is no time to waste. You must
journey into the Court of Dreams and bring back the spell
that will waken his demon." She placed her hands on my
shoulders. "You must journey to the home of the Bat People. It is a long, dangerous path, but there is no choice. It's
the only way if you want to save Kaylin."

Chapter 4

I stared at the Summer Queen. "The Court of Dreams? You seriously want me to go into another plane in search of the *Bat People*?"

Lainule gazed at me. "It's not what *I want*, child. The journey depends on whether you value your friend's life. I would not have you go, except Kaylin plays an important part in your future—that much I can tell you. If his demon does not wake, you will never recover him and this will change the course of the war against the Indigo Court. Whether for good or ill, I do not know, but I don't like playing with the future once it's told me its secrets."

A hummingbird, sparkling green with hints of blue, darted around my head, beating its wings furiously. The creature was beautiful, almost ephemeral. A gust of wind could knock it senseless. A year or two and it would probably be dead. And yet still it fed, and seemed happy, and took no notice of the future.

"To be so carefree," I whispered.

Lainule followed my gaze to the bird. "The hummingbird is no more carefree than you are. She must eat, and eat often. She must build her nest to lay her eggs and hope that predators stay away while she incubates them, and later, while she is off fetching food for the chicks. She must avoid flying into buildings or other stationary objects. She must avoid being caught by birds of prey and cats and anything else that might want to eat her. The world is her enemy and yet . . ." Lainule held out her hand and whistled, and the hummingbird dove for her, perching on her finger, fluttering its wings a few beats every second.

"And yet, she trusts in the way of things. She brings joy in her wake. What lessons can you take from her?" She reached out with her other hand and gently stroked the bird's head, then motioned for me to do the same.

I felt an odd instinct rise up, one I didn't like. A part of me—my owl self—wanted to dart forward and snatch up the hummingbird. It was food, prey . . . And yet I was able to control the predator within and, taking a deep breath, I reached out and ran my finger along the back of the bird, reveling in how small and yet how incredible it was.

"You just faced what will become one of your greatest lessons, I think. When we automatically attack those weaker, we lose incredible opportunities. This is a lesson most of the Cambyra Fae must learn—to hunt only when necessary. What else, child?"

Exhaling slowly, I thought for a moment. "To persevere, regardless of the odds. To take joy in what I can. To attempt what seems impossible. To soar, despite the effort it takes."

"Very good." She flicked her finger and the hummer raced off.

I followed it with my gaze as it soared into the distance. A lazy breeze wafted past, and I reached out on the slipstream to listen. The sound of fading summer ran through the currents, along with the whispering of leaves on the edge of turning color. The faint thunder of winter's drums threatened in the distance. And then I understood. I turned to Lainule.

"Your Court is waning . . . Myst is sucking the life force out of your realm." My voice was hushed. The thought that the Mistress of Mayhem could destroy not only Lainule's people, but her very realm, was terrifying. The long winter had truly come, riding the coattails of Summer, with wolves baying.

Lainule's face—unlined and clear—fell into sadness, and I wanted to reach out, to wipe away the mourning in her eyes.

"Yes, child. She is slowly draining me. She has taken over the Golden Wood, and while I can set up Court elsewhere, the woodland contains the Alissanya—my heartstone. I did not have time to retrieve it when they routed us. There was so much terror that night. So many people screaming and so much blood. My guards fought valiantly, but the blood ran like a river through the throne room, through the halls. Even if we reclaim our rightful home, the scent of terror will never vacate the barrow, and the ghosts of my people will linger. I will forever remember their screams. And I could not stop her. Myst's people fed well."

Shivering, I tried to block out the images, but I could see them—it was as if I had connected into Lainule's memories. The Cambyra Fae, running, screaming, trying to escape as the Shadow Hunters broke through and began to rip them to shreds. The monsters raged that night.

Pushing aside my nausea, I asked, "Heartstone? I've never heard of it. What's a heartstone?"

Lainule reached out and tipped my chin up. "I tell you what few outside of my realm know, but since your father . . . since he's one of my people, I will tell you. And perhaps it will help you against Myst, though I do not want you running off half-cocked. Do you understand?"

I opened my mouth and then stopped. My tongue felt thick.

"I am placing you under a Binding Oath on this one, child. Whatever you promise to me on this matter will hold you to your word." Her voice was solemn, and I realized that my assent would, indeed, give her power over me.

"I promise, I won't do anything rash," I whispered.

"A heartstone is part of a Faerie Queen's heart. When we take the throne, a part of our heart emerges from our body during the ritual and is encapsulated in a gem. The gem is hidden within the depths of our realm. This keeps our land safe; it allows us to shift our lands in and out of the realm of mortals. It is what keeps my realm forever summer . . . it is what helps keep the realm of the Queen of Oceans forever submerged. All Faerie Queens have one."

All Faerie Queens? I knew there were several, but I had no clue how many. "Even Myst?"

Lainule shrugged. "That I do not know. I should think she has to, in order to bring her winter with her, but the ritual may have been tainted, for she did not take the throne until she had been changed by Geoffrey. She was not a Faerie Queen before he got to her."

"And if you lose your heartstone?"

Looking half-sick, she shuddered. "If we ever should lose our heartstone, or if we are driven out of our realm and cannot take it with us, we will fade and become a spirit, doomed to wander the earth like a ghost, and our heartstone will crack. Or . . . if someone finds it, they can destroy it and thus we will die. If Myst finds my heartstone, she can obliterate me."

"And it's still within the Golden Wood." I breathed out a long, slow breath. Lainule was fading, slipping into the realm of spirit because Myst had taken over her land. "So she hasn't found it yet?"

"I guarantee you, if she had, I'd be dead. No, the Alissanya is well hidden still, but it's in the heart of the wood and there is no chance of reaching it without attracting her notice. As it is, reaching the Court of Dreams is going to be dangerous enough because you must go into the Golden Wood to find your way there."

She took her place on the makeshift throne, and I sat cross-legged on the grass next to her, enjoying the warmth from the sun.

"She looks to cover the world in a new ice age, doesn't she?" I asked.

Lainule hung her head. "Perhaps not the world, but her territory, yes. Winter's banging at the door, and unless we can stop her, there will be no summer to balance out the world. Do you understand why Geoffrey and I had to try? Why we hoped this plague would stop her?"

Biting my lip, I nodded. "I do, but . . . Grieve. Please don't tell me to forget him, because I can't promise you. Not like I did to keep silent about the heartstone. I love him, Lainule—he is a part of me and there's nothing I can do to change that. But I will be cautious."

I picked a blade of grass and chewed on it for a moment. "How do I enter the Court of Dreams? How do I save Kaylin?"

Lainule smiled then, and once again the sun emerged from behind a lazy cloud. Summer's tattered robes were still brilliant and beautiful, and not yet fully stripped away. And whatever I could do to keep Myst from destroying the joy of summer, I would willingly do.

"There is a portal in my realm that leads to the Court of Dreams. It is not near the barrow, so if you are cautious, you should be able to reach it. I would not allow you to journey into Myst's territory without good reason, but Kaylin . . . he will be needed before this war is over. Once you find the portal, you can enter the Court of Dreams and seek out the Bat People. Ask their shaman for help—explain what happened."

"Are they dangerous—the Bat People?"

Lainule pressed her lips together for a moment, then took my hand. "Child, everyone in your world is dangerous, including your own self. Get used to it—no matter whom you are talking to, they will be a danger. The Bat People are . . . unpredictable. They can be intimidating and they can be terrifying. But they are not unjust. Use caution, use diplomacy, watch your temper."

"Can I take someone with me? I can't do it alone," I whispered. The thought of facing the journey by myself frightened me. Not only the Shadow Hunters, but also Myst's spiders and the goblin dogs and tillynoks and other creatures pledged to the Ice Queen haunted the woods.

"Take Chatter with you. He knows where the portal is."

As I jerked my head up, she laughed.

"Yes—I know you have him with you. I am grateful you were able to save him. He was always a good servant and playmate for Grieve. And take your friend Peyton. She can help you through the woods. Do not take your cousin or the vampire lackey. I do not fully trust him, and your cousin is too unpredictable in her powers yet. Chatter can run camouflage, you and Peyton can shift into animal form . . . both factors may save your lives."

"I suppose I'd better be quick about it. When should we leave? If we wait till tomorrow morning when the Shadow Hunters are sleeping off their pain, will it be too long for Kaylin?" I didn't want to go into the woodland at night. I really didn't want to face Myst's people when they were awake and hunting.

But Lainule dashed my hopes. "No, you must leave soon. Go as soon as you're home. You may have enough time before nightfall to make it to the portal. I wish I had more help to give, but any additions to your party will call attention. Tell Chatter I entrust your life to his care."

And then the Queen of Summer leaned forward and kissed my forehead. "My kiss will not protect you, but may it gird your heart and when you are afraid, remember, the Court of Rivers and Rushes believes in you. I believe you can do this, Cicely. I have faith in you."

As her guard led me away, I glanced over my shoulder just in time to see Lainule reach her hand up to catch a sunbeam. It traveled down her arm, bathing her in light, and for a moment, I stood, entranced, watching the glory that was the heart of the Golden Wood. And then the portal opened and I stepped back into the snows of winter.

☀

Rhiannon shook her head. "How can she ask you to do this? To send you directly into Myst's clutches? You're insane to even think about it. Who cares what Lainule wants?"

Chatter flashed a surprised look at her. "She is the Queen of Rivers and Rushes. The Queen of Cicely's people, of her

father's people. How can Cicely disobey her? And mind
you, this is not for Lainule's greater good—but your own.
Our own. Kaylin is a powerful ally and you call him friend.
How could you let him drift forever in the mists of his
mind?" He sounded almost hurt.

I held up my hand. Peyton had stayed, and now she,
Rhiannon, Chatter, and I were sitting around the kitchen
table. Leo had gone back out—Geoffrey's errands couldn't
be tabled. And that was fine with me, because I had a feeling he'd object even more than Rhiannon. Leo would want
to go to Geoffrey for help, and this was something I didn't
want the vampires to know about.

"Enough. I've already promised. Chatter, you will come
with me?"

"Of course, Miss Cicely." He smiled softly and quietly
set his hand near mine. "I'll do whatever you need me to."

"Peyton? It's your decision. You are under no obligation
to go, but Lainule seems to feel that you would be an asset
during this journey."

"Hey, how can I open a magical investigations company
if I don't take some risks? Count me in. I'll call Mother and
let her know I'm going to be gone for the night. I won't tell
her what we're doing, though—I just have a feeling she'll be
happier if she thinks I'm just hanging over here with you
guys." She slid out from her chair and headed over to one
corner of the kitchen, flipping open her cell phone.

Rhiannon was pissed, that much was obvious. She
headed for the sink, fuming. I leaned against the counter,
next to her, trying to think of a way to calm her down
as she filled the teakettle. When she was thirteen, she'd
thrown a temper tantrum, accidentally starting a fire that
killed a young girl trapped in a car. Traumatized and eaten
by guilt, she'd repressed her powers until recently, when
they'd flared again. Anadey—Peyton's mother—had been
helping her learn to control them.

"Rhia," I said softly. "I have to do this. We need Kaylin.
He's *your* friend; I'm surprised you're so against this. He'll
die—or worse, become a vegetable—if we don't help him."

Her eyes blurred with tears as she clutched the saucer in her hand. "I lost my mother. I can't lose you, too."

I took the saucer from her and put it in the rack. "I won't let anything happen. I'll come back with help for Kaylin. I promise you."

She leaned against the sink, hands clutching the porcelain, shoulders shaking. "I'm just so scared. I miss my mother. I hate what happened to her and I don't want that to happen to you. What would I do without you?"

I slipped an arm around her. "That's not going to happen, but if by chance anything does, go to Anadey and ask her for help. Listen to what she says. I want you to promise me."

Rhiannon's face crumbled, but she nodded. "I promise. I'm not as strong as you are, Cicely. In some ways, Krystal's lack of care prepared you to handle all of this better than Heather's love ever did me. I'm frightened, but I'm trying to learn to be strong. For so long I hid from myself. I felt tainted. Now, I have to learn how to use my powers and learn fast."

"We're *all* learning. We're all learning how to survive. Rhia . . . more than just our personal lives rest on this. Myst is draining away Lainule's power. Summer will fade and the winter will settle in if we don't stop her. And to stop Myst, we need Kaylin." I took her hands in mine and gazed into her reddened eyes. "I *have* to do this. I'll take Chatter and Peyton with me. You and Leo keep watch over Kaylin and the house. Okay?"

She let out a shuddering breath and hung her head. "I guess we don't have a choice."

"No, we don't. Because even if we run, Myst has other colonies out there, and they will be edging into other towns, and bringing the winter with them, and their hunger . . . no place is safe. Magic-born, Were, vampire, yummanii, we're all on the hit list."

Rhia wiped her eyes with the back of her hand. "Very well, what do you need from me? What can I do to help?"

"That's the Rhia I know and love!" I kissed her cheek. "Can you throw together sandwiches that we can eat on the move? I'm going to change into something warmer." As

I headed toward the stairs, Rhiannon moved to the refrigerator and started taking out bread and ham and cheese. Though her lip still trembled, her chin was set and she looked resolved.

✢

We set out a half hour later, armed with whatever weaponry we could find. Chatter had raided Kaylin's closet and was wearing a pair of white jeans, a black-and-white-striped turtleneck, and a black Windbreaker. He looked oddly out of place in the clothes, but they would provide both camouflage and warmth.

Peyton and I wore jeans with sturdy hiking boots. I'd layered a sweatshirt over a light V-neck sweater, and then topped it off with one of my aunt's Windbreakers. Peyton had borrowed a jacket from Leo's closet—it fit her broad shoulders better than anything Rhiannon or I owned would have.

We climbed in the car and Rhiannon drove us down the road about three miles, stopping at a turnout by the side of the road. Chatter had taken into account the location of the trail we needed to intercept. If we started from this point, the Shadow Hunters—if any were braving the pain caused by the light and were out and about—wouldn't see us coming from the house. And neither would their spies who were watching our borders.

We climbed out of the car. I hugged Rhia and she silently lifted a hand in salute as we headed off the road, picking our way over a rather large snowbank, to enter the thick of the forest.

The sky was overcast with heavy white clouds as the snow lightly floated down, flakes dancing on the currents. Ulean swept around us, trying to ward them off, until I asked her to stop. No matter what, we were going to get wet, and the currents she swept up in trying to blow away the snowflakes were colder than the snow itself.

We plowed through the knee-deep snow, slogging our way under the shadow of the trees. It was going to be a long march and I doubted that we'd get out before dark. For one thing, when we entered the Court of Dreams, we had no clue what to expect.

The forest was silent, except for the kiss of snow on snow. The fir and cedar were bundled in their white coats and reminded me of a Christmas card, but the lack of noise was disturbing. No birds twittered, no sound of animals came breaking through the undergrowth; in fact, there was no sign that any living thing walked the back paths of this woodland.

Our breath came in thick clouds, and my face was already raw with the chill. Chatter walked lightly on top of the snow, barely leaving any footprints behind, but Peyton and I weren't so fortunate.

"It would be so much easier to fly there, but then I wouldn't have any clothes once I changed back," I said, keeping my voice low. Never knew who might be listening behind what bush.

"We already know what their spiders are like," Chatter said. "But beware—the Ice and Snow Elementals are dangerous if they are bound to one such as Myst. You can't really kill them. They'll just re-form if you shatter them."

"Should I have brought Rhiannon, with her fire?"

He shook his head. "She's not strong enough to make the journey. You and Peyton are versed in fighting, and you're both tough. Rhiannon and her beau aren't as skilled or as physically fit." When he said the word *beau* I heard a catch in his voice. Chatter had a crush on my cousin and everybody knew it, but nobody wanted to touch the subject.

"Have you ever been to the Court of Dreams?" I quickened my pace, wanting to be through the woods before afternoon.

"No, Miss Cicely. I haven't. Grieve has, though. He went once, against the Queen's orders. I remember he got in so much trouble." His voice broke again, and he shook his head, as if to shake off the past. "Best not to dwell on times long gone. Even if we win, nothing will ever be the same again."

Peyton cleared her throat. "No, they won't, but perhaps they won't be as dire as you think. Sometimes change brings new growth. I know that sounds like a platitude, but honestly, it's true. When my father ran off, my mother had to change our entire way of life. I was too little to remember most of it, but I do remember we had to move out of our big house into a tiny apartment, and that suddenly, Da was gone. He never came back, and the abandonment still hurts, but we survived. We learned to enjoy life again."

I smiled at her, shivering. "I never had a home, except for the Veil House. It's the only place I ever carried in my heart, because it stood for stability. Heather was the only mother figure I knew. My own mother . . . Krystal was . . ."

I paused, flashing back to all the nights on the run, trying to escape apartment managers after their money, and johns who were angry because Krystal stole from them after she'd fucked them. I'd catch a snippet on the wind and away we'd run. Though my mother hated her magic—and mine—she took advantage of it when it promised to keep her out of trouble.

The only stability during those years came from Uncle Brody, who I met when I was seven and who taught me the rules of survival as best as he could, and the few months we lived with Dane, the man who had tattooed me, and who'd been in love with Krystal. But she blew that one, just as she fucked up everything in our lives, and we were out on the streets again, and Dane died from a gunman's bullet.

I'd learned to use the wind to help me survive. Ulean warned me of danger, warned me when we needed to move or when there was an opportunity I might miss. She—and the wind—kept us alive on the margins of society.

I shook my head. "Krystal was a fuck-up. She was weak and she died because she couldn't face reality. I'll never let myself become like her." A glance at the sky told me the snow was falling faster. "Come on, let's make tracks and get to the portal. Chatter, lead the way?"

As we pushed deeper into the wood, the world faded except for the stark, barren trees, evergreens blanketed with a layer of white, and brush and rocks hidden by the snow. We must have been walking for half an hour when a noise startled me. I motioned for the others to stop.

"Did you hear that?" I kept my voice as low as I could and still be heard. Chatter could hear me if I spoke in the slipstream, but Peyton couldn't.

Chatter nodded, motioning to our left. The noise was coming from deeper in the woods, and whatever it was, it sounded like it was moving closer. I thought for a moment. We could hurry, try to outpace it, but it sounded like it was coming in fast, and we couldn't run through the snow. We could meet it, take the offensive, or we could wait. There was no place to hide, that was for sure—unless Peyton and I shifted and Chatter vanished. But that would require getting naked in the cold, and I didn't fancy that.

I readied my switchblade and fan, and Peyton readied the walking stick she'd been carrying. Chatter took a deep breath and moved into fighting stance.

At that moment, the creature broke through and my heart sank. It wasn't one of the Shadow Hunters, but what we were facing could be far more dangerous. I'd heard of them, but they usually inhabited cold mountaintops or the northern forests.

Ulean, are you ready?

I am here. Be cautious. This one is dangerous. She is old and crafty.

Chatter gasped. "A snow hag!"

She appeared to be a withered old woman, but she was far more than that. Members of the Wilding Fae, inclined toward evil, snow hags were usually magically summoned by powerful entities. *Like Myst.* Far more dangerous than any tillynok or goblin, snow hags wielded dark magic. And this one looked ready to rumble.

Chapter 5

"Crap!" I tripped over a root, I tried to back away so fast. Primal and feral, the Wilding ones were always dangerous, always unpredictable.

But she didn't attack, although she looked prepared to. She eyed the three of us, one of her withered hands scratching her chin. Her limbs were long and bone-thin, and she was gaunt, with one tooth showing that curled out of her mouth and over her bottom lip. Her hair was straggled white and looked like cotton batting, and she was dressed in gray rags, with her equally thin legs bowed out, bending at the knees on large pointed feet.

"What have we here?" Her voice whistled like dry husks. "I smell Cambyra Fae on the both of you." She pointed to Chatter and me. I glanced curiously at Chatter—I knew he was Fae but hadn't realized he was also Cambyra, and now I wondered what he shifted into.

"But you, pretty girl . . . what are you? I smell . . ." The snow hag lifted her nose and sniffed at Peyton, a loud and snuffly sound. "Big cat. Shifter, but a Were. Am I right?" Her keen gaze cut through the snow, piercing.

Peyton glanced at me, looking for a clue. I wasn't sure, so I held my place and watched Chatter, who moved to block the way between her and us.

"Snow hag, what are you doing here?" He stood taller and seemed more commanding than I'd ever seen him.

"You would love to know. But surely you must guess who summoned me. I am in the same clutches you are. But she feeds me meat for my services, at least. Bound I am, unless another frees me, a welcome thought." Her eyes were glinting and I didn't trust her, but Chatter nodded.

He turned to me and whispered on the slipstream. *She's giving us a hint. She wants out from under Myst's control.*

What can we offer her? How do you deal with snow hags? I've heard of them but never had any associations with them, obviously, since I lived in big cities most of my life.

When I'd lived in L.A. and San Francisco, the Fae were common but they were hot-weather Fae who had been urbanized by encroaching society. Vamps also preferred the bigger cities, while the magic-born tended to prefer smaller towns where there was more access to the wilds. But the Wilding Fae—they weren't suited to life among others.

He nodded. *Then let me take the reins, Miss Cicely.*

Be my guest.

The snow hag must have known we were talking about her, but she waited patiently, not moving to attack, simply staring at us with expectant, bulbous eyes.

Chatter cleared his throat. "Someone binds you. Someone else would bind you stronger if you have the will."

"I might, I might at that." She snickered and I wanted to back away from that curiously large head, but I forced myself to stay put.

"Riddle me this . . . what binds a snow hag, but can be broken? Not a solemn oath. Not a blood promise."

"No, no . . . agreed. They are too strong to be broken." Her eyes lit up and she glanced at me.

I looked at Chatter and again sent a message along the slipstream. *What are you doing?*

Remember your history? Oh, that's right—you did not

learn while in the city. She cannot tell us outright. She is one of the Wilding Fae. We must guess until we find what holds her, and then figure out how to break it.

Ah, now I understood. If we wanted her help, we had to break the chains Myst had bound around her without any direct instruction from her. I nodded at him and he turned back to the creature.

"What bonds are soft enough to be broken? My guess would be a bond unwillingly placed?" He cocked his head.

"You might guess correctly on that one."

"Then a spell, perhaps . . ." He paused and—at the wary look in her eye—added, "or perhaps . . . not a spell outright but a *trick*. Let me think . . . Myst is a huntress. Hunters use snares. A magical snare!"

The snow hag cackled. "You might guess correctly again!"

Chatter turned to Peyton and me. "Myst used a magical snare to gain control of the snow hag. Magical snares can be disarmed if we figure out their trigger. They're very much like a regular snare, but if you trip the trigger, you become magically bound rather than physically."

I screwed up my courage and decided to give Chatter's guessing game a chance. I turned to the snow hag. "I'm guessing someone near might be newly trapped. That it hasn't been long since they were ensnared."

She laughed, then. "You would guess correctly, my pretty."

"My guess it wasn't far from here."

"Again, a good and reasonable guess."

"How did you know that?" Chatter asked.

"Myst is able to enchant and bewitch, but the snow hag is obviously not enchanted by her enforced host. So most likely, the snare was set out here, away from the barrow. We should look around this area. Snared or not, the snow hag is dangerous, and Myst wouldn't want her too close, but she thought her powers too good to waste."

We began to look around the area, the snow hag propping herself against a boulder covered with a layer of ice. She looked content, staring off into the distance, as we peeked under shrubs and behind trees. After a few minutes, Chatter held up a broken wire.

"Found it. Now to trace it back to—here we go." He pulled out the magically inscribed peg that had held it in the ground, shaking the snow off it. "I'm not sure if I'm familiar with all these symbols, but a few I recognize."

Handing it to me, he glanced around and, once again, whispered into the slipstream. *We cannot tarry, but if we can gain her help, then we may have an ally for a long time to come.*

I understand. I took the wire and examined it. Some of the symbols stood out clearly to me. Because of the way the magic of the snare spell worked, the wires and pegs usually contained the word to free the ensnared, but it would be invisible to them. I picked through the symbols, reading them as carefully as I could. But something stood out— something in the pattern of the words. And then I realized that I recognized not only the pattern of speech in the spell, but the actual etching itself.

Aunt Heather. Heather had set the snare spell for Myst. I jerked my head up to stare bleakly at Chatter and Peyton.

"My aunt. She's the . . ." I stopped at Chatter's quick shake of the head. He was right—if the snow hag found out who had captured her, she'd go after her. In this case, though, that might not be a bad thing. Heather could never return to her former state. She belonged to Myst. But the snow hag might also seek revenge on Rhiannon—or me— and that, we couldn't chance.

I tucked the snare away. Heather had touched it and so it might be useful in casting a spell on her. "I know the chant to release you," I said to the snow hag. "But riddle me this: Why should I let someone free from a magical snare?"

You never just asked a Wilding one for a favor—that would forever put you at their mercy. But if you played your cards right, you could bargain your way into a deal.

The snow hag frowned, tilting her head. "Someone might have information to share—might play double duty and keep an eye on the enemy. For there are secrets to this forest that even the Mistress of Mayhem does not understand, and there are creatures who do not hearken well to her form of rule."

She was offering to play double agent, to give us information and quite possibly show us something that could hurt Myst.

With a glance at Chatter, I said, "We would have to have a binding oath that Myst will never find out, should someone choose to do this. Blood will be spilled."

"Blood, blood, blood, the juice of life, the drink of the damned. Spill a little blood, spill a little secret. No harm, no foul." Her voice singsonged over the words, traipsing like an arpeggio, a light trill on the wind.

I pulled out my switchblade. That was as close to a *yes* as we were going to get. "Then I would say, a drop of blood for the release word would be a good bargain. A binding oath to keep secret our presence and to tell us truths about this woodland that Myst does not know."

The snow hag nodded. "That would be a fair trade, and a fool would not accept the deal, but one wise in the ways of the world would jump at the chance." She held out her hand and I cut her palm, then my own, and we clasped hands. The feel of her blood on my palm was slippery, and tingled, and I wondered if she had any disease, but it was too late to worry about that now.

As soon as I pulled away my hand, I said, "To free oneself from a magical snare, it might be prudent to whisper the words, *Arcanum, Arcanum, archanumist. Vilathia, reshon, reshadar.*"

The snow hag cracked a wily grin and repeated the charm, and a subtle breeze swept through. I could hear the sound of magical chains breaking in the slipstream. The Wilding Fae tipped her head to and fro, then tapped her nose with one long, jointed finger.

"A bargain offered, a bargain kept. Never shirk a debt, never break a promise. Spill a little blood, now a little secret. Myst would not like this, should she know. Myst is a spider in her sleep, weaving her plans and shenanigans.

But not all spiders are all-clever. Myst does not know about a subterranean pathway that lurks near here. None of her people use it. One could climb in, traipse through the Golden Wood without being sensed, if one wanted to hide."

Chatter snapped his fingers. "Of course—I had forgotten about it! There's a tunnel that runs from barrow to barrow. It's been there longer than I have been alive, and I have no idea what it was used for, but the Queen of Rivers and Rushes closed it up long ago and told us never to play down there. I think . . ." He looked around, then turned to the snow hag. "Riddle me this . . . if there is such a pathway, it would have to have an entrance."

She burped, loudly, and wiped her nose. "A guess that such an entrance would be hidden beneath the boughs of a holly bush would not entirely be incorrect."

"Aha!" Chatter bounded over to a clump of trees where a holly bush poked through as the snow hag cleared her throat and spit out a plug of phlegm.

She sniffed the air. "Travelers wouldn't do well to tarry long on this day, that's a piece of truth for the taking. And Wilding Fae best be off to home and hearth again before the loosened snare is discovered." With that, she whirled in a flash of snow and wind and vanished from sight.

"Hurry, come on!" Chatter motioned us over to the holly bush, where he lifted the branches, wincing as they dug into his hand. I couldn't see anything but dirt protected from the snow by the branches, but Chatter whispered something and there, secreted back next to the trunk of the tree, a faint green light appeared in a square pattern. He quickly slapped the ground three times and the light—and dirt—vanished.

"Down, both of you. It should be safe and it will get us close to the Court of Dreams portal without being noticed." He motioned to me. "You first, Miss Cicely. I have to go last to close it up again."

I hesitantly slipped over the side. "Is there a ladder—" I started to ask but then stopped as my feet felt rungs. They were silver. As soon as I touched them, the metal resonated through my body.

I'd always liked silver, but since I'd first turned into an owl, the metal had started to affect me more and more— gold, too, to some extent, but especially silver. Silver was strong with Fae magic, and gold, too, though not as strongly. When the Fae came in contact with silver it was like meeting a friend who made you shiver with their touch. I hoped I wouldn't develop the bad reaction to iron that most Fae had.

Clinging to the rungs, I slowly let myself down, but I was not climbing through dirt. No, I was moving through some sort of portal, through a dimensional space. All around me was a misty green, swirling like silk, smelling of raspberries and lemonade and warm drowsy afternoons, and it made me want to breathe deep and never let the scent out of my lungs.

I reached the bottom finally, after what seemed like a very long climb, and jumped off the ladder. Peyton was right behind me, and lastly, Chatter. He glanced around. It was so dark I wasn't sure what he could see, but after a moment, he held out his hand and a miniature flame sprang up in his palm, only it was the color of sunlight shining through tree leaves, and it flickered merrily as he held his hand out in front of him.

The light illuminated the passage, but another flicker caught my eye. I took a moment to examine the walls. I had thought them to be dirt and compacted soil, but they were actually stonework—a wall built to shore up a tunnel that was thousands of years old, and yet the air in here was as fresh as the air outside. The walls sparkled: Between the stones and mortar were shards of colored glass. As I looked at them closely, lights flickered from within the pebbles.

"What are these?" I pointed to one particular stone that was shimmering with a fiery color.

"Magic holds up these walls, the magic of summer. The sparkle you see is encapsulated sunlight, woven into the core of the gem." He glanced over at me, his eyes shining in the reflection of the light, and I began to realize just how much the Court of Rivers and Rushes had lost when Myst came sweeping through.

A thought occurred to me, but I didn't want to say anything. Not yet. But what if Lainule had hidden her heartstone down in these tunnels? What if that was why she had sealed them over? Could we possibly find it and return it to her?

My promise to her rang sharply, though, and as much as I wanted to take a look around and see what we could find, I couldn't bring myself to do so. *Bound by oath* . . . she had extracted a promise from me, and I was powerless to break my word. *Right now.* But later . . . when the risk wasn't so great . . .

Gathering my thoughts, I turned to Chatter. "It's close to two P.M. by my guess. We need to get moving."

"Right, but you're going to find that time no longer matters. At least for now."

I wanted to ask what he meant, but he turned away and led us through the winding tunnel. Though it was empty and clear—and actually fairly warm and dry—I felt we were being watched, and it left me uneasy. But I had no sense that Myst or her minions were aware of us. No, it was more like walking through a memory book, where the scent and sounds of old parties and dances that had long ago faded from time played out just on the threshold of hearing.

Even Peyton noticed. "What's that?" She stopped.

"What?"

She turned this way and that, then relaxed. "Nothing, I guess. I thought I heard something, but . . . there's nothing here."

The sudden shifts and currents continued, and as time went on, it felt like we were wandering through a dream. My feet on autopilot, I drifted in and out of the slipstream, trying to catch the voices slipping past in a rush of whispers. There was a peal of laughter, soft words on a dusky summer's night, a shout of recognition. After a while, I stopped trying to understand and simply let them wash over me and vanish.

After a long time, Chatter held up his hand and pointed toward a fork in the passage. "To the left, then another few moments, and we reach the ladder to climb out."

I bit my lip, wondering what might be waiting outside for us. "How long have we been walking?"

"This passage is inside the barrow structure. Time shifts while we're here . . . it bends. There's no telling how long we've been in here, compared to the outer world."

I'd experienced the time shift before, when I entered Lainule's realm over at Dovetail Lake. I'd also noticed a shift when I turned into my owl self. Either time flew by without my realizing it, or I'd seem to be out for hours and when I returned, only moments had passed.

I could never seem to control the time shifts, and I didn't understand them yet, but they were definitely part of my awakening Fae nature. It was as if a part of myself had been locked away, waiting for Prince Charming's kiss— only the kiss had been a pendant and instead of waking from a magical sleep, I woke to a magical form. Until then, like all of the magic-born, I'd followed the time threads of the yummanii and the Weres, although magic-born— like the Weres—lived longer.

We climbed the ladder, Chatter going first, and again, the silver compound resonated through my fingertips, into my body. At the top, he did something I couldn't see, and then we crawled out through the opening, onto the snowy surface. The first thing that struck me was that it was almost dark.

"Crap, the Shadow Hunters will be up and about soon. How far did we come? How far in are we? We can't have been walking *that* long."

Chatter flashed me a ghost of a smile. "We covered well over twenty miles, but I have no idea how long we were walking."

"We're deep into the woodland, then." Shivering, I glanced around. It had been nice and warm belowground, but now the icy teeth of winter bit deep and I shivered, realizing I'd felt safe down in the tunnel. Now I felt terribly exposed again, and terribly vulnerable. "How far to the Court of Dreams?"

"We're near the portal." Chatter pointed toward a rocky foothill that rose through the tree line. "We have to go halfway up, and then a path to the right leads to the cave where the portal is. The climb is rough at first, over the rocks, but that part doesn't last for more than about fifteen minutes and then it's fairly easy going, though all uphill."

We scrambled over the heap of granite boulders that had piled upward. Another alluvial deposit, like back at the creek where we'd escaped Myst and her hunters? No, not a wide enough swath, but I definitely recognized glacial activity here. The Washington mountains were full of rock-fall and sweeping alluvial fans left from when the last ice age retreated from the area.

During the summer, the conies—or pikas, as some folk called them—lived on the rocky slopes. The creatures were within the lagomorph family, like rabbits, but they looked like a cross between mice and hamsters. Pikas didn't hibernate during winter but would be hiding beneath the boulders with their haypiles—the grass and food they'd managed to tuck away for the winter.

I scanned the area, looking for any sign one might be out and about, with no luck. I wasn't sure why I hoped to see one—it would just set off my owl instinct to hunt, but for some reason the thought of the resilient little creatures braving the winter seemed inspiring. And right now, we could use all the hope and inspiration we could get.

We managed to get past the rock slide and finally found ourselves on a snowy slope, leading up through the trees. My legs were burning from the exercise—I'd thought I'd gotten plenty on the streets, running from gang members, irate landlords, and thugs, but the past couple of weeks had put my body to the test and I'd discovered muscles I'd never even known existed. The lactic acid was building in my calves, and I longed to sit and rest.

I glanced over at Peyton. She looked to be sweating as much as I was. "I'm about done in. How about you?"

She nodded, her hands thrust deep in her pockets. "We should have brought walking sticks. Chatter's fully Fae; he can walk on top of the snow, but we have to slog through it."

And slog we did. The higher we went, the deeper the

snow became, and at this point it reached my knees. Each step was like wading through thick mud.

"Chatter, how much farther?"

He glanced over his shoulder, then stopped. "I'm sorry, I didn't realize you two were tired. Not much farther. See that clump of fir ahead? The ones next to the snowed-over ferns?" He pointed to a stand of trees about two city blocks away, up the mountain. "The path to the cave takes off there, and we will be on a trail that runs parallel to the mountain. The going won't be so difficult then, and from there, it's probably another twenty minutes to the cave."

I motioned to the sky. "It's almost dark. Are we in danger from Myst, do you think?"

He bit his lip, thinking, then shook his head. "I don't think her attention is directed toward the mountains. She seems to be focused on the city and the area down below. Remember, we're a good twenty-some miles from your house. I doubt if she sends her spies out this far. And while they might pick up our scent back near the beginning of the underground passage, I used a magical charm to ward the entryway from sight. I might not be a powerful mage, but I'm very good with hiding and camouflage."

Nodding, I motioned for him to lead on. Since we'd gotten him away from the Indigo Court, Chatter had really blossomed out into his own. In some ways, being Grieve's sidekick had kept him cowed. Now he took charge naturally and did not hang back waiting for orders.

"I tell you this," I said to Peyton as we headed toward the stand of fir. "Once we get home, we're hitting the gym a lot harder. If there are any more twenty-mile hikes in our future, I want to be in shape for it."

She laughed, and we continued to trudge through the ever-falling snow.

❋

A half hour later, we stood in front of the cave. It was squat and wide, and we'd have to crouch down to enter.

"Does the portal start when we enter? I mean, is the

cave mouth itself the actual portal?" I stared at the black maw, not certain how I felt about stepping into a dark, dank hole in the mountain. Especially one that might contain, oh, say . . . a bear. Or a cougar.

"No, the actual portal lies within the cave. But don't fret," Chatter said, seeming to perceive my worry. "Animals steer clear of here—they can sense the energy and it scares away most of them. Oh, we might find a rat or mouse or some such creature, but I wouldn't worry about large predators."

"Spiders?" Peyton asked. "I'm not afraid of them but I don't like them."

"This time of year? Unlikely." He brushed away a snow-flake that drifted down to light on his nose and stooped to enter the cave. "Come on, let's move."

The sky had turned deep indigo now, the indigo of twilight, and with the silvery clouds that covered the area, it illuminated the entire valley below with a bluish glow. I gazed at the wonderland. Myst had brought winter with her. Though she might be terrifying and ruthless, she was also beautiful and breathtaking, and so was her season. The air was chill and I listened to the slipstream, lowering myself into it to see what I could pick up, but the only sounds were those of burrowing animals.

As Peyton bent to crawl into the cave, I happened to catch a glimpse farther down the mountainside. Gleaming in the odd light, three Ice Elementals strode through a secluded clearing, their bodies faceted and angular. They were not hunting—I could tell from their stance—nor did they appear to take any notice of our movement. If they were aware of us at all, they gave no sign. They swept through the clearing with strong footsteps, focused on their journey, and against the evening sky they shimmered like diamonds. Another moment, and they were hidden beneath the tree cover again.

As I scrambled to join Peyton and Chatter, all I could think about was the incredible beauty that such a harsh and unyielding season contained.

Chapter 6

The minute I passed through the opening, I was pleasantly surprised. Though the entry was low, the inside of the cavern was not. Chatter had lit the flame in his hand again, and now he blew on it and it flew off, a globe of light, to spread through the air and illuminate the chamber.

The cavern was a good twenty feet high by thirty feet long. Dry and snug against the elements, it was still cold, all right, but the snow did not enter here, and I had my doubts whether rain made it through.

Chatter glanced around.

Peyton tapped him on the shoulder. "What are you looking for?"

He let out a long breath. "The portal. It's hidden to keep yummanii who might be in the area from stumbling into it. I think a few of their shamans know about it, but the Court of Dreams is no place for the unprepared, regardless of background."

After a moment, he stood back and closed his eyes, his hands outstretched in front of him. Taking a hesitant step forward, he faced to the left, then opened his eyes.

"There you are!" With a wave of his hand and a whispered chant that I couldn't quite pick up, an archway appeared against the solid rock. He turned back to us. "There's the portal. Once we cross through, be cautious not to stray out of my sight. It's easy to get lost in the Court of Dreams. There are nightmares there, as well as your heart's desires. And sometimes, they overlap. I know the path to the King of Dreams, so follow my lead. It's not far from the entrance."

We fell in line behind him, with me second and Peyton bringing up the rear. And then, without another word, he stepped through, and we followed.

At first, the transition was black, and everything around me felt like it was swirling in a vortex of endless night. But then I gradually began to make out colors in the wash, sparkling lights that twinkled in and out faster than I could pinpoint them. My stomach rolled with the feeling of being on water, in a big boat surging over the cresting waves. My feet met no solid floor, no sense of resistance, and then it felt like we were traveling a hundred miles an hour, the sparkles turning into tracers.

I could barely see Chatter's back in front of me, and when I tried to ask Peyton if she was still with us, my mouth moved but no sound emerged.

After a time, the kaleidoscope of lights began to subside and then, within a single blink of an eye, my feet hit solid ground and I tripped against Chatter's back. We were standing in a misty valley, with a rolling fog wafting hip-deep.

I quickly turned, relieved to see Peyton standing behind me.

"Are the both of you okay?" Chatter asked.

We nodded. I glanced overhead. The sky was hazy, and no sun shone. I didn't even know if they *had* a sun here, but the land was bathed in a mix of shadows and the colors of sunset. Trees, straggly and barren, dotted the landscape, and boulders jutted out from the fog that swept across the ground as far as I could see.

"Follow me, and do not speak to any who pass you unless I give the go-ahead. There are dangers here I cannot even begin to describe." He looked around, gauging our where-abouts, then motioned for us to follow him to the right.

We moved through the mist, cautiously, unable to see the ground. I was afraid of tripping over a root or a rock, but for the most part, the lay of the land was even and level and Chatter seemed to instinctively skirt obstacles in the path. I followed his lead carefully, and Peyton followed mine.

As we came to a fork in the road, Chatter turned to the left, but something to the right caught my eye. I turned to look and gasped.

Krystal, my mother, was standing there, holding out her arms.

"How . . . what . . ." I stared at her, wanting to believe, wanting so badly to think it was her, and yet I knew she was dead. How could this be? Was she a spirit? Was I hallucinating?

I found myself walking off the path, mesmerized by her sudden appearance. Krystal, my mother. Krystal, the woman who was never a mother to me. But now she was wearing a loose-fitting dress that seemed as ethereal as the fog. Her hair hung loose, but no longer stringy. She laughed when she saw me and her eyes were welcoming, no longer jaded with crack and horse.

"Honey, I've missed you so much. I'm so sorry I had to leave you; please forgive me. Please, give me a chance to make all those unhappy years up to you."

I gazed at her face and thought, *My mother is beautiful*, but then I stopped. Something was off.

Cicely! Cicely—can you hear me? Cicely!

Far in the distance, someone was calling me. But my mother's face filled my vision and I moved toward her, wanting to run into her arms. I was five again, and she was smiling and I felt for the first time in my life that I lit up her world, and I ran into her embrace. She wrapped her arms around me, so strong and caring, and I melted into the love she had never, ever shown me and burst into tears.

Blink. *Wait . . . no, I'm twenty-six, not five . . .*

Blink. *Stay with me forever; you are my little girl. You just dreamed a long, strange dream that you're all grown up. But you don't have to be a grown-up, Cicely. You're my little girl and you can stay with me.*

Thank you, Mama . . . I wanted to love you so much, I wanted to be your little girl but you never would let me. Am I your little girl? Mama?

You're forever and always my baby.

A faint sound in the distance . . .

Cicely! Cicely! A different voice, calling to me, but there was nothing in my field of vision save for Krystal.

Krystal let out a long, happy sigh, and I wondered what she'd say next—all those things I'd waited all those years to hear. But then she smiled, and her teeth were needle sharp, and her eyes burned crimson—the crimson of blood.

The spell began to break, slowly, dreams crashing to the ground.

"Krystal, no—Mother! Mother!" I began to struggle, trying to free myself, but Krystal was strong—a lot stronger than I remembered. And then I realized that Krystal's arms were long and sinuous and she wasn't really my mother.

Cicely! Break free, child. Break free of the illusion! A sudden gust of wind blew away the fog in the area in which we were standing and I gasped, for it blew away illusion, too. Instead of my mother, I was in the clutches of a short, squat, reptilian creature with tentacles waving. I screamed, shattering the last shards of the spell.

Whatever it was, it wasn't happy, and the grip around my arms and waist grew tighter as I pushed away from it. I could no longer understand what it was saying, and I struggled, trying to pry my way free from its grasp.

I felt something jar against my back and glanced over my shoulder. Peyton was stabbing one of the tentacles with a butcher knife. And Chatter was holding his hands out and—*Whoosh!*—a white-hot flame shot out to envelop the creature. The thing made a noise sounding like a scream and let go of me. Peyton grabbed hold of my arm and ran, dragging me along behind her. There was another shriek from behind, and something grabbed my ankle.

I tripped, falling forward, and looked back to see one of the scaly arms wrapping itself around my foot, and I twisted around, lunging forward as I whipped out my switchblade and drove it into the creature's flesh. It uncurled from my ankle and then, with a final thrashing slap, it slammed against me, knocking me down, then retreated.

I lay in the gathering fog, gasping for breath. Peyton and Chatter knelt beside me and helped me stand. Thoroughly confused, I glanced around. We seemed to be right back where we were when I'd seen . . . *Krystal?* Everything came flooding back.

"Krystal? I know she's dead—what the hell possessed me to go over to that thing? What the fuck was that? What happened?" Furious at myself, and bewildered, I looked from Chatter to Peyton, then back to Chatter again.

He rubbed my shoulder gently. "Don't blame yourself— you stumbled over a dreamweaver. They feed on the dreams and secret wishes of others and can look into your mind. The demons live primarily in the Court of Dreams, but now and then you might find one slipping over into our world as well. They tend to haunt the wild places. We don't know what they *are*, only that they aren't Fae."

Nerve-racked, I cleared my throat. "What would it have done to me?"

"Sucked your mind clean. Left you a vegetable." The offhand way he said it chilled me to the bone.

"Let's move on. Maybe you need to tether us together so we don't wander off like I did." I didn't want to meander off the road again. In fact, I wanted to turn around and go home, but the monsters waiting for us there were just as frightening. And Kaylin needed us.

Chatter cocked his head, looking curious. "Cicely, you didn't wander off the path. The creature hid in the fog beside you and caught you in its trap before we could stop it. You stayed on the path the entire time."

I'd stayed on the path, hadn't strayed, and still they

came out of the mist and fog to hunt. Shuddering, I nodded, saying nothing.

Are you all right, child? I tried to reach you.

Ulean . . . *You tried to lead me back to myself. But nothing seemed to penetrate that fog, my friend. Thank you for trying.*

There are so many dangers here. I am glad I came with you. But be wary—creatures like the dreamweaver are hard to fight and they use sweet honey as a lure.

I thought about Krystal, and how I'd always wanted her to be a normal, loving mother. If my thoughts were that easy to read—if my secret hopes about my mother were that clear—then it was a good thing we hadn't brought Rhiannon with us. Steeling myself, I nodded for Chatter to move on.

We headed farther into the shadowy land. I sensed beings going by, catching whispers of sounds on the slipstream, but I couldn't understand the languages, only the emotions . . .

. . . a great sadness, loss . . . melancholy . . .

. . . hunger, seething, angry hunger . . .

. . . fear, constant wariness . . .

. . . so tired . . . so very tired but no place to rest . . .

"This place isn't a happy one," I said after a while, disengaging from the slipstream. It was too depressing.

Chatter glanced back. "No, the Court of Dreams is not a happy place, although some people—like the Bat People— have their own measure of joy. This is the place where old dreams come to die, where jealousy and envy feed, where people lose their way and creatures can take advantage of sadness, insecurity, and hunger."

I had no clue as to how long we'd been walking—though I noticed that I wasn't nearly as tired here as I had been wandering through the snow—when Chatter stopped and pointed. A tall mountain jutted out of the fog, stark against the twilight sky. A large cavern was visible against the side of the granite.

"The home of the Bat People. That's where we're going."

As I stared at the inky opening, a sudden flip in my stomach told me that we had barely scratched the surface of the Court of Dreams.

⚜

There were shadows entering and exiting the cave: tall, thin, bipedal, with wings folded back as they walked. They moved deliberately, as if they were in a procession, knees bent, their movements jerky and strong. I glanced at their hands; long talons shimmered like silver spikes. Whispers raced through the air . . . clicks—hundreds of clicks— echoing on the slipstream to the point where I could barely stand to listen.

Ulean howled around me. *So much energy flowing through the slipstream. Cicely, this is a dangerous place. Watch your step—these beings are not dreamweavers, but they are the eaters of hope and of love and of dreams. They can be wild and wicked.*

One particular shade turned toward us and, in a blur, moved to block our path.

Chatter shivered, but he held up one hand and opened his mouth. He darted his head this way and that to match the bobbing head of our roadblock, and a series of clicks issued forth.

So this is why Lainule bade me bring him along. There was far more to the Fae than being Grieve's sidekick, and I was only now beginning to recognize how talented he was.

After a moment, the blurred figure motioned to us and turned. Chatter moved ahead, gesturing for us to be quiet but stay close. Peyton and I fell in behind him again, and we entered the cave.

I wasn't sure if I was expecting total darkness or what, but the cave was an explosion of light. Globes of light dotted the ceiling, easily a thousand brilliant suns, creating so much light that I instantly developed a headache. The intensity was close to blinding, and I held up my hand to shade my eyes in the white-hot chamber. I could barely see anything, but a strange sensation filtered through my body—that of being analyzed, screened, and cleansed. I glanced down at my skin and saw a fine ash covering my arms. As I shook it off, my arms glowed, and I realized that the light had burned off the layer of dead skin on the surface.

I glanced at the floor. We were walking on a thin mesh—as sturdy as stone, but essentially we were on a sieve that allowed the skin to drop through and far, far below, a flame burned.

More terrified than curious, I moved closer to Chatter and touched his arm. He glanced back and I pointed toward the floor. He just nodded, a cautionary look in his eye. I kept my mouth shut, but moved back to Peyton's side and took her hand. She looked as nervous as I was.

We passed over the mesh and then into a second chamber, as dark as the other had been bright. Plunged into the blackness, I stopped short, unable to see, but then hands—from someone terribly tall and strong—gently rested on my shoulders. Sharpened nails curved around, lightly piercing my Windbreaker, and whoever it was gave me a shove forward.

Too frightened to turn around, I moved as directed. A thick fog began to fill the chamber, and as I inhaled, it felt like I was breathing water. The fog poured into my body like syrup over pancakes, and I started to melt, the same way I had when Kaylin had taken me dreamwalking.

I closed my eyes as the lyrics to Gary Numan's song "Remember I Was Vapour" began to run through my head. I mouthed them as we moved along, gliding, flowing, shifting. I wasn't even sure we were still in body, but it was so incredibly relaxing that I ceased to care, just pouring along the floor.

A waterfall cascaded into my body and washed me clean as I closed my eyes and leaned my head back. Drenching me through, the glistening currents washed away pain and weariness and lingering feelers from the dream beast.

As we came to another door, abruptly I found myself back in my body. My hair hung, soaked—whether from water, humidity, or sweat, I didn't know. I glanced around the dimly lit room and caught sight of both Peyton and Chatter, who looked as wet as I was. And, a ways back in the hall, a tall throne.

Thrones are almost always obvious—they're meant to impress and intimidate. And this one was about as impressive as I'd seen: tall, imposing, and narrow-backed; I realized that it was fit for a king—a king with very large wings.

As Chatter motioned for Peyton and me to scoot close to him, there was a movement toward the back and a tall creature strode forward, knees bent, cloaked in a swirl of smoke, with wings towering above his head. He must have been ten feet tall, stretched thin and gaunt, and the only features on his face that I could see were his eyes, bulbous and faceted. He took his place, wings flanking either side of the tall throne, and pointed to the spot in front of him, then waited.

Chatter pushed me forward, following with Peyton.

He leaned forward and, in a voice so high pitched I could barely hear it, said, "Welcome to the Court of Dreams, Cicely Waters. What do you want from me?"

I wasn't sure how to address him, so I chanced a guess. "Your Majesty, have I the pleasure of addressing the King of Dreams?"

He grunted. "*Pleasure* may not be the best word, but yes. I repeat: What do you want?"

Sucking in a deep breath, I took a small step forward. "Your Majesty, I have been sent by the Queen of Rivers and Rushes on behalf of a friend. He needs help that only a shaman from your tribe can give us."

The King of Dreams did not blink—he did not have eyelids—but his eyes flashed and he tilted his head to the side. "Lainule . . . it has been many years . . ." His voice was soft, almost too soft to hear, and I caught the scent of regret in his words. "What help does your friend need?"

I let out a long breath, feeling suddenly a very small speck in the universe. "I need a spell from one of your shamans for my friend Kaylin. His night-veil demon is waking up and he needs help."

There was a sudden shift in the room and I could hear a

buzz of clicks behind us. The king froze, then reached one long, thin arm in the air and snapped his fingers. Another shadow-bound creature scuttled over to him, listened carefully to a series of clicks, and then nodded, taking off into the gloom.

"Kaylin. I have not heard that name in some time. So he still lives?"

I nodded. "Yes, he's now a grown man and he's slipped into unconsciousness. We cannot wake him." And then, because I could not stop myself, I asked, "Are you one of the night-veils? I know Lainule called you the Bat People, but . . ."

The king let out a loud noise that was either indignation or laughter—I hoped for the latter—and extended his hand to me. "We are not the demons, but the product of them. We are their children. But your friend—he is hybrid, he is unnatural, and there is no predicting what will become of him. We have watched him since his birth."

"You won't take him away from us, will you?" I tried to imagine Kaylin—so full of life—locked away in this gloom-filled world of shadows. Though he might be a dreamwalker, he wasn't cut out for this life. I knew it.

"We will not bring him here, no. He would not survive. We live in the periphery of your vision. We are always a fingertip away from your touch. We speak so quietly that you can hear us whisper but not what we say. We are the shadows that move on their own. We are the people of the Bat, always transforming. Your Kaylin is far too substantial to live among us. But we watch—because there may be more like him out there, and if there are, we need to know what he will become. He embodies the next generation."

He fell silent, motioning for us to move back. Chatter led us to a corner where there was a pile of rocks, and we sat, waiting.

I leaned forward, whispering into the slipstream. *What is this place? I thought the Bat People would be like the Cambyra Fae.*

Chatter shook his head. *No, they are an entirely different race. They take bat form in our world at times, but they*

*can walk through our world in shadow. That's where Kay-
lin gets his dreamwalking abilities. All of these creatures
have night-veil demons merged into their souls. The
demons have chosen the Bat People as their Chosen Ones.
Their children.*

He stopped as another of the Bat People entered the
room. "Ten to one, that's the shaman," he whispered.

I nodded, but inside all I could think about was how
much I wanted to go home. I didn't like the Court of
Dreams. It was too alien, too much of a reminder of how
little humanity—and the magic-born—actually owned the
world in which they lived. The Bat People would forever
make me wonder. Was it a bat, or one of the Bat People,
watching us as they flew out of the cave? And yet . . . and
yet . . . how could I talk? I was also part Cambyra Fae.

Suddenly I longed to turn into my owl self and soar off
into the night. I needed to be in flight, needed to be out of
reach of worry and uncertainty. As soon as we got home, I'd
take wing and leave it all behind. At least for a little while.

"You have the boy? The one locked to the night-veil?"
The voice was so harsh it hurt my ears, and I cringed as the
creature came up to me. The King sat back on his throne,
apparently unconcerned as far as I could tell.

"He's not with us, no. He's back in our world—unconscious. Lainule said that his demon is trying to wake and
that he needs a spell from the Bat People to help him." I
forced myself to sit up and shake off my fear.

The shadow laughed then, an ugly, frightening sound.
His eyes burned, glowing green and sparkling with white
pinpricks. "Yes . . . his demon must wake or he will forever
drift in the depths of his mind. I will give you the spell, but
you must be prepared. Your friend, in his new state, will be
unpredictable. I bear no consequence from waking the
night-veil. Make certain you want to do this, Cambyra. For
once done, it cannot be undone, and I doubt that you can
overcome Kaylin once he's met and accepted his demon."

"Why did it choose now to wake up? I thought it died
when it entered his soul in the womb."

"When the demon first enters the host, it dies, but it leaves behind a hatchling. After a long while, the hatchling begins to wake. It is simply the life cycle of the night-veil demons."

I glanced at Chatter, wondering what the fuck that meant. But I'd come to accept in the past couple of weeks that fear was the worst reason for holding back. Fear paralyzed. Hesitation was deadly.

"Give it to me. I'll take it to him and cast it, if I can."

The shaman clicked a series of notes, then held out a fetish—it was of a grotesque, twisted creature, and I had the feeling it represented one of the demons.

"To call forth his demon to waking, cast a circle round him with salt and then inside that, a ring of crystals—quartz—and lastly, a ring of belladonna. Then follow these simple steps," he said, giving me the rest of the instructions.

"Thank you. We need Kaylin, and he's our friend."

"Think you friend, think you foe. Either way it can go. But you must not tarry. If he lingers too long in the world of dreams, he will never wake, and his body will fade." And with that, the shaman abruptly left.

I tucked the fetish inside my pocket, making sure it was zipped shut. As we stood, I turned to look back at the King of Dreams. He was standing now, his wings outstretched in a terrifying wingspan that filled the area around the throne.

"Cicely!" His voice echoed through the chamber. "Go now. But do not forget—we are watching. And you have now caught the attention of the Court of Dreams. Lainule owes us a favor. As do *you*."

And then, with a swirl of shadow and fog, he was gone and we were outside the cavern.

Shuddering, I turned to Chatter. "Get us out of here. Now."

He nodded. "I think it best we leave. Come."

All the way back to the portal, we kept silent, moving as quickly as we could. We entered the cavern, stepping into the vortex of the portal, and everything became a spinning top of energy as we passed out of the Court of Dreams and back into the cavern on our side.

When we exited the cave, we found morning had arrived.

I was dragging butt. "We were there all night. That's kind of a good thing," I said. "The Shadow Hunters will be hiding from the light."

"Yes, but we have to hurry. I have a great sense of urgency." Chatter pushed us forward, not allowing us to rest. By the time we were partway through the underground tunnel, I was walking in my sleep, so tired. Peyton didn't look much better, but Chatter seemed fueled by an inner fire.

The snow was falling thickly when we emerged from the tunnel and began to work our way back toward the road. We'd walked a good fifty miles—since, I supposed, the day before, although time wasn't fixed in the realm of Faerie—and my body ached. My mind was running on autopilot and I ignored the quiet hush of the snow as it layered deeper and deeper.

As we neared the road, there was a rustle in the bushes and my wolf began to howl. I pressed my hand against my stomach and turned, knowing in my deepest core that he was there—watching me.

And there he was. Panting with pain, leaning against a tree, Grieve stood, his gaze fastened on me.

Oblivious to common sense, I raced toward him, my muscles screaming as I pushed them beyond their limits.

He opened his arms and I fell into his embrace. "Cicely, oh Cicely, my Cicely," he whispered, covering me with kisses. "I can't stand this. I miss you. I need you. I have to have you."

And I knew then, I was lost.

Chapter 7

"Grieve!" I closed my eyes as he embraced me, his lips covering mine, his tongue parting them as he pulled me ever tighter. His hands raced across my back, my ass, my hair, as he held me against him. I pushed him back, cupping his face in my hands, searching for some sense that things were okay again. But the wild streak in his eyes frightened me.

"I couldn't stay away. I sensed you in the woods; I had to be near you. I needed you," he panted, trying to hide from the daylight, and my wolf whimpered in pain. "I can't stand this. I can't stand being apart from you, but she forces me. She controls me, Cicely—and she'll kill me if she finds out I'm here with you. But I'd rather be dead than call her my consort."

He was broken. I could see it in his eyes. Myst had broken him. Or at least she was making a good attempt.

"Hold strong, don't let her win. I won't let her have you. Can't you break free and come with me? We can lock you in the basement during the day. I can . . ." And then it hit me. Lainule and Geoffrey were working on an antidote.

I could get hold of it somehow. I could save Grieve. I could take away his rage at—and inability to withstand—the light. *If it worked*. Then it would be easier to get him out of Myst's clutches. "I may be able to help you."

"My lovely Cicely, you have a death wish, don't you?" His eyes were cunning, but behind them his love stirred. I could feel it wash over me: his longing, his desire, his hunger. I leaned toward him and he wrapped me in his arms again, lingering against my lips with his own, plying them with his tongue.

"Let me drink from you. You give me strength. You give me hope. You are my all, Cicely Waters. You are the only reason I have to live." And he dipped his head toward my neck. "You're shaking," he whispered.

How could I tell him that he terrified me? That I feared him as much as I loved him? I swallowed my fear and looked into his eyes at the emotions waging war within him. The clash of tension, the clash of swords, the desire to hunt and the desire to love, all played out across his face, and all I wanted to do was hold him tight and wipe away the pain.

"Grieve . . . will she know? If you drink from me?"

He shook his head. "She is not all-powerful, though she is a force and fury. She is cruel, and vicious, and I'm terrified I'll become like her. I can feel myself shifting, every moment I'm with her. She is the corrupter, the Snow Queen with the heart of ice. And she means for me to be her king." His hands shifted and he leaned down again. "May I drink? It will help me keep my sanity—for a little while longer."

"Cicely, get away from him." Chatter's voice echoed through the snow and I glanced over at him. "Let her go, Grieve. If you truly love her, let her go."

Grieve stared at Chatter for a moment, snarling. "You would become a turncoat on me, too? You would forsake the one who saved your worthless life?" His voice was harsh and cruel.

I struggled against him as his hold changed on me. He laughed. "Cicely, my own little Cicely. Oh, Myst would have such fun playing with you."

"Grieve, no—please. Please, hear me with your heart, not with the haze of her madness." I reached up, stroked his face, forced him to look me in the eye. He quieted then, and again my wolf whimpered in pain, making me want to weep.

Ulean swept around me. *He is dangerous, like a wounded animal. Use caution, Cicely. Do not provoke him.*

But he let out a shuddering breath and hung his head. "Chatter is right. I'm dangerous. If I drank from you now, I don't know if I could stop."

I shook my head, running my fingers through the platinum locks that cascaded down his back. "You *will not* hurt me, Grieve. Our love runs through lifetimes. Remember . . . remember that. You and I were together before, and we'll be together again. We are soul mates, stronger together than apart."

And then . . . flash . . .

※

Grieve and I were standing there, together, on a mountain, scanning the vegetation below. Only he was Shy, not Grieve. "Can you see them? Are they coming?"

I shaded my eyes and searched the area. "I think so, but we are far enough away. We routed them, my love. We tore them to pieces."

He flinched. "You tore *them to pieces. I still can't fathom your fury, Cherish. But we are free from the chase for at least a little while. My mother will never rest until you are dead . . . and me. I am a traitor to my people, because of you. But I choose you—it has always been you. Only you."*

And my heart swelled, as tears began to run down my cheeks. I dropped to my knees. "And you, my love. Only, always you. Traitors . . . we both bear the label. My mother will torture me in front of our people, if she catches me. I have dishonored her. But I am not like my people . . . at least not without reason."

The memory of the guards, dismembered, bloody to the bone, tasting sweet in my mouth, filled my body, and I murmured a gentle moan. Their flesh was tender between my teeth, their blood still staining my lips. I'd taught them a harsh lesson about interfering with me.

Grieve-who-was-Shy knelt down and gathered me into his arms and slowly kissed me, long and deep, and the taste of blood mingled with the taste of his gentle breath. I slid my legs around his waist and he entered me, rocking gently against the mossy ground, as we mated. The sky shone crimson and yellow overhead, the sun high in the sky, and the feel of him on me, deep inside me, swallowed my anger.

"I will be with you forever, Cherish. We are fated together. No one else will ever measure up. You are my soul mate and we will never let them take us alive."

"We'll escape. Somehow we'll escape and go to a place where our union is not forbidden. Now, take me. Love me," I whispered. *"Make me forget who I am. Who my people are. Who my mother is." And he did.*

❧

Grieve shuddered in my arms, then inhaled a deep breath and gently pressed his lips against mine. "We are soul mates," he murmured. "Together forever." And then he dipped his lips to my neck and lightly nipped the skin, quietly lapping the blood that began to flow.

The pain was exquisite, and I flowed into his pleasure as my wolf let out a high pitched yip of joy. I wanted to lay him down, to straddle him in the snow, to feel him deep inside me, but this was not the place or the time. And Grieve seemed to sense it.

He voluntarily lifted his head, his eyes gleaming black, filled with stars. "You are mine, Cicely Waters. And your blood will sustain me. I can resist her, for a while longer. You are mine."

"I am yours," I whispered. "Keep her at bay, speak not to her, avoid Myst at all costs. And I will come for you—I promise, I will find a way."

"Do not make promises you can't keep, my sweet." And then he turned, and like a ghost he was gone through the woods. And my wolf bayed in the waning light.

"We have to go." Chatter was looking pissed out of his mind, but he said nothing. Peyton just glanced at me as we hurried through the snow, over the snowbank. She put in a call to Rhiannon, and after a couple of minutes, her car came rolling up the road and we scrambled in, exhausted and bone-weary.

�֎

"Did you make it to the Court of Dreams?" She sounded frantic.

"What happened? I can tell something happened. And yes, we did. I have the spell to help Kaylin."

"Thank gods—I was afraid Myst might have caught you. You were gone two days." She flashed me a worried smile. "Last night, a group of vampires and a group of Myst's hunters got into a rumble downtown. It was bad, Cicely—very bad. Several of the townsfolk were nearby and there were deaths."

"Holy crap. How many dead on each side?" I didn't want to know, but it was like taking off a Band-Aid; better to just rip it off quickly.

"Three vamps, two Shadow Hunters, and five passersby. Including two police officers who didn't know enough to stay out of it." She sobered. "It was pure carnage down there. A bloodbath." After a pause, she added, "Oh, and Lannan's furious—he's been looking for you."

"Oh wonderful. Just what I need." The thought that Lannan was looking for me made me feel as cozy as a bed of nails. It wasn't time for my tithe, so whatever the hell he wanted had to be some other plan his perverted mind had come up with. "I guess I have to tell them about our trip."

"*All* of it." Chatter's voice was somber as he leaned forward. "Grieve was out in the woods, waiting for Cicely on our way home."

Rhiannon jerked her head toward me, then back at the road as we swerved on black ice. "Grieve? Oh, Cicely."

"We're linked . . ." I shook my head and stared at my hands. "I have to save him, Rhia. I can't leave him to Myst—

he hates what he's becoming. I can't let him turn into a monster. And he will, if we don't get him away from her." I suddenly stopped, angry that I had to defend myself against my family as well as the vampires and Lainule. "I love him. I know it's risky, but I love him. If you can't handle it, I'll move. I'll find another place where I don't put you in danger."

"Stop this." Peyton's voice came from the backseat and she leaned up, nudging Chatter out of the way. "The both of you, stop it. Grieve and Cicely are what they are and there's nothing we can do to change it—or change them. They will go on seeking each other out because they bound themselves together on a level far deeper than a promise. So we have to deal with it. Even if Grieve spills that he saw Cicely, what's he going to tell Myst? That we were out in the woods? *Big fucking deal.* They don't know *what we were doing.* So might I suggest we go home and concentrate on helping Kaylin?"

Rhiannon blinked but nodded. "You have a point."

Chatter fell back against the seat, his arms crossed, looking mournful. "Grieve will never give up. He's always gotten what he wants, and he wants to be with Cicely. I still think she's in grave danger."

"We're all in grave danger," I said, ending the conversation. "There's nothing in this world that's safe for us now." And that finished that.

*

At home, Leo was stewing. "I can't believe you took off like that without telling me. Geoffrey was asking where the hell you were—and so was Lannan." He was in my face, making me angry.

I poked him in the chest. Hard. "The vampires may own me, but they do not spend every moment of my waking day telling me what I can and cannot do. Kaylin needed help. You were off somewhere, busy. You weren't any help. But most of all, you need to remember that I don't play by your rules, nor are you my big brother or uncle or father. So chill out, dude."

Leo looked about ready to blow, but I skirted him and

went up to the room Kaylin had claimed for his own. He preferred the attic, which was a comfortable nook. I knelt beside him and took out the fetish.

"Kaylin? Can you hear me? We're going to bring you out of it—we're going to help you." I looked up, motioning to Rhiannon. I was exhausted, but the shaman had warned me that we had very little time in which to perform the ritual; that Kaylin would retreat further into his mind if we didn't rescue him and wake his night-veil demon soon.

"What do you need? And are you sure we should do this now? You look absolutely out of it." She pressed her lips together, a worried expression on her face.

"We have to. Can you bring me a sandwich first? Then we need a pound of sea salt, enough belladonna to ring the circle, and a dozen quartz spikes that are at least two inches long each."

I slumped on the floor beside Kaylin's bed, wanting nothing more than to drag myself to my room, crawl into bed, and crash for a week, but it wasn't going to happen. As I leaned back against his bed and rested my head on the mattress, closing my eyes, all I could see was a swirl of colors. I let them play out, following them on the screen of my closed eyelids, as they whirled and dipped. Red, green . . . a splash of yellow . . . and then they began to take form.

A creature, winged and fierce, appeared out of the sparkles, and it homed in on me, flooding me with panic. I wanted to move, but I couldn't, and it latched hold to my shirt and began dragging itself up, its claws holding tight to the material. I couldn't open my eyes but I could see it nonetheless, and I knew it was headed toward my face—and toward my mind.

What are you doing? What do you want? Who are you, Cicely Waters? Do you remember who you were?

The words flooded my mind and I stammered, trying to answer, but I didn't understand the questions. *Who are you? What are you doing to me?*

Are you prepared to unleash me? Are you ready to accept the consequences for what you're about to do? And then it was face to face with me, and it leaned close. All I could see were flashes of light everywhere.

Ulean! Help me! What is this thing? I can't break free.
I was struggling, trying to disconnect from its energy, trying to shake it off. But it had hold of me on a psychic level.

And then, as Ulean swept into the room and rattled the door and shook the pictures on the wall, the creature let go and moved off. I opened my eyes, trying to catch my breath. As I looked down, the front of my shirt was rumpled and I knew I hadn't been dreaming.

What was that?
I believe it was a manifestation of Kaylin's demon.
Do you think I'm doing the right thing, Ulean?
I believe you have no choice. There are murmurs on the wind. Kaylin must live. We need him. And she would say no more.

Rhiannon brought me a ham-and-cheese sandwich, and she also handed me an energy drink, which I slammed down. I wolfed down the food, and then, as she and Leo—who was still simmering—brought in the ritual items, I went into my room and changed into a loose gown. Nightgowns were fine for ritual, and I needed to get out of my clothes. I held up the fetish, staring at the image of the creature. Sure enough, it was the same thing I'd seen in Kaylin's room. A night-veil demon.

I closed my fist around the figurine and brushed my hair back, slipping a headband on to hold it back. Picking up my stiletto dagger, I double-checked to make sure I was wearing my moonstone pendant. Then, I returned to Kaylin's bedroom.

"Help me get him in position. He needs to be on his back, arms out at his sides, legs not touching one another, naked." We stripped him, and I stopped when we pulled off the loose kimono that Leo and Rhiannon had dressed him in. He was toned, muscled but not muscle-bound. I automatically scanned his body and I found myself wondering what it would be like to touch that smooth, inviting skin . . . to feel him touch me.

My wolf growled and I gasped, pressing my hand to my stomach. *Never worry, Grieve . . . I might like to look, but you know you are my only love, my soul mate and lover.* The wolf settled down but felt restless and antsy. And I . . . I wondered once again where this was all leading, and how I could possibly save Grieve when I wasn't even sure I could save myself.

I motioned for all of them to leave. "I need one of you—Chatter, will you stay? Otherwise, the more people there are, the more it will complicate the ritual."

As Leo, Rhiannon, and Peyton filed out—the first looking ready to revolt—I shut the door and turned to Chatter. "You need to have my back. I have to release the demon but keep it contained within him. The only way I can do that is to struggle with it and break the fetish against his heart once it fully wakes. The shaman gave me its name, and with that I can control the creature, but it will try to attack me."

"I thought it was already part of him," Chatter said.

"So did I, but apparently what happened was that as it merged with his DNA and died, it left behind a hatchling. And it's ready to hatch."

"Ah." Chatter nodded. He looked like he wanted to say something else.

"What is it? And don't say 'nothing.' You're upset about Grieve."

"You should not count on him. I love him perhaps more than you—he's like a brother to me, but I'm practical. Grieve belongs to Myst, and Myst won't take lightly to anybody tampering with her toys."

I let out a short sigh. "No offense, but I don't give a fuck what you—or Leo—or Rhiannon thinks. You know that Grieve and I've been together before, in another life. I was part of the Indigo Court, he was Cambyra Fae. We were in love and we were hunted down and we bound our souls together before we killed ourselves. We're here to even the score, we're here to find each other. *I will not lose him again*, do you understand?"

Chatter's eyes flashed and he leaned in—the closest to

angry I'd ever seen him. "Of course, I know perfectly well that you were together before. I was *there*. I am as much a part of this whole mess as you are."

I didn't want to look at him. I knew what he was talking about but hadn't yet admitted it to myself. I didn't want to think about the truth—it was too raw; it made me too angry. "I don't want to talk about it."

"One of us has to say it—and you have to accept it. You were Myst's daughter and both you and I know that she's out to destroy you for betraying her! Grieve is her bait— she doesn't want him, she wants *you*. If you go charging in, she's just going to capture you. That's why she's keeping him. You can't really think she loves him. She loves no one." He leaned back, arms crossed.

I stared at him as his words ricocheted through the room. "No, no—I was part of the Indigo Court but I was never her daughter! You lie!" But my protest was weak. He was telling the truth. I'd known since my first flashback a week or so ago, but I hadn't wanted to admit it to myself. "I can't face being Myst's daughter. She isn't my mother. Krystal is . . . was . . ."

He was on the floor by my side in the blink of an eye, gathering me into his arms. I leaned against his body, closing my eyes as he murmured an apology.

"Oh, Cicely, of course you aren't—not this time around. But before, when you were with Grieve, you were Myst's daughter, destined to take the throne in the future when she died. You defied her . . . you ran . . . you dared to love one of the enemy. You have to accept that part of yourself if you hope to beat her this time."

"You were there. Which side were you on?"

"I was Shy's brother. Don't you remember?" His words hit like a sledgehammer, and I started to cry.

"No, no . . ." But the room started to fall away, and I went spiraling into the past.

※

Grieve and I were standing there, only he was Shy and I was Cherish, and now I could see myself for who I was—Myst's daughter. We were poised, waiting as the first front of those hunting for us came up the slope. Shy turned to me and blinked, his long lashes dusted with a lazy skiff of pollen from the deep grass in which we'd been lying. We were in Summer's land, and the Queen was hunting for us. Or rather, her servants were.

"Stop!" A man who looked very much like Shy stepped to the forefront. He carried a long, razor-edged silver-plated dagger and was wearing the armor of the knights of Summer. "In the name of Lainule, I command you to stop. Shy, return to us now, for punishment. The girl may go if she departs our lands and never returns."

Shy glanced at me, and I could tell he was nervous. "You have a chance to survive. If they take me home, I'll be punished for treason. But you—my Cherish, my love, you can escape."

I stared at him, my heart racing. "Surely you jest. Leave you to them? Leave you to death? Never. We fight together and if necessary, we die together."

"But love, they'll crucify you if you fight and falter." His eyes were wet, and he looked so forlorn that I wished once again we'd never met. It had been instant attraction, a deep and abiding need to be together that burned its way through my heart. Through his, too.

"Then let them do their worst. I will not leave you." I paused, resisting the urge to just go barreling into the fray with teeth sharp and jaws unhinged. I could mow down a good five or six of them before they had a chance to blink. But I was trying to resist instinct, trying to use reason.

There was one other factor to think about. "He's your brother," I said slowly. "Can you resist him? Do you want to? If you truly wish me to go, I will."

Shy bit his lip, glancing from his brother back to me, then back to his brother again. He pressed his lips shut, pulling me to him. "I cannot give you up. Not now. Not ever. We belong together, and if they can't see that . . ."

We turned, facing his brother, who was leading the band of warriors, and steeled ourselves for the attack. Shy's brother caught my gaze. I readied myself. And when they charged, he fell first under my attack . . . and the bloodlust raged, and soon, the field was soaked in their life force as Shy and I stood triumphant, with tears falling, unwilling victors against a force that would destroy our love.

❧

"No . . . Chatter—I would *never* hurt you—"

"Sshh . . . but you did, Cicely. Or rather, Cherish did. And Shy was not innocent in the act." He gently stroked my forehead, then my face, searching my eyes with a terrified look. "Please don't hate me for forcing you to remember. But you have to know the truth—you have to have all of the information you can in order to make clear decisions."

I blankly shook my head. "I don't hate you. How could I hate you, Chatter? But . . . she knows, she really does know that I was her daughter. That's why Myst is out to destroy me as much as she's out to destroy Geoffrey, isn't she?"

"She'll hurt you in any way she can. And she knows Grieve was your lover back then—how best to hurt you except to steal him away and turn him into the monster *you* were supposed to become?" He tightened his embrace. "Grieve did his best to deflect her from you, and I think even now he tries. But the more you and he connect, the more arsenal she has."

I gazed up into his face. He was so like Grieve and yet so unlike him. "What are you, Chatter? I know you're Cambyra like Grieve . . . like . . . me . . . so what are you? What kind of shifter?"

He let out a long sigh. "I do not shift into animal form like you and Grieve. My powers are different. I can't show you here."

"How come?" I was beginning to relax into a drowsy state in his arms. It was almost as if Grieve were holding me, without the intense pressure between us.

Chatter leaned close and whispered in my ear. "Because I turn into a pillar of fire. I'm deadly, Cicely—when I change, I have no control over my actions. Fire lives to burn, and when I transform, all I want is to consume."

That broke the spell. I jerked my head up to stare at him. "Fire? Is that why you are so pulled to Rhiannon?"

He blinked. "You can tell?"

"I can tell a mile away that you've got it bad for her."

"No," he said softly. "You misunderstand. I'm pulled to her flame—it sings within my own heart. But Miss Rhiannon, she is a gentle soul and I would never intrude on her relationship."

You're lying to yourself, I thought, but said nothing. Instead, I let his information settle. Chatter, who seemed so quiet and unassuming, turned into a raging inferno.

"When was the last time you transformed?"

"Years ago. I started a wildfire and burned one of my friends. Grieve, actually. It was long before you were born, and I meant no harm, but it hurt him for a long time. I swore then I'd never take a chance on hurting someone else I cared about. But it's not the same as Rhiannon repressing her powers. When the magic-born do not practice their magic, it backs up in them, and eventually it will implode. With the Cambyra, it's not as much pressure." He sucked in a long breath, then let it out. "Don't tell her—please. And don't tell Leo."

"Leo wouldn't like the connection." I frowned.

"No, he wouldn't."

I let out a long sigh. "We'd better get this done. Thank you—for everything. I'll think about what you said, but . . ." As I stood, it was all I could do to shrug. Nothing could make me give up Grieve.

Chatter nodded, his eyes dark and glowing. "You will do as you see fit. But Cicely, Myst will use anything against you she can. You were her blood. And you betrayed her."

"And she remembers . . . even if I don't." I shrugged off the weight of his words and turned to Kaylin. "We need to start the ritual. Are you ready to start?"

He nodded. I explained what we needed to do and we began to forge the magical circle of salt, then belladonna and lastly, the quartz. I crawled on the bed and straddled

Kaylin's naked body, feeling inappropriate, and yet something within me stirred as I sank down, sitting on his stomach.

Slowly I began to chant.

Demon waken, demon dreams,
demon days, demon wings,
night-veil, creature of shade,
wake to your host, fulfill the pact you made.

Chatter stood beside me, his voice weaving with mine, providing a countertonal response. Surprised, I glanced at him—he had an excellent voice and could have easily been a professional singer.

Waken to life, waken to death,
Waken to void, waken to breath,
Waken to the world, waken to the grave,
Waken to your host, wake and be saved.

Kaylin began to stir. Or rather, he began to convulse. I motioned to Chatter, who hurried over to my side. Kaylin was shaking and it was all I could do to keep him down. He frothed at the mouth, his eyes rolling back in his head, and I leaned forward, pressing his shoulders down, holding him still. He'd be bruised and sore, but it would be worse if I just let him flail.

Chatter pulled out a little bottle that the shaman had given me before we left the Court of Dreams and dropped three drops of the potion into Kaylin's mouth. Kaylin let out a long scream—really more of a howl—and I felt his arousal as he began to wake. Crap. This could end badly.

Kaylin thrashed and I suddenly found myself flying through the air, onto the floor, as he stood. He rose up, standing over me, erect and hair flowing, his eyes flashing with an odd light. Chatter backed up, reaching down to grab my hand, pulling me out of the way.

As if he'd never seen himself before, Kaylin held out his arms, examining them, then glanced down at his erection and let out a low, throaty laugh as he turned toward me.

"Thank you for waking me, Cicely. Let me show you just how grateful I am." The look on his face was insolent and yet—and yet—there was Kaylin, behind the new attitude.

"Kaylin—do you remember what happened?" The thought ran through my mind that maybe this hadn't been the best idea, but Lainule had insisted we needed him and how could I leave him in a vegetative state? I might as well have killed him as done that.

"Oh, I remember," he said, slowly stepping toward me. "I was sleeping for a long, long time and then . . . something stirred and it was time for me to wake."

"You're the night-veil—where's Kaylin? I see him in there. Let him through. It's his body and you only share it."

"Share it? No, I think not. I'm going to take this body and thoroughly enjoy the freedom." The demon laughed, holding out his hand. He made a fist and brought it up, gazing at it joyfully.

"Cicely—you have the fetish!" Chatter frantically motioned to my hand.

Crap! I was supposed to break the fetish against Kaylin's heart! Otherwise the demon would be free to control him. I scrambled to my feet, nodding.

"Help me, Chatter—I can't do it by myself."

The demon snorted. "You think I'm going to let you carry through with the rest of the spell? I know perfectly well what you're up to and it's not going to work."

I glanced at Chatter, wondering if we could take him. We didn't dare let him loose. "We have to," I murmured. And so, without another word, we both jumped Kaylin, trying to take him down.

Chapter 8

Kaylin burst out in laughter again and he swung his fist, connecting with my stomach to send me reeling across the room. I landed hard on my tailbone, feeling like my midsection had met a sledgehammer. But I still had hold of the fetish. I wheezed, struggling to right myself as Chatter landed a blow on Kaylin, my wolf growling low and long.

"Cicely! Chatter! What the fuck's going on in there?" Leo pounded on the door. "Open up!"

"Stay out until we call you!" I didn't want them in the way of those fists. As it was, my midsection was going to be sporting a nasty bruise for a couple of weeks. I rolled to my feet while Chatter and Kaylin engaged. Chatter was stronger than I was, but Kaylin had suddenly developed a strength that could match—or best—one of the Shadow Hunters. I glanced around the room and suddenly remembered my street-fighting days and the advice from Uncle Brody: *When facing the enemy, think dirty. Anything for a weapon.*

I grabbed a bottle of cologne off Kaylin's dresser and aimed it for his eyes, then pressed the button. The scented spray of Spice hit him directly in the face, and he let out a roar as he covered his eyes with his hands and stumbled back.

Chatter tackled him, knocking him to the floor as I scrambled over to his side and brought the fetish down hard against his heart. The clay figurine shattered into pieces and I leaned over him.

"Egrend . . . Egrend . . . I command you to submit your will to Kaylin. You are no longer in control. Merge, and become one."

Kaylin's eyes jerked open, glowing with a pale yellow light, and he struggled, but after a moment the light faded and he slumped on the floor, breathing softly. I looked for any sign that the creature was playing possum, but I was fairly certain the spell had worked.

Chatter gathered him up and laid him on the bed. "He's exhausted, I think. Being ridden by a demon can drain a person in no time. And when his demon woke, it rode him like a horse."

"Yeah," I said, staring down at the bed. "It was out for blood, all right. I wonder how this will change the Kaylin we know."

"There's no telling. Not yet. We just have to hope for the best. If we hadn't done this, Cicely, he would have faded and never again been able to wake. You saved his life." Chatter placed a hand on my arm, and I smiled gratefully.

"Then why do I feel so strangely guilty? Like I've just altered him forever?"

"Because you have. But we had no choice. Come on, let him rest. He's no longer unconscious, just asleep. I can feel the difference." Chatter led me to the door and, with a backward glance at Kaylin's slumbering form, we left the room.

Leo and Rhiannon were both looking terrified, although with Leo, an undercurrent of anger ran through his worry. We told them what happened, and he just shook his head in disgust.

"I thought we were working together on this—why the fuck did you shut us out? Or at least *me*. And you put

Rhiannon in danger." The muscles on the side of his neck tensed and his ears were turning red.

I had to nip this attitude in the bud. "Listen to me, Leo. I did as Lainule asked. She told me to take Chatter and Peyton with me, that you and Rhiannon couldn't handle the journey, and she was right. Until you get up to speed on your fighting skills, deal with it. You're a healer—we need you in the background. You are vital to the continued health of our group, and that's not a front-line job. If you get hurt, it hurts all of us. Got it?"

Though I'd started off trying to appeal to his ego, I realized that what I was saying was true. If Leo got hurt, none of the rest of us could work healing magic or knew what to do with the herbs that my aunt had so carefully cultivated.

I led them into my room, away from Kaylin's door, and dropped onto the bed. "Listen, I'm exhausted. I have no doubt Peyton is, too—and even Chatter is looking worn out. We had a long trip and haven't slept since we left."

"Don't try to make me feel better," Leo grumbled.

"I don't have the time or energy to patronize you. What I'm saying is true. You're the only one who knows what to do with that huge stash of herbs down there. We can't rely on anybody else. Who knows where Myst has sent her feelers through this town? And the vampires aren't going to give a fuck about our health. You know that."

He bit his lip, glancing over at Rhiannon, who nodded, then plunked himself down on the window seat. "Whatever. I never thought about it that way."

"No, you didn't." Peyton stretched and yawned. "You just tripped over your ego like most guys. But she's telling the truth, you big goofball. So accept that you have a vital place in the group and act accordingly." Peyton wasn't particularly verbal, but when she did speak, she usually had something to say.

"Honey," Rhiannon said gently, "they're right. They aren't shutting us out, they're protecting us. I'm not all that competent either when it comes to fighting—I'm still learning the ropes. I can handle short skirmishes like with the goblin the other day, but I couldn't have taken on this trip. I know it. We'll be up to speed soon enough."

A smile broke over Leo's face and the gloom lifted. "Yeah, yeah . . . okay. Quit making me sound like some pathetic basket case. I'll quit being such a jerk. Now that Kaylin's back . . ." He stopped. "He *is* back, isn't he?"

I shrugged. "I hope so. I did what the shaman of the Bat People told me to do. And trust me, that was one freakshow of a trip. If someone will go fix us some dinner, Peyton and I will take showers and then eat and then sleep for a week."

"Not a week." Leo frowned again. "As I said, Lannan's been asking for you. He's pissed that you up and disappeared. I'm worried about what he might do to you for running off like that." He gazed at me, a bleak expression on his face. Leo knew what Lannan wanted from me. What Lannan had *already* done to me. And he knew the vampires better than any of us.

I swallowed the lump that formed in the bottom of my stomach. "Nothing I can do about Lannan's wrath right now, unless I want to drag myself over to his place, and in this condition, there's no way I can face him."

"No, but you'll have to confront him soon. And . . . as I said, I'm afraid what he might do to you." This time, Leo's words were soft, almost consoling.

"Crap. Yeah. Well, I'll deal with that when it gets here. Meanwhile, some eggs and ham and waffles or pancakes would be great, before I crash. Peyton, you should stay here. I don't trust you driving. Why don't you call your mother and let her know you're home and then use the downstairs shower?"

She smiled. "I already called her—while you and Chatter were busy with Kaylin. But thanks anyway. I'll definitely take that shower and a place to crash. I'm starting to feel the lost time catching up with me."

She wasn't the only one. My body was suddenly aware I'd been on my feet pretty much for two days and had walked for at least forty to fifty miles. Not to mention the cold that had set into my bones, and the adrenaline rush from the entire journey and the blow from our fight with Kaylin.

I waited till Leo and Chatter withdrew, then took off my clothes. Rhiannon and Peyton gasped as they eyed the bruise blossoming across my midsection. My wolf paced—or would have if the tattoo could have gotten up and walked off my stomach—and I knew that Grieve had felt the blow to me and that he was angry and feeling helpless.

Be cautious—he may be out tonight and he will surely be looking for whoever hurt you. Ulean swept around me, a gentle cloak against the raw nerves that jangled.

Hell, I can't let him in here. If he got hold of Kaylin while he's sleeping, Grieve could eat him alive—literally. And if Kaylin's awake, then they might do each other irreparable harm. What should I do?

May I suggest you calm your wolf down and take a mild sedative to relieve the pain?

I laughed. Leave it to my Wind Elemental to think of the most practical course of action. *Good idea . . . thank you.*

"Rhia—can you go ask Leo if he has something for my bruise and to help me sleep? I have to calm my wolf down before Grieve comes here to find out what the hell happened to me. We can't risk him getting hold of Kaylin. Meanwhile, I'm heading into the bathtub."

Peyton headed downstairs with my cousin as I filled the bath with some of the bubble bath my aunt had made before the Indigo Court caught her. As I eased down into the warm suds, lying back against the porcelain, my body groaned and then let go. I was so tired, my eyes were beginning to play tricks on me and I was seeing sparkles—tracers that spiraled and looped as I followed the sparks of light with my fingers. I rested my head against the back of the tub and gave in, closing my eyes as I softly breathed in the gentle scent of lilac and lavender.

※

"Cicely? Cicely? Wake up, Cicely." My cousin's gentle voice broke through the cloud of sleep and I opened my eyes. I was still in the tub, only most of the bubbles were gone and the water was lukewarm. "Come on, let's get you out of the water and into a nightgown."

She helped me out of the bathtub as I tried to keep my eyes open. We returned to the bedroom, where she gently towel-dried me, then slid a flannel nightie over my head.

"I brought a balm for your stomach, and your food. And some chamomile tea with valerian tincture in it. I figured you'd be too tired to come downstairs. I found Peyton asleep in the tub, too."

Laughing, I pulled up my nightgown and let her gently rub the soothing balm across the flowering bruise that covered part of my wolf. The colors were spectacular—brilliant black and blue, in a rose pattern.

I managed to corral my thoughts long enough to ask, "How's Kaylin?"

"Sleeping like a baby. Here, eat this and drink the tea—it's meant to ease pain in the muscles and joints and will help your general fatigue." She guided me over to the desk, on which sat a tray. The plate was stacked with pancakes and two eggs, scrambled, along with six slices of bacon, a glass of orange juice, and a cup of tea in a cute cat mug.

Spearing a piece of egg, I popped it into my mouth and the rising scent woke my stomach. "I'm starving," I said, shoveling in the food. "I can't believe how hungry I am. I thought I was too tired to eat, but . . ."

"You haven't had food for two days and you wore out your body. Of course you're hungry. I bet you lost about five pounds out there."

"Not the way to lose weight, and I don't want to lose muscle. Next time I go on a trip with Chatter, remind me to take some protein bars." I bit into the golden pancake. "Umm, a piece of heaven. I love maple syrup."

"Me, too." Rhia paused, then said, "Not to bring up distressing thoughts, but what do you think Lannan wants?"

I took a long sip of the tea, grimacing at the bitter aftertaste from the valerian, but I knew it would soothe me and help me sleep deep.

"I know what he wants—he wants to fuck me, humiliate me, and make me grovel. He gets off on it. But other than that? I'm not sure. I don't trust him, but he can help us and I'm bound to him by contract. And contracts with vampires are enforceable by law."

"Yeah, I know." She played with the napkin she'd put on the tray, twisting the corners. "Drink the rest of that tea— Leo said it will help."

I nodded, chugging down the orange juice first, then sipping the scalding hot tea. It smelled faintly of licorice, and of earth and rock and root. But the taste was slightly bitter, with a hint of summer infusing the chamomile. The herbs settled in my stomach and my wolf stopped growling as both balm and tea set in to soothe the aching muscles.

"What I'm wondering is how this is going to affect Kaylin. The night-veil demon that we woke—it's powerful, Rhia. Powerful, and very chaotic, and it didn't want to knuckle under." I shrugged. "This is going to change the Kaylin we knew, and whether that change will be for the better or worse—I don't know."

My eyes were closing and I could barely keep them open. Rhia pulled down my covers. "Get into bed, and don't worry about it for the night. Don't worry about anything. You need sleep."

As she gently covered me up, tucking me in like I was a little girl, I could hear the great horned owl hooting in the oak, whispering for me to come and play. I drifted off before I could answer his siren song.

❧

"Cicely . . . Cicely Waters."

I blinked, expecting to see the morning light, but as I sat up, I found myself in the middle of a swirling vortex. A creature sat at the distant center, reeling me in, and I had a sudden squirming in my stomach that told me I wanted nothing doing with him or what he represented.

"Bring her here," he said, crouching like a spider. "Bring her forward and let me read her future."

"As you wish." The smooth voice by my side was too smooth—too polished—and I whirled around to find myself facing Lannan. He gave me a slow smile and wink. "My lovely young juice box. Guess where we're going?"

And then I knew—he was taking me to see Crawl, the Blood Oracle.

"No—I won't go. You can't make me go back to see that freakshow!" I struggled, trying to get away from Lannan, but he held me tight and drew me in, his black-as-night eyes flashing with fire.

"Give yourself to me. Kneel before me. Acknowledge my superiority. You resist me and it drives me crazy. You refuse to bend to my power and it makes me want to reach out, to break you. You are not my better—you are not above me!" He threw me to the ground, and I began to whimper as he began to unbuckle his belt. "I'll give you something to whimper about, my pretty one."

But then, creeping through the slipstream, came Crawl's raspy voice, like the wind sweeping through hollow husks on a cold autumn night.

Bring her to me. She is a fulcrum to this war. Bring her to me and do not tarry. We have no time. Blood is streaming like the sands of time and our people are in danger. The girl is our key to victory.

Lannan glared at Crawl, then down at me, and then he buckled his belt again and grabbed me by the wrist. "Just wait," he whispered as we headed toward the center of the whirlwind. "I've got so many special things planned for you. You're not going to be sitting down for a month, girlie. And I *will* have my satisfaction."

I began struggling to get away, but the whirling spiral pulled us in ever farther. As we approached the Blood Oracle, I began to scream and scream . . . and my voice echoed in the night.

❋

"Cicely! Are you okay?" Once again, I was being shaken awake, but this time it was Kaylin, his eyes dark and flashing with an inner light.

I struggled to sit up, both terrified by the dream and leery of him. "Kaylin, what are you doing here?"

He sat down on the bedside and put a light hand on my shoulder, pushing me back against my pillow. "You were having a nightmare. I came to wake you."

When I realized he wasn't going to clobber me again, I stopped resisting and scooted back against the headboard. "Was I screaming?"

"No, but I could feel your unrest." Once again a flash of light echoed through his eyes, and I felt a sudden rush of apprehension. "When you summoned my demon to wake, you created a connection. I can feel your dreams now."

Hell. I hadn't seen that coming. Nor did I want it—I already felt bound to too many people. Grieve, through my wolf; Lannan, through blood. Now Kaylin, through dreams. What would this mean?

"How far away can you feel me when I sleep? I have some pretty . . . interesting dreams at times." I blushed, but he didn't seem to notice.

"I don't think distance is a factor. I don't know if it will last, and don't fear—I won't intrude," he said, leaning in, his voice husky. "Not unless you want me to."

And *that* was not an innocent remark. Of that I was sure, but I decided to ignore it for now. "Um, okay. Listen, how are you? What time is it? How long was I asleep?"

Kaylin glanced at the bedside clock. "It's five in the morning. I've been awake since three. I have no idea when you went to sleep."

"Around nine." I stared at his face, searching for signs that the night-veil was in control, but all I could see was Kaylin. After a moment, I blurted out, "I dreamed about Lannan, and Crawl. He was taking me to see the Blood Oracle. Dragging me, rather. And Crawl was saying that I'm a fulcrum in the war and their victory depends on me."

Kaylin considered my words, then gave me a slow nod. "I think your dream was predictive. It sounds like something that may come to pass."

I cringed, thinking of Lannan's part in it. I didn't want

it to be predictive; I wanted it to be a nightmare. I decided to keep my mouth shut about the rest of it—no use getting everybody stirred up over something that might not happen.

But a voice inside whispered, *You know what Lannan wants, and you know he'll stop at nothing to get it.* And that was worse than thinking Crawl wanted to see me.

"Was it hard?" Kaylin asked, and I stared at him for a moment, trying to figure out what he was asking. All I could think of was Lannan and his sick fascination with me.

"Hard? What?"

"Forcing my demon to submit to me?"

I did blush then, and because I knew he'd find out one way or another, I pulled away the cover and showed him the bruise on my stomach. By now it was the size of a cantaloupe.

"Did I do that?" His voice was quiet, and he looked taken aback.

"Yeah, you did. But really, it was your demon. You never would have punched me like that if you'd been in control."

He pressed his lips together and turned to go. Over his shoulder, he said, "I'm sorry, Cicely. I'll find a way to make it up to you. I would never deliberately hurt you. I hope you know that."

But even as he left, I silently padded to the door of my room and locked it. No use taking any more chances.

I went back to sleep and slept dreamlessly until ten in the morning, when a splash of unexpected sunlight filtered through the window to land on my face. Blinking, I sat up, rubbing my eyes, and slipped out from beneath the covers. My breath came in cold puffs and, as I padded to the window to look over the frozen world below, it occurred to me that I'd need to turn up the heat. The house had central heating, and usually the second floor was a lot colder than the first.

I shoved my arms into my bathrobe and gazed down on

the wonderland that spread out across the backyard and forest. The snow was beautiful, picture-perfect, and the sun glinted across the white diamonds covering the world and through the icicles hanging off the roof of the house. One icicle had grown all the way to the ground and must have been a good thirty feet long. The sunlight reflected through it, fracturing into prisms that skittered off the frozen cascade of water.

Delighted, I let myself sink into the beauty of the season, trying to put Myst out of my mind for a little while. If she weren't around, we could enjoy the winter so much more.

If she weren't around, the winter would be warmer and raining, not a thick layer of snow. Ulean swept up behind me, gently hugging me with her currents.

You were Myst's daughter, you fool! She's out to destroy you for betraying her! Chatter's words came tumbling back as I gazed over the woodland. I had pushed them out of my mind, focused on the job to be done but now . . . now in the clear light of morning, after sleeping and regaining some semblance of clearheadedness, I couldn't ignore them.

Chatter said that Myst was my mother . . . in the other life.

Ulean let forth a sigh, which rolled over me like a cool wind on a spring morning. *Chatter should not have opened his mouth, but he did. Yes, it is true. You are—were—Myst's daughter. You were on the verge of figuring that out on your own, though, so don't blame him for telling you.*

I'm not sure what to do with that. I shook my head, not sure how to process the information . . . not sure what it meant for the future. *I'm not Indigo Court now, am I?*

No, you are Cambyra Fae and magic-born. But you bear the trace markers in your soul of that time—which is how Myst recognized you. Do not worry, you don't have their nature. Even then, you didn't have their nature—not unless your loved ones were threatened. You were a misfit, miscast in your role as the Queen's daughter. Ulean

enfolded me in her gentle breeze. *You are a good person,
Cicely. Do not doubt that.*

I closed my eyes, trying to summon the memories, but
they were hidden still, and the only glimpses I had were
those that had already come to me. But knowing who I had
been—knowing what I'd been capable of—terrified me.
What if my nature from then came back? What if Myst
wanted to turn me, to use me against my friends like she
was using my aunt?

Too many questions spinning in my head, I pushed
away from the window as clouds began to sock in and a
light flurry of snow started. It was as if Myst could read my
thoughts and had come to douse any hope the sunlight had
promised.

"Cicely? Are you awake?" Rhiannon's voice echoed
from outside my door as she tapped on it lightly.

I hurried over to unlock it. "Yeah, I'm awake."

"Come down to breakfast. Leo's out and about, and he
left you a message." She looked pale, and I wondered if the
strain of all of this was getting to be too much on her.
Heather, her mother, had been captured and turned by our
enemy. Rhiannon was struggling to control her own powers and heritage. And from what I could tell, she wasn't as
strong as I was.

I cinched the terry-cloth robe tighter and slid into a pair
of fuzzy slippers, following her downstairs to the kitchen.

There, next to a big breakfast of sausage and eggs and
toast, sat an envelope with a bloodred rose seal, and my
name on it. I recognized the slanted writing—it was from
Regina, Lannan's sister.

I stared at it, not wanting to open it. Not wanting to
know what the vampires were demanding from me now. I
was their pawn, their hope in this war, and after my dream
about Lannan and Crawl, I longed to crawl away and hide
somewhere. Finally, I opened the flap and pulled out a single sheet of linen paper, along with two checks.

The writing was, again, Regina's.

Cicely: Your monthly stipend is enclosed. Also: We request your presence this evening at a small soiree at Geoffrey's, along with Leo Bryne and your cousin Rhiannon. Formal cocktail attire—use the enclosed to buy something appropriate for yourself. Lannan requests you choose something in black with red accessories. A limousine will arrive for you at 7:30 P.M. Attendance is required. Best, Regina.

I swallowed a bite of toast, staring at the two checks. One, for twenty-five hundred dollars, was my monthly pay, for my second month of indentured servitude. The other was for three thousand dollars, and as I stared at it, I realized the writing on it was not Regina's, nor was it Geoffrey's—his I recognized on my monthly paycheck.

Lannan . . . it had to be from Lannan. Which meant that he was planning something and I was his target. Angry, I folded the checks and slipped them into my purse. I had to obey—they practically owned me. But that didn't mean I had to like it.

"Heads up," I said to Rhia. "You and Leo and I are required to attend a cocktail party at Geoffrey's tonight."

She shuddered. "I wonder just what kind of cocktails we'll be expected to drink. Can vampires eat or drink alcohol?"

"I dunno," I said, softly. "But contract or no contract, I'm not drinking any Bloody Marys while I'm there."

Rhiannon broke out laughing. "Me either." She glanced at the clock. "I keep thinking I have to be at work, but the school's shut for winter holidays from now till the New Year, so what do you want to do today?"

I thought about the money burning a hole in my purse and shrugged. "Since we were gone longer than we expected, Peyton and I put off opening our headquarters. She has to work for Anadey today. What say you and I go shopping? My treat." And with that, for the first time in a while, I felt like smiling. Lannan be damned . . . Even though I hated giving him a reason to feel smug, the thought of spending a few hours shopping with my cousin, and maybe taking in a quiet lunch, seemed like heaven.

"Sounds good," Rhia said. "Finish your breakfast and then get dressed while I do the dishes." So I cleaned my plate, shimmied into a pair of jeans and a turtleneck, and in no time, we headed out for the mall.

Chapter 9

The New Forest Mall was like most malls in the country: a mixture of the bland but necessary (think Limited Express, Jean Junkies, Sizzle), to the yummy (Pizza Ria, KFC, Brent's Ice Cream Palace), to the esoteric (Leather & Lace, Sharpen, Versailles Vamp, Magic Forest).

There were quite a few people out and about—though no vamps, of course—but everybody seemed to be paired up, or walking in groups, and a feeling of tension reverberated through the air. Which was no surprise, given the recent spate of brutal deaths.

Rhiannon and I deftly maneuvered our way through the main drag until we came to Slither. I swallowed my reluctance and entered the store, Rhia behind me. The shop was geared for clubbing, and the outfits were pretty much what I figured Lannan wanted me to wear. The money rankled. I had no intention of decking myself out to be his toy, but I had to at least meet him partway or I'd be in violation of my contract, and I knew his punishment would be swift and terrible.

The entry was through a set of beaded curtains, and

once we were inside, the light dimmed, with spotlights aimed toward the merchandise. Mannequins wore tight-fitting jeans that rode so low on the hips it was hard to imagine how they stayed up, and skirts so high you couldn't hide your panties if you tried. Sequins and glitter abounded, as well as spikes and rivets and studs.

"I like leather, but this isn't my style," I said, staring at the clingy, revealing clothing. "I don't mind showing some leg or cleavage, but I'm just not comfortable with this crap."

"What about this?" Rhiannon motioned to a black dress with gold threads running through it. It had a plunging key-hole neckline, which, though it showed off the cleavage, didn't leave me with the feeling of *tits on parade*. The back was draped, reaching the top of the butt, and the dress was snug and form-fitting. But at least it wasn't so short that I couldn't bend over without worrying—and around Lan-nan, bending over wasn't such a good idea.

The material was knit and it even had a cute little butterfly charm that held the keyhole shut. I flipped through the rack until I found one in my size—most were made for girls the size of young boys, and I was most assuredly not that—and carried it into the dressing room.

A glance at the price tag took me aback—fourteen hundred. But he'd given me over twice that amount with which to shop so what the fuck?

Rhiannon followed me. I shimmied out of my jeans and top, then dubiously assessed the dress. Finally, I sucked it up and slid it over my head, thankful that it had no sleeves. It made it easier to slide it over my curves.

"Oh man." Rhia gave me one of those *Wow* looks. "Look in the mirror."

Dreading the sight, I obeyed, and I blinked as I stared at my reflection. *Wow* was right. The dress hugged my body in a flattering way, showing that I had an hourglass figure as well as muscle. It was lightweight and comfortable, and yet I definitely felt dressed. Some dresses left me feeling naked.

"I can sit okay." I demonstrated, then knelt down, squatting to pick up a thread off the floor. "I can crouch down without my ass giving a peep show."

"It looks wonderful on you. All you need is a shawl and some heels to go with it." Rhiannon shook her head, smiling softly. "I could never wear that. I'd be far too self-conscious. But I have a beaded cocktail dress I found in Mother's closet and it fits me, and it still looks new."

"You think *you'd* be self-conscious? I know that Lannan just wants to watch me in something like this. I know all too well that he wants me because I won't succumb to his vampire charms, and I won't knuckle under. If I gave in, he'd probably lose interest."

And there was the rub: If I did what he wanted and had sex with him, Lannan would probably stop bothering me. But that would compromise my essential nature. I didn't want him—at least not when he wasn't using his charm on me, and even then only my body responded.

"I don't know about that, Cicely. You never know why people get obsessed. Sometimes giving them what they want only makes it worse." Rhia bit her lip, then said, "I wish I'd never let you agree to the blood tithe. I wish we'd waited—Myst was going to turn Heather no matter what, and I just couldn't face it. But now, every time Lannan makes a play for you, I feel guilty. You could have avoided that part of the deal if you hadn't been trying to help me."

I sat down beside her on the narrow bench and took her hand. "It's not your fault. Heather's my aunt; I was going to do everything I could to help her. How could I ignore the fact that she was in danger? I screwed up on the time limit thing with Geoffrey, but that was my own fault. I've never dealt with vampires much . . . not till now. But Lannan . . . No, I think even if he hadn't horned in on the deal, he would have been coming after me."

She let out a long sigh. "I guess you're right. Everything is just so fucked—and nothing's settling long enough to catch my breath. Don't you feel like you're in the middle of a whirlwind and it won't stop spinning?"

Grinning, I gave her a quick kiss on the cheek. "Rhia,

my mother saw to it that I've been on a carnival ride since I left here at six years old. Come on, help me get out of this. Then we'll go shoe shopping, look for a shawl, and go out to lunch."

With a grateful smile, she helped me ease the dress over my head, and I slipped back into jeans and my turtleneck. Truth was, everything did seem like one big blur to me. But I decided to be the strong one. Rhia needed me, and even though I was the younger cousin, I felt so much older, in so many ways.

∗

On the way home, we stopped by Anadey's Diner for lunch. The snow was coming down hard as we gingerly parked next to a snowbank and hurried for the door. The lights on the Christmas tree glimmered out through the window, reminding us that the winter solstice wasn't far away. I had my doubts about how much of a celebratory mood we'd be in, and if Myst didn't stop with the snow, there wouldn't be longer days to look forward to . . . not for a long time to come.

Peyton waved at us as we pushed through the door and stomped the snow off our feet. She was cooking, as usual, while Anadey waited tables. Anadey had become our touchstone since the Indigo Court took Heather, and we clung to her as we'd cling to a surrogate mother.

She brightened as we entered the diner and motioned to an empty booth. I glanced at the counter. Werewolves from the Lupa Clan . . . *crap*. Why they ate here, I didn't know—considering how much they detested the magic-born—but a few had become regulars and were in here every time we dropped by.

They snarled as Rhiannon and I walked by, and I ignored them. It was dangerous to engage the Lupas, and we did our best to pretend they didn't exist. I slipped into the booth on one side, Rhiannon on the other. Anadey came by, pulling out her pad.

"You girls want hot coffee?"

Rhiannon shook her head. "No more for me today. Tea, though—strong, with milk."

I glanced up at the older woman. She was pushing sixty, but in pretty good shape even though her bones creaked and her muscles hurt from the long hours she spent on her feet. Anadey crackled with magic. She was one of the shamanic witches who could work with all four elements—unusual, and they were usually loners.

"I want a hot mocha, please. Triple shot, with whipped cream and chocolate shavings, please." I smiled at her and she laughed.

"Oh, Cicely, you and your chocolate shavings. Every time you order hot cocoa or mocha, you ask for them. Very well. You girls hungry? Do you need menus?" She automatically wrote *allergic to fish* on the order pad—as she did every time I came in. I gave her a grateful smile, and she shrugged.

"I think I know what I want—what about you, Rhia?"

Rhiannon nodded.

"We're ready to order. I want your turkey plate—turkey, dressing as long as it's not oyster based, cranberries, mashed potatoes, and green beans."

"You want pumpkin pie for dessert or Yule log?"

I grinned, suddenly feeling happy. When times were dark, you had to take happiness where you found it, and right now it was in the form of a whipped-cream-stuffed chocolate cake with mint icing. "Yule log, please."

She chuckled as she wrote it down. "Thought so. Rhiannon? What can I get for you?"

My cousin pondered the question. "Chicken soup, toasted cheese sandwich, pickle on the side, and for dessert, I want some of the Yule log, too."

"Check. I'll get this right in, girls. Rhiannon, do you want your soup now or with your sandwich?"

"With my sandwich, please."

As Anadey headed for the back to put in our order and fix our drinks, I leaned against the back of the booth, watching the fall of snow outside the window. The past couple of weeks, it had seemed like New Forest was cut off from the world, silent in its shrouded wonder, alone in the universe. But all over the world, Myst's people were beginning their war, making inroads, looking for prey. How many of the Vampiric Fae existed? How many were out there?

"What are you thinking about?" Rhiannon asked. "You look so pensive."

"Myst and her people . . . how many do you think there are? How many small towns are feeling their encroachment, uncertain of what to do? How many people have they killed in their feeding?"

She shook her head. "I don't know. I don't know if I want to know. In some ways, I wish we were the only place they were attacking—then we could run away. But we can't ever really run away, can we?"

"If I did, the vampires would come after me. Or Myst." I glanced up as Anadey brought our drinks. "We have to destroy her, you know—"

A crash from the counter interrupted me. We all turned just in time to see one of the Lupa Clan members throw his plate toward the kitchen. He had a bottle of beer in hand and it looked like there were two empties on the counter.

"Fucking slut! Can't you cook something worth eating?" His words were slurred, but that didn't stop him from jumping up and heading around the counter toward the door to where Peyton was cooking. She'd stopped and was holding a cleaver in hand.

Anadey rushed after him. "Tim Wylde—you stop right there before I summon Ranger."

He ignored her. Lucky, one of the older assistants who had seen more than his share of days but still looked rugged enough to rumble, blocked the door into the kitchen.

"You just get your ass back over to the other side of the counter, *Lupa*." Lucky was one of the yummanii and he didn't care whether a person was Were, magic-born, or vampire as long as he didn't have to scrap with them. But let them cross the line and the older man was leathery tough.

"Get out of my way, *human*. You're no match for me."

Tim smashed his bottle on the counter, holding up the broken edge.

Lucky eyed him with a speculative look. "I would advise against it, boy."

"Don't you *boy* me, *human*. You're weak and sniveling, almost as bad as the magic-born." Tim lunged for him with the bottle.

Dodging the attack, Lucky pulled out a short rod from beneath the counter. It sparkled. *Silver.* Lycanthropes hated silver as much as vampires. He swung it, connecting with Tim's drunken face, and the Were screamed and went down on the floor, shifting even as he did so. The resulting wolf was huge, and as he came up, a murderous look filled his eyes.

I jumped forward and closed my eyes. *Ulean, bring the wind—please.*

Ulean slammed open the door with a strong gust of wind, and the snow drifted in as the currents of air sliced between the man and the wolf, knocking both off their feet. As man and wolf struggled for footing, I glanced over at Tim's buddies, both of whom were starting to turn. If we didn't stop this now, Anadey's Diner would be the home of a bloodbath.

Just then, a burly man strode through the open door. He was Were—you could smell it coming off him, strong with glittering eyes, topaz ringed with black. The men at the counter immediately turned to him, and Tim rolled over on his back, showing his belly.

"Tim, Alder, Snell . . . get the hell back to the compound. *Now.*" For a moment, the man looked like he was about ready to take out everyone, and then he pulled up short and took out his wallet. His eyes never leaving Anadey's, he fished out five twenties and tossed them on the counter. "For any damage my boys did, ma'am. I told them not to come here, but they insist you make the best burgers in town. I'll suggest takeout from now on." The words seemed to stick in his throat and his hands were shaking, but he finally turned away and swept out the door behind the three Lupas.

Anadey stared at the money on the counter, then finally

flipped through the bills and slid them into the cash register. Lucky was already on his feet, looking ready to kill. He glanced around the diner to see if there were any other potential troublemakers, then put away the silver rod.

I stared at the departing figures making their way through the storm. "Who the hell was that?"

"Ben Sagata. The alpha of the Lupa Clan." Rhiannon shook her head. "He rules them with an iron paw, I gather. Rumors are he's vicious and cruel, but he tries to keep his people on the right side of the law. Most of the time."

"Whatever the case, I would not want to meet him in a dark alley." But then again, I'd already had a run-in with two of the Lupas my first night home, and one of them had been taken out by the Shadow Hunters. "I wonder how he knew . . ."

"You mean that there was trouble? Probably the clan connection. Most Were clans have a connecting thread that runs through them."

I glanced over at Peyton, who had joined us. She tossed her apron to Lucky, who took her place behind the grill. "Do you?"

"Do I what?" With a long sigh, she wiped her forehead, leaving a small streak of grease. I picked up a napkin and gently reached up to brush it off.

"Do you have a connection with the werepumas of your father's tribe?"

She shrugged. "Da ran off years ago. Left us alone. He never took Mother home to meet his family—I don't know if they even knew he married her. The werepumas are strong with magic, but unlike the werewolves they don't tend to approve of interracial marriage, and since my mother is one of the magic-born, there's a chance they don't even know I exist. I've never gone to them to find out. I think I'm afraid they'll reject me."

"Do you want to meet them, ever?" I was curious. I wanted to meet my father, perhaps because my relationship with my mother had been so rocky and my father had given me the gift of flight. *Especially now*, since I had learned that Myst had been my mother in my life before. I wanted some feeling of roots, and the only ones to provide that had been Heather and Rhiannon. And now, Myst had Heather. Whom would she strip away from me next?

"I don't know . . . as I said, I'm afraid they may reject me. But someday . . . if I marry and have children and any of them turn up with strong Were blood, I suppose I should, for their sake." She looked uncomfortable, so I backed off.

"We should head home." I motioned to Rhiannon.

"But you didn't get your lunches," Peyton said.

"Can you wrap them up for us?" The thought of a cozy lunch out had been pretty much disrupted by the Lupa wolves, and the world felt harsh and too bright with the snow. I wanted to go home, light a fire in the fireplace, and try to find some time for peace and solitude. I needed to meditate, to clear my mind and search for some semblance of inner peace.

Peyton nodded. "I'll be over tomorrow to finish up on the shop front with you. I can't come tonight because Mom needs me to help her with the housework." Peyton was a good daughter, helping Anadey as much as she could.

"No problem, Geoffrey's insisted on seeing me tonight. I'm not looking forward to it, tell you that much." I let out a long sigh at the thought, wanting to chuck everything and go hide my head under the covers.

"Lannan summon you, too?"

"Gods, I hope not." As Anadey brought us our meals, wrapped in recyclable containers in a paper sack, I handed her a twenty and motioned for her to keep the change.

"You look tired, my dear." She gave me a quiet smile.

"I am tired."

"You need to fly. Go home, meditate, and stretch your wings. Rhiannon—tomorrow, you come over for your lesson." And with that, Anadey was off, serving the rest of her bustling diner, all signs of the fight with the Lupas extinguished.

I picked up the sack of food and turned to Rhiannon. "Let's get moving."

"The snow is piling up awfully fast." She struggled to push the door open and one of the busboys came out after us with a snow shovel and shoveled our path to Favonis.

On the ride home, I stared at the bleak winter as the wind howled around the car. *Ulean, is Myst growing in her power to harness the weather?*

She is, my friend, she is. And if you don't stop her, the winter will never end. She is the season, Cicely. She is the dark night of the year.

⚜

After lunch, Rhiannon went to lie down for a while and I retired to my room, determined to spend the afternoon in flight. I needed to transform so badly that my body ached, and my spirit felt trapped, locked up like a canary in a gilded cage.

I slipped out of my clothes, shivering as I opened the window and crouched on the sill, my pendant around my neck. Closing my eyes, I reached for that feeling of transformation, of the winds lifting me aloft. A swirl of snow caught my breasts, but I ignored it, focusing on a silver light that grew from somewhere deep within me. The light started as a narrow beam, a laser point, and grew, spreading like the blast from an atom bomb. As it spread out to encompass my toes and then my feet, the sensation worked its way up my body, spinning me around.

I tensed, gritting my teeth as I leaned forward, and then the ground whistled up to meet me as I let go and swan-dived out the window.

Within a blink, I was in owl form. The shift came easier each time.

I rose on the wind, Ulean shrieking with delight as she flowed along beside me, sparkling currents on the slipstream. The air slid past, ruffling my feathers as I dipped and turned, screeching in pure joy, my wings slowly flapping two or three times before I stretched them out to glide on the updraft.

The ground stretched below, a panorama of white, and the house and forest seemed at the same time so huge but so small as I circled overhead, reveling in the freedom flight brought me.

And then, there he was—the great horned owl—swooping in from the side to match my movements. We flew, synchronizing movements as he encouraged me to turn on the wing, to glide like a shadow over the yard.

You are out during the daylight—not usual, my friend.

He tipped, wing to ground, as he turned and I followed suit. *I kept watch for you. It's dangerous out here for young owls. I would not have you get hurt.*

Who are you? Are you one of the Cambyra—the Uwilahsidhe?

There was a silence. And then: *I will teach you to hunt now. You may never need this skill, but if you get stuck in your owl form, you should know how to take care of your needs.*

Inside, I grimaced. I didn't really relish eating a mouse or rat, but then something in my blood stirred and I followed him without protest as we headed over the yard. Not that I really expected much prey to be out—the snow had started to fall more thickly and the flakes were sticking to my wings.

As we glided over the backyard, the great horned owl suddenly made a slight motion with his head and turned sharply, homing in on a movement on the snow. Two rabbits were there, beautiful and white against the ground, hidden by the camouflage of their coats. I stared in horror as the owl began a hunting pass, but then my blood stirred and all I could see was a red haze and the hunger hit me.

I targeted the smaller of the rabbits, who suddenly looked skyward and then started to run, but we were faster and I flew low over the smaller of the pair, instinctively bringing my feet forward and extending my talons. With one swipe, I grabbed the screaming rabbit by the scruff of the neck and powered myself back into the air. Exhilarated, I rose and followed the owl as he flew to the great oak.

There, he led me to a hollow in the tree, where he dropped the rabbit and began to feed. I could feel his ravenous hunger, and my own rose up. I stared at my prey—now dead and glassy-eyed—and suddenly it seemed a beautiful feast. As I held it with my claws and began to rip into it with my beak, the hunger grew and the taste of blood and meat raced down my throat as I swallowed strips of meat. We fed in silence, and all felt right with the world.

✥

I ate for a while, then stopped, satiated. As I gazed at the horned owl, I knew he was more than he seemed. No regular owl would let me share his nest without wanting to mate. But he seemed to cut off my questions too quickly. A sneaking suspicion began to form in the back of my mind, but I didn't want to say anything prematurely. Maybe I just didn't want to be disappointed. I decided to let the matter drop for now.

I should get home. I have to get ready for the vampires' party tonight.

You should be wary of vampires, Cicely. They are dangerous, far more predatory than our own kind. Owlfolk love the hunt. Vampires revel in it. His words carried an air of disapproval behind them.

I take it you don't like them?

Vampires are parasites. Ultimate hunters, but parasites nonetheless. And they are unnatural to the world. No, I don't like them. Look at what they did to the Vampiric Fae. Myst did not start out the madwoman she's become.

You sound like you knew her before she was turned.

Again, silence. I did not press. *I will be careful.*

Good, we cannot afford to lose you. Not to the vampires. Not to the Shadow Hunters. And then he hopped out on the bough near his nest. *You should go now before the snow gets too thick for you to fly in.* Warning: *The rabbit may not settle well once you return to your two-legged form. Be prepared—the results won't be pretty, but you don't have time to wait for regurgitation.*

That sounds delightful. But thank you, for everything. I hopped out behind him onto the branch and sprang off, soaring toward the house and the open window in my bedroom. As I landed on the sill, then hopped to the floor, I let out a soft shriek and let go of my winged form, and within seconds I was sprawling forward on the floor.

I always came out of the transformation shivering and icy cold. As I lay there for a moment, gathering my wits about me, my stomach began to churn and I scrambled for the bed, pulling myself to my feet. I staggered slightly, still dazed, but there wasn't time to grab my robe as my stomach lurched again. I rushed out into the hallway, naked, and ran into the bathroom across the hall, slamming the door as my gag reflex lost it. I barely had time to lean over the toilet when the rabbit came spilling out, bits of fur attached.

As I heaved up what would have become my first owl pellet, I felt a perverse sense of pride, as if I'd just been initiated into a secret society. Finally done—and realizing I'd eaten far less of the poor decapitated bunny than I'd thought while in owl form—I flushed the mess and slid down on the floor.

The owl didn't like vampires, that much was certain, and I sensed a slight empathy for Myst in his words. Which told me . . . not much, since Myst hated owls and he was always warning me against her. But it did bring up questions: Had he known her before she was turned? If so, then whoever he was, he was several thousand years old, which would make sense if he was Cambyra Fae.

And thinking about that brought up a sudden thought—I was part Fae, as well as half magic-born. Being magic-born, I'd have a life span longer than most of the yummanii—or humans—but since I was half Cambyra Fae, was I going to live for a thousand years or more?

Wishing I could talk to Lainule, I brushed my teeth and swished mouthwash around in my mouth, then filled the tub with vanilla-scented bubble bath and slid into the embracing warmth. So much to think about, but in the forefront, the image of Lannan danced in my head, with Crawl sneaking behind him like a spider, desperately gaunt and dangerous. A sense of dread overcame me as I tried to wash away the fear of Lannan's hands on my body.

Chapter 10

As we were dressing, Rhiannon and I remained quiet, letting the stereo do the talking for us. "Around the Bend" by The Asteroids Galaxy Tour was playing, and I head-bopped to the beat as I thought about my flight with the owl, and how each time, I went further into the life and didn't want to come back. Though I loved Grieve and my cousin and friends, everything seemed so dark that it would have just been simpler to fly off to a distant wood, to live out my life on the wing.

But that's what your mother did. She ran away from her life, ran away from her fears. Though she ran from her powers, retreating into one facet of your life would be akin to the same thing.

Ulean danced in tune to the music, the air sweeping this way and that. Though I couldn't see her from this plane, I could feel her. And I knew what she looked like—a pale being, sparkling with light, the currents of the slipstream like a wild head of hair that moved as she moved. Even her gender was a misnomer—I assigned it to her because she reminded me of a woman, but Elementals had no real gender like people.

My mother was afraid of her powers, not her life.

Don't lie to me—or yourself. Your mother was afraid of everything. Do you really want to follow in her footsteps? If you retreated into owl form and stayed, you'd be turning your back on every challenge coming your way. And you'd be leaving Grieve behind forever.

I hate it when you're right. Frowning, I slid into the tight dress I'd bought at Slither, tugging it down to hug my body and curves. As I smoothed it over my belly, my wolf let out a low moan and I could feel him—awake and in pain.

Grieve . . . where are you? What's going on?

But all I could see was my prince's face, tormented, as a wave of pain slid over my back, and then another and another. The stinging blows raced through my body and I sank to the floor, curling into a ball, whimpering. The hail seemed never-ending and Grieve let out a howl, my wolf echoing back to him. And then Rhiannon was shaking me out of the haze of pain.

"Cicely! Cicely, come out of it—come back to us."

As I opened my eyes, I saw that I was surrounded by Kaylin, Chatter, and Leo. Rhiannon gathered me into her arms and I screamed as a white-hot lance raced across my skin.

"What? Your back!" She leaned me forward and I heard the men murmur.

"What about my back? Other than it hurts like a son of a bitch." All I could think of was that Grieve had taken one hell of a beating and I'd tuned in to it. The thought of him out there, lost to Myst and her beatings, made me queasy.

"Your back is covered with raised welts. Like you've been whipped."

They helped me up and to a mirror, where I looked over my shoulder to see the red thin weals crisscrossing my skin.

"Fuck. Oh motherfucking son of a bitch." I stared at the oozing cuts even as Leo raced downstairs. "Grieve was being beaten—I felt his pain. I didn't realize . . ."

"You took on his pain for yourself. Cicely, this bond you have with him—it could be terribly dangerous. What if Myst decides to kill him?" Kaylin took my chin in his hand, forcing me to stare into his eyes. "We have to break the connection."

"No! Grieve is mine . . . he's mine . . . she can't have him!" I burst into tears as I folded into Rhiannon's arms. She held me quietly.

"Shush . . . we'll figure something out. We'll find a way . . ."

I knew she didn't believe it, but hearing her say it made me feel a little better. Leo returned with a jar of salve in hand, and as he smoothed the ointment over my back, the sting and pain began to recede. After a few moments, it vanished.

"There, it all soaked into your skin. I don't think we can bandage them—the marks cover your back, but I also don't think that it's going to leave marks. They're fading a little already. I think because these were sympathetic magic, they'll disappear a lot quicker than actual lacerations would." He let out a long breath. "I hate to sound pushy, but we've got to get moving. Geoffrey and his crew don't brook lateness, and Lannan will use any excuse he can to get to you. You don't need that right now."

I nodded, swallowing the lump that had risen in my throat. Rhiannon helped me up and gently helped me adjust the dress. I winced, but at least the fact that it was backless kept it from brushing against the welts. I hoped Lannan wouldn't notice and ask questions. I'd wear a shawl, and hopefully that would cover the marks until they faded.

Heartsick, wondering how Grieve was, I applied my makeup and then slid into stiletto black patent leather ankle boots. Brass padlocks ornamented the side zippers, and I slowly clicked them into place. Then I added a red chunky bracelet and necklace. If I wore silver to a vampire soiree, I'd be asking for trouble.

When I was finished, I slid a black shawl laced with sparkling red threads around my shoulders and picked up my clutch. A look in the mirror told me too much—I washed up pretty good. Which normally would make me feel wonderful, but in this case, I knew Lannan would be there, watching and waiting. As I headed for the door, I tried to push him out of my mind, but the vampire was there, and he wouldn't let go.

⚜

Geoffrey's mansion was sparkling as we pulled up in the limo he'd sent for us. The crowd overflowed, out the main doors, a scintillating *Who's Who* of the bite-me set. As Rhiannon, Leo, and I walked through the crowd, I felt like a walking invitation to an all-you-can-drink party.

Rhia wore a blue ankle-length cocktail dress, sparkly with sequins and about twenty years too old for her. I had to get her to stop plundering Heather's wardrobe. The two were nearly the same size—tall and willowy—but Aunt Heather had dressed sedately and Rhia looked older than she was in Heather's clothing.

Leo was the surprise of the night. He was wearing a pinstripe zoot suit, with the matching white-and-black shoes. And it looked good on him. He grinned at me as he caught my eye.

"Geoffrey said I need to break out of my style rut. I decided to take his advice, especially since he pays the bills." He touched the brim of his felt hat and winked at me.

"Geoffrey calls the shots, doesn't he?" I eyed Leo cautiously, thinking that for a magic-born healer, he really enjoyed working for the vampires.

Leo's smile disappeared. "Geoffrey pays both our salaries. I think it would be best to shelve this conversation for a more suitable time." He wrapped his arm around Rhiannon and waved to one of the guards, who motioned us through without even searching our purses.

The mansion was a glitter of sparkling lights. Though Geoffrey and his kin didn't usually celebrate holidays as the living did, he'd still taken advantage of the season and a giant tree filled one corner, glistening with a thousand lights.

The swirl of vampires filled the hall and I noticed that one of the bigger rooms was closed off. No doubt their playhouse—the vamps had a predilection for orgies, and having been witness at one, I had no desire to join another.

I glanced around, looking for Regina or Geoffrey. The foyer was filled with bodies, all incredibly seductive regardless of shape or size. Sensuality came with being a vampire. It was an innate ability, like drinking blood or fading into shadows or—for some ancient vamps—turning into a bat or wolf or spider.

The music swirled around us. Buffalo Springfield, Nine Inch Nails, Marilyn Manson, Black Rebel Motorcycle Club, Nirvana . . . I closed my eyes, swaying slowly to the beat. The heavy scents of perfume drifting around us clouded my senses, and the smell of musk in the air was intoxicating. Ulean couldn't come with us—the vampires didn't like Elementals, and so there was no one to wash away the lingering smell of sex that permeated the room.

And then, at my elbow, Regina appeared. Her gold hair was swept up into a chignon, adorned with a black-and-red lace comb covered with Swarovski crystals. She was wearing a jacquard bustier in crimson and a black chiffon pair of lounging pajama pants, with five-inch stiletto sandals.

She coiled herself around me, her fangs showing slightly as she smiled. "You look lovely, Cicely. I'm sure my brother will appreciate the effort."

"I didn't do it for him. I don't give a fuck what your brother thinks about my looks." I couldn't stop myself. I was worried about Grieve and my back hurt like hell. Well, that was a lie. I did care what Lannan thought about me. I just didn't want him to *like* the way I looked, though I knew that was too much to hope for. "I was ordered to dress, and I did. Simple as that. I'd rather be in my jeans and a comfortable sweater." Or one of Rhiannon's gypsy skirts and a tank top, I thought.

She shook her head. "We need to have a private talk. *Now.*" Grabbing me by the elbow, she threaded through the room with me in tow. Leo and Rhiannon watched us go, but Leo was smart enough not to attempt a follow-and-rescue.

Regina dragged me into a small room off the main foyer and slammed the door. I glanced around and realized that what I'd thought was a smallish parlor was actually a huge bathroom. Must be for the bloodwhores, since vampires

didn't need to use the bathroom, unless it was to wash off
the blood.

She slammed me against the wall and I gasped—all
vampires are strong, but Regina was stronger than most.
My back sent a shiver of pain through me and I moaned as
she leaned in, all too much like Lannan, and slowly reached
out with her tongue, licking gently along my cheek.

"You are delicious. Lannan is right. You're a sweet treat
on a tiring night, a gumdrop or sugar cube to a man who's
hungry. Why, I bet that even your blood . . ." She reached
out and, with the sharp fingernail of her index finger, cut
me with just enough force to leave a thin red mark. As a
weal of blood rose up, she lightly traced it with her tongue.
"As I imagined. Your blood is sweet, too. My brother calls
you his ambrosia. He says you're ripe . . ."

She pressed her lips to my lips, forcing her tongue
between them. I melted under her kiss—so foreign and yet
so inviting. Regina shifted, pressed her breasts against my
own, and part of me wanted her to continue, while the logi-
cal side of me was screaming, *Stop! Stop!*

After a moment, she quietly pulled back and crossed her
arms.

I stared at her. She was beautiful in a frightening way, so
pulled together, so confident. But then, she was thousands
of years old and Emissary to the Crimson Queen. And she
was far more ruthless than her brother. Even I knew that.
Lannan was a creature of impulse. Regina was calculating.

"One of these days, I'm going to tell Lannan to drain
you dry and make you one of us. Or maybe we should do it
together, become your joint sires. Because what my brother
wants, I make sure he gets. And your attitude begs for an
adjustment, which you would so very much get if you were
sprawled prone at our feet."

She pressed against me again and I flattened myself
against the wall, wincing at the pain from the lacerations
on my back.

"I like little girls like you, Cicely. I eat them out for
breakfast and fuck them for lunch. You remember the party

a couple of weeks ago? I can make that look like a play date at the park. I could strap you down and fill every orifice in your body with my *toys* . . . I have my own harem, you know. I like watching them ravage limpid young women. Do you understand me?"

I nodded, breathless. She was stunning and her charm was working its way through my body, but I still had sense enough to be terrified. I also knew she was referring to her retinue of lesser vamps as a bunch of toys, which told me just how far up the food chain she was in the Crimson Court.

"Yes. I understand. I'm sorry." When in doubt, apologize.

"One of these days an 'I'm sorry' won't be enough. But perhaps you'll learn and won't disparage my brother in public again. And you'll think twice about your demeanor when he arrives. You'll enjoy his company. You'll laugh at his jokes and flirt with him when he winks at you."

I nodded, silent.

She snorted. "Yes, I'm sure you'll do your best. You're smart enough to listen to me. But perhaps not *wise* enough? Think on this: Leo knows his place, and he is properly subservient to Geoffrey. You have not learned the manners you need with which to survive vampire society. Let us hope that you take etiquette lessons as soon as possible. It would be a shame to lose your services and see you become just . . . one of the throng."

And with that not-so-veiled warning, Regina turned and smartly strode out of the bathroom, her heels clipping on the tile with precise rhythm. I peeled myself off the wall, leaving a trail of salve and blood, and straightened my dress. Breathless, turned on, and yet petrified, I decided I'd better toe the line and followed her out.

"Lannan! Darling, you're here." Regina's voice filtered through the crowd first, and by the time I squeezed through the throng of vampires surrounding her, her tongue was deep in his throat. His hands were cupping her butt and I watched, both fascinated and repelled, as the brother-sister team were all over each other like puppies in heat.

Leo and Rhiannon found their way to my side and gave me a questioning look. I shook my head and smiled nervously. A waiter came by, stopping to serve us. His tray held goblets of both blood and white wine. He offered us our choice, and we all quietly accepted the wine. He gazed at us for a long time before moving on.

Rhiannon moved closer to Leo, but as I watched him, he seemed to take on a different demeanor. I'd noticed it before. Leo, when he was in Geoffrey's presence, seemed more imposing, a little more threatening and control-oriented. And dressed in the zoot suit, he made the perfect addition to the scene. He blended in, which scared me. I still hadn't figured out how much he was in Geoffrey's back pocket.

A sudden movement behind me and hands wrapped around my waist as a low voice whispered in my ear. "Oh, my Cicely. How wonderful of you to dress for me tonight. You remembered my request."

Lannan. I glanced over my shoulder. Dressed in jeans and a tuxedo jacket with tails, juxtaposed against the formal background, he stood out. The golden tumble of his hair down his back made him even more eye-catching.

I shuddered but, remembering Regina's admonishments, stood still. I swallowed my desire to spit out some nasty remark and instead slowly smiled. Lannan's face was inches from mine. His eyes—the purest jet—gleamed, fixated on me, and the tips of his fangs sparkled as he gave me a sinuous smile. My stomach lurched as my body reacted to the sight. Even *I* couldn't deny that the vampire was gorgeous, but I hated the loss of control when he was around. I had no ability to keep my body from responding.

"Did you miss me, wherever you disappeared to?" he murmured. "Or did you just decide to vex me, to not answer my call? Hmmm?" He cocked his head, showing a bit more of his fangs, as he pressed against me. I could feel him, straining at his jeans, hard and rigid and waiting for the slightest provocation.

"I'm sorry I didn't answer." It took everything I had to

keep my voice civil. "I had an errand to do . . . one assigned by Lainule. There was no time to tell anyone where I was going."

He perked up, his smile growing by a fraction of an inch. "Lainule? An errand, you say? I wonder what this errand was? Did it have anything to do with your *wolfen lover*, perhaps?"

As I shook my head, he crowded closer and, in a tender voice, said, "Tell me, have you ever fucked Grieve when he was in wolf form? If so, I want to know every detail. And I'll know if you lie. Remember that, Cicely. I'll *always* know if you lie to me. And I'll punish you."

Horrified, I whirled around, only to find myself fully in his arms. "No," I said hoarsely. "No, and I never will—I am not of the wolfen Cambyra."

He laughed. "You're blushing! How delightful. What a little priss you are. I'll just have to find the perfect way to corrupt you. And what fun that will be. Now, be a good little slave and kiss me, Cicely. Give me enough reason not to drink you down tonight."

I could see Rhiannon and Leo watching from the side. Rhia looked on the verge of tears, and Leo—it was impossible to read his expression. He'd donned a pair of sunglasses and I couldn't see his eyes. A glance to their right showed Regina watching with a triumphant look. A sick feeling in my stomach, I allowed Lannan to lean in for a kiss.

My wolf began to whimper as Lannan pressed his lips against mine. The taste of the grave, of dust and old embers and bonfires long dead, of death and silk and apple brandy filtered into my mouth along with his tongue. A heat began to burn in my legs, working slowly up my body as I shifted against him. Against my heart, I was kissing him back, rubbing against him as his hands cupped my back and ass. He was intoxicating, passion incarnate, and my body lapped up the feel of his energy like kittens lapping cream.

And then he rubbed his hand along my back and the pain broke through the haze. I let out a little cry and he let go.

"You didn't resist me. I rather miss that," he whispered.

"But what's this?" He pulled my shawl away and peeked at my back. "What—who did this to you? What happened?"

I stumbled for words. "I don't know. It was . . . a magical attack."

"You're lying." His voice was flat, warning me.

"I . . . someone attacked Grieve and his pain became mine."

Lannan stared at me for a moment, then let out a harsh laugh. "You are so very linked to him that you take on his pain? How brilliant. How utterly precious. Perhaps we can put a stop to that. I will not have you marred by someone other than myself. It's not becoming."

I wanted to protest but then shut my mouth as Geoffrey and Regina motioned to us. Lannan joined them.

Geoffrey pointed to me. "Come." He glanced at Leo and Rhiannon. "You two enjoy the party. Don't get yourselves in trouble."

And with that, I followed the three vampires into Geoffrey's office.

Geoffrey took his place behind his desk, while Regina sat on the corner of it, crossing her legs so that the smooth pale skin of her thigh flashed through the slit in her skirt. Lannan motioned for me to sit on the love seat and then parked himself beside me, his hand on my knee.

I stared at it for a moment, imagining what it would be like to stick a silver pin through his palm, which led me to smile and laugh out loud.

"You have a joke you'd like to share with the rest of us?" Regina asked.

I blinked and lowered my gaze. "Not really . . ."

"So, we have a situation. We need to ask Crawl, the Blood Oracle, for help. But you must be present because you are the fulcrum; you are the closest connection we have to Myst and her secrets. You have locked within you the memories of when you were part of the Indigo Court . . ."

I stared at them. *They knew.* They knew I'd been Myst's daughter, just as Chatter knew. "Am I the last one to find out? You know, don't you?"

Geoffrey searched my face, then nodded, a pale smile crooking his lips. "Yes, my dear. We know. You were Myst's daughter. We weren't going to tell you, but obviously you've discovered the truth. Or remembered?"

I shook my head. "No, I didn't remember. I was told."

The Regent turned a frown on Lannan. "Not from one of us, I presume?"

Lannan snorted. "Retract your fangs, Geoffrey. I didn't tell her. But you're right, she needs to visit Crawl. As much as I dislike the messiness of politics, it seems we will not be allowed to live in peace as long as Myst continues to make a nuisance of herself."

"Nuisance?" I sat up, pulling away from him. "That's how you think of her? Myst and her people are killing the magic-born and yummanii alike. And she's coming after you, as well as me. If you haven't figured out her plans, let me spell it out, Lannan: Your bloodwhores? Your favorites? All targets. Myst is strong. Terribly strong."

"Cicely is correct," Regina said. "We cannot ignore Myst and you know it, my brother. The Mistress of Mayhem is out to kill all of us. Winter's next move is coming, and we must be prepared. We need to know more about her. When you tried to turn her—"

Here, Regina stopped and looked at Geoffrey. He blinked and shrugged. "Yes?"

"When you tried to turn her, Myst was lost to our spies and over the eons, we've barely been able to keep track of her. Now we have the chance to find out how strong she's become since she was turned. We can probe Cicely's mind, and because in one life, she was Myst's daughter, Crawl should be able to see back to that time and find out more about our enemy. Not all the information will be up to date, but we can at least get a feel for some of the abilities she gained after we lost sight of her."

Regina's words struck terror in my heart. *Crawl.* My dream came rushing back to me and I leaned over, moaning as I rested my head in my hands.

Lannan's hand slid around my waist and he slowly

raised me back up to a sitting position. "Oh, still the water-works, girl. Crawl is . . . who he is. One of us will be there with you, to make sure he doesn't wrap you up and suck you dry like a mosquito caught in a web."

I turned a bleak eye to Geoffrey. If anybody would be sympathetic, he would. "Do I have to? Crawl gives me the fucking creeps." I didn't care if I offended them. The last thing I wanted to do was to visit the Blood Oracle again.

"I'm afraid so. We need to see into your memories—and since you can't give us a clear view, we need his help. It won't be pleasant, but it won't hurt you as long as you don't resist. And as Lannan so succinctly put it, *one* of us will be there to ensure your safety." As he stared at me, once again, his words rang in my head.

I'm offering you my protection again, girl. Join us in our world. I will sire you and keep you safe.

His look was low and sultry, and I felt myself wavering. Being under Geoffrey's rule wouldn't be as rough as deal-ing with Lannan, but then, before I could entertain the idea, a spark of sanity crept in and I shook my head. There wasn't much I could say. I had no intention of letting any-one turn me into a vampire. Besides, I had the feeling it would spark off a war between Lannan and Geoffrey, with me suffering the consequences.

No thank you, but—thank you, for the offer. If I were to ask anyone to turn me, it would be you.

He inclined his head at the same time that Lannan clamped his hand around my waist. "Then we take you to Crawl. And *I* claim the right to see you through the ordeal. Can't have you losing your way, now can we?" And with a look that spoke volumes, he told me exactly what I already knew: If Geoffrey ever turned me, Lannan would be out for blood.

"I think perhaps we'd better let Geoffrey take her. I have another engagement and you, my brother, tend to set Crawl off on his tangents." Regina stood and smoothed her skirt.

But Geoffrey, his face humorless and taciturn, let out a rough laugh. "No, let Lannan take her. I have guests to attend to." And with a last look at me, his thoughts were clear.

I offered you safety from him, but you obviously prefer Lannan's ministrations to mine. Remember: Being a vampire is not altogether unpleasant.

Taken aback, I let out a little cry. *No—don't leave me to him. I'm part Cambyra Fae; you would turn me to something akin to Myst and I could not bear the thought.*

You are only half Cambyra . . . I doubt very much that you would shift over to one of the Indigo Court. But this is your choice. Do not come crying to me when he tears you down, although if you change your mind, I am here.

I stared bleakly as he left the room, the door closing behind him with a soft hush. Regina waited for a moment, then turned to me.

"My brother will take you to Crawl." Her look was almost one of pity, but she, too, turned to follow Geoffrey. With one last look over her shoulder, she added, "Lannan— do not lose her. She means too much to us. And do not let Crawl touch her. You know, as well as I do, that he lives to feed on flesh again, but we dare not let him touch a mortal . . . be they magic-born, human, or Fae. *I mean it*—you are under strict orders from the Crown. She comes back in one piece, with her mind intact."

Lannan laughed. "I hear you, sweet sister. But that doesn't mean we can't have our fun, now does it?"

"Then do as you please." Regina shut the door behind her and I was left alone with Lannan.

Chapter 11

Crawl. Lannan was taking me to see Crawl.

Who knew if I'd come back whole? Who knew if I'd ever come back at all? I wrapped my arms around me, shivering. Lannan circled me and I knew he was waiting for me to speak, but I couldn't say a word.

"What are you thinking, Cicely?" Lannan slowly reached out and lifted my chin so that I was forced to stare at him.

I swallowed, the feel of his fingers on my skin making me breathless and angry. Finally, after a moment, I told him the truth. "I'm afraid. Crawl terrifies me. You terrify me."

Lannan smiled, slow and seductive. "Good. So very good. You *should* be afraid of us. But never fret, my luscious. I will protect you from the Blood Oracle. He is my sire, you know—as he is also Regina's. He was a vampire for far longer than he's been the Blood Oracle, but two thousand years ago, he underwent the ritual that changed him into what he is now."

"He really is a seer, isn't he?" And as I asked, it hit me like a ton of bricks: It wasn't just Crawl I was afraid of; it was what he might see.

"Yes, he is." Lannan's voice was suddenly hoarse and he brushed a flyaway strand of hair out of my eyes. "Crawl is the eyes of the Vampire Nation, as our Crimson Queen is the heart and fist. You fear his words. You fear his visions—but everyone dies, Cicely. If that's what you fear he might say, remember: There are those of us who've come through death and returned."

"I don't know if it's death I fear," I said softly, pulling away and turning toward the heavily draped window. "I faced it every day on the streets with my mother."

"Then what do you fear?" His hand crept along my shoulder.

I wanted to shake it off but forced myself to just stand there. "Losing Grieve again. Losing my cousin. Seeing them hurt."

"Are you truly so selfless? It's my observation, through thousands of years, that few of the humans, few of the magic-born, are so generous. There's always an agenda, Cicely. You think I have one and you're right. But so do you. You don't help us out of the goodness of your heart. You signed the contract—"

"I signed the contract because you threatened me. *Yes*, it was self-preservation. I personally don't give a fuck if you and the Indigo Court kill each other off, but I also know that they hold the advantage, and dealing with you is a lot more palatable than dealing with the Vampiric Fae. Myst is a hurricane bearing down on our shores. You . . . you are the shark in the water."

"Ha! You still have your sense of humor." He laughed, then pulled me to him and planted a long kiss on me, his tongue prying my mouth open as he ran his hands over my butt. "I want you. You make me burn."

"You want me because I don't want you." But my words were a gasp on the wind.

"I can make you want me. I can make you beg." But then he slowly let go. "But first, I must take you to see the Blood Oracle. Do you remember Regina's admonishments from before?"

I wanted to say, *How could I forget?* but then decided that it might be better to ask for a refresher. So much had happened—and it couldn't hurt to be cautious. "I think so, but please, refresh my memory."

"No sudden moves. Never address him directly—ask all questions through me. Never let him stare you down." He stopped, then abruptly sniffed me and asked, "You aren't on your period, are you?"

Blushing, I shook my head. It was useless to resist.

"Good, because the smell of menstrual blood drives him into a frenzy." Lannan grabbed my hand then and pulled me over to the bookshelf. This time I watched closely and took note of the name of the book he used to open the secret entrance. A copy of *The Secret Garden.* Never knew if I'd need the info someday, but I didn't say anything. Vampires liked their secrets.

The door opened and we slipped inside. The room was as dark as I remembered it, and the table still sat in the center, the single lightbulb illuminating it from overhead. Magic lived here. Magic deep and old, like tentacles creeping in the dark.

Like Crawl, I thought.

I kept within the field of light. The shadowed corners promised to hold danger. Scuttling things, things that might eat me alive and spit out my bones. On the center of the table rested a crystal, floating above a crimson slab of glowing glass. The first time they'd taken me to see Crawl—before I pledged myself to working with the vampires—I'd seen it, and I'd been too petrified to say a word.

This time, I turned to Lannan. "What is that?"

He gazed at me softly, then, with a pout, shrugged. "I honestly don't know. Nobody's ever seen fit to tell me." A slight edge to his voice told me that he wasn't all too happy with the situation. "My sister, as much as I love her, doesn't think I can keep my mouth shut. And Geoffrey . . ." He stopped, his face clouding over. "You might think Geoffrey is your savior, waiting to rescue you from me, but there's far more to the Regent than you think. *Once a warlord, always a warlord.* Remember that, Cicely, when it comes to picking your sire. Or your sides."

I coughed. "I'm not planning on picking a sire. I have no intention of becoming a vampire."

But Lannan continued as if I hadn't said a word. "My guess: Either you'll be forced into Myst's servitude, or you'll choose one of us. I recommend me, for obvious reasons, but if you hate me so much, then choose my sister. She's safer to be around than Geoffrey, though you may not believe me right now."

He pushed me toward the table and leaned over the crystal, his gaze totally caught up in the spinning crimson lights that began to emerge.

"Take my hand. *Now.*"

I obeyed, reaching out to clasp his cold fingers. Like a hurricane, the energy began to spin, whirling into a giant eye, and we were caught in the maelstrom. And without further ado, we went sliding through the rabbit hole.

⚜

Peeling pages off the calendar, we went sailing through the ether, buffeted by gale-force winds to every side. We were the fence posts caught by the tornado, a boat caught in storm surge, trees crowning from wildfire. I clung to Lannan's hand, no longer caring who he was—he was a lifeline and if I let go, I knew I'd be lost.

It could have been seconds or hours, but the spinning lights died down and we came to rest in a room I remembered all too well. Crawl's temple. Huge, reverberating with energy, the chamber stretched beyond my sight line, the ceilings well over thirty feet tall. The walls were a blur of crimson—I'd thought it paper the first time I was here, but now it looked like blood, staining the hall. Benches lined the walls, magical sigils covered the floor, and the scent of ancient magic filtered through every corner, every inch of the temple.

Lannan put his arm around my waist, and for once I did not resist as he led me forward, toward the dais. The walkway was Tuscan gold, but unmarred by magical symbols, and I knew better than to step off the path. All the while, I held back, not wanting to approach the raised platform. I knew who waited, and one visit had been enough.

But then, within a blink and a skip, we were there. Lannan stepped in front of me and, much to my surprise, knelt at the foot of the dais covered in curtains.

"Rise, son of Crawl. The Blood Oracle recognizes you. Stand, Wild One, and beseech. Answers will be offered for payment." The voice came from behind the curtains, rasped and harsh, the whistle of the wind through ancient ruins, the sound of ghosts on the wind.

Slowly, Lannan stood. "My Master. I come seeking your help."

And then, he was there, at the edge of the platform. *Crawl*. The Blood Oracle. The vampire every other vampire revered, perhaps even more than their queen. *Crawl*, almost unrecognizable—if he'd ever been human, it didn't show. *Crawl*, who was more a force than a being anymore.

Bent and twisted, Crawl crept rather than walked, like a bug or a spider. His skin was blackened, charred by some unseen fire that burned from deep within him, his hair falling in clumps of dreadlocks long lignified.

In front of the dais, rising up to his reach, stood a fountain of bubbling blood, ringed by unwavering flames. The blood was fresh, smelling fetid and cloying, and it sounded like a brook. Crawl's lidless eyes gleamed with a sudden intensity when he saw me standing behind Lannan.

"Her blood—the Oracle remembers the smell of her blood." His tongue darted in and out of pasty thin lips, and with one bony finger he reached out, pointing at me, his hand shaking. "Give Crawl her blood. Sweet and thick in the mouth. Quickly, son of the Oracle, cut the flesh and make offering!"

Lannan grabbed my wrist and gave me a look that froze any objections I might have had. Regina had used my own blade to cut me, but Lannan just held out his fingernail and ripped a gash in my forearm, then motioned for Crawl to move back.

Crawl stared at the blood dripping down my arm, his

dark eyes gleaming. Before Lannan or I could move, he stretched out one of his incredibly long arms and grabbed me by the hair, pulling me up onto the platform with him.

Lannan let out a shriek and scrambled to catch me before Crawl could yank me up on the dais, but he failed and I found myself lying beneath the Oracle, staring up at him. I began to scream as his long nails dug into my shoulder and he leaned over me like some giant praying mantis, his head turning from side to side as he contemplated me like a Happy Meal. I rolled, trying to get away, but he quickly straddled me, holding me down.

Crap. I had to get away because I knew that Crawl was about to take a big bite out of me . . . or at least sink his fangs into me, and who knew where those fangs had been? I struggled, pushing against him, but he was incredibly strong, his thin arms anything but brittle. He leaned in, his teeth chattering at me, eyes burning with hunger.

"This one is dessert. This one is sweet. This one makes the Oracle's belly rumble. This one is ambrosia. Lannan has done the Oracle well to bring such a sweet treat." Crawl smelled like decaying wood and mothballs, and I beat against his shoulders.

"No, no! You can't drink from me!" I was frantic, even as I saw Lannan leap up on the platform. "Lannan, help me! Please!"

Lannan gave me a vague smirk, but he looked worried as he knelt beside the Oracle's side. "The Master perhaps remembers the rule of the Crimson Queen? The one rule she extended to the Blood Oracle?"

Crawl leaned down and trailed his tongue along my arm, sucking up the blood where Lannan had cut me. The rasp of his licking felt like wriggling insects against my skin. I let out a sob, wishing it were over, just praying it would all go away, but the stench rising from the Blood Oracle overwhelmed my senses and I just wanted to go *poof* and no longer exist. If this was what life was going to be like from now on, could I handle it, even for the love of Grieve?

"My sired child should keep his comments to himself."

Crawl glanced back over his shoulder at Lannan, hissing at him. "The Blood Oracle is hungry and it's been so long since he fed. Sweet flesh before him, a temptation too hard to ignore." And he turned back to me, opened his mouth, and bit hard on my shoulder.

The pain was blinding—heat and fire seeping into my body as his fangs sank deep and he began to drink from me. The sensation of the blood leaving my body made me queasy. This was not like when Grieve drank from me, or even when Lannan had fed on me. The blood flowed like a river, and Crawl was reveling in my life force. I closed my eyes, willing myself to fight, but the pain became all there was—a white-hot haze of fire blurring my vision.

Everything retreated to a distance and I found myself staring down a long tunnel, and there, at the end, was Lannan, holding his arms out to me as he called my name. I turned but could not move.

My wolf moaned, then let out a long howl, and I reached to comfort it but there was no comfort there—only a gash ripping the space between my love and me. I sought Grieve out on the slipstream, calling to him.

Grieve, Grieve . . . where are you? Why aren't you here to help me?

And there he was—but he was at the end of a long narrow ravine, running toward me, though I could tell he couldn't see me. He was screaming my name, looking for me, and I couldn't break through the fog that rolled along the snow, for everything was icy and pure and brilliant. I tried to run to him. All I wanted to do was to be safe in his arms, to let him enfold me and protect me from the energy that was sucking the blood from my body drop by drop.

Cicely! Where are you? I can't find you!

I'm here, Grieve! Grieve, can you hear me? But he couldn't, and defeated, he turned into his wolf and began to race toward the wood, howling and snarling.

No, Grieve! Please, come to me. Come back to me.

But it was dark and the moon was rising over the snow-laden forest, and he was gone.

"Cicely! Come back. Come back to me, Cicely!" And then Lannan appeared again, at the end of the tunnel, and I turned and began to journey the long distance toward him. As I drew near, he shoved me behind him and I stumbled into darkness as his voice thundered through the void and the tunnel began to recede.

"By the power of the Crimson Queen, you have no right to feed!" Lannan's voice echoed with an authority that shook the walls.

Crawl let out a shriek. "You dare to command your sire? *I am Master*. I am the Blood Oracle! And you, who are you to order me off my feed? You are not your sister, impudent whelp. I should never have sired you. I should have killed you where you stood. You are weak; you like the magic-born and human too much. They are cattle."

But even as he spoke, Crawl began to loosen his grip on me and I opened my eyes, feeling weak. I glanced at Lannan for a clue, and he shook his head, motioning for me to stay still. I obeyed.

"Old Father, I beg of you, remember the treaty. Remember the rules of the Crimson Queen. Remember what you are and how you became that way." Lannan held out his hands in supplication.

Crawl stopped, breathing heavily, then squatted back on his heels. He stared into my eyes, as I lay there, panting, bleeding. No compassion, no mercy would ever cross that face again—if indeed, it ever had—but I suddenly realized that I was staring back at him: So not a good thing. In that moment, I felt my father's blood rise up and I latched onto my owl and imagined myself flying, free and beautiful and aloft. And in that moment, Crawl retreated to his cushioned throne and Lannan cautiously lifted me off the platform and retreated a safe distance.

He looked at me, forced me to meet his eyes, and then without another word, turned and began to walk down the path leading to the archway.

Crawl's voice echoed behind us. "Son of the Blood Oracle, listen well to these words. You set yourself up for a downfall if you care too much about these mortal beings. Let your desire be for blood, not for the body, or you will find yourself an outcast."

Lannan said nothing, not even as Crawl began to laugh.

"Then, young fiend, if you will not take advice from your elders, listen to this. The Blood Oracle knows your questions before you even speak, even though you were not one of his favorites."

Lannan stopped, holding me, listening but not turning.

"I read her memories as I sucked her veins. Myst has one thorn, one vulnerability: her anger at the girl. Betrayal has become her enemy and offset her vision. Use the girl as bait, set mother against daughter. Geoffrey will know what to do. Or bring her to this temple and the Blood Oracle will feed and turn her. Either way, the war has begun. There are too many variables yet to predict the outcome. But blood shall run, like a river to the ocean."

And then, after a pause, Lannan started walking again, and we exited the room. I passed out the minute we began to shift back into the crystal chamber and woke up to find myself on a sofa in Geoffrey's office with Lannan kneeling beside me. Everything was spinning and I felt like I was half out of my body.

"What . . . I'm so . . ."

"You're weak. I know. Don't try to talk." Lannan seemed almost tender, but I didn't trust that look. "Here, you've lost a lot of blood. We have to treat you or you risk passing into the shadow, and becoming one of Crawl's shadows is not something you should ever wish."

I blinked. "What? I don't understand . . ."

Lannan held his wrist up and with one long nail slit it expertly. A drizzle of blood formed on it. "You must drink," he whispered. "My blood will strengthen you, keep you from passing into the veil. And you do not want to go into the veil, my Cicely. No matter what you think of me, it's a thousand times worse there."

I didn't know what he was talking about and tried to

push his wrist away from my lips, but I couldn't move my arms and then I realized I was paralyzed.

"I can't move—!"

"I know, but the paralysis will stop if you drink. You are under Crawl's thrall now; he has a hold on you and only by drinking my blood can you break the charm. If you were to die now, you'd come back as a shadow tied to the Blood Oracle."

"I don't want to be a vampire . . ." I began to whimper. "Just let me die . . ."

"No—if you die you will be far worse than a vampire. And you will not become one of the Vampiric Fae . . . not at this point. I am not trying to turn you. My blood will strengthen you. So for fuck's sake, *just drink it*, woman." He slammed his wrist against my mouth and I had no choice; the scent of the blood was suddenly tantalizing and I sucked eagerly, feeling the warmth slide through me, race through my body in a sensuous trail of droplets.

The heat started in my feet first, my toes suddenly awake and aware, and trailed up my legs, leaving a luxurious feeling like I'd just woken up after a long, long nap. I ached, but it was a hungry ache, and as the heat reached my pelvis, all I could think about was fucking. I was so horny that I thought I was going to scream, and I shifted slightly as the heat traveled still farther, to my breasts and arms, and finally through my head. Letting out a low moan, I pushed myself up on my elbows.

Lannan was kneeling there, looking radiant and gorgeous, and his hair was the color of spun gold. I reached out and played with the strands, suddenly no longer afraid of him.

"You have the most glorious hair," I whispered, wondering why I'd resisted him for so long.

He tensed, like a coiled cobra waiting to strike. "Cicely . . . don't tempt me. I won't hold back."

I could hear the rush of blood through my body. Everything around me seemed enhanced to the point of ultra-clarity, and every breath of air on my body was like a sensual caress. I sucked in a deep breath, reveling in the feeling of breath in my lungs. My thoughts were a blur, but I knew that I was hungry and that I wanted the touch of a man on my body.

My wolf began to growl, but I ignored it. Grieve couldn't find me. Grieve couldn't save me. Grieve was lost in the woodland and I couldn't do anything to help him. Not now. Not until I found a way to defeat Myst.

Lannan's smile grew dark and triumphant and he slid one hand up my thigh. I shifted as the cold touch of his skin made me shiver. He laughed, low and sultry, as he walked his fingers under my dress and toward my inner thighs. I gasped and parted my legs as he tipped me back on the sofa and moved against me, his weight making me catch my breath.

"I'm going to fuck you so hard you'll forget anyone you've ever slept with before. There will only be me, Cicely. I am your master, I am your lover, I am your everything." His lips nestled in the crook of my neck and I felt his fangs trail along my skin. "I won't drink from you tonight—you've lost too much blood. But oh, the next tithe, I can barely stand the thought of waiting."

I let him slide between my legs, thinking only with my body. The white heat burned so strongly within it clouded every other thought except that of being touched, being stroked, being nibbled on and teased and held down by the weight of this glorious golden vampire as he fucked my brains out.

He shifted and I heard him working his zipper. "I've waited for this. Tell me you want me. Tell me, Cicely. Say it."

"I want you," I whispered, my hands running through that glorious hair, which was as soft as it was golden. "I want you to put that gorgeous cock of yours inside me and take me away from all the blood and death and darkness, Lannan of the golden hair. My angel of darkness, make it light for me."

Lannan moaned, and ripped at my dress, and I was suddenly naked. He began to circle one nipple with his tongue and I let out a shriek, coming quickly and sharply, but as soon as the orgasm hit me, another wave built and I felt the heat curling up inside, a serpent forcing me ever higher.

"Is this the way you always feel? This desire?" I whispered to him.

He gazed down at me and nodded. "Always, forever eternally. Some learn to corral their feelings, but I choose to give them free rein. I do not deny my nature."

Gasping, I sought for him, letting out a low cry as his icy-cold shaft plunged deep into me, sliding up to the hilt. But even as he entered me, the door slammed open and he quickly pulled away, hissing over his shoulder.

"What are you doing to her?" Rhiannon's voice echoed through the room and, in a haze of lust, I tore my gaze away from Lannan and stared over at her. Her mouth was hanging open and I wanted to scream at her to get out, to leave me alone, but then I saw Leo, and behind them Geoffrey and Regina, and a thin trickle of common sense began to race through me and I realized what the fuck I was doing.

"No . . . no . . . what . . . Lannan, let me up."

He slowly moved back, smoldering, but I could sense unspoken communication between the three vampires. I sat up and caught sight of myself in a mirror. I was naked; my mouth was streaked with blood, as was my arm where Lannan had cut me and Crawl had fed. My hair was wildly askew and I was bruised and battered from where Crawl had slammed me to the floor.

"No . . . oh no . . ." I tried to stand up but fell, still weak and caught in the haze of lust that Lannan's blood had fed into me. "I need to go home . . ."

Geoffrey motioned to Leo. "Let me carry her. You cannot take her out there, reeking of pheromones like she is. Every vampire in the house would descend on her and ravage her. She'd be drained before you made it to the door." He motioned to Regina. "Go get the limo. I'll bring them out through the French doors. Lannan, you attend me to make sure no one protests. We'll discuss this later."

Lannan nodded, giving me a long look. He leaned close. "We'll finish this later, Cicely. Trust me, there's no going back from here. I've had one taste of you, and I will have the rest. I will forever be your angel of darkness."

I bit my lip as Geoffrey wrapped me in a blanket, then silently carried me out through the doors, with the others following. We swung around to an empty part of the driveway and within seconds, a limousine had pulled up. After he deposited me on the seat, Regina climbed in beside me and motioned for Rhia and Leo to take the front seat.

At my questioning glance, she turned to me and said, "To make sure the driver minds his manners." And then, before another word could be said, the door slammed shut and we were on the way home, and all I could think about was how desperately I needed to release the fire burning within.

Chapter 12

Regina said nothing, but I could feel the tension as she made me lie down with my head on her lap. My stomach churned; it felt like I was cramping from the fire within. I didn't want to talk about Lannan. Even though my mind rebelled, all I could think about was the feel of him inside me, the ache that raged through my body, and how much I regretted the interruption.

A sudden wave of fear rushed over me. "Crawl can't get out of the temple, can he? He can't come after me?"

She glanced down at me, frowning. "What do you mean?"

"He drank from me, he yanked me up on the dais and he held me down—"

Regina let out a mumbled curse. "I should never have allowed my brother to escort you there. I adore Lannan, but he isn't equipped for delicate procedures. Tell me what happened to you."

So I did—I told her about Crawl and about Lannan ordering him off me and forcing me to drink from him. "I didn't want to, but he said I was too weak and would pass into shadow if I didn't."

"He was right," Regina said. I could hear Rhiannon from the front seat—she let out a little mew. "So you drank from my brother . . . no wonder you burn with the fever. We should have left you alone with him to finish your tryst. One of the few ways to release excess fever brought on by drinking vampire blood is to fuck your brains out, Cicely. I'm afraid that if you don't have sex tonight, you'll get sick. I can send Lannan over if you like."

"No . . . I can't . . . I thought . . . I don't know—everything is so mixed up."

"We'll take care of her." Leo's voice came ringing from the front seat. "Don't bother your brother, Emissary."

"I doubt he would see it as a bother." Regina shook her head. "You invest too many emotions in the act, you know. Sex is a bodily function."

But I just shook my head. "No, please, no."

"Very well, but either Leo or one of your friends had better soothe your passion or you're going to be a very sick little girl tomorrow." Regina let out a short laugh. "At least Lannan remembered the way to harness the Blood Oracle's thirst."

"Tell me—if you would . . . why is it against the rules for him to drink from the living?" I looked up at her face, which was unreadable. She was stroking my hair, gently playing with it in an almost endearing way.

Regina pressed her lips together, then abruptly said, "That should never have come up in your presence. You'd do best to forget it. But you have nothing to worry about. The Blood Oracle never emerges from his temple. He will not come stalking you." She paused, then added, "See, here we are—your home. Leo, you and your lady friend should get Cicely inside quickly and call us tomorrow night should she fall deeper into the blood fever."

The limo waited as I scrambled out of the car and, with Leo and Rhia's help, I made it through the snow, up into the house. Then it pulled off into the night and we shut the door behind us.

I dropped on the sofa, still burning from Lannan's blood,

from his touch. "I need water. I need . . . a cool cloth." The blanket Geoffrey had wrapped me in was driving me nuts and I wanted nothing more than to tear it off.

Kaylin took one look at me and motioned to Rhiannon. "Get a towel and an ice pack." He knelt beside me. "Cicely, I can feel your blood, it's racing through your body. Did you drink from a vampire tonight?"

I nodded, stammering out what happened as best I could.

"She's got blood fever." Kaylin swept me up and carried me to the sofa. "I can't stem it, but I know someone who can. I'll head out and bring her back. Meanwhile, keep her temperature down." And with that, he was out the door.

I thrashed as Rhiannon placed the ice pack on the back of my spine and a cool cloth on my forehead. All my instincts were on overload, my mind clouded with a haze of lust and pain from the intense sensations flooding my system.

Leo stood behind the sofa, shaking his head. "I don't know what to do—everything's going to hell and I can't stop them from touching her, from doing what they want with her."

"Then why are you still working for them? How can you stand by and watch them do this to my cousin?" Rhia's voice was harsh against my ears, her emotion too much for me to handle.

"Argue somewhere else—I can't bear listening to you." I shot up, my skin crawling. "I need it dark and quiet. This is just too much. I should have just finished fucking him and gotten it out of my system."

Rhiannon shot Leo an angry look. "Carry her up to her room and then come down to help me prepare a cooling poultice for her." She grabbed the already warmed wash-cloth off my forehead and marched out of the room.

Leo collected me and carried me up the stairs, his lips pressed tight. He gently laid me atop my bed covers and whispered, "We'll be back, with help. I'm sorry, Cicely. I'm so sorry."

As soon as he left, I was able to calm my thoughts enough to search for Ulean. *Are you there? I need you.*

I'm here . . . oh, Cicely, I wish I could help you, but there's nothing I can do.

Stay with me.

Cicely—Cicely . . . A different voice echoed off the slipstream and my wolf shifted. I pressed my hand against my stomach and almost cried, the desire and hunger were so great.

Grieve . . . are you there? I need you. I need you now.

Come outside. I'm here for you. I can feel you. Hurry.

I pushed to my feet and staggered to the window, where I shoved it open. There, in the far corner of the backyard, I could see the figure of a wolf, huge and silvery-gray, gorgeous and wild. He was staring up at my window, waiting.

I shuddered as the blast of air met the prickling of my body. My breasts quickened in the wind, nipples stiffening as I raised my nose to catch the scent of ozone and snow. Even the chill couldn't dampen the heat flowing through me—I was a wild horse, aching to be broken, and nothing could stop the fire that burned through my veins.

Except . . . except . . .

I crawled onto the sill and, with only my pendant hanging around my neck, closed my eyes and dove. I came up, pulling aloft, spiraling over the yard, reveling in my flight. And then I dove toward Grieve, pulling up short to land gently on his back.

He glanced over his shoulder, his wolfen eyes glowing, and as I held tight with my talons, he loped into the bushes with me astride him, not into the Golden Wood, but to the other side of our property. As soon as we were out of the yard, I hopped off his back and shifted back into myself, as he did the same.

Grieve was full Fae; he could fashion his clothes out of magic if he wished, but I was naked and shivering under the slow drift of flakes that floated down to blanket the yard. He was wearing a fur cloak, and he pulled it off. As he wrapped it around my shoulders, I lost all caution.

"I don't care, I don't care if you kill me. I just need you—now, forever, in my life. I need you to be with me, to touch me, to love me." I burst into tears. "I can't stand this—I'm in pain."

"I felt you call. I heard your shriek on the wind. What happened to you?" He turned me around, lifted the cloak, and crumbled to the ground. "How—how did your back get marked up?"

"I felt you being whipped. The blows transferred."

He pulled off his shirt and turned. There were no marks on his body. "Myst was furious. The blows did not take. She couldn't figure out how, and neither could I. Oh, Cicely, you took my punishment into yourself. I can't let this happen anymore. I can't chance hurting you again. We have to break the connection."

"No," I whispered. "Please, don't. I can't stand the thought of life without you. Myst is out to torture me—I know, Grieve. I know she was my mother when you and I were together before. I know she remembers and hates me for it. She's trying to destroy everything and everyone I love."

He gathered me in his arms, pulling the cloak around my shoulders to protect me from the cold. My breasts pressed against his body and I sought his lips. His teeth were sharp, needle-like, and he let out a soft gasp as I wrapped my arms around him and kissed him, deep and soulful. He tasted of dark wine and burnished leaves, and cinnamon and the promise of haunted moons rising high in the sky to light the ancient autumn.

Our kiss turned darker, and I dropped my neck back as he burrowed his face in my hair, trailing his lips along my skin, gently tugging at the skin with his teeth. And then I moaned and sought his belt.

"Please, I need to feel you inside me. I can't stand this pressure any longer. I almost . . . I can't go back to the house without release. Please, fuck me, Grieve. Make me forget about Lannan, about Crawl, about Myst . . . about the darkness that haunts both of our lives."

And he laid me down on the fur cloak, and was naked in a flurry of sparkling light, and then he was over me, touching me, running his hands across my breasts, down my sides, sliding his fingers into my secret recesses. I let out a moan, opening my legs, hungry for him. Hungry and aching as the waves pounded against the shore, I reveled in the feel of his back under my hands as I pulled him between my thighs.

He gasped, kissing me again and again like he was a drowning man and I was his life preserver. "Cicely, it's only you. I service Myst because I must, but it's only you. I can't touch her again—I hate her. I hate the rage that hits in the morning light. I hate the taste of blood in my mouth, but I crave . . . oh, how I crave."

He slid into me, smooth, a perfect fit, and we rocked on the ground under the long winter's night. I began to cry.

"Grieve, I have to get you out of there. If I can find a way, please, let me rescue you. I can't stand that she perverts you day after day—you are not Vampiric Fae. You are Cambyra and that she turned you sickens me."

A flash and there was a feral grin on his face, dark and clouded. "But I do crave, Cicely. I hunger for your blood even now. I want to drink from you."

I shivered. I'd been drunk from far too much already. "You can't," I whispered. "I'm still low."

"Low?" He pulled back, looking both angry and afraid. "What do you mean, low? What happened to you tonight, Cicely?"

And so I told him—almost everything. I did not tell him it was Crawl who had drunk from me, but that an elder vampire had gotten his fangs in me, and that Lannan had forced me to drink from him. I didn't tell him that I'd let Lannan inside me, though. That would be a truth too far.

"You have blood fever," Grieve whispered. "No wonder you're so dry and parched. I won't drink from you—not tonight. But I swear to you, one day and it won't be long, I will personally rip Lannan Altos's throat out and stake his heart and hand it to you on a silver platter." And he began to fuck me hard, like I needed, thrusting deep and long and rough.

"Oh please, don't stop," I begged, reveling in the feel of his body against mine, of the grind of his hips against mine. We rolled over, and I was atop him, straddling his body. I threw his arms back, holding him against the snow, and he did nothing to stop me.

"I want you," I whispered. "I want you forever, I want you in me, around me, with me. You are my beloved, no matter what Myst says. I will have you back." And I drove myself down on him, head thrown back, letting our motion take me higher and higher. The heat in my body was channeling through me like a serpent, rising up to coil and strike.

"Myst can never hold a candle to your light," he said, his arms wrapping around my waist as he moved to my rhythm. "It has always been you."

And then the burning within rose to a head and I thought I was going to die, gasping for breath as I came, screaming like a wild creature in the night, letting out all my pain and anger and frustration in one rush that spiraled me up toward heaven, then dove back down into the depths.

As I fell onto his chest, spent, I glanced into his eyes. He murmured softly and wrapped his arms around me.

"I want you to drink from me. I want the last fangs of the day in my body to be yours, not Lannan's or . . ."

"Or whose?" Grieve looked at me expectantly.

I gave him a quick shake of the head. "Never mind. But feed—drink, even just a few drops, please. Make me remember who I truly belong to."

Grieve sat up, pulling me astride his lap. The fire within me still raged but the most painful part had been quenched, at least for now. "You're sure about this? I will not hurt you."

"I want to feel you drink from me. I want you to mark me."

He slowly licked his way up from my nipple to my neck, then, with closed eyes, sank his needle-sharp teeth into my flesh. I cried out, but this time it did not hurt. This time it was ecstasy. The passion of pain, the passion of being owned, of feeling my life force enter his body . . . it all fell into one kaleidoscopic orgy and I came again, laughing wantonly as Grieve coaxed the blood from my throat.

As we sat there in the snow, his erection rose again, hard

and eager, and I slid onto him, straddling his lap, rocking gently as he drank in droplets of my blood. I felt like one of the sacred harlots, finding my communion through fucking, the divine and sacred joy of merging bodies and spirits.

And then, slowly, we eased down from the heights. Grieve's eyes were dark—the obsidian of the vampires with the sparkling stars of the Vampiric Fae, and I lost myself in the swirl of galaxies. After what felt like forever, I could hear someone calling my name from the house.

"I'd better go. Won't you please come with me now? We can lock you up, keep you from the light."

He shook his head. "She would hurt you and I wouldn't be able to stop her. Not yet. If you can find a way, I'll come, but I can't be around you when the light-induced rage hits—I would stand far too much chance of injuring you or your friends. And Cicely, if I hurt you, I might as well kill myself. It's all I can do to keep myself in check now. I love you, but I'm not safe and you know it."

He put the cloak around my shoulders and pushed me toward the open yard. "Go, I will make sure you get inside without being harmed. And then, I must hie myself away before Myst discovers where I am."

And then he pulled back into the shadows. Unwilling, I headed toward the house. Rhia saw me coming first and raced into the yard barefooted to guide me toward the door. Leo insisted on wrapping his arms around me and carrying me inside. As soon as we hit the light, Rhia cried out.

"You were with Grieve!"

I gave her a long look. "I had to be . . . it was either that or return to Lannan. And so help me, if that happened . . ."

Kaylin was back, motioning from the living room. As Leo deposited me on the sofa, the cloak fell away and I grabbed for it.

"I'm naked, dude."

He ignored me. "I could not find a healer willing to come, but one did give me this." He handed me a small vial of orange liquid. "This will manage the blood fever until it burns itself out of your body."

I stared at it. Part of me didn't want to drink it. The intensity I'd felt with Lannan, with Grieve, as my owl self, begged me not to quench the fire. Now I understood the appeal of being a vampire—if life continually burned so brightly, if every sensation led to a shiver, the temptation would be hard to resist.

After a moment, I looked at him.

"I know your struggle," he whispered. "I can feel it. You are torn."

"Yeah." I held up the vial. "Is this safe? Do you trust who made it?"

He nodded. "Yes. She is safe."

With another pause, I flicked open the lid and upended it down my throat. As much as the blood fever beckoned, my common sense won out. As soon as I drank it, the pounding waves of my pulse began to subside almost immediately.

Cicely, can you hear me?

Ulean—it was Ulean. *Yes, I can. Why?*

Because while you were outside with Grieve, you could not. While you were deep in the blood fever, you couldn't hear me, though I could feel you. Now I know why vampires don't like Elementals. We can sense their moods, but they can't sense when we're around. That is an interesting piece of information we should not forget.

I glanced at the vial. "Is this a cure?"

"No, but it will keep you calm until the fever burns out. Muted like this, it will only last another fifteen to twenty hours. You drank from an old vampire. Lannan is many things, but he is not young and he wields more power than you would give him credit for." Kaylin settled in, looking grim. "This will appease the blood fever but not the other ramifications of drinking from him."

"What are those?" I couldn't imagine much worse unless . . . "He didn't enthrall me, did he?"

"Briefly, yes, but it will subside. However, the fact that you drank from him will make it easier next time he drinks from you to bewitch you. And if you drink from him again, you will fall deeper under his spell." His lips were set, grim. "Vampire blood can heal, but it can also enchant."

"Yes," I said softly. "I understand that . . . I've never before grasped the allure of the bloodwhores, but if they drink from their masters regularly, I can see . . . I can see how easy it would be to get addicted."

"And addiction it really is." Leo handed me an afghan and I wrapped it around me and curled up on the sofa, exhausted. "What most people don't know—and the vampires try to keep under wraps—is that their blood is as strong as heroin. It only takes a few times in a row before you're hooked. Withdrawal symptoms are bad. If you drink it two or three times over the period of a year, it won't enthrall you, but two or three times in a week? You're done for . . . hooked."

Rhiannon brought me a cup of tea and I sipped it, reveling in the quiet my body felt. Grieve had taken a big bite off the edge of my passion, and the serum Kaylin had brought was doing the rest. I could think again, and remember. Blushing, I shook my head, not wanting to talk about Lannan and drinking his blood anymore and how good he had felt inside me. I didn't want to face my own reaction to him.

"What I want to know is why they won't allow Crawl to drink from mortals. You should have heard Lannan when he was ordering Crawl to back away from me. And the Blood Oracle obeyed."

"I haven't come across anything in their history regarding that, but then again, it's a dense book and much has never been found out. Several researchers died in procuring the information contained in *The History of the Vampire Nation*." Leo shrugged. "But yes, it's something we should look into."

"Do you think it might weaken him somehow?" Rhiannon picked at a cookie, crumbling it on her plate.

"I doubt it," Kaylin said.

As the others joined in the discussion, my thoughts drifted back to Grieve. I had to get him away from Myst. Lainule and Geoffrey were working on an antidote. If I could get hold of some of it . . . it would be worth a try.

Grieve couldn't go on the way he was. And he couldn't try to escape until he was free from the infection. But how? Neither Geoffrey nor Lainule would give me a bottle of it if I asked. Of that, I was sure. And Lannan hated Grieve.

But Lannan wants me . . . and he's going to want me more even now . . . I could offer a trade . . .

I shook away the thought. I didn't even want to go there.

Don't. You can't bargain with him. You already sold yourself in so deep to the vampires that they own your life. Don't give Lannan a reason to own your body, too. You love Grieve, but it's too dangerous.

Ulean was right. I could go to Lannan and ask him for the antidote, and he'd fuck me and torment me and turn me into his whore. But would Grieve want me then? Would he want me to save him that way?

No . . . I had to think of something more clever. I had to figure out a way to get hold of the antidote without anybody knowing. I had to save Grieve on my own, because nobody here—or over at Geoffrey's—was going to help me.

"I'm tired," I said, a terrible fatigue settling through me. "I need to sleep."

Kaylin picked me up and carried me upstairs, and I didn't even care that my afghan slipped. He seemed more reserved than he had before his night-veil woke up, and I wondered how he was doing. But asking would have to wait for morning. Grieve had sated my passion; being with him had given my heart a little boost. The serum had quenched a good share of the fire, and I was left spent.

As Kaylin laid me under the covers and closed my window and made sure the protection wards were affixed to it, I slid into my dreams, and stayed there till morning.

Chapter 13

Next morning, I was torn. My heart urged me to sneak over to Geoffrey's, to break in and find the antidote. But it would require far more stealth and planning than I could pull off by myself. I had to accept that rescuing Grieve wasn't going to happen in a day. And killing Myst wasn't going to happen in a day, either. The blood fever was a mild bed of embers and I was able to ignore it as I rose and dressed, then headed downstairs for breakfast.

Today Peyton would come over and—as hard as it would be—we'd finish up our business fronts and be open for calls. I fretted, but Ulean brushed through my hair and shushed me.

You cannot win wars in a single day. You cannot build plans askew. Give yourself the time to think. Don't rush out in a half-baked attempt that will only get you killed.

As I poured myself a bowl of corn flakes and added milk and sugar, Rhiannon glanced at me, her expression pained. "How are you doing?"

I paused, considering her question. Memories of Lannan and Crawl crept through my thoughts like earwigs rustling through cornhusks, but I managed to brush them away. The tryst with Grieve had done much to soothe me, at least for a little while. He loved *me*, not Myst. He hated her. And he wanted to be with *me*. Those thoughts alone kept me going.

"I need to get ready—Peyton will be over in an hour or so and we're going to finish tidying up and then open to business this afternoon. Maybe that will keep my mind occupied." I paused, shaking my head. "I wish we could just leave. Pack up and run. But Lannan would trace me down. You can't just walk away from a contract with the vampires."

"Myst would trace you down, too. If what you say is true, then she's out to hurt you—not just kill you, but actively hurt you."

I shrugged. "I betrayed her. I betrayed her when she was my mother. Now I understand why she's out to get me—it's more than I turned my back on her Court. I was the heir apparent. I turned my back on her in front of everyone. And now you're in danger. Everyone I love is in danger."

"I'll take my chances," Rhia said softly. I glanced up at her and she was smiling. "I'm here to help you see her die. She took my mother, you know."

Slowly nodding, I slipped into a chair and spooned my cereal into my mouth. What would Rhia say if she knew I was planning on rescuing Grieve? Would she help me? Leo would be furious and might tell Geoffrey. Kaylin . . . who knew what Kaylin would do? He seemed to have returned to his old self, but I knew that wasn't true. I could feel his demon, just below the surface. He looked at the world through eyes we recognized, but behind there . . . inside . . . he had changed. And Peyton . . . hmm, what about Peyton?

"What's going on in there, Cicely? I know something's up." Rhiannon sat down beside me, espresso in hand. She handed me a homemade latte and I gratefully sipped at the steaming caffeine. "What are you thinking?"

"I want to tell you something, but I'm afraid you'll try to stop me." I shook my head. "Maybe it's best if you don't know."

"We're family, Cicely. I've got your back. It's something

about Grieve, isn't it? I know you were with him last night and I know that it helped ease your pain. I promise, I won't say anything to anybody else." Her eyes were wide as she crossed her heart. "Cross my heart and—"

"Don't finish the rhyme," I said softly. "Grieve told me that long ago. Never promise your life away."

"Then what is it?"

I bit my lip. "If I tell you, you *cannot* tell Leo or Kaylin. At least not until I give you the okay. It's important."

"I promise."

Taking a deep breath, I let it whistle slowly between my teeth. "I'm planning on how to rescue Grieve. Myst is tormenting him, and unless we sever the connection, I'll just keep taking on his pain every time she hurts him. And I refuse to break the bond. Grieve and I . . . there is no life without the other. I never used to believe in soul mates or twin souls until . . . until I came home and realized how tightly we are linked."

"How can you rescue him, though?" And then she stopped. "*The antidote* . . . you plan on getting hold of the antidote that Geoffrey and Lainule are making and you're going to give it to Grieve, aren't you?"

I blinked. Rhiannon was more astute than I'd thought. "Yeah. That's what I'm thinking. But I have to figure out a way to get into Geoffrey's house, and then to find the damned thing."

"That's not going to be easy. And if Geoffrey finds out, he might take it out on Leo." At the expression on my face, she hurried to add, "Don't worry—I'm not going to tell him. But we'll have to think carefully."

"*We?* I'm not asking you to help me, Rhia. It's going to be dangerous."

"And our lives aren't dangerous now? Don't be ridiculous. Of course I'll help you. I wish you could walk away from him, but I understand." She paused, then slowly added, "You have something with Grieve that I don't know if I'll ever have with Leo. I love him dearly, and he loves me. And I'll be happy to spend the rest of my life with him but . . .

but we weren't destined for each other. I know that in my heart. I always thought there was someone out there waiting for me until he came along and then I . . . I wasn't sure, anymore. And we grew close and then I fell for him and now . . . we mesh. We aren't a complete fit, but we mesh."

"Maybe that's all we can hope for and anything else is gravy. In my case, painful gravy." I cupped the latte with my hands, feeling the warmth of the mug seep into my body. A knock on the door interrupted my thoughts.

Rhiannon motioned for me to stay seated. "I'll get it."

She returned with Peyton in tow.

"Sorry I showed up early, but I was just too excited about getting things moving and I figured you'd be up." She slid into a chair and put her purse on the table, looking dour.

"Are you sure that's the reason? I mean, it's fine but you don't look very happy."

She shrugged. "I had an argument with my mother and needed to get out of the house."

"What about?" Anadey and her daughter were both strong willed. It wasn't hard to imagine them getting into a spat.

"I got a letter." Peyton let out a long sigh and opened her purse, pulling out a thin envelope. "Mother wasn't happy about it." She tossed the letter on the table and shrugged. "It's from my father."

"Your *father*? But I thought he ran off and left you years ago!" I stared at the note and then at Peyton's face. "This is the first time you've heard from him since then, isn't it?"

She nodded. "Yeah. He wants to be a part of my life now. He's sobered up, been in AA for three years, and he wants to get to know me. He's got himself a job in Seattle and he's pulling his life together. I didn't know he'd been an alcoholic when Mother kicked him out. She never told me." And then she promptly burst into tears. "I don't know what to think. I don't know if I want to see him—he left us. He left us high and dry. But now . . . what if he's changed?"

She leaned forward, resting her face on her hands, crying softly.

Rhiannon scurried around to give her a hug, and I leaped up to get her a glass of water and the tissue box. Peyton fumbled for a Puffs tissue and blew her nose, then looked up, her face red.

"Mother tells me not to trust him. That he'll just skip out again on me. She won't allow him in the house and says that if I want to see him, it's up to me but she doesn't want to hear about it." She bit her lip. "I know he hurt her, and left her with a baby and no money. I know what he did was horrible . . ."

"But he's your father and you want to see him. You want to know if he loves you." I whipped up a quick latte and slid it in front of her. "Drink this. It's okay. Rhiannon and I understand. We've never even met our fathers. I know the name of mine but nothing more than he's Cambyra Fae."

"That's more than I know. I used to ask Heather about my father when I was little," Rhia said, sliding into the chair next to Peyton. "She wouldn't tell me anything. I used to get so mad at her." She paused, then added, "I'd almost forgotten—I set a fire once when that happened. I didn't mean to but I was so angry that one day I stomped outside and was sitting on the back porch and my mother's rosemary bush went up in flames. I know it was my doing because I felt the fire shoot out from my heart. But I hurried to put it out with the hose and she never asked me what happened."

I glanced at her. "Was this before . . ."

She nodded. "Yeah, before the accident."

Peyton bit her lip. "I don't know what to do now. If I contact him, I know my mother will be upset. I think she really hates him. She won't stop me from seeing him, but she won't support me, either. He hurt her pretty badly, I guess."

"Give her a little time; maybe she'll come around." I let out a long breath. "Meanwhile, let's get started early. It will help both of us to keep busy."

We headed into the back parlor and finished tidying up. Our sign had arrived via UPS the day before and I stared at it—it was ready to set up in front of the house, by the road.

"This makes it real, you know." I glanced up at her. "Think we should take out an ad?"

She shrugged. "Why not? We don't have overhead costs in terms of rent since we're using your house and the mortgage is long paid. I can easily come up with a couple hundred for a spot in the *New Forest Times*."

I nodded. "Me, too. Okay, let's do it. What should we say?"

After about half an hour, we'd pounded out a classified ad to go in the local paper and phoned it in. I handed Peyton a check and she used her credit card to place the order. I picked up the sign and a hammer.

"Let's go hang our shingles."

The sign was like one of those FOR SALE signs, but instead of advertising a house for sale, it read, WIND CHARMS— MAGICAL NOTIONS & SPELLS, and below that, MYSTICAL EYE INVESTIGATIONS. I carried it out the front door, Peyton following, and we stopped by the mailbox at the side of the road.

"Here we go." I gave her a crooked smile. "It's not like we're going to have a hundred people on our doorstep the minute we put this up but you know, it feels so very official, doesn't it?"

She nodded, a glint in her eye. "Yeah . . . who knows where this will lead for both of us?"

As she held the sign, I pounded it into the ground, first scooping away a good foot of snow to reach the dirt. As we finished and stood back, I realized that in some weird alta-verse I'd been hoping that a throng of people would descend on us, but for the moment, we were alone, standing in the snow. I brushed back my hair and glanced up at the sky.

The clouds were rushing by, white cotton mixed with gray haze, and always the ever-present silver sheen that accompanied snowstorms. They were billowing by in the stiff breeze and the temperature was steadily falling. I turned, slowly, staring down the street, across the road, at the woods.

Everywhere, a silver and blue wasteland. The Ice Queen held the world in her grasp, and she was steadily squeezing tighter as her magical storms passed through. We were up to a good four feet of snow in parts of the yard. Drifts were higher. In Seattle, they were reporting the coldest winter in recorded history, with fifteen inches to two feet depending on how far out the neighborhoods were.

And in that moment, I knew. "She could do it."

"Who could do what?" Peyton glanced around, then at me.

"Myst. She could bring on another ice age. I can feel it in the wind—I can feel the shifting of currents and the cooling gusts racing around the world. She's sent her people into all corners of the northern lands. And they all carry her magic."

"Ragnarök."

I glanced at her. "Not quite. That's the twilight of the gods. This could be the twilight of the mortals. And this will be ice, not water."

"Stopping her won't be easy." Peyton stared at her feet. "When she held me captive . . . Heather and I were put into the same cell and Myst came to me. She was so beautiful . . ." Her voice drifted off. "I couldn't believe how beautiful she was. But so cold, and so . . . inhuman."

I nodded. "She has no more humanity in her than a rock."

"Yeah. She was so aloof. It wasn't as though she cared, one way or another. We were just . . . objects. She made us get down on our knees—or her guards did. And then she walked up and said, 'One of you will walk out of here alive. One of you will join my court. It's up to the two of you, which one.' And then . . . and then Heather stood up and faced her and said, 'Take me. Let Peyton go.' Myst shrugged and motioned to her guards and said, 'As you wish.' And then she just turned and left. The guards threw me across the room. As I slammed into the wall, they forced Heather to leave with them."

I hung my head. We hadn't heard about this before, though we had some inkling of what had happened.

"Heather saved me—at least for the time being. If you hadn't rescued me, I doubt I'd still be alive. I owe your aunt—I owe you everything." Peyton reached out and brushed her hand across my cheek. "Whatever you need me to do, however you need me to back you up, you've got it."

I felt shaky. So much had gone wrong. To have someone on our side, clearly, ready to take up the battle flag without complaint, meant so much. "Thank you," I whispered. "I've been feeling so mired. And after last night . . ." I told her what had happened with Crawl and Lannan and Grieve.

"I'll help you get the antidote. Whatever you decide, I'm in on. Just tell me what to do. I'm your soldier." She gave me a *buck up* smile and, throwing her arm around my shoulders, turned me toward the house. "It's cold. Let's go in before we catch our death."

By afternoon, we both had our first customers—Peyton had a tarot reading walk-in, and I was talking to Dorthea, a local woman who was frightened because her neighbor had been one of the ones killed in the theater incident. She wanted a protection charm to wear, and one to put in her house.

Dorthea looked like she didn't have much money—she was dressed in a faded housedress, and her eyes had a look of hunger in them. New Forest had its share of poverty-stricken individuals, and this woman fit the bill.

I took her name and then, with a momentary hesitation, followed Marta's instructions in her *Book of Shadows* and took Dorthea's hand. I cautioned her to be silent and lowered myself into the slipstream, trying to suss her energy.

As I listened to the currents, I could hear whispers surrounding my client.

A plaintive child's voice. *Mom, I'm hungry—what's for breakfast?*

You've got to get a handle on the spending. I can't make enough to keep up with the bills if you don't start cutting corners. The gruff sound of a man on the edge, trying to keep his temper.

I'm doing the best I can. What do you expect from me? Dorthea herself.

Then, the crack of flesh on flesh, a whimpering cry, and a man's voice. *I'm sorry—I didn't mean to do it. I promise— this time I mean it. I won't do it again.* Only the energy behind the voice didn't ring true. It was only a matter of time before it happened again—and worse.

And . . . the faintest sparkle of magic, hidden deep within, unnoticed and buried through the years. I opened my eyes and let go of her hand. As I stared at her money on the table, I let out a long sigh and pushed the ten-dollar bill back to her. "Keep it."

"But the charms—"

"I'm giving you a charm to protect you and your child. Use the money for food, or to get yourself and your son to a women's shelter. Don't let him have another chance at you." I knew it wouldn't do any good. Dorthea wasn't ready to hear that it wasn't her fault, that she couldn't change her husband. But I had to try—had to reach out.

Her eyes went dark and I could feel her shut down as she slammed up her barriers. I shrugged and pushed the charm across the table. "Tie this over your front door, and use this oil on the window latches and any other doors to the outside in your house. It will keep the monsters out."

But only the monsters that you haven't already allowed in your house. I wanted to blurt out another warning—that he would hit her harder next time. That maybe he'd take it out on their child.

Ulean swept around me, a soft cloak against the frustration I was feeling.

You can't save the world, Cicely. You can't stop her from going home to her husband. You couldn't save your mother and you can't save every woman in danger. You do what you can, and you accept the fact that you aren't a goddess. You aren't a superhero. All the magic in the world can't help someone who's not ready to listen.

I nodded, softly. *Thank you, my friend. It's a hard thing to face.*

I know.

Dorthea picked up the charm, hesitating for a moment. She looked at the money I'd pushed back across the table. "I . . . are you sure?"

"Ten dollars can buy soup, macaroni and cheese, a loaf of bread. Put it to good use, please." I gave her a soft smile, even though I wanted to reach across the table and shake her by the shoulders.

She pocketed the money and, with another smile, headed out the door, charm and oil in hand. I sat back, wondering what Marta would have done. Would she have taken the money? Or turned away the woman? Or would she have done what I did? This was new territory, and I had the feeling it wasn't going to be easy to pick my way through the landscape.

After a few minutes, Peyton waved to her reading, and as the woman left the room, we turned to each other. Her face had the same stricken look as mine.

"Rough reading?" I pushed back my chair and stood up, shaking the cobwebs out of my brain.

She nodded. "Woman wants to find love, has a bad habit of self-destructing in good relationships and going for the bad ones. Had to tell her that Prince Charming is more likely to be wearing a pair of geeky glasses than riding a Harley, but she didn't want to hear."

I let out a long breath. Were we all lost and confused, searching for our loves, searching for the answers when they were there in front of our faces?

"I think we need a drink. Can I make you a latte?"

"Mocha would be better." Peyton grinned. "I need me some chocolate!" She glanced around. "Where are the guys?"

"Out and about. At least Leo is. Kaylin might be with Chatter, wherever he is. One mocha, coming up. Iced or hot?"

Peyton glanced outside at the blowing drifts. "Hot. Today I need warming inside—something to convince me that there's hope and sunlight around the bend." We headed toward the kitchen.

"Sometimes I think it would be a whole lot simpler to be a vampire, you know? They don't feel the cold or heat, they have their own agendas, they . . ." I stopped. "Geoffrey offered to take me into his stable, to turn me."

"No! You can't let him do that. I know you're upset, but Cicely—that's not the answer." Peyton looked horrified.

"No, it's not," I said slowly. "But . . . what if he thought I was interested? What if I asked him to show me his stable of vamps, to introduce me, so I could think about it? And what if I brought you and Rhiannon with me, and while Geoffrey was off with me, you guys just happened to find the antidote? I know it's a long shot. I know it's dangerous, but damn it, that's the only way I can think of to get invited into his house without waiting for him."

Peyton stared at me, her mouth agape. "I dunno about that. It sounds like a setup for a bad end. You know I'll do whatever you need me to, but are you sure you want to put your cousin in danger? What if they catch us?"

Reality hit with a sledgehammer. "Yeah . . . I know. A bad idea all the way around, I guess—"

"What if *who* catches us?" Rhiannon entered the kitchen, cocking her head to the side. "What's going on? What are you planning?"

I frowned. "I thought of a way to go after the antidote. But Peyton's right. I can't risk you guys." I quickly explained Geoffrey's offer to her. "If I could get in there, keep him occupied, maybe . . ."

"Too dicey. But what about this? It's still dangerous, but . . ." She hesitated.

"What is it? Dangerous I can handle, as long as there's a chance of breaking through."

"Kaylin took you dreamwalking once before. Suppose you go dreamwalking through Geoffrey's mansion and find out where he's keeping the antidote? If you can find it, and nobody's guarding it, maybe you can manage to steal some for Grieve?"

Rhiannon looked positively shocked at herself, and I almost laughed. She had spent so long keeping her nature under wraps that it was going to take some time for her to get used to putting herself out there.

"That's actually got a chance of working. It means getting Kaylin on our side." I bit my lip. "But it's the only way I can think of. It also means I have to find a safe place to keep him once we have him free, because even though I love him with all of my life, I won't chance you guys living in the same house with him. I'm not that stupid. Even without the light-rage, he's still plenty dangerous."

I thought of Leo, of how he'd react. "We're going to have to tell all the guys, but we have to put up a united front or they'll let testosterone get in the way. This isn't up for a vote. I'm going to do this . . . well, *if* Kaylin agrees."

"Leo will be home in a few minutes for an early dinner. He's got some evening chores to attend to for Geoffrey. I guess I'll go get Chatter and Kaylin." Rhiannon pulled out a frozen pizza. "Here, stick this in the oven. Make sure we have something sweet for dessert. You know the best way to influence men is through their stomachs, and we need all the help we can get."

Then she took off to look for Kaylin and Chatter. Peyton unwrapped the pizza while I dug through the cupboards and found pudding mix and cookies. I whipped up some instant chocolate pudding and topped it with whipped cream, then set it in the refrigerator and opened the cookies.

"Do you trust Leo?" Peyton suddenly asked, her voice low.

I glanced at her, surprised. "He can be a butthead, but yeah, I guess. Why?" Actually, I'd had nagging doubts over the past week or so, but ascribed it to my own nerves.

"I don't know. He's in thick with the vampires. He owes his loyalty to Geoffrey—and every time we bring up your connection with the vamps, he seems defensive, like he thinks he's being edged out." She shrugged. "Maybe I'm imagining things, but I am a little uneasy with the way he acts."

I blinked. I'd had the same thoughts but hadn't wanted to articulate them because they sounded petty. Coming from Peyton, they sounded reasonable.

"I . . . I'm not sure. I kind of wondered, but Leo's in love with my cousin. They're engaged to be married. I can't just up and ask him, 'Are you jealous because I'm indentured to Geoffrey and Regina? And Lannan, by default.'"

"Yeah, I guess not. If he were, he wouldn't admit it. And if he's spying on you for them, he's not going to tip his hand."

Now I was nervous. The thought that Leo might be

spying on me for Lannan made me queasy, and I would have wiped the thought right out of my mind if I were sure about him. But honestly, I didn't know. I couldn't say for sure how much I trusted him.

Stricken, I stared at Peyton. "What if you're right? What happens if he runs back and tells Geoffrey what I'm planning?"

"Then I guess we'd better be ready for the shit to hit the fan. Because I don't think we can pull this off without everybody in this house knowing what's up." She began to set the table as I checked on the pizza.

"Fifteen more minutes." I stared out the window. We were all in the midst of personal crises. And things didn't seem to be lightening up any. "Have you decided what to do about your father?" I finally asked, pushing the matter of the antidote to the side.

Peyton nodded. "I'm going to see him, but do you mind if he visits me here? I can't ask him to come to my house, not with my mother there. And I'd rather chat someplace where we'll have more privacy than a coffee shop."

I nodded, absently wishing my only problem were meeting my father for the first time, then immediately felt guilty for thinking that. Peyton had a lot riding on getting to know her father.

"Sure," I said, glancing over at the door. Leo was scuffing the snow off his boots out on the back porch. "Well, I guess we're about to find out which way the cookie crumbles." I flashed Peyton a strained grin. "Let's just hope the crumbs all fall close to home. Hansel and Gretel had it easy compared to me."

"Yeah." She gave me a thumbs-up. "Because if Lannan so much as gets a whiff of the gingerbread house, he's going to be on your tail like white on rice."

"Or snow on snow," I added softly, staring out the window at the drifting banks that continued to grow ever taller.

Chapter 14

Leo was grumbling as he came through the door. "Damned snow. I wish it would give it a rest." He looked up and saw Rhiannon entering the kitchen, with Kaylin and Chatter right behind her, and the frown turned into a smile as his face lit up. "Hey, honey, I'm home!"

As he enfolded her in his arms for a long kiss, I hoped to hell that I wasn't going to be a wedge between them. I also hoped that Peyton was wrong about Leo—and that my own secret suspicions were off.

I sliced the pizza and slid the pie on the table while Peyton poured drinks all the way around and set out the pudding and cookies. Kaylin and Chatter slid into their places and I stared at Kaylin, wondering what he'd say. He'd been against my dreamwalking with him the first time, but a lot had happened since then. He glanced up to meet my gaze, unblinking. A dark smile fell across his lips as he lifted his beer and slowly saluted me with it.

As we all fell to eating, I glanced over at Rhiannon. She nodded. No time like the present. I leaned back and licked the melted cheese off my fingers.

"Guys, I need to talk to you about something. I need your help."

"Peyton and I have already agreed to help her in this, and we're not changing our minds, so I suggest you think twice about turning her down." Rhiannon swallowed her pizza and blinked. "Kaylin, we especially need your help."

"Why do I think I'm not going to like this?" Leo frowned, pushing his food around on his plate.

"Because you feel it's your duty to protect us even when it's not. But we're here to help each other, and no single one of us is strong enough to protect the others." Rhia gave him a playful kiss, but he scowled at her.

"What's up? I can feel something coming." He reached for another slice of pizza.

I took a deep breath. "I'm planning something. I need your help, Kaylin, but if you aren't comfortable then I'll find another way. No matter what, I'm going through with this." In a rush, I spilled out, "I'm going to steal some of the antidote and give it to Grieve."

Leo choked on his pizza, coughing so loud I thought we were going to have to thump him on the back. I glanced over at Kaylin, who raised his eyebrows but didn't say a word. Chatter looked at me like I was crazy.

After a moment, Leo pushed his plate back and stood up. "This is insane. You're going to get all of us killed."

"I'm not asking *you* to help. I'm not asking Rhia and Peyton to go in with me. I'm just asking you to keep your mouth shut about it. As far as you're concerned, you don't know anything."

"If Geoffrey finds out that I'm keeping this quiet, he'll rip my throat out—and yours, too!" Leo slammed his hand on the table. "You can't do this! I know you're hot for Grieve, but face the fucking facts: He belongs to Myst now. You lost him, he's gone. Buh-bye!"

I slid out of my chair, staring at him, unable to believe the extent of his anger. Leo seemed mild-mannered on the surface, but he'd shown a nasty temper more than once now.

"Excuse me, but you don't own this house and you don't

own me. You're not my brother or my keeper. Grieve means more to me than you can ever comprehend. If you can't accept the fact that he and I have been bound for lifetimes, then you never will."

"We don't always get what we want." He turned a cold eye at Chatter, then back at me. "We don't always get *who* we want."

He was jealous. Chatter had a crush on my cousin, and Leo knew it, so he was taking it out on all of the Cambyra Fae.

"You're threatened—Grieve and Chatter threaten you!" I shoved my finger against Leo's chest. "Grieve scares the hell out of you and you'd do anything to keep him out of my life. And Chatter—you don't want him near Rhiannon."

"Fuck that! I'm not scared of some freakshow Fae. What I am scared of is having a member of the Indigo Court under the same roof as me. A member of the race that killed my sister. That killed my fiancée's mother. *Your* aunt, might I remind you! And I take my job for Geoffrey seriously. I owe him—"

"You owe him what?" Rhiannon turned on him. "A paycheck? He's one of the *vampires*, Leo. I don't mind you working for them, but I'll never trust them."

"At least the vampires keep their word—"

"Yeah, right. And they use every trick in the book on us. Look at the contract I signed with them." I waved my hand, accidentally knocking over my juice. I ignored it as it trickled across the table. "Lannan's not going to keep his word—he'd love a chance to humiliate me, especially now. You think they have respect for you just because you play toady for them?"

"Don't you ever call me that again!" Leo knocked his chair over as he backhanded me across the face.

I reacted instantly, kicking him in the stomach and knocking the wind out of him. "You *ever* touch me again like that and I'll make you wish you hadn't."

His eyes wide, Leo slid to the floor. "I'm sorry . . . I didn't mean to hit you . . ."

"Bullshit. You knew what you were doing." I rubbed my

cheek. "And for your fucking information, dude, I've been thinking about alternative places where I can keep Grieve. I value my cousin and Kaylin too much to chance having him in the house with them. *You*—I'm not so sure about right now."

Rhiannon stared at him, horrified. "I can't believe you just did that. I thought I knew you."

"Please, don't look at me like that. Honey—sweetie . . . I didn't mean to hurt her." Tears in his eyes, he turned a dark gaze on me. "Geoffrey *does* respect me. And since that seems to be all the respect I get around here, then maybe I should move back to my apartment. Rhiannon, come with me. Get the fuck out of this place and cut your losses."

She shook her head, slowly backing up from his outstretched hand. "Leo, what the hell are you doing? I know you're upset, but nobody touches a woman like that in this house. Cicely, are you okay?"

I nodded. My jaw was sore, but he'd grazed me rather than hit spot on. "Yeah, I'm all right."

Leo stared at the table. After a moment, he said, "I can't excuse myself. I can't take it back, but Cicely, please. I didn't intend to hit you. I don't know what I thought . . ."

"You'd better leave—" Rhiannon started to say, but I stopped her.

"No," I said, moving between her and him. I faced him down. "There's nothing more I'd like to do than throttle you, Leo, but we can't afford to divide up. Myst would come after you in a heartbeat. Not only are you a day-runner for the vamps, but she assumes you're a friend of mine. I'm no longer sure she's right, but you're a sitting duck. However, understand this: I will rescue Grieve if there's any chance of doing so. You're going to have to get over your fear and learn to accept it."

He smoldered but then ducked his head and nodded. "I don't like it. And I won't pretend to."

"You don't have to. You just have to stay alive, and your best chances of doing that are while you're here. Got it?"

Rhiannon was staring at him, arms crossed. After a moment, she turned away. "So, Kaylin, after all this, are you going to help us?"

Kaylin let out a quiet snort. "Whatever you like."

I turned back to him, searching his face. The old Kaylin would have objected, but he seemed blasé about the whole matter. Everything felt like we'd been shifted onto quicksand; the landscape was changing even as we walked through it. "Thanks."

"No problem." He reached out and slid another piece of pizza onto his plate. "You might want to wash the blood off your face."

I reached up. Where Leo had hit me, a trickle of blood trailed down my cheek. Without a word, I headed to the bathroom. He'd been wearing a ring that had grazed my cheek, slicing a thin weal down the side. As I washed it off and slathered it with antibiotic ointment, I wondered if Myst was going to sit back and watch us tear ourselves apart before she even had a chance.

As I returned to the kitchen, Leo was talking in quiet whispers with Rhiannon, who was shaking her head. After a few minutes, he grabbed his coat and slid into it.

"I've got work to do."

"Are you going to tell Geoffrey?" I turned to him. "Tell me the truth."

After a long pause, Leo shrugged. "Not right now. No, I won't. But you're being a fool. And I don't want any part of it." And with that, he headed toward the door, but before he could get there, his phone rang. He answered, listened for a moment, then flipped it shut.

"Shit, we have problems." He glanced out the window. "It's almost dusk but not quite enough for Geoffrey's people to come out."

"What's going on?"

"Vampiric Fae, spotted heading into the parking lot at Anadey's Diner. Probably light-crazed."

"Mother!" Peyton grabbed her coat and I was right behind her.

Without another word, we headed out into the growing dusk.

❧

I floored it and we swerved into the parking lot of the diner. The door was ajar and there was a ruckus coming from inside. I pulled out my fan as Peyton raced to the side, transforming into her cougar self even as she ran.

Leo reached into the pocket of his trench and I let out a sharp breath as he pulled out a Beretta . . . by the look of it, an M92. Dane—my mother's boyfriend—had showed me his collection when we lived with him, and I'd soaked up all the knowledge I could about guns from him.

Slapping in a high-capacity magazine, he cocked the gun in wait. Whether bullets would work against the Indigo Court, I didn't know, but the fact that he owned one and hadn't told us caught me by surprise.

As we neared the entrance, screams echoed into the evening air. Kaylin rushed through and I followed.

The diner was a bloody mess. Four of the Shadow Hunters were enough to take on a diner full of people. One of the Lupa Clan was in a fight for his life with one of the Vampiric Fae, rolling on the floor trying to push the Shadow Hunter off as the creature began to transform atop him.

A second Shadow Hunter was feasting on the remains of a woman, and her blood ran thickly across the floor. The doglike monster looked up, a long scrap of muscle hanging from his mouth, but his eyes were intelligent—crazed, but far too smart for our safety. The woman was still screaming—he was devouring her alive. My stomach lurched.

Still another pounded against the ladies' room door, trying to break through, and we could hear screaming from inside. The fourth was headed toward the kitchen, where Anadey was wielding a huge cleaver.

"Stop him!" I shouted, but Peyton was two steps ahead, leaping on the Vampiric Fae and knocking him to the floor.

I motioned for the others to stand back and swept my fan three times.

Winds don't fail me now. Gale force.

A gust howled through the diner, raging more than one hundred miles per hour, catching everyone off guard, toppling everything not nailed down. Plates went whipping like Frisbees, glasses smashed against the walls, the hurricane-force winds caught up the chairs from the front tables and sent them sailing through the windows. The lights flickered as screams erupted—the Shadow Hunters were not happy with me.

As soon as the winds died, Kaylin rushed in, aiming his shurikens with deadly accuracy toward the head of the creature who was feasting on the woman. She had passed out—or died—and was a bloody mess of torn flesh. The Shadow Hunter screamed again and rushed toward the dreamwalker.

As Leo aimed and fired off a half dozen rounds, Rhiannon held her hands out and sent a blast of flame through the air. Both the bullet and the flame caught hold of the Indigo Fae and he fell to the floor, transforming as he did so. As he shifted back into his normal form, he jumped up, blackened from the fire and bleeding slightly from the bullet, which had gone directly through his shoulder. But the bullet hadn't seemed to slow him down any, and he aimed himself directly for Rhiannon.

Her eyes went wide as he launched himself and jumped. Leo dove between them, but not before the Shadow Hunter caught Rhiannon and took her down. At that point, the Shadow Hunter pounding on the bathroom door broke through the wood, and the one heading toward the kitchen ducked as the cleaver came flying out from behind the stove.

"What kind of game are we playing now?" A familiar voice rang over the chaos from the door of the diner and I whirled around to see Lannan enter the room, leading a group of eight vampires. They were dressed to kill, in black leather, and their fangs were gleaming in the dim light. For once, I was relieved to see the bloodsucker.

Without another word, the air blurred as the vamps sprang into action. They were all over the Shadow Hunters and the blood began to flow.

A hiss here. A shout there. The lights flickered again. Outside the snow was falling at a steady clip and people passed by, their car doors locked to keep the monsters at bay. The woman on the floor was dead—one of the vamps had gotten distracted and was licking up her blood. Lannan had the Shadow Hunter by the throat—the one who'd grabbed Rhiannon—and was holding him off the floor, squeezing as hard as he could. Rhiannon scrambled out of the way.

Two of the other vamps had routed the Indigo Court Fae from the bathroom and as I watched, one of them plunged a cast-iron spike through the Shadow Hunter's heart. He shrieked and dropped, dead.

So iron stakes can kill them.

Ulean swept around me. *Yes, they can, it appears. Be cautious of using your fan, Cicely. It has powers that you do not yet realize and they can captivate—*

But I shook off her warning. At that moment, Anadey stumbled out, helped by none other than one of the Lupa Clan. She looked dazed. At that moment, the other two Shadow Hunters raced out of the diner, followed by five of the vampires. There were screams from the parking lot, and then all was silent. One of the vamps returned a few minutes later.

"All taken care of."

I stood very still, keenly aware of how much blood was staining the diner, and how easily it could set off the vampires. I stared at Lannan, who swaggered over to me. He said nothing, but reached down to cup my chin. I waited. He planted a long, slow kiss on my lips and, still in shock, I found myself responding. As I pulled away, he whispered, "You can thank me for saving your cousin later."

And then, as quickly as they'd come, the vampires disappeared into the darkness and we were alone, knee-deep in carnage. The night closed in and Winter howled her wrath.

✤

Anadey slowly came around the counter to the front. "All right, who's hurt?" She stared down at the woman's torn body and shook her head, her expression fractured between shock and pain. "That was Eva. She comes in here every night for coffee and pie . . ." She turned away, looking over the remains of her restaurant.

A handful of people filed out of the restroom. They looked bruised but no worse for the wear. A couple of people were hurt; one man looked seriously injured, but it wasn't apparent whether it had been the Shadow Hunters who'd hurt him or the broken glass from the windows. As Anadey picked up the phone to call for an ambulance, Leo sidled up to me.

"And you still want to bring one of them into the house. You like fucking danger, don't you? I bet you even want Lannan—you protest, but you weren't putting him off last night. He was all up inside you—I saw it. I'll bet you get down on your knees like a dog for him—" He whispered low enough so that Rhiannon didn't hear me, but I whirled around and smacked him across the face.

"*Better him than you.* Just give it a fucking rest, dude. I told you I wasn't planning on bringing Grieve into the house, but you just fucking didn't bother to listen."

He let out a long sigh but made no move to return my blow.

Peyton padded over and growled at both of us before transforming back into herself. She stood, naked. Her clothes were on the floor in the flurry of debris and she began hunting them out. One of the women standing nearby helped her find them and she dressed, then went to help her mother.

Rhiannon brushed a strand of hair out of her way. "Leo, I heard what you said to Cicely and believe me, if she hadn't backhanded you for it, I would have."

"The antidote won't turn him back into what he was. It

will only take away his vulnerability to light and make him stronger. And who knows what side effects it's going to produce?"

I stared at him, wanting to flail him a good one, but his eyes registered fear. Leo was scared. He was terrified, and nothing in the world would take that away. I let out a long breath and pulled one of the chairs up off the floor where my windstorm had tossed it.

"I understand your fear, Leo. I just wish you could understand what I'm saying."

"You did have sex with Grieve again," Kaylin said, wandering up. "Remember—every time he bites you, you're under his charm a little bit more."

"He wouldn't let me bring him back. He said he didn't want to put you in danger," I muttered.

"This isn't about gaining access to the house," Kaylin said. "It's obvious he's fixated on you. You're soul mates, he wants back with his other half. And his nature is highly dangerous right now. Just remember: The venom from his bite can cloud your judgment."

I swallowed, and it was a bitter pill. Kaylin was right about that. Every time Grieve bit me, his saliva injected a toxin into my system that brought me a little bit further under his dominion.

"But you were willing to help me get the antidote." I stared up at him bleakly, totally confused.

"I believe he can harness his nature, but it's going to take a lot of work. We need to find a safe place to keep him. Somewhere he can't break out of."

"You mean lock him up?" I let out a long breath. "Like an animal."

"You know what the Shadow Hunters can do. Even if he wasn't born to the nature, if Grieve does lose control . . ." Kaylin knelt beside me and took my hand. "I'll help you, but this isn't a Cinderella story and you aren't rescuing a fair princess caught by the minions of darkness. You're rescuing one of the minions, and one who may just get terribly, terribly hungry."

I nodded, silent. I had to find a haven for Grieve—a place where I could hide him, yet keep myself and the others safe. I couldn't ask Geoffrey; that would tip him off to my plans. It wasn't like I had access to dungeons or cells or anything like that, and most apartments weren't built to keep someone in.

And then I thought about my earlier plan. I had one ally who might be able to help me, who wouldn't feel the need to blab to Geoffrey about my plans. And he might be able to help us get in and get hold of the antidote. But was I willing to pay the price? Could I face myself in the mirror again?

How far am I willing to go to save Grieve?

Cicely—don't do it, please. There has to be another way.

I'm running out of options, Ulean—I'm running out of time.

Quietly, I turned to Anadey. "What's the damage?"

She pressed her lips together, then let out a strangled sound. "One dead, three severely wounded and I hope they don't die before the ambulance gets here. Four others hurt, but they'll live. What do we tell the emergency techs?"

Geoffrey's whole tactic about wild dogs did not sit well with me. I stared at Leo, who was glowering at me, and said, "Tell them the truth. A group of deranged Fae broke in and tore up the joint."

"You can't—Geoffrey would object—" Leo started but I swung on him.

"I don't give a flying fuck about what Geoffrey would say. People need to know that there's danger out there in the woods. For the sake of the gods, they *already know it*, but nobody's doing anything and they feel abandoned. Geoffrey controls the town; let Geoffrey fucking step up to the fucking plate and do something about it. Passing off urban legends about wild dogs is just going to get a bunch of pets killed. And you can tell Geoffrey exactly what I said. I don't care!"

With that, I pushed him aside and swung out into the chill air. I needed to get my head straight. Kaylin joined me.

He shoved his hands into his pockets and stared up into the sky. "Snow won't stop till we stop Myst."

"I know. So what do you suggest? Where should I hide Grieve when we rescue him?"

"A secret place—hidden and hard to escape from." Kaylin began to whistle, gently, and I turned to him.

"What do you know?"

"I might have access to such a place. You'll remember, I've spent the past year off the grid. Before I moved into your cousin's house, I hid in a number of places that might do the trick." He gave me a contemplative look. "I'll help you but I advise you not to tell Leo where you're stashing the Fae. In his anger, he might take it upon himself to . . ."

"To rid the world of one more member of the Indigo Court."

"Exactly."

"What do you want for helping me?"

Kaylin slowly put his hand on my shoulder and leaned close. "Not everyone is out to use or abuse you. Not everyone has an ulterior motive. You suspect my demon, I can feel it, but not everything that lives in shadows is an automatic threat. Though I can be deadly, I'm not necessarily out to get something from you."

I raised my gaze to meet his. "You didn't answer my question." I'd learned from Lannan and Geoffrey. "What will you ask in return?"

He flashed me an insolent smile, but it wasn't snide nor was it patronizing. "Only that when I need help, you'll be there. I watch your back, you watch mine."

Feeling like a drowning woman clutching at a life preserver that might or might not come from an enemy, I nodded. "Deal. What next?"

"Tomorrow, while the vamps are asleep, we go dreamwalking and find out where that antidote is." And with a laugh, Kaylin threw his arm around my shoulder and we headed back to the diner.

Chapter 15

As I'd expected, the cops showed up, took the report, and left without a word. No crime scene investigation team, nothing. Either Geoffrey had them firmly cowed or Myst had them charmed. Or maybe a little bit of both. The rest of the patrons wandered off, looking dazed.

Leo headed for Geoffrey's from the diner while the rest of us offered to stay and help Anadey clean up. She shook her head.

"Go home, kids. You've already helped so much. There's not much left for you to do . . ."

"Yes, there is," I said, righting a chair. "We can at least clean up and see how much actual damage there is."

I began tipping tables upright, and Kaylin jumped in to help me. Rhiannon and Peyton pulled out mops and buckets and began cleaning up blood. Anadey looked like she was going to cry.

I said nothing, convinced I was to blame. Anadey was my friend. But she must have noticed my mood because she put her hand on my shoulder.

"This isn't your fault, Cicely. Myst has it out for all of

the magic-born, and remember: She killed my mother to keep her out of the way. We're all targets. Never let anybody put the blame on your shoulders, regardless of who they are."

Rhiannon heard but pressed her lips shut. I knew she was torn about Leo's attitude and accusations, and I decided that I had to put at least some of the tension to rest.

"Guys, gather around a moment." When they were listening, I took a deep breath. "Kaylin made a valuable point and it's one I tend to forget. Grieve's bite enthralls me, and I may act stupid because of it. It's not Grieve deliberately trying to control me—I'm sure of that. But the fact is, I don't think things through. I still plan on rescuing him, but I told you that I won't try to keep him at the house and I want you to know I fully intend to keep my promise."

"We know that." Rhiannon rubbed my shoulder. "And Anadey's right—this isn't your fault. The Shadow Hunters were taking over the town before you arrived home."

"Well, Leo's certainly pissed at me and while I seriously want to smack him down, I get it. Though . . . I have to admit, I'm not sure how much I trust him." I glanced at Rhiannon and gave her a sad smile. "I'm sorry, Rhia . . . but after he hit me . . ." I shrugged.

"I never expected him to explode like that. I've got a lot to think about," she said quietly.

"Let's get this place back to some semblance of order." I returned to clearing up the debris, and with the help of the others and the kitchen staff, we were done in a little over an hour. It wasn't spotless, and Anadey'd need to bleach the place down because of the blood and call in the health department to check the biohazard level, but at least she wouldn't return to a mess in the morning. We waited with her while the emergency glass-repair guys came out and boarded up the windows, and then we headed home.

Peyton went with her mother—Anadey needed her.

As we gathered in the living room, I looked over at Chatter. "I suppose you're against me trying to rescue Grieve, too?"

He surprised me. "Not anymore. If Myst keeps him there, not only will she destroy what control he has left, but she'll be able to hurt you through hurting him. I think our only choice is to get him out of there. Either that or . . ."

"I know, I have to sever our connection—if I even can—and give up on him. And I can't do that. I just can't. And it's not my hormones or his venom talking. Grieve and I . . ."

"Cicely's right. She can't sever the connection." Chatter looked over at Rhiannon and Kaylin. "I was there when Grieve and Cicely were together, before. It was a terrible battle—I remember the aftermath when Lainule found out Shy—Grieve—was in love with Cherish. She flew into a rage and that just strengthened their resolve. They became so entwined together that nothing in the world could separate them—not Myst, not Lainule, not even heaven itself. I died trying. I was Grieve's brother back then."

"I'm sorry." I stared at him. "There's so much I still don't remember, but if there's anything I regret, it's hurting . . . killing . . . you."

Chatter bit his lip. "I wish I could tell you everything, but Lainule would have my head. She's convinced you need to figure this out for yourself. But I witnessed the devastation the two of you caused in your wake. And though by then I was dead, I now know that the potion you took was created by one of the most powerful sorceresses of that time period. The effects brought you back together in this lifetime, across time and space."

"I know that—" I started to say, but he shook his head, cutting me off.

"No, you still don't understand. You're bound together, and nothing but death can keep you apart. When Grieve is hungry enough for you, he's going to tear through Myst's guards until either he's dead or they're in shreds, and then he'll come for you. If we can get him out, so much the better. Because I've done some research. Cicely, that potion you took? It did more than simply bind you."

"I know—it brought us back together this time around."

"It did more than that," Chatter said.

A pit in my stomach opened up. How many times Grieve and I'd been together in past lives, I didn't know and wasn't sure if Grieve even knew. But our time together as Shy and Cherish had been strong enough to bond us forever. At the end, when we were cornered by our enemies, we'd taken a potion to bring us back together in the next life. But now something tugged at the back of my mind—something I felt I should remember.

"What did it do? Tell me."

Chatter let out a long sigh. "When one of you dies this time, it will take the other with them. That potion bound you together *forever*. Not just for the next lifetime."

"Holy crap," Rhiannon said. "Then if we don't rescue Grieve . . . if Myst kills him . . ."

"Myst will also kill Cicely. *That's* why Cicely took on Grieve's scars from the whip. And if she's terribly hurt, he'll be the one to bear her pain." Chatter looked unhappy. "When Grieve first told me—as Shy—that he intended to have the potion made, I tried to stop him. I tried to persuade Grieve not to go through with it, but he wouldn't listen. He was blinded by the venom of your bite."

I stared at him, breathing hard. No . . . no . . . I *couldn't* have enchanted him. "We loved each other," I said, hoarsely.

"Yes, you did, just like you love him now. And I'm surprised you're keeping it together so well this time. But Kaylin was right—you're sucked in by the intoxication; you can't help it, just like he couldn't help it. Another few bites and your common sense may flee."

That scared the hell out of me. I exhaled and slumped back into the chair. "How do I keep my head clear? What should I do?"

"We can try some sort of counterenchantment." Kaylin shrugged. "There are some powerful spells that might counter the venom's effect without breaking your connection to Grieve. Leo was talking about the idea earlier to me. He said that Anadey may know of a way. He asked me to bring it up, because he thought you wouldn't listen to him if he did."

That was an even scarier thought, but the more I mulled it over, the more sense it made. I loved Grieve, but my obsession could all too easily put friends in danger. "All right. I'll ask her. But damn . . . I hate this."

"I know. But don't be afraid of breaking your connection—from what Chatter says, I don't think there's any real way to do that. You guys are linked, like it or not."

I picked up the phone, not wanting to bother Anadey after the tragedy at the diner, but this was too important to ignore. As I punched in her number, I realized that I dreaded the thought of countering Grieve's enchantment over me. Suppose Chatter was wrong? Suppose my love for him died away? Suppose I found out that the venom of his bite was the only true link we had left? What if I emerged from the spell not caring about whether he lived or died?

Anadey picked up the phone and I explained what I wanted. "Leo said you could help. Can you?" I held my breath, hoping she'd say no.

"I think so . . . at least, I can give it a try. Come over now and we'll see what we can do." She hung up, sounding tired.

I stared at the receiver. Kaylin was watching me closely, and I realized everybody was waiting to hear what I had to say.

"Yeah, she says she can help." I reluctantly replaced the receiver on the cradle and let out a long sigh. "I don't like this, but to make sure you guys are safe, I'll do it." I grabbed my keys and slid into my jacket.

"Do you want us to come with you?" Rhiannon asked.

I shook my head. "Nah. Unless you're afraid I'm not going through with it." I gave her a long look, challenging her to call me a liar. Of course, Rhia wouldn't, but I was feeling under the gun and really itching for a place to lash out.

She gazed at me softly, then touched my arm. "Come with me."

I followed her into the parlor. "What?"

"Cicely, I know you think we're against you but we're not. Leo's being an ass, and I am so sorry for the crap he's given you—if you want, I'll put him out. But we all want the same things: Myst dead, the town free, Grieve home safe. And"—she lowered her voice—"my mother . . . I want her to rest. For good. I can't stand the thought that Myst turned her into a vampire."

I hung my head, trying to swim up through the depths of depression. Everything was so fucked up that I couldn't see the bottom from where I was standing. Enfolding my cousin in my arms, I patted her back and kissed her hair.

"I'd give anything—even Grieve—to be able to give you your mother back again. Remember: I loved her, too. She was the only steadying force I ever knew in my life, aside from Ulean. Please, never think I'm angry at you. I hold my anger for those who deserve it. Myst—Lannan . . . even Leo. Right now, I could take them all out. Well, maybe not Leo, but I'd like to give him a bruised butt. But you . . . *chica*, we're family. We're twin cousins—remember?"

She smiled then, tears in her eyes. "I remember when we were young. How much fun we had. Life seemed so full of promise, until Krystal took you away. After that, I still had fun, but there was always something missing. And that missing piece was *you*. Cicely, we're solstice babies; I'm the light, you're the dark. We balance each other out."

I nodded. "Wipe your eyes. Get some dinner. I'll be back later. We'll see what Anadey can do."

As I let go of her and moved to the door, she clasped my hand. "I know this is hard for you—"

"The hardest thing I've ever done."

With that, she let go and I headed over to Anadey's, to see if she could release me from something I'd give anything not to let go of.

❧

Anadey was wearing a long black robe when she opened the door, and she looked as tired as I felt. She stood back and I entered the house. Peyton was in the corner, curled up with a book, and waved when she saw me.

"Are you sure you're up for this, so soon after . . . what

happened at the diner?" The last thing I wanted was to cause Anadey more pain.

"It will help me take my mind off today." Her voice was grave. She motioned for me to sit down. "Tell me everything."

I did, including our plan to rescue Grieve and hide him in a safe house. Anadey said nothing while I spoke, just blinked her way through what I had to say. After I finished, I sat back, waiting.

"I think I can help you. In fact, it won't be that difficult. But you have to trust me. Do you trust me, Cicely?" She gazed at me with those brilliant eyes of hers. Anadey: the daughter of the most powerful witch who had ever lived in New Forest. Anadey: Peyton's mother. Anadey: one of our only allies. And I was about to put myself in her hands, to let her work her magic on me.

I paused, holding her gaze. After a moment, I slowly nodded. "I trust you."

"Then go into the bathroom and bathe—I've set up a ritual bath for you. After you finish, return, naked. Peyton—you must leave. You shouldn't be in the house while we're working. Be careful, though—the Shadow Hunters could be anywhere." She gave her daughter a long look.

Peyton bit her lip, then turned to me. "Are you sure you want to do this, Cicely? Think about it . . ."

"Don't you trust me to treat your friend right?" Anadey turned to Peyton. "After all we've been through, do you doubt my word? Is that your father's doing? Did he lie about me to you in that letter he sent?" She sounded bitter.

"No, damn it! I just want to be sure Cicely realizes what she's doing. This has nothing to do with you—or my father!" Peyton grabbed her jacket, then turned back to me. "Give the word and I'm out of here. I will support whatever you choose to do, but I want to hear it from your own lips. I just have a bad feeling about it."

I gave her a faint smile. "I love you, too, Peyton. And thanks—for caring. But I have to do this. If I don't, I put everybody I love in danger."

She nodded. "That's all I needed to hear. I'll see you later, lady." To her mother, she glowered, but said, "I'll be careful. You better be, too."

When we were alone, Anadey let out a long sigh. "I wish she'd quit blaming me for being angry about her father. He's a sleaze and a drunk. He ran out on us, leaving me to cope with a young girl, and never once checked in to see how she was doing. Never once did he send support for her—I had to fend for the both of us on my own. And now he wants back in her life? I'm convinced he'll try to take her away from me."

I lightly put my hand on the older woman's arm. "Don't do this to yourself. You know Peyton adores you—she loves you so much. How can you believe that someone who's a relative stranger could come in and destroy your relationship with her that easily?"

She wavered, and I could see she was thinking about what I'd said, but then she shook her head. "It's just too dangerous . . . I can't chance it . . ."

"Chance what?"

"Never mind." Her smile returned and she pointed toward the bathroom. "Here, drink this. It will put you in the right mood. Go immerse yourself in the bath and clean with the soap I put there. Then return here, naked."

I downed the drink—it tasted like apple juice—and then excused myself and went into the bathroom. The walls were soft rose-petal pink, and the bathtub and fixtures were painted porcelain. The tub was filled with steaming water and a froth of bubbles that immediately calmed me down. As I stripped down and slowly lowered myself into the water, the heat seeped through my muscles and I leaned back, letting the magic of the herbs work their wonders.

All my angst and worry seemed to drift away, out of my muscles, out of my heart, and I relaxed for the first time in days. The blood fever felt like it had worked its way out of my system, and I slowly bathed with the soap that Anadey had left. It was a golden brown, and as I smelled it, I recognized honey and oatmeal, valerian and comfrey, lavender and newly mown grass. I lathered up and then, holding my breath and closing my eyes, slid beneath the surface, letting the water cover my head before breaking through again. I gasped, then wiped my eyes on a hand towel.

Cicely, something doesn't feel right.

Ulean? I didn't know you'd come with me.

I think you need to get out of here right now.

I bit my lip, wavering. *What do you sense? Is there anything riding the slipstream?*

A pause, then: *No. But I just have an uneasy prescience about this. Please, leave. Go home.*

Wondering what was up, I slowly emerged from the tub and wiped off. As I draped my pendant over my head, I began to notice that I was feeling lightheaded. I sat down on the bench to the side of the vanity and tried to collect my thoughts.

Ulean, I don't feel well—I'm feeling woozy.

Cicely, get out of here. Now!

I stumbled up and tried to gather my clothing but kept dropping pieces. Finally, I tried to shove myself into my jeans but couldn't manage the legs. I threw on my jacket, ignoring my bra and top, which were somewhere on the floor. As I opened the door and staggered out, Anadey was there to meet me.

"Anadey—something's wrong. I don't feel so good. I think I'd better go home."

"Nothing's wrong, Cicely. I just had to make certain you were relaxed. This is a delicate spell. Now, take off your jacket and let's get on with the casting. We don't have all day."

Everything seemed terribly normal, but when I stared into Anadey's eyes, I saw a flickering light that I didn't like. It was the light of betrayal. I pushed past her, attempting to make my way to the door, but once again I stumbled, and this time she grabbed me by the arm and jerked me back. She was horribly strong against my drugged state.

Off balance, I crashed to the floor. The room was spinning now, and I was blinking, trying to clear my sight, which had gone blurry. "What did you do to me, Anadey? What did you put in the drink?"

She tugged my jacket off me and then, grabbing me beneath both arms, half-lifted, half-dragged me into a circle of salt and herbs that she'd laid out in the middle of the living room floor. When we reached the center, she dropped me onto the floor, then stepped out of the circle and whispered a few words.

I forced myself to my hands and knees, crawling slowly across the twisting floor, to the edge of the salt. But try as I might, I couldn't force myself to cross the barrier. I tried to scatter the salt, but my hand met an invisible force field as it neared the edge of the circle.

"You might as well quit trying," Anadey said, glancing down at me. "The drink I gave you will last through the ritual. I'm sorry, Cicely, but I cannot chance having my fucking ex come here and take away my daughter. He tried, you know, once before. He tried to kidnap her when she was still young, and I stopped him. He still bears the scars of that lightning bolt. But now he's gained powerful allies, and I have been offered a choice. I won't lose her."

I forced my gaze up to meet hers and saw stark fear emblazoned across her face. "Anadey—what are you doing? Are you going to kill me? Hand me over to Myst?"

She stopped, her eyes wide. "Oh no, my dear. I'd never do that to you—please, don't think I mean to hurt you. I'm just going through with the spell we agreed on, with a twist. I'm going to take away your love for Grieve. Forever."

As she lightly stepped in the circle again, I tried to catch her by the hem of her robe, to trip her up, but it didn't work, and I let out a little cry.

"You can't break the connection—you'll kill us both."

"Don't be ridiculous," she said, kneeling down. She stretched my arms and legs out, tying me to four pegs that she'd hammered into tiny holes in the floor. After that, she began to draw on me with a brush dipped in red ink. *Dragon's Blood ink*. I shivered as the bristles tickled their way over my skin.

"It's true, Anadey. Please, believe me. Talk to Chatter—"

"He'd just make up a story. He misses his friend. No, we have to go through with this and then you and your cousin will be safe, and so will my Peyton. It will work out best for everybody."

"What are you doing to me?" I whispered, my voice falling mute even as she drew. "Peyton—does Peyton know what you're planning?"

"No, she doesn't, and I'm doing what I was told. This is the only way I can ever ensure that Rex won't get his hands on Peyton. You have to trust me, Cicely—please trust me. I won't hurt you, I promise. I would never hurt you."

But even as she continued to emblazon the symbols across my body, I knew that what she was doing would hurt me far worse than any beating I would ever endure.

Ulean, Ulean, help me. Can't you please help me?

But no answer came. Ulean couldn't hear me—or I couldn't hear her.

"Just a little more, and then I can begin the ritual." Anadey stood, and, eyeing me, gave a little nod. "Done."

As she stepped out of the circle, I felt a rush of energy surround me, and for the first time in a long while, I felt totally isolated. There was no one here to help me. I focused on my wolf, calling to Grieve, but he was nowhere to be sensed. *Truly alone. I am truly alone.*

Anadey waved her hands as she began to circle the ring of salt. A faint bluish mist seeped out from her fingers and drifted lazily into the circle with me, filling my lungs with the scent of ocean waves and salt brine.

Water to water, wave to wave,
Love built through time, I seek to stave.

A flush of energy rushed over me and I was breathing water, choking on the liquid as it rushed through my body, cleansing me fully, seeking all corners of my heart and soul, looking for inroads to fill me full with its briny depths.

I began to cry as it dislodged feelings and thoughts and began to buoy them up on its ever-encroaching currents.

"Anadey—stop—you're stealing my memories!" I tried to scream, but my words were so many bubbles floating up to the surface of the flood that flowed through me.

Anadey returned to the beginning of the circle and began a second sweep.

Earth to earth, stone to stone,
Sever connections that have been sown.

The mist turned to green, and as it flowed into the circle, it felt like a landslide, rumbling. And then I was looking up as a billowing cloud of mud and rock towered over me. I gasped but there was no air to breathe, only the deep gases of the earth, only the dust and soot-laden clouds that swept around me. As the energy began to seep through me, it uprooted connections and bonds, and I felt numb. Empty, and so truly alone.

Anadey returned to the beginning of the circle, to commence a third sweep.

Fire to fire, flame to flame,
This questing love, the sparks shall tame.

Crimson . . . the mist was a crimson cloud and smelled of bonfires and graves, and hearth fires. It burned as it neared, chafing my skin, and brought with it the crackle of embers. And it ate—gobbling up the will of my heart, the love I felt inside, my desire to be with Grieve. As I felt my need for him seeping out of me, I opened my mouth to cry out but there were no words. My lips were silent.

Anadey paused, staring down at me. I looked at her, pleading. After a moment, tears in her eyes, she began her final sweep.

Air to air, gale to gale,
Travel now, beyond the pale.

As the mist faded into white, I felt myself melting, as a rush of air buoyed me up, and then—a sudden jolt and I was gloriously free, rising up in owl form to hover near the top of the ceiling. Anadey gasped, and the mist began to retreat.

"Cicely—get down here! You can't break the spell, not this way—it will backfire in hideous ways if you don't allow me to finish it."

But I didn't give a fuck what she was saying. As far as I knew, Anadey was my enemy, as surely as Myst. Even more so than Lannan.

At that moment, Peyton broke through the door.

"Cicely! What's going on! Mother, what the fuck are you doing?" She gasped. "What's all this?"

She'd no sooner spoken than I took a chance and dove for the door, winging my way out and up into the sky, and then headed for home, free and wondering just what the hell Anadey had done to me.

Chapter 16

I flew into the night sky, winging my way into the heavens as Anadey and Peyton shouted from below—Anadey yelling at me, while Peyton was shaking her mother's shoulders. No way was I going back and chancing getting caught by Anadey again. Shaken, confused from the drugs and the spell, I headed in the direction I thought was home, terrified I'd transform midflight and go tumbling to the ground.

As I soared over the streets, my head began to clear and all of a sudden, I could hear Ulean. She was riding the currents beside me.

Cicely, Cicely? Can you hear me yet?

Ulean! Oh, Ulean, help me. I'm so confused and not sure where I'm going.

Keep on in this direction and I'll get you help.

And then, her presence was gone. I focused as best as I could, following the breeze as it carried me aloft. The night was chill, but no snow was falling and the clouds parted to allow the moon to shine through. What was I going to do? She could have killed me. She could have killed both Grieve and me if she'd succeeded with her spell. But how much damage had she done?

And then it hit me. I thought about Grieve, and my heart didn't skip a beat. I thought about my love, and realized that I felt numb. I tried to summon my wolf, but in owl form I couldn't connect with it. Thoroughly defeated and afraid, all I could do was keep flying.

At that moment, another owl came gliding in from behind me. The great horned owl. Ulean was riding the slip-stream along beside his wing.

Help me—something's happened to me and I don't know what.

Follow me. His thoughts came through clear and he turned, heading toward Dovetail Lake. I turned on my wing, following him, able to take direction better than make my own decisions at this point.

We flew under the moon until we reached the lake. A shimmer resonated through the night and the great horned owl flew into the light. It glimmered like summer, like warm leaves and dusky dreams, and a steady breeze that carried roses and night-blooming honeysuckle soothed my senses. I followed the owl through the portal and blinked as the land beneath us opened up, with rich grass untouched by snow, and lakeshore waters lapping gently.

The owl slowly spiraled down to land on a low branch near Lainule's throne, and I followed suit. I'd never been in the realm of Summer while in owl form and now, every breath, every sound, every movement was magnified.

A moment later, the Queen of Rivers and Rushes appeared, dressed in gossamer white. She steadily approached the throne and looked up at the two of us. After a moment, she let out a long sigh and slowly inclined her head.

"Cicely, take form."

I flew to the ground, and then, trying to focus through the fear, I shifted back into myself, naked and cold and shivering. As I stood, I found I wasn't ashamed or even

embarrassed—I was too worried and miserable to care
about what I was wearing. Or *not* wearing.

Lainule considered me for a moment, then removed her
own cloak from her shoulders and gently wrapped me in it.
The thin shawl was surprisingly warm, and my breath
slowed as I began to let go of my immediate fear. She nodded to the great horned owl and he flew to the ground. A
moment later, I was staring up at a gorgeous man with jet-
black hair. He wore clothes, so he must be full Cambyra
Fae—but his clothing matched the shimmer of Lainule's
own gown and as I gazed at him, I realized that this was no
ordinary Fae.

Lainule pressed her lips together and looked terribly sad,
but then she tossed her hair back and straightened her shoulders. "Cicely, say hello to my Consort, the King of Rivers
and Rushes. He has been guarding you since you returned.
Bow before your father, Wrath, Lord of Summer."

I let out a sharp gasp as her words ran through me like
an electric current. *My father, Wrath.* I'd had some inkling
the great horned owl might be my father—I hadn't been
sure, but the thought had crossed my mind. But . . . Wrath
was the Lord of Summer? Lainule's consort?

"Aren't you going to say something?" She gave me a
short look, and I wasn't sure if she was perturbed or merely
curious.

"I . . . I'm not sure what to say," I whispered, looking up
into Wrath's eyes. They were kindly, but stern. Ancient and
wise, as were Lainule's, and lit by a vivid light that knew
no sense of mortality. "I was hoping to meet you . . ."

"I did not want this meeting to happen yet—there is too
much at stake, but my Lord would never bring you here
were matters not grave."

And with her words, Anadey's betrayal came sweeping
back and I slid to the grass, tears flowing down my face.
"Everything's so dark right now. I can't find my way.
Anadey did something to me—the spell didn't fully take,
but I *know* she did something to me."

"Tell us what happened, Cicely. We have all the time in

the world to discuss the fact that I'm your father. But this . . . you say Anadey betrayed you?"

I nodded, my face red and hot. "I trusted her." And then, before I could stop myself, I spilled out everything. My plan to rescue Grieve, my need to be with him, the worry over hurting my friends because of being ensnared by his venom, Leo's suggestion that Anadey might help, and the choice I'd made to see if we could neutralize that effect. "I just wanted to be thinking with a clear head. But now . . ."

Placing my hands on my wolf, I sought for him, sought for the connection, but there was nothing. The tattoo was so much ink on my belly.

"Describe the spell that she cast." Lainule neither comforted me nor chided me.

Biting my lip, I did my best to describe everything that happened. So much was fuzzy—the drug she'd given me had been strong, but here in the realm of Summer, it seemed to be negated and I was able to focus more easily.

Lainule glanced up at Wrath and I could sense some conversation, unspoken, going on between the two. After a few moments, she stood. "Stay here. Talk with your father for a few moments. I am going to bring you something that will help."

She glided away, a mist of shadow in the night.

Wrath watched her go, his eyes longing and loving. As I stared at him, all I could think of was one question. "Why my mother? Why, when you are Lainule's consort, would you sleep with my mother?"

He turned to me, his smile steady but firm. "Because my love requested it. We have watched over your family for years. The boneseer told us you should return to life in this family as a half-breed, and so we chose the time and place of your birth. Myst has been waiting for your return all the years since you and Grieve—Shy died. If she found you first . . . it would not be good."

I bit my lip. My birth had been planned. "You seduced my mother?"

"Not a difficult task. She was comely, if terribly shy and

self-conscious. I could not stay with her, of course. Nor could she know who I was. We did not expect her to run and take you with her. However, perhaps that was best. Myst came to find both Geoffrey and you, but you were not here. So she turned her sight on the vampires and left it at that for a while."

"Ulean said that she belonged to Lainule before she was bound to me."

"Ulean was Lainule's personal Elemental, as the fan you carry was hers. The pendant, I enchanted. We knew you would come home, Cicely, and did what we could to prepare for your return."

I wrapped my arms around my legs and stared up at the sky. "Can I stay here? Can Rhiannon and I just come live in the realm of Summer and be safe?" It was a wistful question, I knew, and futile, but I had to ask.

"You have bound yourself to the vampires, so no—we could not let you shirk your oath. And you and Grieve must find one another again."

"How did I meet him in the first place? My mother was Myst . . ."

"You will remember in time. This is no war that can be won lightly. This is no skirmish. We are in for the long haul. The important thing is to mitigate our losses as much as we can at this point." He laughed and stretched out on the grass beside me. "You grew up lovely, my dear. I'm so glad that I was finally able to tell you. Cicely Waters, you are the daughter of a king. And yet you have not asked me for anything—for money or jewels or power."

I stared bitterly into the darkness. "Money will not buy freedom for Grieve, nor jewels. And power . . . power corrupts. I hate the fight I'm immersed in, but I will persevere. Because there's no other option. I am not the daughter of a king, with all respect, Your Majesty. I prefer to think of myself as the daughter of a witch and an owl-shifter. That suits my nature far more than the robes of a princess."

He reached out then and took my hand. His fingers were long and thin, with sharp nails, and he squeezed gently.

"Your answer pleases me more than you can possibly imagine. And just so you know: Lainule does not resent you. I speak the truth when I say your birth was her idea. We are not so beholden to having only one mate in the realm of Rivers and Rushes. You and Grieve are somewhat of an anomaly."

Just then, Lainule returned, a serving girl behind her who carried a steaming mug that smelled like raspberries and lemon. She handed it to me and when I inhaled, the scent washed through me.

"Drink deep. I give you my word of honor, it will only help you, not hurt you. Leave Anadey to me. Do not pursue the matter."

"She mentioned this had something to do with her ex-husband, Rex, and the fact that he's got 'powerful allies' and is back in town. I think she's afraid he'll lure Peyton away from her after all these years." I hesitantly brought the drink to my lips and sipped. The flavor ran through me like sweet wine, and I upturned the mug and emptied it down.

As the liquid spread through me, it felt like it was undoing knots and gnarls in my aura, and I relaxed a little. I found myself smiling, feeling free, and my wolf began to warm again. I placed my hand on the tattoo and felt a low rumble.

"Grieve . . . he's back . . ."

Lainule reached out and shook my shoulder. "I have reversed her spell, but you must listen to me. You *must not* follow through on your plan to rescue Grieve. I offer you this bargain: We will rescue him, but in our time, in our own way. Until then, pretend that Anadey's spell succeeded. We want to ferret out who she's working with, and if they see that it didn't take, they might fade away to avoid being noticed."

That made sense, although something felt off, but I couldn't put my finger on it.

"All right, I promise." Again, the feeling that I'd been locked in, thoroughly and tight, rang through me. Promises to the Fae, even by a half-Fae, were binding.

I thought about what it entailed—lying to Rhiannon and

the others—but I couldn't take the chance that one of them might be working against me. Leo, for example. I wouldn't put it past him to have been behind this mess. Now that I knew Anadey was all too willing to betray me, I couldn't be sure of anybody. Suddenly feeling much more alone in the world, I hung my head.

"I can't trust anyone now, can I?"

"You can trust yourself, child." Wrath patted my shoulder. "I'm proud of you. You've struggled against so many hardships over the years, and look at the strength that you've evolved. You make me proud to be your father."

Gazing up at him, I saw the kindly fire in his eyes. He'd never be one to hug me tight, or take in a ball game with me, but he meant what he said and that was more important to me than all the father-daughter outings in the world.

"Thank you," I whispered. "But what will I say to them? I ran out on Anadey."

"Keep away from her. She was trying to remove your connection to Grieve. Do your best to pretend that the venom enchantment has been severed. Let them see it's led you to reconsider rescuing him. Continue with your business. If Grieve tries to contact you, don't tell anyone and instruct him to do the same."

I told them what happened when Myst beat Grieve. "I took on his injuries."

Lainule pressed her lips together, then let out a long sigh. "Obviously, we cannot just leave him with her. Not if it's going to hurt you. I feared this might come to pass. We have to move quickly. Go home, do as we bid, and we'll be in touch with you soon. And meanwhile, keep your heritage secret. If Myst finds out you are Wrath's daughter, she will throw all her efforts into capturing you. She would ignore the vampires and come after you directly."

"This is why you didn't tell me about my father isn't it? You were afraid I couldn't keep my mouth shut?"

"No, Cicely," Lainule said softly. "I feared she'd torture it out of you and then all would be lost."

Wrath walked me back to the edge of the portal. "You

will have to tread carefully with what has happened. One misstep and we all lose. I wanted to tell you earlier, you know—about the fact that I'm your father—but we couldn't take the chance letting you know. Now you do."

"Now I know," I repeated softly. Then, without thinking, I threw my arms around him and gave him a long hug. "Thank you. Thank you for being my father."

"Don't thank me yet, Cicely. It's too soon to tell what the fallout of everything is going to be. But know I am watching over you—that's why I spend so much time in owl form."

He opened the portal. A dark green sedan was waiting for me. I frowned, staring at it, then looked back at him.

Wrath nodded. "The car will see you safely home. Don't ask questions, don't tip the driver. Just get in, be silent, and leave silent."

I slipped into the backseat and as the driver glanced at me through the rearview mirror, I caught a glimpse of his face. Whatever he was, in the mirror it didn't translate as human. But I said nothing, just nodded, and as the car pulled out from the parking lot, I settled back for the short but silent ride home.

⁂

After I climbed out of the car, I stood watching it speed off into the night. Then, turning back, I stared up at the Veil House. Had Leo been in on Anadey's little plan? Who was backing her? All answers I needed to know. Steeling myself, I entered the house.

Peyton was there, along with Rhiannon and Kaylin, both of whom looked terribly worried. They rushed over as soon as they saw me.

"Cicely—I'm so sorry. I drove your car home for you and brought your clothes and purse. What did my mother do to you? I knew something was wrong. Why the fuck did I leave when she told me to?" Peyton's eyes were glittering with tears.

I bit my lip. The last thing I needed was for Peyton to

confront Anadey. I hated lying to my friends, to my cousin, but there was no help for it until we found out who might be working with the older witch.

"Your mother broke the venom enchantment, like we wanted. I just don't like the way she did it—she scared me. I want nothing to do with her for now." I held her gaze, willing myself to go through with this. "She pissed me off, although I can't remember much of what happened."

Peyton paused, sucking in a deep breath. "I'm so sorry. How are you feeling, physically?"

I hesitated, as if searching my feelings, then slowly shook my head. "I don't know. Numb, I guess. All I know is she drugged me and tied me down—isn't that enough? No spell should involve that sort of behavior, not when it's cast on a friend."

It bothered me to keep it from Peyton that Anadey was working to ensure that her father was out of commission, but there was too much at stake to come clean over that.

Peyton waited another beat, then slowly nodded. "Yeah, I hear you. Loud and clear. Maybe I'll stay over here for the night—that is, if you don't mind me being here after what happened."

I shrugged. "No, you weren't the one who did that to me."

Rhiannon and Kaylin pummeled me with questions, but I played dumb and managed to get out of any protracted conversation by pleading exhaustion. Rhia followed me upstairs, and as I drew a bath, she pulled out my nightgown and robe for me. I wanted to break down, to tell her everything that was happening, but a spark of fear held me back.

Lainule and Wrath were going to rescue Grieve, and they were going to find out who was behind Anadey's bizarre behavior. I couldn't sell them out just because Rhia was my cousin. I felt like I was walking a razor's edge—so many conflicting forces, so many potential enemies. But as soon as they gave the okay, I would sit her down and tell her everything.

My wolf growled slightly, but I forced my hands to keep away from my stomach. I pulled off my clothes and stepped into the bubbling tub of lavender and lemon, sliding down into the comforting water as the steam loosened my joints. Rhia sat on the edge of the tub.

"Do you want me here?" She bit her lip, looking torn. "I can leave if you want to be alone."

"Nah, that's okay." I blinked back tears, thinking I'd cried all too much in the past few weeks. But these were tears of weariness and of joy. Meeting Wrath had brought with it an underlying sense of peace, even though it left me with more questions than ever. Such as: How had he enticed my mother? Had he cared for her at all, or was it simply a mission to ensure that I return as Cambyra Fae? And Krystal . . . had she fallen for him, only to be left alone and pregnant?

"Anadey . . . I don't know what to think about this. Did her spell work, though? Do you think the venom from Grieve will still intoxicate you? Or did she . . . did she do anything else to you?" Rhia was astute, that much I already knew. And she knew something was going on.

I closed my eyes, leaning back against the warm porcelain as the water soaked through my aching muscles. After a moment, I shrugged. "I doubt the venom will be a bother anymore."

"Peyton says you flew away into the night. Were you wearing your pendant? I thought you left it at home."

"No . . . I had it with me. But the transformations are getting easier." I sat very still.

"You're changing, evolving. Very quickly. I hope it's not too much for you."

"I think I'd like to just relax now," I said, closing my eyes. "Can you light a candle and turn off the overhead on your way out?"

Rhia stood, brushing the front of her skirt nervously. "Cicely, are you going to go after Anadey for what she did to you?"

And then I realized she was afraid I'd attack the older woman, that I'd go off half-cocked and kill her or something. I laughed softly. "No, don't worry yourself over that. Trust me. I don't really consider her a friend right now—not after drugging me—but attack her? No." *At least not now.*

With a sigh of relief, Rhiannon lit a candle and turned to leave, softly closing the door behind her. As soon as she was gone, I let everything go and suddenly found myself weeping, silently and uncontrollably. I let the tears run down my face, not bothering to wipe them away. I was crying for Grieve and our people—the Cambyra Fae. I cried for Chatter, whom I'd betrayed in my former life. And for Rhiannon and Heather. For Anadey, who had proved herself to be false-tongued. I cried for Leo, so caught up in his need for validation that he'd actually slap a woman. I cried for Kaylin, tied to the Bat People, who seemed so very harsh.

And lastly, I cried for myself . . . because I had no clue how we were going to come out of this with any sense of happiness. In fact, happiness seemed a million miles away.

Chapter 17

I slept uneasy, guarding my dreams. The thought that Kaylin might be able to slip in, to sense them, bothered me more than I thought it had. I wanted something private, that was my own, and each time someone linked to me, it took a little of my privacy away.

Early in the morning, I woke to the sound of the owl outside my window. Wrath was perching in the oak. I opened the window and saw that he was carrying a note in his beak. Cautiously, I crawled out on the snow and ice, shivering, and he flew by, dropping the paper on the roof, then soared off to the tree line again.

I snatched up the folded paper and headed back inside, slamming the window again. As I unfolded the thick, papyrus-like paper, a thin spidery writing leaped out to catch my eye. Not from the vampires, that was for sure. The paper reeked of Fae energy. Glancing at the signature, I saw that it was from Lainule.

It read:

Cicely, I'm going to talk to Geoffrey about these issues. Keep strong. Keep to our agreement.

Tucking it away in a desk drawer, I stared at myself in the mirror. I looked haggard. My wolf growled and I gently rubbed across it, sending soothing thoughts to Grieve. Thank the gods that Anadey hadn't been able to complete her spell or I'd be dead.

With that thought, I took a quick shower, dressed, and ran down the stairs. As I shot into the kitchen, I skidded to a halt. Everybody was gathered around the kitchen table: Rhia, Leo, Kaylin, Chatter, and Peyton. They all looked up at me, as if expecting a thundercloud to break.

"What? What's going on?"

"How are you doing?" Rhia looked uncomfortable.

I shrugged. "Fine, I guess. I feel a bit discombobulated, but it was probably just Anadey's magic. It's different than my own."

"Did you want to go dreamwalking at Geoffrey's today?" Kaylin gave me a long look, speculative, and I realized he didn't believe me.

With a shake of the head, I let out a short sigh. "No, there's too much at stake for us to chance it right now." Before anybody could say anything, I turned to Peyton. "We'd better make sure the parlor and waiting room are clean. Our ad hit the paper this morning and my guess is that we're going to have a busy day."

At least, I prayed it would be a busy day—that way I wouldn't have time to think. I wolfed down my breakfast, waffles and eggs and bacon, without looking up at the others, even though I was all too aware of their attention focused on me.

"But I thought you needed to get the antidote as soon as possible?" Rhia asked slowly.

"I've decided to wait—just not a good idea. Leo was right." I looked up at him, a faint smile on my face. "It's too dangerous."

"The day I'm right around you women is the day hell freezes over," Leo said. He glanced out the window. "And it looks like it has. I'd better get back outside to shovel the walks again. I feel like crap, but it has to be done."

"Let me do it," I said. "I need the exercise." Truth was, I just wanted to be alone for a while. "Peyton, would you mind watching over the fort? Call me if anybody comes in and I'm still on shovel detail."

"All right," she said, frowning. "Cicely . . . are you sure you're all right?"

I nodded, vigorously, forcing a smile to my lips. "Yeah, I'm fine. Good breakfast. Thanks to the cook." As I pushed myself to my feet, I noticed Leo watching me, a thoughtful look on his face. I engaged his stare, feeling altogether too hostile, then turned away.

Grabbing the snow shovel, I headed out the front door. The cold took my breath away, but I cautiously began scraping the snow off the steps leading to the walk, making sure to scatter rock salt to melt the underlying ice.

Myst's winter had hit and hit hard. A good two feet of snow blanketed the front yard, but where we were shoveling the walk, we'd built snow banks over three feet high. I slid the edge of the shovel under the layer of white and began to scoop it away. Too bad we didn't have a damned snowblower, I thought. I should ask Regina for one. She'd probably buy it for us.

As I scooped shovelful after shovelful of snow away and tossed it on the ever-growing pile, I began to calm down. Breakfast had been difficult, but this was no different from the scams we'd run on the men Krystal attracted. All it came down to was playing a part. And I'd developed into a pretty good actress over the years. I'd had to learn— that was how I won my 1966 Pontiac GTO in a game of street craps. Bravado and bluffing was what it was all about.

After a while, the cold settled into a gentle numbness and I worked silently, clearing the sidewalk. The sound of a car made me stop, and I leaned on the shovel, watching as a long black limo eased down the cul-de-sac. It crept toward me, and I waited, a tingling racing down my fingertips. As the limo stopped, easing into the driveway, I caught my breath. Myst's people didn't drive, as far as I knew— they hadn't assimilated into society that far. Or at least

I thought so. And it was daytime, so it couldn't be the vampires.

The door opened and a lean, wiry woman stepped out of the car. She looked yummanii, but the sense of magic tingled around her. She was one of the magic-born. As she swept up the sidewalk I'd just cleared, I found myself tensing.

Watch what you say, watch what you do. Ulean's warning came sharp and clear.

I gave a gentle nod.

"You are Cicely Waters?" The woman's voice was husky. She wore an ankle-length dress, almost Victorian in nature but made from a warm purple jersey. Over the top, she was wearing a white fur coat, and her hands were swathed in ivory gloves made from brushed suede. And she was carrying a briefcase that looked like it had been fashioned in the early 1900s.

"Who wants to know?" I didn't mean to be belligerent, but her nature put me off. She had a nosy energy about her, and my instinct was to head inside and lock the door. But she wasn't vampire, she wasn't Fae . . .

"I am not here to play games. I'm Ysandra Petros, from the Consortium, and you'd better answer me quickly if you have any wits about you."

Oh crap. The *Consortium.* Had they gotten wind of Myst? Geoffrey's warnings came rushing back as a swell of panic rose up. I had to get her inside. We couldn't chance her sensing something from the Golden Wood.

"Come in. Yes, I'm Cicely. Please, let's get out of the cold." I hastened her inside and showed her into the living room—the parlor now being a place of business. "I'll be right back. Would you like some tea?" Without waiting for a *yes* or *no,* I hurried into the kitchen, yanking off my coat and gloves and tossing them on the table. A spark of good luck: Everybody was still gathered around the kitchen table eating.

"Trouble with a capital T. We have a member of the Consortium out there. Chatter, don't you dare come out. I'll handle this—we have to hustle her out before she finds out about Myst. Geoffrey warned me about the Consortium and on this, I trust him fully."

The color drained out of Rhiannon's face, and both Peyton and Leo let out little gasps. Chatter frowned, but said nothing, and Kaylin sat there with a smirk on his face. He slowly pushed himself to his feet.

"I can be useful in this matter," he said.

"Are you insane? You're bound to a demon. Doesn't the Consortium feel it necessary to bind demons or something like that?" I stared at him, wondering if he'd gone bonkers.

He shrugged. "Perhaps they do, but I am not so easily read, not by magic-born and not by yummanii. Trust me on this, as you trust Geoffrey. Tell her I'm your husband."

Without a clue as to what to do, I nodded. "Then make a quick pot of tea and bring it in, please. I offered her tea for some godawful reason."

I washed my hands, then hurried back into the living room, where I found Ysandra sitting primly in one of the chairs. She glanced up at my entrance.

"I'm sorry. My . . . husband"—the word rolled oddly off my tongue, but for some reason I had the feeling Kaylin knew what he was doing—"will be in with tea in a moment. Please, to what do we owe the honor of your visit?"

Though her visit was anything but an honor, there was no good way to ask her to leave without catastrophe. I'd told Geoffrey the truth when I said I knew about the Consortium. They were a powerful community, and one in which I did not wish to be embroiled. But it looked like I wasn't going to get my wish. At least not right now.

"Heather Roland owns this house?"

"Heather's my aunt, and she's away on a sabbatical. My husband and I are staying with my cousin, Rhiannon, who is Heather's daughter. We're house-sitting." The mixture of truth and lies rolled out one after another, and I prayed she didn't have a truth spell handy.

"I see. Is Rhiannon available? I'd like to talk to her, as well." Ysandra blinked, and it was obvious her request was a demand.

I cleared my throat. "Of course; wait here, please." I hurried back into the kitchen, where Kaylin was finishing up the pot of tea. "She wants to see Rhiannon as well. I told her that you and I are married and house-sitting with Rhia, because Heather's away on sabbatical."

Rhiannon, still pale, nodded, and followed Kaylin and me back into the living room. She motioned for us to put the tea on the coffee table and graciously reached out to shake Ysandra's hand.

Kaylin nodded, giving the woman a short bow, then sat after Rhia and I positioned ourselves on the sofa. "Miss . . . ?"

"I am Madame Ysandra Petros. You must be Rhiannon Roland?"

Rhia nodded. "Yes, you've met my cousin Cicely, and this is her . . . husband, Kaylin Chen."

"Ma'am," Kaylin said, pouring the tea. "Sugar, milk, or lemon?"

"Lemon. Thank you." Ysandra accepted the cup and sniffed the steaming beverage, smiling for the first time since she'd arrived. "Tea does a body and soul good, with the horrible weather we've been having."

"What can we do for you?" I asked, after giving her a moment to warm her hands on the china cup.

"There have been rumors of strange activity in this area—odd magical happenings. And we've not heard from one of our members in a long time. Marta Vekos. I stopped in at her house but nobody's home and so I thought I'd come over to ask Heather what's going on."

Ysandra seemed to relax a little, but I knew better than to be caught off guard. She was taking in every nuance. I could tell because she was doing exactly what I'd trained myself to do while growing up. Uncle Brody's rule number fifty-four: Become hyperaware of your environment. The skill had kept me alive more than once.

I put on a sad face. "Marta was killed by wild dogs a couple of months ago. At least the police seem to think there's a pack of wild dogs on the loose. She left me her business. If you'd like to see what I'm doing with it, we can go into the parlor."

A flash of pain echoed across the woman's face. "Marta is dead?"

Rhiannon nodded. "Yes, and the Thirteen Moons Society has fallen apart. She was the heart and soul holding it together. A number of the elders moved on. Her daughter, Anadey, and granddaughter took over her house."

We were dancing with the devil, but at least we knew it.

Ysandra let out a soft sigh. "So that's why my summons went unanswered. Anadey has little love for the Consortium and would not have notified us." After a momentary pause, she added, "Marta was a good friend of mine. She will be sorely missed. But seeing that you inherited your business, you are responsible for taking the appropriate actions. All magical businesses must be registered with us, and the owner must join the Consortium."

Oh hell. Then I remembered: Marta had belonged to the Consortium. Apparently, I was also expected to become a member. What the fuck were they going to do once they discovered I was half Cambyra Fae, and working for the vampires?

"And what about Mystical Eye Investigations? Do you run that, as well?" Ysandra gave me a long look.

I slowly shook my head. "Marta's granddaughter does. We decided to join forces, so to speak."

"Then she must become a member of the Consortium, as well. I will leave you both the necessary forms. You must fill them out and send them in with the appropriate fees, and then when we summon you, you must stand before the CCC to win final approval to obtain your licenses."

"CCC?"

"Consortium Chamber of Commerce. We control all magical businesses of any note. Since Marta did not pay her quarterly tithe, the CCC sent me to find out why. Now I know." She opened her briefcase and took out two packets of paper. "Here are the forms. You have one month to fill them out and mail them back to us. We will contact you after we've gone over them."

She finished her tea and stood, her hand shading her eyes. "I wish to pay my respects to Marta's daughter, but I'm pressed for time. Please convey my sympathy. Marta . . . she and I went way back. We roomed together at the Conservatory when we were in school."

And right then, Ysandra ceased to be a terror and suddenly became a very humane, if magic-born, person to me. I looked in her eyes and saw the glimmer of tears, and realized that everything else—all the brisk business and no-nonsense part of her persona—had paled compared to losing an old friend.

I reached out and pressed her hand. "I'll let her granddaughter know. We're good friends, and I'll make sure she passes on the message."

"Marta's daughter, Anadey, was always sour about the Consortium. I understand she might not want to hear from me, but my sympathies are there if she wants them." As Ysandra started to gather her things, she paused. "Oh, and you'll be starting the Society up again, of course."

"Say what?" I stared at her. "Why would I do that? The Society disbanded with her death."

"You inherited her business, and therefore you inherited her place as elder. Since the Thirteen Moons Society disbanded, it's up to you to choose up to twelve other members and bring it back to life—with a new name, of course. That goes with being the witch chosen to watch over any particular village or town."

"I'm confused. What do you mean, chosen?"

"Marta was chosen to lead the Society, and her business was not only to sell magical potions and charms, but to watch over New Forest. She knew that by choosing her successor, she would automatically pass on the position. Usually it would be a direct lineage, but since her daughter chose not to involve herself with the Consortium, apparently, you were her choice. I'm surprised she didn't choose your aunt, but she must have had her reasons. Heather was always Marta's right-hand woman."

"My aunt . . ."

"Mother is so busy with her studies that she had to bow out of the Society for now." Rhia spoke up, her voice steady and calm. "And the Society never recognized me, so I was not a viable candidate."

Ysandra gazed at her, silent for a moment. "Yes, we never understood Marta's position on that. You will be accepted if Cicely chooses to include you in her roster."

And with that, she headed toward the door, briefcase in hand. "Get me those forms as soon as you can. I'll be in charge of your applications, so mark them to my attention. It was nice meeting you, and you, too, Kaylin. You make a lovely couple. Since you're married, you'll have to provide me with a copy of your marriage certificate so it can be recorded. All partnerships by members of the Consortium are on record, whether they be poly or monogamous."

Before we could respond, she swept out into the frigid air, down the steps, and her dark sedan glided up the street again.

I stood there, gaping at the door. "What the fuck do we do now?"

Kaylin laughed from behind me. "Get married, I suppose."

❧

As we gathered back around the kitchen table, I accepted a cup of tea from Kaylin, who had returned the still-full pot back into the kitchen.

Rhiannon brought the others up to speed while I gulped down the scalding drink, supplementing it with a piece of cold toast.

"We have to keep them from finding out about Myst, and yet we're supposed to join their little club?" I shook my head.

"The Consortium is no 'little club,'" Peyton said. "And now I have to join, too? Mother's going to love that."

"Your mother's got more problems than you becoming a member of the Consortium," I muttered, but I shook my head when she asked me to repeat what I'd said. "Nothing. But we need to fill out those forms. You *don't* ignore the Consortium. Tonight, I'd better talk to Geoffrey and tell him what's happened. The vampires are going to have to know."

"Why would it be so bad to have the magic-born on our side? Why don't the vampires want them to know about Myst?" Peyton asked.

I shrugged. "The Consortium is rife with greed and so swamped in politics that it's likely they'd mire down any action in arguments and debates. But they'd also try to squeeze out the vampires' help—the magic-born don't tend to like the vampires as a whole. Everything would end embroiled in turmoil and arguments. And though the Consortium is big, don't forget, there are one hell of a lot of vamps in the world, and they might take umbrage at being pushed out of what they consider their own private war."

"Politics, then."

"Politics between two very dangerous forces. I have no idea which side the yummanii would come down on— probably the Consortium, but either way, it could get very sticky." I glanced over at Leo. "You've been awfully quiet."

"My sister Elise belonged. She kept trying to get me to give up my job so I could join the Healers' Society, which is sanctioned by the Consortium. There's not a lot of love lost between them and the vampires. I never even wanted to be a healer."

Rhiannon jerked up her head. "What? I thought you loved it."

He shrugged. "I don't mind the healing arts, but it's not what I signed on for. But I've got the talent, so I figured I might as well learn how."

"What *do* you want to do?" She stared at him, her lip quivering. Apparently, the healer side of him had appealed to her.

"You want to know? Honestly?" Leo looked at her, then at the rest of us. "I wanted to be a cultural anthropologist and study vampires. This way, I get the best of both worlds. I'm working for them—so I get to see their culture in action, and yet I don't have to give up my life to become one of them."

I stared at him for a moment. He wasn't telling the full truth, that much I could tell. He wanted more . . . but just what, I couldn't fathom.

Rhiannon blinked. "What? Is that why you're a day-runner?"

"Hell, yeah. You thought I'd do this just for the hell of it? Too dangerous, but I like the ability to study them up close. Someday, I hope to write a book about my experiences, though they don't know that." He grinned, then his smile faded again. "But the way things are going, I'm not sure what to expect."

A dark flash ran through Rhiannon's eyes. "Me either," she said quietly, and I knew she was talking about Leo and her relationship with him, as much as she was commenting on the situation at hand.

"Peyton and I are going to have to join the Consortium. Does that mean anybody I choose for the new Thirteen Moons Society—or whatever we end up calling it—will have to belong?"

"Yeah, most likely. Though I'm not totally sure." Rhiannon frowned. "Heather belonged. But I think a couple of the members weren't Consortium members." She shook her head. "It looks like Marta meant for you to revive the Society. Do you think she planned all this?"

Peyton drummed her fingers on the table. "Could be. She knew Mother would never take over the shop. But . . . Anadey had to expect they'd be paying you a visit . . ."

"I'm not so sure about that. I think your mother has focused on other things besides the comings and goings of the Consortium." *Like how to prevent your father from stealing you away from her.* Which brought us right back to the case at hand: I had to rely on Lainule and Wrath to rescue Grieve now, without telling the others that Anadey had damned near killed me.

"So how do we sort this all out?" Rhia said.

"First, Peyton and I get these forms filled out and sent off. I guess we'd better get serious about our businesses because we're going to be tithing to the Consortium. I guess Kaylin and I have to get a marriage license somewhere, and I'll bet they're going to check on it to make sure it's real. What the fuck was with the idea of telling them we're married?"

Kaylin grinned. "It kept them from asking further questions about me, didn't it?"

Again, the feeling I was out of the loop on something flickered through my mind but I knew better than to ask Kaylin what he was keeping to himself. He'd flat-out refuse to tell me.

"Whatever you say. After we get things in order, I'll sit down and figure out what I want the new Society to be like. I'm not calling it what Marta did, though—I'm too superstitious to give it the same name. I don't have to add all thirteen members at once, I suppose, so we'll start out with . . ." I glanced at them. As much as I wasn't sure about Leo, I couldn't leave him out. It would make for an uncomfortable situation. "I guess with five—the five of us."

"Five, for the five points on the pentagram," Rhiannon whispered.

"Earth, that's Leo; Fire, you, Rhia. Water—Peyton, you can handle that. Air, me. And Kaylin, I guess that leaves you for Spirit—for the shadows you walk in. We have enough to invoke the Elemental Watchers. Ulean can guard the gates of Air. Chatter can keep watch overall." I'd never really worked formal magic, but it looked like I was going to learn. And it looked like I was going to learn faster than I'd ever imagined.

"We can do this whatever way you want, Cicely." Rhia shrugged. "Since you're the heart of the group, you call the shots." She sent Leo a stern look, and he paled but nodded. "Whatever you say goes."

"I still don't know how the hell they'll handle the knowledge that I'm part Cambyra Fae. I thought only the full-blooded magic-born were allowed memberships." I played with the crust of my bread.

"Apparently not. They have to know something about your background. Either that or they've changed their rules. One way or another, we'll find out." My cousin gave me a soulful look. "Whatever you need, we have your back."

"Thanks." But in my heart, I wondered if that was true. Were they all loyal, or was Anadey working with one of my friends? Everybody in this room knew that if she'd managed to neutralize my love for Grieve, it would destroy one of us. So her spell would have killed me. If somebody tried to help her . . . they knew they'd be party to murdering me.

And what the hell was I supposed to do about Kaylin, now that the Consortium thought we were married? We couldn't fake a license. They'd be able to check on that without any problems. We'd have to actually get married, pretend to be husband and wife, long enough to placate them. Because if they found out I'd lied about that, they might discover I'd lied about other things. Like Heather being on sabbatical, and Marta being killed by wild dogs.

Somehow I didn't think the Consortium would forgive lies of omission. With these thoughts in mind, I finished my tea, then went into the parlor to try to focus on work.

Chapter 18

Peyton and I were silent as we tidied up the parlor and took our places. I was sorting herbs and gemstone chips into little plastic bags to sell, while she was playing mutely with the cards. The silence was awkward, but what was there to say? I had to keep quiet about what had actually happened at Anadey's, and I knew she was feeling guilty and angry over the whole incident.

But after a few moments, she broke the ice. "I want to move in, if you'll have me."

I jerked my head up. "What?"

"If you have room, I'd like to move in. I'm not going back to the diner, and I'm not going back to my mother's. The look on her face when I broke into the circle last night was terrifying. I've never seen her look so angry, or so . . . secretive. What the fuck did she do to you?"

I shrugged. "I guess . . . what we talked about."

"She did more than that. This morning, when Kaylin asked if you wanted to go dreamwalking to find the anti-dote, you shrugged him off like he'd asked if you wanted to go stroll through the forest and take Myst a basket of muffins."

I sucked in a deep breath. How to handle this? Sometimes avoidance was the best route. "We should talk about something we can control, like the Consortium and how we're to go about working with them. I had no clue they oversee magical businesses. It seems odd that they came out here just as we opened our doors, doesn't it?"

"Not if they've been trying to get in touch with Marta. They're probably running a bit behind, like any bureaucracy. But that aside, how do you feel about joining them?" Peyton brushed her hand across the soft cloth of the table. "Mother's going to have a fit when I do."

"I'd rather have a few teeth pulled, but I guess there's no help for it. And it's not like we could hide anything—our sign was right out there by the side of the road when she got out of the car." I shook my head. "I've never been good at joining anything or following rules. Creating a society like Marta did is going to be hell on me."

I preferred to rely on myself. But then again, perhaps we could create a group that was strong against Myst and the Indigo Court. Ysandra had given me no clear rules. What if I wanted to include Fae, or even vampires in it? She hadn't said that I couldn't. I was about to say as much when someone walked through the door for a reading. As Peyton invited the woman to sit down, I turned away, focusing on my work.

I sold five protection charms that afternoon, and Peyton had one other customer. She talked to her for a bit, then called me over.

"This is Luna. She has a problem that I thought you might hear." Peyton introduced the woman, who was probably about thirty-five. She was short and plump, with long dark hair, and her eyes were ringed with silver sparkles. Pretty, in a way that appeared soft on the surface, but beneath I sensed a huge reservoir of strength.

"Hi." I shook her hand, surprised by the strength of her grip.

"Hello." Her voice was even and low, sultry almost. She slid back into her chair and as she lowered her head, a sweep of movement caught my eye. I closed my eyes and listened on the slipstream.

She is marked. Her energy is marked. Keep her here, do not let her go out into the wilds tonight. The Hunters are following her—I can hear them on the slipstream. Ulean whirled around me, frantic.

I turned back to Luna. "What's going on?"

"I feel like I'm being followed. The past day or so, especially during the evenings, I've felt something outside my house. I haven't gone out to check—I'm not stupid—but my cards have warned me that something dangerous is waiting for me. I don't know what to do. I have nowhere to go. I saw your ad in the paper and thought I'd ask if you could investigate. And maybe fashion a protection charm for me. I can make them myself, but my fear is overwhelming my sense of accuracy."

I glanced over at Peyton. "They're after her."

"Who? Who's after me? You know already?" Her lip quivered. "I live alone and I'm not sure what to do."

We couldn't take in everyone whom the Shadow Hunters were after, but damn it, we had a chance to save her life. And for some reason, Luna struck me as useful. As someone I might want to know better.

"Luna, tell us a bit about yourself. Then maybe we can help you better."

She let out a long sigh. "I'm single, I'm a singer—well, part time. I work in a little thrift shop to make ends meet, and I occasionally attend a psychic fair and do readings."

Then it hit me; she wasn't magic-born like I'd suspected, but yummanii. And she had some very strong magic of her own. The magic-born didn't bother with psychic fairs, but the yummanii, especially those who had magical abilities . . .

"You're yummanii." I held her gaze.

She nodded. "Well, mostly. There is mixed magic in my family. My grandmother married into the magic-born. After that, the abilities of the children and grandchildren grew stronger. I'm the strongest in the family. But it mostly comes out when I sing or play an instrument. My songs . . . I can sometimes make things happen."

A bard. Luna was an old-fashioned bard. And that would be very useful to Myst. She'd be able to charm in people with a bard-turned-vampire in ways that she couldn't now. Influential people, who might listen to Luna's songs and fall under her spell. And if Luna belonged to Myst, then she'd obey without question.

"You can't go home, not alone. At least not for tonight." I bit my lip, trying to think of what to tell the woman.

She will believe the truth. Her energy . . . you must not let her fall into Myst's hands. Ulean was adamant.

Are you certain? She's mostly yummanii . . .

The yummanii are no less at risk than the magic-born, especially one with her abilities. She came to you for a reason. Don't turn her out or you will be signing her death warrant.

Taking a deep breath, I let it out slowly and gave her a slow smile. "Have you ever heard of the Shadow Hunters?"

She slowly shook her head. "No, should I have?"

"That depends . . ." And so we told her about Myst, and the vampires.

❦

The afternoon passed into shadows and faded away. Luna listened to our story and—after a few probing questions—accepted what we had to say.

"My grandmother warned me that one day something might happen. She was one of the historians who worked on writing *The History of the Vampire Nation*. At least, the condensed volume."

I jerked my head up. "Condensed volume? You mean there's more than one book?"

"Oh, yes. There's a fifteen-volume encyclopedia that was written about their history. It's under lock and key—only two copies of it still exist. My family owns one of them; the other is deep in the vaults." She let out a little gasp and pressed her fingers to her lips.

"Vaults? Luna, you need to tell us what you're talking about."

Looking chastised, she grimaced. "I should never have mentioned them, but . . . given what you told me about Myst and the Indigo Court, it might become necessary for you to know this. I'll tell you, but please, don't let the vampires know . . . or Myst."

Peyton and I gave our word.

"There's a society, they keep track of all the goings-on in the world. A group of historians known as the Akazzani. They are magic-born and yummanii alike. And they watch. They are born nine to a generation, and they are taken when young and trained for their jobs. They live in a hidden fortress and from there observe the goings-on of the world. They are the preservers of knowledge, the guardians of the ages. They do not interfere, nor do they direct matters, but they record all that has gone on, and all that will be. My sister was chosen by them. I only remember her from when she was very small, before the Akazzani took her under their wing."

"Does your family live in the area?" Peyton gave her a soft smile.

Luna shook her head. "No, they are originally from Ireland, though some of them migrated over toward the Italian shores. My own mother and father chose to come to the States when they were younger. I was born here."

I made a snap decision, going on instinct. "You can stay here. I'll have to ask my cousin, but I'm sure she won't mind when we explain the situation. I'm glad you came to us today."

If she had not, tonight she would die. Ulean swept through the room. *She can hear me, if I choose for her to. Her voice sends magic through the slipstream when she sings. You can teach her to talk to the wind. It might be a handy skill for her to have.*

You act as if she's going to be around for a while.
Keep her away from Myst's hunters and she will.

Luna glanced out the window. The clock was chiming six and dusk had fallen. She closed her eyes, then shuddered. "They are out there, aren't they? Hunting for magic, hunting for people."

"For blood and life force, yes. And they leave very little of their victims. They are killing machines—make no mistake and do not let them charm you, should you ever encounter them. Myst's people are sharks of the land, and they do enjoy their carnage. They dance with death and deal it out by the handful."

"I will stay, if you'll put me up."

I stretched. "Then welcome. Can you cook?"

"Can a bird sing?"

"Good, because we can manage, but it will be nice to have a change of pace."

As Peyton led us out of the parlor, the doorbell rang. Rhia answered, glancing briefly at Luna, then came back from the door, an envelope in hand.

"For you, Cicely."

I stared at it, recognizing the handwriting. After a moment, I ripped it open and pulled out the card.

"Your presence is requested at my home tomorrow night. Formal dress. A limousine will arrive for you at 8:00 P.M. Come alone. Geoffrey."

I wondered if Leo knew about this, then silently slid the card back in the envelope. Best leave it for now. I shoved the summons in my pocket and, asking Peyton to take Luna in the kitchen for a snack, pulled Rhia into the living room and told her about the woman.

"We need her. Ulean is certain of it, and certain she will die if we let her take off again."

Rhiannon peeked around the corner, then let out a long sigh. "We are gathering allies, you realize."

"And losing some." I thought of Anadey. "But Luna, she's yummanii and a bard—with a touch of magic-born blood in her background."

"She seems swathed in an aura of mist. There is more to her than meets the eye," Rhia said. "You are sure of this?"

"Ulean is sure. And yes . . . when I think about it, it feels right that Luna join our group. That will be six. I must bring the group to a full thirteen—of that Ysandra was positive. I wonder who they'll be."

"Not Anadey."

"No."

"You aren't telling me everything. I know that much, Cicely. But I won't ask you what or why. You have your reasons, and I can only imagine what you must think of me, after Leo hit you like he did. I can't ever apologize enough for his actions—"

I waved her words away. "It's not up to you to apologize. He knew what he was doing."

"I don't know what to think. I'm second-guessing myself about him. Ever since he laid hands on you, I haven't been able to let him touch me. The thought of him hurting a woman makes me sick to my stomach. It could have been me, Cicely."

I bit my lip, not knowing what to say. The fact that Leo had found it acceptable to hit me bothered me, too, a hell of a lot. And I wondered: If he could hit me, could he beat my cousin, who couldn't fight back easily? Or who might lash out with her fire and burn him terribly?

"I can't give you an answer. All I know is that Ulean said we'd need him. So for now . . . we lead an uneasy truce because I know he's still thinking I'm going to betray you all by bringing Grieve here." At the mention of my love's name, my wolf shifted and I forced myself to hold my hands steady.

"What happened with that? Why won't you let Kaylin take you dreamwalking to look for the antidote?" Rhia pleaded with me, begging to understand. "I know I wasn't going to ask questions, but I can't help it. Talk to me, Cicely."

"I cannot. I cannot speak, not now. Trust me, it's for the best. As we descend further into war with Myst and her people, there will be more secrets and hidden agendas and we'll have to get used to gathering our information in bits and pieces. For now, let's make Luna welcome, and Leo better not frighten her off, is all I can say."

Rhia followed me into the kitchen, where Peyton was starting dinner. Luna was helping her, dicing herbs and vegetables for soup as Peyton browned cubed beef.

"Did Peyton tell you I'm deathly allergic to fish?" I asked. "No fish at all—even shellfish—allowed. So never, ever bring any into the house, please."

"Does that extend to never giving you a hug if I've just eaten a tuna sandwich?"

"If you give me a kiss I could go into anaphylactic shock. Hugs probably aren't the best idea after a tuna sandwich or crab cake." I pulled out my EpiPen. "I have to keep one of these around."

"Then I'll start eating chicken or egg salad." She smiled, and I wanted to hug her for understanding. So many people acted like it was such a big hassle for them to skip eating tuna for the day when they wanted to see me. Over the years, I'd gotten used to snide comments about how I should just "get over it," and I'd learned to just brush them off, but they still irritated me.

We cooked side by side, at first Peyton directing the preparation, the three of us punctuating the silence with get-to-know-you comments and questions.

"Do you have a boyfriend?" I asked, after a moment.

Luna paused, then shrugged. "No, not right now. I had a boyfriend, but he left me two years ago and I've been nervous about trying to meet someone new. I'm not quite what the fashion mags order up for a date, you know."

"You're gorgeous," Rhiannon burst out. "I can't believe you don't see that. You look a lot like Jane Russell."

Luna laughed then, her voice clear and ringing through the kitchen. "I'm about forty pounds heavier than she was, but yeah, I can see it."

"You wear the weight well," I said. "Here, the tomatoes are diced. What should I do with them?"

"Slide them into the skillet with the mushrooms, onion,

and bacon. Then when they've sautéed we'll put them into the soup base." She stirred the broth containing the beef—already browned—and potatoes. A heavenly aroma rose from the pot and I found my stomach grumbling.

"How long till this is done?"

"About half an hour. Enough time for us to make biscuits." Luna took over the kitchen the way Rhiannon took over the herb garden. We were suddenly at her bidding, fetching flour and butter and baking powder and greasing pans as she rolled out dough and cut it into rounds with a cookie cutter.

By the time Leo, Chatter, and Kaylin came trudging in, we'd found out that Luna had two sisters that she hadn't seen in years, that her parents lived in New York, that she'd come to New Forest because of her love affair with West Coast culture and her ability to get a job teaching music at the New Forest Conservatory, and that she had once sung on stage at Carnegie Hall.

We also found out she hated living alone and that her roommate had recently vanished without a trace. She'd reported the incident, but the cops—as usual—had merely nodded, then said they'd take a look for the woman and never bothered to get back to her. When she called to check on the case, no reports had been filed, no action taken.

Leo greeted her politely enough, but I could tell he wasn't all that delighted about another person in the house, although his interest picked up markedly when he smelled the soup and bread. But his possessiveness over this place was starting to get to me. The Veil House was Rhiannon's—not his. And after Rhiannon, it would be mine. He was a guest here and it was time he started acting a little more gracious.

Kaylin, however, had noticeable eyes for Luna. From the moment he took her hand, I could see that he was attracted to her. She seemed to sense it, too, and I could almost see the sparks of interest flare between them.

As we sat down to dinner, I wondered if there was any way I could get away without Leo finding out about my impending visit to Geoffrey, but as always, he seemed two steps ahead of me when it concerned the vampires.

"I heard you're due out at Geoffrey's tomorrow night. You need a ride?" He glanced over at me, and for the first time in a couple of days, his voice sounded friendly.

I shook my head. "Thanks, but I've got one already."

He shrugged. "Whatever, but if you want somebody to go with you, I'm there."

I wanted to make some nasty retort, considering how he'd behaved lately, but then he pushed back his plate and gave me a soft smile.

"I really am sorry, Cicely. Geoffrey got wind of our argument. I don't know how, but he swears it wasn't you, and I have no choice but to believe him. He dressed me down something royal. I apologize for the way I've been acting, about you—and about Grieve."

For a moment I panicked. "You didn't tell him that I planned to break in and steal the antidote, did you? Because that plan has . . . gone by the wayside."

He shook his head. "No, I didn't say a word." He let out a long breath. "I'm not supposed to tell you this, but damn it, I feel like I owe you one. I overheard Geoffrey and Lainule talking. They're working on a plan to rescue Grieve."

The light in his eyes didn't look as friendly as the words falling out of his mouth, but I chose to let that go. His ego was probably still smarting from the dressing-down Geoffrey had given him.

"Thank you," I said, feigning surprise. It occurred to me to warn Geoffrey to watch his back as far as eavesdroppers went . . . but then, if I did that, it would expose Leo to trouble. "That's wonderful! But don't let anybody else know—please. Not just yet."

Leo gave me a sharp look. "You're excited, right? Grieve will be back with you."

If he'd been in on Anadey's attack, he'd have to know that her spell hadn't taken—I was still alive. Unless they really believed the connection could be broken without hurting either one of us. But the others would wonder if I didn't show excitement. Feeling in a pickle, I opened my mouth, searching for something to say.

Peyton snapped around and interrupted. "So, Cicely, have you decided on a name for the new society yet?"

I flashed her a thank-you. "Yeah, I think I have. We're fighting shadows. We're fighting Myst. My thought is the Moon Spinners. Because the moon will expose them. The moonlight can ferret them out."

"The Moon Spinners . . . I like it." Rhiannon began serving the soup as Luna passed around the biscuits. Everything smelled warm and cozy and for a brief moment, I could almost pretend that we were just a group of friends, hanging out on a cold winter's evening.

❦

As I lay in bed that night, aware of the sounds of the house around me, I heard a whisper on the wind. I sat up, suddenly afraid, but Ulean seemed unperturbed.

Do you hear that? I hear something on the slipstream.

Ulean paused. *You're right, but I sense no danger. Only that someone is seeking your attention. It is not Myst, nor her kin. That much I can tell you.*

Grieve?

No, or it would have Myst's signature behind it.

I slipped out of bed and wandered over to the window, gazing out at the Golden Wood. The unhealthy glow that had settled over the forest remained, a thin green light that wavered and shimmered like an aurora. Only this aurora was sickly and felt infested with buzzing insects and rotting things that crawled out of the dark. I focused, turning my attention toward the energy emanating from the woodland, but the summons was not coming from there.

As I turned back to my bed, I caught sight of a shadow creeping along my wall. There was nothing for the shadow to be attached to.

Who are you? What do you want? I sent my thoughts forcefully on the slipstream, tired of games and pretenses.

It's me, Kaylin. I'm dreamwalking. I need to show you something. May I come into your room?

The whisper echoed and I realized it hadn't been off the slipstream, but somehow through the tiniest link of connection we'd forged while dreamwalking a week or so ago. The lines of communication were still there.

Relieved, and yet a little irked, I nodded. "Come in, but use the door."

A few moments later there was a tap and then Kaylin entered the room, in the flesh. He was dressed in black, head to toe, and his eyes were luminous—more so than usual. He slipped over to my side and drew me to the bed, sitting me down.

At first I was a little nervous, remembering his behavior and threats when his demon had been in control, but he didn't try anything. Instead, he simply put his hand on my arm.

"I was out dreamwalking and found something. You need to see it. Truly—I can't exactly explain what it is, but I feel you would know. Come with me? I can take you along."

"I know you can." I frowned, wondering if it was safe to give in to him, to take off dreamwalking again, especially now. But the urgency in his voice convinced me he'd found something, and I gazed into his eyes. "I have been betrayed twice this week by people I thought were friends. Why should I trust you?"

"Because if I wanted to kill you, I would. If I wanted to fuck you, I'd have raped you by now. You know I have the power to do both and yet, I did not. I truly mean it when I say I have no ulterior motive with you, Cicely."

"But why help me? I am walking in danger."

"Yes, you are, but I've always walked beside death. I am a dreamwalker; I have a demon bound in my soul. I understand the night, and the dangers within. I understand what calls you under the wilding moon, Cicely Waters. I understand your drive to fly away, to be free."

I gazed into his eyes, and I knew he was telling the truth. "Where are we going?"

"To the outskirts of the Golden Wood, but outside the boundaries of Myst's hold. In a far corner. I've been exploring—trying to find something of use to us. Let me take you there. Dreamwalking . . . we can get there in no time. We won't be discovered."

I slipped into a warm turtleneck and a pair of boots. "Do you think I'll need a coat?"

"I'd wear one. We may be dropping out of the shadows when we get where we're going." He was wearing a Windbreaker, I noticed, along with gloves and earmuffs.

I grabbed my jacket out of the closet and pulled on gloves and jammed a knit hat down on my head, then made sure I had my fan and my blade.

"You really have to get a better blade than that. We'll go shopping over the next day or so." He motioned to me and we lay down on the bed.

"Does anybody else know we're heading out?"

"No, and I don't think they need to. Not till you've seen this." He held out his arm and I rolled into it, silent and waiting. And then, slowly, we began to blur, merging together, into the universe.

Dreamwalking. What can I say? It's like melting from the outside in. From the toes up to the top of the head. Everything begins to dissolve and it's easy to lose the sense of separation between self and everything that surrounds. Fingers and toes blur into legs, and arms blur into a nebulous energy as the lines of distinction vanish. Within a blink, I become part of the bedspread, part of the bed, part of the air and the floor. Breathing stops, and the fight-or-flight reflex kicks in, but then—after a moment when the body realizes it no longer needs to breathe—there is calm . . . and then, the dreamwalking begins.

I opened my eyes and sat up, drifting lightly on the slipstream. Kaylin was beside me, and now I could tell just how much the demon's awakening had affected him. His aura, which had been brilliant and strong before, was now glowing like a neon-infused Slurpee. He was supercharged. Not sure how that would translate over to practical application, I decided to pass on mentioning it until later. The first time he'd taken me dreamwalking, I'd been petrified and almost panicked myself into a frenzy. This time, I'd been prepared.

After a few minutes, my own shadowy form came into view and I was able to move around without feeling like I was going to float off. My room looked nebulous, but over on my dresser, where my magical tools lay, a haze of energy surrounded them—sparkling and crisp and clean.

Let's move. Kaylin motioned to me and I followed him. I wasn't sure how we'd get out of the building, but for us, the house didn't fully exist and we were able to drift through the sparkling atoms that made up the physical form of the Veil House. As we reached the snow and hovered lightly over it, I turned.

The Veil House. Oh, the Veil House. Superimposed over the material structure was a web of energy that was threaded so intricately I almost couldn't see the house for the lines. And a channel ran right below it, and a cross-channel. The Veil House stood on two ley lines that crossed paths. Powerful, old, ancient as the hills, the land beneath our house was like a reactor.

I gasped, but no air hit my lungs and once again, I startled. Kaylin's hand rested on my shoulder, blending into my energy and calming me down.

The land here . . . the land is a powerhouse . . .

The land, but not the house. However, that's not what I want you to see. However, it doesn't hurt to know that you're sitting on top of one of the strongest nexus points in this region. But come—we have much distance to travel. We can sweep there in no time, but take my hand or you might get lost in the astral turbulence.

I took his hand. Last time I was on the astral I'd almost gotten lost to the dreambeast's appetite. But this wasn't the same plane—this wasn't the Court of Dreams, and I had Kaylin with me. As my hand touched his, our fingers blended together and we were off, sudden and swift, flying through the night, running through tree and wood and snow without leaving a mark.

I caught a glimpse of several Shadow Hunters, seeking prey, but they didn't notice us and I wondered if any of them were Grieve. But then all thoughts of Myst and her people fell away because we were in a clearing, a clearing I'd never seen before. It seemed outside the barrier of the Golden Wood, but for the life of me, I had no clue as to where we were.

In the clearing, in the midst of the snow, a statue rose well over twenty feet. The statue of an owl, carved from marble. And around the statue, a group of men and women danced around a slab of stone to which was tied one of the Shadow Hunters . . . but he was not fully of the Indigo Court. He was also one of the Cambyra Fae—I knew it with the core of my body and heart.

The dancers were Uwilahsidhe. *My people*. And leading them was my father—Wrath, the King of Rivers and Rushes. As he danced wildly around the marble slab to a hail of pounding drumbeats, his followers matched every move. Standing to the side, I caught sight of Geoffrey and Lainule, standing silent, watching.

And Grieve, tied to the slab, looked terrified, in fear of his life.

Chapter 19

Grieve! My first instinct was to leap forward, but I managed to stop myself. I held back, waiting, watching. My wolf didn't seem in any pain, and though Grieve looked terrified, the wolf wasn't whimpering. Perhaps he had given up. Or perhaps his subconscious sensed they weren't going to hurt him. At least I hoped that was what it meant.

And truthfully, they didn't seem to be focused on killing him. Nobody carried a weapon that I could see. All the while, Geoffrey's invitation rang in my head. The fact that he was here led me to believe this was what it was about. They'd caught Grieve, that was obvious, and they were doing something to him.

I motioned for Kaylin to wait, and then I began looking around. As I tried to gauge where we were, I realized that we'd passed through a portal while dreamwalking. This was part of the Golden Wood, yes, but nothing the Shadow Hunters could see or touch.

As I relaxed, trying to focus on seeing through to the physical, I began to notice something behind the owl statue. It was a figure, hidden in the shadows of the night.

Not a Shadow Hunter . . . no, this was too . . . corporeal for one of the Vampiric Fae.

I moved closer to get a better view and gasped, motioning for Kaylin to join me. Behind the statue, hiding himself so he could not be seen, was Lannan Altos.

What the fuck is he doing here? And if he's supposed to be here, why is he cloaking his presence?

A sudden swell of danger rose up on the slipstream and I tensed. The dancers were raging now, wild and filling the air with their chants. Geoffrey held up a needle and walked into their center, leaning over Grieve.

The antidote. He was going to try the antidote.

Grieve looked up at him, at the syringe, and clarity filled his face. He stopped struggling and I could hear his words through the music, through the dancing and drumming. On the slipstream they flew, from his lips to my ears.

Whatever happens, I love you. Whatever they're doing to me, I sense you near and I will love you forever, Cicely.

There was no recrimination in his voice, no sense of fear, only brilliant love. And I fell into his heart, tumbling head over heels. If Grieve died from this, so would I, and I wanted to live, but I wanted him with me.

Geoffrey jerked his head up, looking directly at me.

He can't see us, can he? Vampires don't have the natural ability to see out on the plane of shadow and smoke, do they?

Kaylin's fingers rested gently on my shoulder, blending with my own essence. *No, he cannot see us, but he seems to know something's up. Perhaps he heard Grieve talking?*

That must be it. And if he'd heard Grieve talking, either he would think it delirium or he'd know I was prowling around out here. Either way, I chose to remain right where I was.

And so we watched, as Geoffrey finally lowered his head back to Grieve and leaned over my suffering prince. He held up the syringe, almost as though he wanted me to see it, and brought it down toward Grieve's arm.

"Stop! What do you think you're doing?" Lannan stepped

out of the shadows. Even from this distance, I caught the glare on his face.

"Lannan. I don't remember requesting your appearance here. What are you doing?" Geoffrey stopped short of injecting Grieve, and I tried to catch my breath but was once again rudely reminded that I was in shadow form, not breathing.

Lannan held up his hand. "Don't do this. Let the Vampiric Fae die. Let him rot in the moldering mess that *you* started so many years ago. Don't even pretend we need him—we don't. The only reason you could want him alive is to win over Cicely to your side because Lainule put an end to your *other* scheme. Well, I can guarantee the current one won't work either, not once she finds out what plans you have for her and her beloved feral boy toy here. She's mine, Geoffrey, and I don't share well with others."

Geoffrey snarled at him. "You do not have the authority to alter my decisions, nor do you have the balls to fight me. *Don't even try, Golden Boy.* I can stake you like a tomato. I didn't become the most feared warlord in history by backing down to sycophants and hedonists. The land ran red under my rule and my people learned to fear me."

Lannan took a step back, and I could see his eyes grow wide, the shining black orbs glistening in the dim light.

"You've never understood the finer points of living. You thrive on bloodshed, and this time is not kind to warlords. You've outlived your place, Geoffrey. You should just walk into the sun while you still have your dignity."

With a low growl, Geoffrey strode over to clasp Lannan by the collar and lift him off the ground. Lannan didn't resist, and though I was glad to see him get smacked down, the fact that someone could force him to endure such an indignity scared the fuck out of me.

Lannan let out a short laugh, but Geoffrey choked it off. "Laugh if you will, for now, boy. But don't *ever* forget how we met. I took down a hundred of Regina's men, single-handedly. I bloodied your palace and captured Crawl for the Crimson Queen. I had the Oracle on a collar when I took him to the Queen, when she laid the curse on him. And you . . . you and your sister crawled on your bellies at my feet, begging for your lives. Regina has her position solely with my backing, and you live only because she has a passion for you. Interfere with my plans, and you'll watch your stable die one by one, before I make you my whipping boy."

Lannan let out a short sound, but quieted, and Geoffrey lowered him back to the ground.

"Tsk, tsk, Regent. Best watch your temper. If our Cicely finds out about your past—your present—truly, she's not going to want to cooperate with you." Lannan shook his head and turned away. "I won't interfere, but I won't help you, either. Not unless the Crimson Queen directly orders me to. I know too much about you."

He looked up, turning my way, and for a moment I thought he could see me. As he stared in our direction, he added, "Geoffrey, you'd best walk softly. Myst is out for your head, and there are many who would serve you up to her on a silver platter. And Lainule, I urge you to be cautious. I would not see you hurt—you are too bright, too beautiful. Don't trust this blood-monger. And don't trust that breeding won't play true. Cicely was Myst's daughter. Do you truly believe her soul energy can't outweigh mere blood?"

Lainule, who had remained silent through the vampires' altercation, shook her head. "She will not revert. I have seen her heart, as have you, Lannan Altos. You seek to defile her; I seek to uplift her. Geoffrey is the fulcrum, a middle balance. And though I had to dissuade him of his original plan, the current one bears more promise. We have no hope left but to try it. *Myst* . . . you know nothing of the Queen of Shadow and Winter. She is evil incarnate. She is the long, dark deep of the winter. She is the shadow of the moon and the chill of bone and blade. I know her—she is my counterpart. She is my alter ego, my doom. Cicely is the key—her decisions set in motion events leading to an ending of this war. Geoffrey may have started it by himself, but he cannot finish it alone."

"I sincerely hope for your sake that you're right. And for your information, I do not seek to defile the girl. I enjoy toying with her because nothing can quench her spirit. I've seen both sides within her—the dark and the light. Which way she turns remains to be seen." Lannan turned and began walking over the top of the snow, his feet leaving no prints on the surface of the glistening white.

I shivered. Everything was in a tailspin, and I felt like I was falling into darkness, into the shadows, into a vortex of decisions needing to be made. Geoffrey—was he truly a warmonger? Did Lannan actually mean what he said? And just what influence did Geoffrey have with the Crimson Queen? Or Lainule, for that matter?

Kaylin tapped me on the shoulder, and I glanced over at him. His aura flared with energy, some golden, some dark red, and I knew he was angry for me. I nodded that I was okay, although I felt anything but, and turned back to watch as Lannan strode out of sight and then a great black bat filled the sky, flying off.

Geoffrey turned back to Wrath, who stood, arms folded, waiting. "Continue. I'm sorry for the interruption. Will this cause a problem in proceeding?"

"Tell me what you plan with my daughter."

Geoffrey would not answer, but Lainule spoke up, her voice smooth. "There is no need to fret, husband. I have approved the plans and they will not be in vain."

Wrath shook his head. "As you will, my love. We will need to recover the energy before continuing. It has seeped away, and the only manner in which to be certain the antidote takes is to build the cone once again. So you must wait for a few more moments, Regent, before administering the serum."

"I still think this is premature, but we must take steps before Cicely insists on doing something rash. For she is as headstrong as her sire," Lainule said, then laughed. "My Wrath, you begot a daughter to be proud of, even if she is a handful. Lannan Altos is wrong. She is now ours, fully and forever. And if it took our finding Grieve again in order to bring her spirit to us, then that is a small price to pay. His love for her will not go unrewarded. Nor hers for him. If she but agrees to the plans Geoffrey and I have made, all will be well."

"We have much to speak of, my lady," Geoffrey said, turning to Lainule. "You owe me for this, remember."

Lainule inclined her head. "The Court of Rivers and Rushes never forgets its debts."

Confused, but convinced that it was better if I found out what they were talking about on my own, rather than be seen and have them angry I was spying, I motioned to Kaylin that we should leave. He took my hand and we slipped away.

As we were headed back to the house, still on the plane of shadow and smoke, a blur and a flash interrupted us. Kaylin stopped short, slamming me in back of him, and stretched out his arms.

"Do not attempt to pass. She is not one of the Bat People, nor of their children. You cannot claim her."

"I need to settle—I need a host." The words echoed through me with the force of a sledgehammer and I caught a glimpse of the creature over Kaylin's shoulder. It reminded me of something . . . the fetish! The twisted creature, part bat, part—something else—had to be one of the night-veil demons. Oh crap, was it thinking it could nest in me?

"Then you must find a host elsewhere. Go to the Court of Dreams; find a host among the Chosen Ones. She is not yours and never will be yours." Kaylin clapped his hands and the energy reverberated through the air, sending the night-veil head over heels, gusting away from us. It howled once, a pained shriek, then raced off.

"What did you do to it?"

Kaylin glanced back at me and, even in his murky, shadow-stuff form, I caught sight of those glowing eyes. He smirked. "I told it to go away."

"So you did, so you did." I debated pressing the matter. Kaylin was strong—I already knew that—but I'd never seen him use energy like that. "Ever since your demon awoke, you've been different."

"Yes, I have." No denials, no defensiveness. Just a calm, clear statement.

"It's your demon doing this, isn't it?"

"My hatchling is under my control now, so no—it's me doing it, but the demon gives me the power. We work together." He frowned. "If you're concerned, you needn't be. I'll continue to evolve, but unlike the Bat People, I am not enamored of the night-veil demons. I simply accept them for what they are, a tool to an end."

"A tool? But they are sentient—they have a will of their own. Yours decked me a good one and I have the bruises to prove it." I wasn't sure how I felt about anyone referring to another creature as their *tool*, even a demon.

"They are what they are, Cicely. There are so many aspects to this universe that you do not understand—that none of us understands. There is no absolute black or white. Even Myst has a side to her, somewhere, that walks in shades of gray. You may see it one day, and I pray it won't be your downfall."

I bit my lip. Nothing could make me feel sorry for Myst, but even as I thought the words, I decided not to utter them aloud. No sense in jinxing myself. Besides, Kaylin would just argue with me.

"Let's go home. I have a lot to think about before meeting with Geoffrey and Lainule tomorrow night."

We headed back to the house, and Kaylin helped me leap off the astral, back into the physical realm. I shivered, icy cold. Before he left my room, he brushed back the strands of my hair and smiled softly.

"You brought Luna into the house. For that I thank you. I feel a pull to her, as I've never felt a pull toward any woman. I only hope she isn't spoken for."

"She's not," I said automatically, before thinking I should have kept my mouth shut. She might not be interested in Kaylin—although if I read her energy correctly at dinner, there had been mutual sparks. But whatever the case, the cat was out of the bag.

"That's all I wanted to know." He paused. "Cicely, don't

worry—if she's not interested, I won't press the matter or make her uncomfortable. I'm not the one you have to watch out for."

He left, closing the door behind him. I locked it, hating the fact that I felt like I had to lock my door now, that I didn't know if I could trust everyone in the house. After Anadey, I had lost confidence in my ability to know whom to trust. What if Luna wasn't who I thought she was? What if Leo really was in cahoots with . . . well, at this point, was Lannan worse than Geoffrey? And Geoffrey had seemed nice compared to the others, but Lannan's words rang in my head. And so did Geoffrey's own—how he had bragged about the swath of destruction he left behind him.

I crawled back onto the bed, pulling the quilt around my shoulders and wrapping my arms around my knees. As I huddled, another knock sounded at the door.

"Am I Grand Central Station tonight?" I grumbled to myself, but then called, "Come in."

"It's locked."

I clambered out of bed and opened the door.

Peyton entered the room. She followed me back to the bed and—without the pretense of small talk—sat down beside me.

"What did my mother do to you? You have to tell me."

I thought about what Lainule had ordered and shook my head. "Don't want to talk about it."

"I know it was worse than you let on. I know she fucked you over a good one—and I know that it has something to do with me." Her eyes flared. "I'm moving out for good. I've talked to Rhiannon, and she said I can move in here. I'll be taking the downstairs maid's bedroom. I can't trust my own mother, and if I find out she put you in danger . . ."

"Stop. Stop right there." I was furious at Anadey, but the last thing we needed was for Peyton to go all wild child on her. "I can't say anything right now, but yes—she did try to fuck me over. And yes, it does have something to do with you." I paused, remembering Anadey's rant about Peyton's father. "Have you talked to your father recently?"

Peyton shook her head. "I was going to call him, set up a time to meet him here."

"Call him now, but hold off on the meeting for a few days. Do not tell *anybody* else about it, and do not use your own phone. Use Kaylin's phone." Anadey had access to Rhiannon's cell phone when she helped her with her magic, and she'd have access to Peyton's cell phone without any trouble. Who knew whether she'd messed with mine while I was there? But Kaylin—she barely had anything to do with Kaylin. "Go ask him to borrow it now, then come back here."

I waited for her. After a few minutes, she returned. I prayed her father would still answer—if Anadey had been using me to . . .

"Dad? This is Peyton . . ." A pause, and she frowned. "What? Where are you? Why . . . okay . . ." A pause, and then a longer pause. After a few minutes, she whispered, "Please, be careful. I'll call you back when I've thought of what to do." As she hung up, she gazed up at me. "You knew he was in danger, didn't you?"

I bit my lip. "I suspected. I don't know the details, and as I said, I can't tell you everything that happened . . . yet . . . but you have to warn him to be careful. Don't try to see him yet. He needs to lie low and not tell anybody where he is. And whatever you do, don't talk to him on your phone or on Rhiannon's phone."

After a moment, a light flashed in Peyton's eyes. "Mother. Mother's behind whatever is happening to him. He told me that he's been followed for the past two days— that he was almost sideswiped by a black limousine today and only managed to escape by driving into a parking lot and losing himself in the crowd. He grew suspicious and decided to go into hiding."

"I think Anadey *is* behind this, but she's working with someone and we're trying to find out who. You absolutely have to keep quiet. Anybody could be in on this."

"By *anybody*, you mean Leo. Black limousines? Come on, that has *vampire* written all over it."

I realized that she thought Leo might have been the one driving the car that tried to sideswipe Rex. The thought hadn't occurred to me—I'd just assumed it was some vamp for hire that Anadey had come in contact with. But now, the idea that it might have been Leo loomed large in my mind. Anadey had been trying to strip away my connection to Grieve, and Leo had been on a real bender lately about that same subject. Suppose he'd promised her something in return—such as Rex never getting to see and talk to Peyton?

"I really hope you're wrong. I want Leo to be a good guy. I want him to have our back. But . . ." I rubbed my cheek where he'd backhanded me. "Any man who hits a woman out of frustration . . . I just can't trust him, even if that's the only bad thing he ever does. I'm nobody's punching bag."

Peyton bit her lip. "I think I'd better do a little private sleuthing on Leo—what's his background? How much do we really know about him?"

"I only know what Rhia has told me, and what Leo's said. For all I know, he comes from Mars and secretly phones home once a month." I pointed toward her phone. "You'd better call him back, warn him to lie low."

She punched in the number and mumbled a few words into the receiver, then hung up again. "Okay, done. I didn't tell him why I wanted him to hide out, but he seemed to agree it was a good idea. As soon as they give you permission to talk about what happened, you better tell me. Anadey's my mother, and if she's fucking up, I want to know. I've always trusted her . . . it kills me to think that she might be a traitor."

"Or maybe, just a very worried Mama . . ." I stared out the window. "I'll know more tomorrow night. Go to bed now, and try to get some sleep."

As soon as Peyton left, I slid out of my clothes and into my bed. I was worn through, but it took me a couple of hours before I could take my own advice. Once I dropped off, though, I slept like the dead.

✧

With morning came an e-mail from Lannan. I glanced at the time stamp—he'd written it shortly before dawn. Or, at least, he'd sent it around then. I hesitated, my cursor hovering over it before I finally decided to open it.

> *I'm going to tell you this once, and once only. I've hinted before as to Geoffrey not being all he seems. Tonight, you will find him charming, witty, and he'll give you your heart's desire. You will probably trust him and come to doubt anything I have to say. But I say it anyway: Don't be a fool. Listen to your head, not your cunt—perhaps odd advice coming from me, but truly, for a breather, I've come to enjoy your company. I'd prefer to meet you in the flesh than to remember you in spirit. Lannan.*

I stared at the e-mail, then printed it out, tucked it away with my magical supplies, and deleted it. I then emptied my Deleted Items folder and cleared my cache. Of course, Lannan had no clue that I'd seen what had gone on. Like Lannan or hate him, I suspected that I could trust his word more than Geoffrey's. The feeling unsettled me.

After I showered and dressed, I wandered downstairs. Rhiannon and Luna were cooking breakfast. Kaylin was reading through *The Rise of the Indigo Court*, searching for something we could use. The book was slow going, though, dense and filled with arcane facts and obscure references. Leo was outside, shoveling snow, and Chatter was staring out the window at the Golden Wood, a pensive look on his face.

"Where's Peyton?"

"She was up early and headed out. She said she'll be back around ten A.M. to open up for business. Is she really quitting the diner?" Rhia shook her head. "Whatever Anadey did, it must have been bad." Her voice lingered over the words, but she didn't ask any questions.

"Trust Peyton." As I buttered my toast and spread jam on it, there was a sudden whisper on the slipstream, and my wolf let out a low rumble, not a howl, not pain, but a slow stream of yipping noises that sounded almost joyful. I stared down at my stomach.

Grieve! It was Grieve and he wasn't in pain—and it was daylight. I pressed my hand to my stomach and focused, but all I could feel was the joyous dancing of my wolf. Before anyone could notice what I was doing, I stopped and reached for the orange juice, trying to remain low-key.

Leo came stomping in, looking red in the face from the exertion. He nodded when he saw me, unwrapping the scarf from around his neck and sliding out of his jacket.

"We're having the winter from hell," he said, panting.

"Of course we are. Look who's bringing it in." I motioned toward an empty chair. "You should sit down. You don't look well."

He fidgeted, tugging at his collar as he coughed. "I don't feel so good. I'm really sweating, and my throat hurts." As he winced, Rhia crossed to his side.

"Open your mouth," she said. He did and she peered down his throat. "As I thought. You've got a nasty swollen throat. The beginnings of strep throat or laryngitis at best. Get out of your clothes and up to bed."

"Geoffrey expects me to take care of his errands today—" Leo tried to push himself to his feet, but he was so unsteady that he almost fell. Rhia caught him on one side, Kaylin from the other.

"You aren't going anywhere. What's so important that it can't wait?"

"I've got a list here . . ." He waved his notebook around, but then the fever took him and he dropped it and slumped back in the chair, mumbling.

I picked up his Day-Timer and flipped it open. A number of errands, yes, but nothing that couldn't be taken care of by any one of us.

"We can do this, dude. You get your butt up to bed. Rhiannon, Kaylin, make sure he's under the covers. I'm going to see Geoffrey tonight; I'll just take his dry cleaning with me."

Besides, I thought, it would give me a chance to learn a bit more about the Regent. There weren't any exclusively secret operations listed, but some of the errands would perhaps shed some light on just who I was dealing with.

As Rhia and Kaylin struggled to get Leo up the stairs, I went back to my toast and jam, wondering what I was going to find out—if anything. But in the back of my mind, Lannan's e-mail played itself over and over, and I hated the fact that I believed every word he'd written.

Chapter 20

The first few items were easy, and rather boring. I stopped at Cheri's Alterations & Dry Cleaning and picked up Geoffrey's clothing, marveling at the rampant textures and colors of the Regent's smoking jackets. There were ten. He must change clothes twice a day, I thought, to go through this many.

As I pulled out of the mini-mall's parking lot, Favonis purred and I cruised along the streets, watching passersby. It might have been any other year, any holiday shopping rush, except people walked in groups, and cars were no longer single-occupant. Carpooling had suddenly become popular in New Forest.

I turned up the music—"Napalm Love" by Air pounded out of the speakers and I thought about Lannan's note. There were no demands in it, no orders to pay him back for his advice. For once, I had the feeling he might be stepping outside his comfort zone and doing something altruistic.

Don't believe it. He has an agenda: keeping you alive. He wants you, and he can't have you if Geoffrey wins you over.

I sighed. *Ulean, sometimes you're a killjoy. But yeah, I hear what you're saying.*

As I pulled into a parking lot at the next stop, I glanced up at the store. Leo was supposed to pick up a package for Geoffrey here—that was the only notation, so I guessed that whatever it was, was ready. I slid out of the car and pushed through the door to the little shop.

The store turned out to be an art shop, and the package I was to pick up was a framed print. The cashier motioned for me to have a seat at one of the desks.

"I'll just get your print and you can approve or disapprove the framing job. One moment, please." She disappeared into the back.

Nervous now—what if I approved something that was fucked up? Geoffrey would be furious, and Leo would be in trouble.

Just go through with it. There is something important here for you to learn, though I don't know what it is. The energy on the slipstream is crackling around this shop.

I nodded, sliding into the chair to which the woman had gestured. As I waited, I glanced around the shop. The walls were filled with frames—all sorts from inexpensive plastic to what looked like ornate gold-leaf embossed etched frames. There was a huge table next to the cash register with a variety of measuring tools on it and what looked like several projects in the middle of completion.

After a moment, the woman returned with a bag. She withdrew a painting that was about ten by ten inches, not including the frame, and placed it in front of me.

"I hope you and your employer will like this. It was a joy to work with the Regent, and we're grateful that he trusted our shop to get the job done." She paused, staring at the painting, then at me. "You were wearing a lovely costume."

"What?" I took the painting and stared at it. Sure enough, there I was—or rather . . . someone who looked a lot like me, in a gossamer gown. And next to the woman stood Geoffrey, wearing what looked like a costume from long ago. His arms were around the woman's waist, embracing her, and they were both laughing. I could see his fangs and—holy crap! I recognized the woman now. She was fuller, not so thin, and not quite so . . . stretched . . . but it was definitely her. Myst—but without the cerulean cast to her skin.

The more I looked at the painting, the more I realized that it had to have been painted before Myst had been turned. Or rather . . . I touched the canvas lightly. This was a print. A picture of a painting. The original was probably in a vault somewhere.

"Thank you," I murmured. "Is there a balance due?"

She shook her head. "We charged your account. Or rather, the Regent's account. Please, if there's any problem, don't hesitate to let us know."

I took the receipt, slid the painting back into the wrapper, then slowly returned to Favonis. After I slid into the front seat, I took another look at the print. Sure enough, that had to be Myst—before she was turned. She might have been Unseelie at that point, but she looked far more human . . . far more *humane* . . . than she did now. And the way Geoffrey was holding her waist . . . almost like a lover.

A thought occurred to me and I tried to brush it away, but it kept coming back. What if Geoffrey had tried to turn her *with* her permission? What if he hadn't captured the Unseelie, but the rumor had gotten started that he had? What if they'd been lovers and she'd agreed to let him turn her, but something had gone horribly wrong?

As I started up the car, I gave one last glance to the print before tucking it back into the sack. Myst and I looked alike, all right. And Geoffrey had offered to sire me. I wasn't sure what was up, but whatever it was, I had an uneasy feeling about it.

※

None of the other errands revealed anything more worth noting, other than the fact that Geoffrey's servants or stable apparently liked chocolate mint—I ended up picking up five pounds of chocolate mints at one store. When I was finished, I thought about dropping in at the diner and giving Anadey a scare, but the fleeting chuckle I got was immediately replaced by a sense of sadness and anger. We needed her, and she had turned her back on us. On me.

I spotted a drive-through a few blocks away and pulled in. Since I wasn't sure if their French fry fryer was dedicated or whether they fried fish fillets in it, I just ordered a strawberry shake and a cookie. As I scarfed down my sugar fix, I thought about what Geoffrey would say tonight when I delivered the picture. Was it safe to mention what I'd noticed? It began to occur to me that I might have made a serious mistake—Leo would have been the one picking it up and Leo had never . . . wait a minute.

Leo *had* seen Myst. He knew what she looked like, and Geoffrey had to be aware of it. Which meant, if Leo picked up the picture, he'd have to have dropped it off. And surely he'd recognize Myst in it and know that . . .

Shit. I slammed my shake into the cup holder. Leo constantly defended Geoffrey. And that alone meant he knew more than he let on. I wondered if Geoffrey confided in him, but that seemed out of character. Then again, Leo had worked for the vampire for quite some time. Chances were Geoffrey forgot he was in the room during some conversations. Yummanii and magic-born were a lot like furniture to the vampires.

Glancing at the print again, I pressed my lips together. There was something I wasn't getting—parts I couldn't put together. The equation didn't add up, and I was afraid that by the time I fully understood, it would be too late.

I finished off the shake and, unable to figure out anything more than I had, pulled out of the lot and headed home. Now I just had to decide whether to confront Leo or lie low. But I was sure as hell going to show Kaylin the print—and Peyton. My cousin was still in love with Leo. And I wasn't sure. I wasn't sure about anything anymore.

At least I didn't have to worry about Leo insisting on going out—he was out cold, a jolt of Heather's cold medicine down his throat. Kaylin and Peyton weren't around, so I helped Luna clean the kitchen and made sure she was doing okay before heading upstairs to change for Geoffrey's.

"How is Leo doing?" I asked, peeking in on him. Rhiannon was just gathering up a bowl and a washcloth. She motioned me out of the room.

"He's got a horrible sore throat, but I don't think it's strep. I got his fever down to a manageable level, and now he needs sleep. A lot of sleep. He won't be getting out of bed for a few days, though. Can you tell Geoffrey tonight . . ." She paused, staring at me. "What happened?"

"Nothing. Or . . . well . . . I don't know yet. I need some time to figure it out."

"So many secrets lately. Anadey and Peyton's father and now this . . ." Rhia shook her head. *"I am half-sick of shadows . . ."*

". . . Said the Lady of Shalott." I smiled softly. When we were teens and I visited, we'd read poetry to each other and that had been one of our favorites.

"We haven't done anything fun like that in years." She gazed at me, her doe eyes softening. "I missed you so much while you were gone. I hated Krystal for taking you away. Then, when you phoned to tell us she'd died, I secretly dreamed you'd come back. I fantasized about it—daydreamed that you would come back and marry Grieve, and I'd marry Cha—I'd marry someone . . . and we'd settle down and raise babies and be the two old witches of the village when we grew old."

"Chatter? You started to say Chatter." I cocked my head. "Rhia . . . please, promise me you won't settle. That you won't tie yourself to someone you aren't sure about."

She bit her lip, staring at the floor. "I know . . . I know . . . but what is love? Love brings pain and sorrow. Isn't it better to marry someone you consider a good friend rather than getting your heart broken?"

I pulled her close, kissing her cheek. "Oh, Rhiannon . . . whether they're friends or lovers or both, we'll always have broken hearts. When they reject us, if they love us and then leave . . . if we live with them a hundred years loving them, and then they die—our hearts are bound to break. Why cut yourself off from the wonderful part just to avoid the sad?"

She shivered. "What if . . . what if I throw away something good to find I'm chasing an illusion? What if I discover that I've built something up in my mind? Can I hurt him, because I just maybe *think* I might be in love with someone else?"

"You're walking on a tightrope. Please promise you'll talk to Chatter? Find out how he feels before you say anything to Leo?"

She glanced at the closed door behind us. "That feels so wrong. Like I'm going behind his back."

I bit my lip, not sure what to say. "Just promise me you'll think long and hard before you actually get married. Breaking an engagement is a lot easier than five years down the line when you're filing for divorce."

Rhiannon let out a low sigh. "Yeah, I know. I'll think about it." She shrugged. "Come on, let's get you dolled up."

As we entered my bedroom and I closed the door, Rhiannon sat cross-legged on the floor next to the bed, resting her elbows on her knees. She played with the hem of my blanket as I slipped out of my clothes and into my bathrobe.

"I'll be back in a few—I just need a quick rinse off." I headed into the shower and, dropping my bathrobe, called out to Rhiannon. "Can you find me something nice to wear? I'm not sure what, but it's not a party, as far as I know, although he said formal dress."

When I finished soaping up and rinsing off, I climbed out of the shower to find her holding up a gorgeous cobalt blue sleeveless dress. Low cut, it was made of a simple jersey, with gathered shoulders and a woven black belt. I stared at it, struck by its beauty. The color was rich—so rich it was hard to look at.

"Where did you find that? I know full well I don't own anything like that."

She grinned. "I raided Heather's back closet. This never fit her—it was too short and too . . . well . . . a couple sizes too big. But it looks like it's made for you. I think she bought it for you on your last trip home, but you didn't stay long enough for her to give it to you. Not after you and Grieve . . ."

"After we broke up." I'd taken off, wanting nothing more than to get out of New Forest, to forget the look of pain on his face when I'd told him I wasn't ready to come home. Now I'd give anything to go back to that moment in time, to take it back. But then again, would I? Would I give up being who I'd become?

I shook off the thought. "Let me try it on." I dried off and fastened my underwire bra, then slipped the dress over my head. It clung in all the right places and was just the right color for my skin and hair. As I gazed into the mirror and saw the beaming smile of Rhia behind me, a crack in my mood started to fracture. I tried to repress it, but within minutes, like a glacier calving, the façade fell away and I sank to my knees, in tears.

Rhia was by my side instantly. "Cicely, what's wrong? Are you okay?"

I shook my head, weeping into my hands. "I want to tell you things, I want to so bad, but I'm afraid to because of Leo. Because I don't know where your loyalties lie. I want to talk to you, but I can't . . . I can't trust anybody but myself—and I feel so alone. I'm walking into a vampire's lair tonight and I don't trust him. But I have to go, and I have to go alone."

"I'll go if you like—I'll be there with you."

"No, Geoffrey told me to come alone. Oh, Rhia . . ." I turned to her, grasping her hands. "I know Leo trusts him. I know Leo works for him, but Geoffrey's not the fair, just leader we think. I know. Trust me, I know. And I'm afraid that he's using me for something . . . something that could lead to everybody's destruction."

"What are you talking about? I promise you—I give you my word to keep it silent, upon our mothers and our grandmothers. On the Veil House itself . . ." She held up her hand to swear.

I quickly grabbed her fingers. "Before you do that, you should know—I saw the Veil House from the astral. This land is almost a living being. Its energy is brilliant, a beacon in the night. We live on top of Grand Central Station— we're the blue-light special at Kmart. If you swear on the house, the land will hear and hold you to it. Don't say anything rashly."

She nodded, serious now, and pulled her hand away. After a moment, she held it up again. "I swear to you on the memory of our mothers, on our legacy with this land and this house, on flame and fire, on the Veil House itself, I will not betray your confidence. You are my cousin and we are in this together. Neither love nor men nor circumstance will sway me from my oath. You have my back, Cicely. And I have yours."

A pale light, orange and flickering, formed around her hand. I stared at it, feeling a pull I'd never felt before. I held up my hand opposite hers.

"I swear to you on the memory of our mothers, on our legacy with this land and this house, on wind and air, on the Veil House itself, I will not betray your confidence. You are my cousin, and we are in this together. Neither love nor men nor circumstance will sway me from my oath. You have my back, Rhiannon. And I have yours."

From my hand spun a whirlwind, tiny and gray; it began to increase, as did her flame, and the two met in the air, producing a firestorm of sparks, but none that stung as they landed on our skin. We brought our hands together, clasping them. The energy spiraled around us and as we held tight, we were dancing through a vortex, through a spiraling tunnel that wended with flame and cloud.

And then, we were aloft, spinning in a dance through the stars, while the pounding beat of drums in the night surrounded us.

"We are powerful together," I whispered. "We can move mountains."

"We can take down armies. We combine our powers and we are the sun and the moon."

"The night and the day. The summer and winter." I let my head drop back and laughed wildly as we began to spin faster, and then I was standing outside myself, watching as we spiraled even higher. I glanced to one side and saw Rhiannon's spirit there, too, watching, laughing joyfully. And then, before our spirits could journey too far from our bodies, we were back in the room, dancing, laughing, stomping on the floor until we collapsed in a pile in the center of the room.

After a few moments, I looked up, surprised no one had come to find out what the fuck we were doing. Rhiannon looked just as confused.

"I guess . . . we were hearing everything on an internal level?"

"Could be," I said. After a few minutes I sat back and stared at her. "Okay, you want to know what's going on? Lainule and the rest of them be damned. I'll tell you, but you can't tell anyone at this point."

"I promise. What the hell happened with Anadey?"

I slowly started, and then the words spilled out and I told her, told her everything. About Anadey drugging me and tying me down and trying to strip away my feelings for Grieve. About Wrath being my father, and the plan to find out who Anadey was working with. About the picture with Myst—who looked like me—and Geoffrey. By the time I finished telling her about what Kaylin and I had witnessed, she was staring slack-jawed, shaking her head.

"I can't even begin to put it all together, but, Cicely, I'm afraid. You know *too much*. You're walking into a lion's den. And somehow, I don't think Lannan is the lion in this cage."

I nodded. "You think Geoffrey was behind Anadey's actions?"

"I don't know, but I don't like you going out there by yourself."

"I can't take anybody—the vamps would be pissed and the last thing we want to do is stomp on any vampire egos. Lannan . . . he tried to warn me in that e-mail and if I hadn't seen what Kaylin took me to see, or the print . . . I wouldn't have believed him. I'd have thought it was yet another trick to get me into his clutches. But now, I don't think so."

"Don't trust him too much, Cicely. He's not one of the good guys."

"I don't. I know he still wants me and will do what it takes to get hold of me. But now—alliances are running deep and hidden, and I'm realizing there's a lot more to this than what's on the surface." I stood and straightened the dress. "This is really pretty. I wish . . . I wish I could have thanked Heather for it."

"I wish so, too," Rhia said. "I miss her so much. I hate that she's out there, a spawn of the Indigo Court. I hate that they transformed her. She was so wonderful and now, now she's Myst's confidant."

"That's another thing," I said. "Myst has to be fuming. Wrath and Lainule managed to capture Grieve. Myst will be on the hunt for her chosen one. And she's going to blame me for his disappearance. You have to keep watch—the wards may not hold out against an all-out assault. And you can bet that tonight, Myst will realize Grieve is gone, and she may send her people."

I braided my hair back in a French braid, slipped on some simple gold hoops and a pair of black pumps, and whisked on a quick, five-minute face for evening. Standing back, I observed myself in the mirror.

"You look elegant." Rhiannon hunted through the closet and pulled out a simple black velvet cape. "Here, this will make the outfit." She stood back as I slid my arms through the slits and fastened it by the single button in front. "There, see—you look incredible."

The cape transformed the outfit. I paused long enough to slide the moonstone pendant over my head. "I wish I were going to visit Wrath and Lainule instead of Geoffrey."

"I know. I wish we could go with you. I wish you didn't have to face them alone." She opened the door and handed me my purse. "Call us if you need us. We'll be there . . . in fact, I'll ask Kaylin and Peyton to drive out and park nearby. They can hide in the car and wait in case you need them."

"Normally I'd say no, because the Shadow Hunters will be out tonight in full force, but I think I'd feel better if you did that. Tell them to be cautious, though, and keep a low profile. Don't hang out on the streets. Take weapons."

I wish I could go, my dear Cicely . . . watch how much you reveal. Sometimes silence brings life and to speak is to die.

Ulean couldn't attend me—but I had learned the secret why. The Elementals could sense the vampires but not the other way around. Until now, we thought the vamps just didn't like them. I thought about asking her to go with me now that we knew the truth, but the chance that someone there might be able to sense her—perhaps one of the bloodwhores—and rat us out was too great. I didn't dare tick off Geoffrey.

I sucked in a deep breath and swallowed my fear. "I have survived worse fears before. When you're six, facing the streets with a junkie mother tends to leave you immune to lesser threats."

Besides, I would—if I read things right—be seeing my beloved Grieve tonight. And that . . . that one fact alone was enough to sustain me. I followed Rhiannon downstairs and peered out the living room window. Geoffrey was sending a limousine and I wanted to meet it outside rather than wait for them to come knocking.

A glance over at the Golden Wood told me that Myst had most likely discovered Grieve was missing. The forest was lit up like a house afire—the sickly glow that permeated the area was shining brightly, flaring with fits and sparks. I looked for Wrath, but he was nowhere in sight and I could only hope that he'd be there tonight when I arrived at Geoffrey's. I wanted someone on my side who I felt I could believe in, and among all the major players, my father would be most likely to take my part. Lainule was ruthless in her own way, and the vampires were using me to their own ends, but Wrath . . . he was my father. And he'd been watching over me since I returned to New Forest.

A black sedan pulled up in our driveway and out stepped one of the vampires that I recognized by now from Geoffrey's mansion. I exhaled slowly, steeling myself for the coming meeting. Picking up the bags with Geoffrey's laundry, the chocolates, and the framed print, I stepped out into the icy night. I was headed straight into the arms of destiny. I only hoped she'd cover me with kisses, instead of flogging me with her whip.

As we pulled out of the driveway, I looked back at the Veil House, wondering how much longer we could hold the front line against Myst. Our wards were strong, but her desire was stronger.

Chapter 21

As I entered the mansion, I felt conspicuous. For one thing, there was no crowd this time. I was standing all alone in the foyer, with Butler-Vamp. A few people came and went—some of them vampires, some bloodwhores and servants—but for the most part, the house seemed empty.

"Follow me," my guide said. I picked up the bags and obeyed.

We reached a door I'd never been through before, and as I entered the room, my wolf trembled and whimpered. I whispered comforting words to calm it and, heart pounding, turned to face Geoffrey.

He was sitting there, alone, and he looked hungry. I dropped the bags by my feet and glanced over my shoulder as the door behind me shut, and I heard the sound of a lock turning.

"Geoffrey . . . what did you want to see me about?" I wasn't sure how to broach the picture—or anything, to be honest. It was unnerving to be in a room alone with the Regent, especially after what I'd seen and heard at the Owl People's circle the night before.

He slowly stood, then languorously wandered over to

my side. Without a word, he circled me, then came to a stop right in front of me. "Cicely, do you know where Leo is?"

I sucked in a deep breath. "Yes, he's home very sick. He fainted this morning from a fever. I . . . I did his errands for him since I knew I would be seeing you tonight." I pushed the bags forward with the toe of my shoe.

He glanced down at them. "Domestic, aren't we? Playing fetch so Leo does not get into trouble? Or for another reason?"

Shivering, I hesitantly reached down and picked up the bag with the picture. I slowly held it out to him. "What's this?" My voice barely above a whisper, I was shaking so hard I could barely form the words. "Were you and Myst . . ."

"Ah, so you've seen it. I did not mean for you to. There are reasons that we hire day-runners. Leo should have called his contact this morning and asked for a stand-in. I shall have to have a chat with him about that."

"Please, no—he was delirious."

"Sometimes the magic-born remind me of humans. Weak . . . but necessary. So, you have seen my secret and you now wonder. Were Myst and I in love? No. Were we star-crossed? No. Were we lovers? Yes." He took the picture and cast the bag aside. "She was so beautiful. She looks a lot like *you*, you know." His jet-black eyes fixated on me and his nostrils flared.

I took a step back. "What . . . why . . . you tried to turn her but it wasn't the way it said in the history books, was it? You were partners . . . she wanted it."

"We could have become a force that no land could withstand. We planned to rule the world together. If things had gone right, we could have conquered innumerable lands. But the turning changed her. She became . . . what she is. She was no longer willing to share power. She became more dangerous than I ever dreamed she would." He glanced up, a dark look on his face. "She betrayed me, and I tried to destroy her."

"And that is why the war . . . the other vampires think it's about her anger at being turned, but she's really out for *your* head. To grind you into the dust."

"As she is you. We're in the same boat, my dear. You were her daughter and betrayed her. I was her lover and gave her the keys to the kingdom. And now, she needs no one . . ." He stopped. "Which is where my plans for you come in. Cicely, before I bring your tortured love in for you—and yes, we have him back—I offer you a chance that you will never have with anyone else."

Something about his look, his voice, frightened me more than anything he'd done or said before. "What is it?" I stumbled back as he stepped toward me.

"Cicely, take Myst's place. Fulfill her original plans. Let me turn you, and become my partner. You will be part Indigo Court, but more. You are half magic-born, and that will help you to control the ravaging nature. If you embrace the power, together we can destroy Myst, and together we can take this land by storm. I know you are not cut out for ruthless rule, but you don't have to be that way—you can rule with a just hand. And you can still have your Fae Prince for a lover. I would not object."

I stared at him. The light in his eyes told me the warlord was still lurking beneath the surface, that you could take the warmonger out of the Dark Ages but you couldn't take the Dark Ages out of the warmonger.

"I can't believe you just asked me to do that."

"You were Myst's daughter. To see you go up against her, a queen in your own right, would be a blow hard for her to ignore. It would unsettle her and she'd make mistakes."

"You want to use me for psychological warfare, you want to turn me into what she is, only you hope to control *me* because I'm only *half*-Fae. What would Lainule say if she knew?" I stumbled back toward the door, half-afraid he was going to grab me and drink me down.

But at that moment, Lainule and Anadey appeared from behind a screen in the back of the room. Lainule looked pained. Anadey looked sullen.

"I told you not to approach her until we were here and could explain matters to her." Lainule shook her head. "You'd better hurry. Regina was just down the hall and may come in here. You don't want her finding out what you're up to before we've had time to prepare."

I stared at Lainule, as it dawned on me that she'd known all along what Geoffrey was up to. But had she also been behind Anadey's little stunt?

"Lainule, you know what Geoffrey asks? You can't approve! I'm Cambyra Fae—I am not Unseelie! How can you even dream I'd agree to this? And where's Grieve? Were you the one who tried to force Anadey to strip away my feelings for him?"

"Your lover is with us, young daughter. Do not push your luck. You may not be Unseelie in your own heart, but many of the Uwilahsidhe are on the darker side of the Court. I am the Queen of Rivers and Rushes, and I am the heart of Summer's realm, but not all of my people are bright and beautiful of spirit. The world is made of shades of gray, young Cambyra."

"Did you know what Geoffrey wanted of me? Did you help Anadey?"

Lainule looked pained. She shook her head. "No, I did not help her. It would have killed you, and she will be taken to task for her actions."

Anadey shifted, looking at me through shaded lids.

Lainule ignored her. "As for Geoffrey, yes, long ago he convinced me of the wisdom of his plan. You can still have your lover, Grieve, and do as Geoffrey asks."

Her gaze was cool, and I remembered how ruthless she could be. She would sacrifice anyone in her court to destroy Myst—and that included Grieve. And it included me. If she thought this alliance with the vampires would work best, then she'd back it all the way.

"Do I have a choice?" I asked, my voice flat. If they decided they wanted Geoffrey to turn me, I wasn't likely to get out of here alive.

But she surprised me. "Yes, you do. But think long and hard before you decide whose side you wish to stand on."

Geoffrey let out a hiss, but Lainule shushed him. "I told you—I will agree to this only as long as it is voluntary. But if the child refuses, I turn my back on her. Cicely, you have the chance to sacrifice yourself to rid the world of Myst. If you choose your life over this . . . we have little to say."

"This is why you insisted Wrath impregnate my mother. You foresaw this coming. All along, you planned this with Geoffrey." I stared at her, certain I was right. And she gazed back at me, unmoved, unmoving.

"Some wars are fought in minutes, others are in the planning for generations. We knew Myst would resurface. We knew that you would return to be with Grieve. What better way to defeat Myst than to create a force who could equal her power and yet retain control over her desires? You are the perfect choice. You were her daughter—and you have her soul-mark in your own soul. Yet you do not seek the power she craves. Your potential is vast and untapped."

At that moment, Wrath strode into the room, slamming the door open against the wall. "Stop! You will not do this—you will not force her to make this move." Grieve and Lannan were behind him. Grieve looked ragged and worn, but alive. Lannan looked dark, hostile, and angry.

I let out a little cry and ran over toward my father, wanting to go to Grieve but sensing now was not the best time. "They want me to let Geoffrey turn me—to set me up against Myst by his side."

"You are one of the Uwilahsidhe. The Owl People abjure the Queen of Spiders. You will not let them do this to you. *I will not allow it.*" Wrath turned an angry face on Lainule. "My beloved, what can you be thinking? This is madness. You listen to the bloodsuckers too readily."

"This is why I did not tell you the plan—you are too softhearted, my husband. We will not force her, but if she turns aside, then she is no use to us. We must defeat the Winter. Cicely and Geoffrey can do so, together. Cicely is only now coming into her powers. Think of what she could do if she combined her magic, her strength as one of the Uwilahsidhe, and the power of the vampires." Lainule reached toward Wrath, but he shook off her touch.

"That was attempted once and look at what it engendered—Myst, herself. No, this will not happen. And perhaps, if we have to go to this length, then Summer is not meant to stand against Winter. There are other ways, other avenues to defeating an enemy." He stared at Lainule for a long time. "My love, you are courting danger. You risk becoming as dark as the Mistress of Mayhem. I fear for you."

"She stole my kingdom. She killed my people. *Your people.* You are Uwilahsidhe. You court the path of the Unseelie all too often, and you would dare to lecture me? Be gone—King of mine. Out of my sight. I cannot bear to look upon you." Lainule turned her back on Wrath, who looked as though she had struck him.

He turned away, then to Lannan. "You were correct. I had no clue this is what they planned."

Geoffrey slowly swung toward Lannan, who glanced in my direction, then stood definitely, facing them. "Lannan . . . you told Wrath our plans? I thought we agreed there was no need." He raised one hand. "You haven't, by chance, been speaking to your sister, have you?"

Lannan snorted. "I care nothing for the Crimson Queen nor her court . . . but my sister cares about her position. I'm sure she would *love* to hear your plans to usurp the Crimson Queen's position."

"You'd damned well better keep your mouth shut. If you don't, I will remove your head. I've warned you before. Your stable, everything you own is in danger. You know I won't hesitate to destroy you *and your sister* in the process. Keep quiet, both of you live. Speak, and both of you die. Again and this time, for good." He turned to me. "I know how you feel about Lannan. Would you now align yourself with him, hating him as much as you do?"

I stepped back, looking at all of them. "I choose for myself—and as much as I hate what Lannan has done to me, at least he is honest about what he wants. He sees reason. I will not allow you to turn me. Not for all the summer nights in the world."

"Then leave and be damned. Take your lover with you,

and Lannan, as well. Altos, you are outcast—pariah in my lands. I strip you of your job and your place in our society. I'm going to tell Regina you've gone on a trip for me. Keep quiet, and *she* will live."

Lannan wandered over to stand beside Wrath, Grieve, and me. He gave Grieve a contemptuous look. "I have made my choice. Myst can only be stopped by an alliance of forces, not by the rise of a long-forgotten warlord. Geoffrey, you only seek to use Cicely for your own ends. You would never share your power with her once the dust settled. You would destroy her, as you plan to destroy Myst. The world is large; I happen to believe that the Fae and the vampires can coexist, but I don't believe for an instant that you agree. But know this: If you touch one golden hair of my sister's head, I will raise an army and obliterate you and your world."

"We seem to be at a standstill. I will not harm your sister if you keep quiet, and you stay away in return for her continued well-being."

I turned toward Lannan, wondering. Could he really believe what Geoffrey said? As much as I wanted to stake him, Lannan was taking my side. I sidled over to Grieve and quietly took his hand. I wanted to kiss him, to hold him and ask how he was, but we both knew better. This was not the time for a reunion.

"Lannan, leave my house. Cicely, you, too. I wish you luck in keeping alive without our protection. Tell Leo he must choose—either work with me, or align himself to you and your cousin, but he cannot do both. If he does not report for work tomorrow, tomorrow night he will be taken off the rolls. Just pray you do not meet me on the opposite side of the battleground. Lainule, attend me."

Geoffrey turned away and stormed out the door.

Lannan let out a sigh. "Geoffrey has always been—and will always be—a warlord. He misses the battle, he misses the conquest. He may be Regent, but once the Crimson Queen understands how deep his ambitions lie, I can only hope she's not too late in putting a stop to them. Because the day he can, he will topple her from the throne and take control. And my sister will be next in line to die."

At the door, Lainule turned back to us, her gaze fastened on Wrath. "Be cautious—you have no allies. Return to the fold; accept that only through solidarity can we defeat the Winter."

"Not at the sacrifice of my daughter," Wrath said.

"Then prepare to meet your doom—but never at my hands." She motioned to Anadey and they slowly followed Geoffrey out of the room.

I turned to Wrath, Lannan, and Grieve. "What the fuck are we supposed to do now? I couldn't do it . . . I couldn't let Geoffrey turn me."

Wrath shook his head. "I have been the King of Summer for eons, but my Lady doesn't always tell me her plans. And she is terrified—her heartstone still lies within the boundaries of the Golden Wood. If Myst finds it . . ."

"She'll destroy Lainule." And there it was—the fear within Lainule was born of self-preservation.

"What if we get it back?" Grieve turned to me. "Cicely, my love . . . I am cured of the light-rage, but I am still part of Myst's people. I will do my best to control my impulses. And if I can't . . ."

"Then we will have to destroy you," Lannan said. "I must figure out a way to warn my sister so she can get out before Geoffrey does something to her, but we can't tarry here. Geoffrey will return and he will kill us if we're still around. Of that much, I guarantee."

Grieve slowly turned. "*You.* You're the one I smelled on her—you filthy bloodsucker! What have you been doing to my Cicely?" He shoved Lannan back and took a step toward him.

Lannan laughed. "Not as much as I want to." He made an obscene gesture with his hands.

"Stop it, both of you." Wrath lashed out and within seconds had separated both men. "We cannot afford to be divided. Leave it for now. We'll sort everything out once we're away from here. Come, let us leave."

"What about Lainule?" I glanced at the door. "Are you just going to leave her?"

"I'm afraid we don't have much of a choice. We're running on borrowed time, whether it be from Geoffrey or from Myst." Wrath led us out. The butler gazed at us, unreadable, but he did nothing to prevent us from leaving.

"I didn't bring my car," I said, pausing. "I came in Geoffrey's limo."

"I've got my BMW here." Lannan motioned us toward it. He flipped open his phone, trying to contact Regina, but after a moment, hung up. "She's not answering. I don't like this."

Grieve hung back. "I won't get in the car with him. Cicely, how can you?"

In tears, frustrated and confused, I swung on him. "You'll get in the fucking car. Do you know how much we risked for you? And now we're on our own. We no longer have the backing of the vampires, and trust me, to defeat Myst, we need as many allies as we can gather. So shut up—both you and Lannan—and just get in the damned thing. Lannan— we'll keep calling Regina, trying to warn her."

Lannan rolled his eyes but said nothing. Grieve stared at me, his lips full, and I wanted again to rush into his arms, to feel his heart beating against mine. After a moment, he inclined his head.

"Very well. I will obey."

"The machine will be painful, but I can withstand it for a short time," Wrath said. "We have a long night ahead of us."

But before I could climb into the car, my cell phone rang. Exasperated, I flipped it open. "Hello?"

"Cicely, can you get home, now? And bring help." Rhia sounded frantic.

"What's wrong?"

"The Shadow Hunters have broken through the wards and they're on the way toward the house. We can't fight them alone."

Crap! "We're on our way. I'm bringing Wrath, Grieve, and Lannan with me. Get whatever weapons you can together."

"Lannan?"

"Yes, *Lannan*. We'll tell you all about it when we have the time. Now just get off the phone and be fucking careful."

I took off for Lannan's car. "Myst broke through the wards. They're in danger." The squabbling stopped as they followed me. I shoved Lannan away from the wheel and took over. "I drive faster than you."

"I doubt it," he said, but he let me get behind the wheel.

We sped through the dark streets as I counted off the minutes. As we rounded the corner onto Vyne Street, I closed my eyes.

Ulean, are you there? Can you hear me?

I am here—the Shadow Hunters are circling the house, coming closer. They seem cautious, as if they expect a trap.

Is everyone still okay?

Yes, so far. But there are seven of the Indigo Court out there—and the energy on the slipstream is roiling with anger. Myst is awake and hunting for Grieve.

And I was bringing him right to her. I thought about how we'd make it into the house—all my weapons were there. "We have to fly in. Grieve, you and Lannan will have to make a run for the door, but Wrath and I can shift and fly in the upper windows." I tossed Lannan my phone. "Call them and tell them to be ready at the front door and my bedroom window."

Lannan put in the call and, whatever he said, it was brief and to the point. I wasn't paying attention. I was focused on the battle ahead. I had my fan, of course, and my switch-blade, but that alone wasn't going to be enough.

"Iron stakes. We need them—they'll work on the Shadow Hunters."

Wrath peered over the backseat. "The gate. There's a gate made of iron in front of the house next door. But neither Grieve nor I can touch the stakes. You can, since you are only half-Fae—you don't seem bothered by the iron. Even this car hurts me, but I bear it because of necessity."

"I can get them." I said. "And Lannan can."

Lannan leaned forward. It was disconcerting to have him at my shoulder but not to be able to see him in the rearview mirror. "Are you willing to put your life in my hands? I can rip the stakes out of the gate. You fly in with your father. The Prince will have to make a run for it on his own."

I bit my lip. "Are you sure you can make it without getting caught?"

"If you cause a distraction, yes. Once you're inside, do something to draw their attention to the back of the house."

I sucked in a deep breath. "Okay. That's how it is. Grieve, when you hit the ground, don't stop running. Meanwhile . . ." I cringed. "I'm going to have to take off my clothes before we get there if I expect to be able to transform into owl shape. Lannan, I guess you'd better take the wheel." I abruptly pulled to a halt and we played musical seats, with me running to the back of the car and Lannan leaping into the driver's seat.

I began to yank off my clothes and had the distinct feeling Lannan was watching me through the rearview mirror, though there was no way I could prove it, since I couldn't see him other than the back of his head. I slid beneath a throw in the back of the car and pulled it around my shoulders as we drove off again.

Grieve simmered, but he simmered at me, his eyes drinking their fill as I disrobed. Hard as it was, I forced myself to hold back, to keep from tumbling into his arms. But I did kiss my fingers and press them against his lips.

"You make me want to—" Lannan started, but my father interrupted him.

"Be cautious, vampire. That's my daughter you're talking to," Wrath said, his voice thick with warning. "You will behave like a gentleman."

"You may be the King of Summer, but Cicely owes me more than you want to know and I intend to collect. And chill out, Wolf Boy, because I know she only has eyes for you." Lannan's words took on an edge as he added, "She's made that all too apparent."

I pulled back, not wanting to start any more arguments. Grieve gave me a curt nod, but his eyes promised me that once we were finished, if we managed to come through this alive, he'd prove to me just how much he missed me.

Ulean, we're near. Did you hear our plans?

I did—your thoughts were clear.

Can you start a distraction in the backyard?

I can, but if you can get to your fan, we can wreak much more havoc together. You have yet to use the most powerful force that it can summon.

I've created a tornado before—and gale-force winds; what more can there be?

Hurricane force. Typhoon. But beware, Cicely—it can devastate an area.

We may have no choice. I'll meet you in my bedroom.

And then we turned on to Vyne Street. As we raced along the silent asphalt, I shivered, more out of fear than cold. Before we arrived, I leaned over and pressed my lips against Grieve's. He gathered me close and I ached, wanting him to reach out and touch my breasts, to slide his hands along my body. But, mindful of my father's presence, he simply pulled me close, and I found myself falling deep, sucking under, into the spiral of love and lust that permeated our connection.

And then we were there, and the car screeched to a halt. We slammed out of the doors, Wrath and I transforming into our owl selves and winging into the sky. Last I saw, Grieve was racing for the house as Lannan began yanking iron stakes off the neighbor's gate. And then, as I neared my bedroom window, I could see them out back—the Shadow Hunters, gauging the house.

It was official. We were at war.

Chapter 22

I swooped high enough to stay out of range should they have archers, but low enough to fly directly in the window, which was open, with Kaylin waiting to slam it shut the minute I was through.

I landed on my dresser, then hopped to the floor and quickly transformed, my moonstone pendant lightly hitting against my breasts. As I spilled forward, Kaylin quickly handed me a pair of jeans, a bra, and a turtleneck. I wriggled into my clothes.

"We have big trouble—but we don't have time to tell you. Just know that Lainule, Anadey, and Geoffrey are no longer on our side. Lannan and Wrath, however, are. Grieve's back, too."

At his startled look, I shook my head. "Don't ask—it's just too complicated right now. Have the Shadow Hunters made any attack?"

"Not yet, but I think they were waiting for you. They made themselves obvious, and then held off, keeping us in the house."

"They must have seen me leave earlier. And Myst knows we have Grieve—how can she not?" I slid on a pair of lace-up steel-toed boots and then strapped my blade to my wrist and grabbed my fan. "I need a better blade."

"What about the obsidian one? The one we caught when we fought Myst and her cronies last week? Remember?"

I thought back. When we'd rescued Peyton, we had picked up an obsidian blade off one of the Shadow Hunters. "Oh hell, yeah. And it wants blood. Bring it to me."

Kaylin hurried out of the room, returning with the sealed box. I cautiously opened it and pulled out the blade. Obsidian, it was fashioned with a bone handle. I cautiously reached out to touch it. The one time before when I'd picked it up, it had immediately tried to possess me, but I had the feeling that now that I knew about my heritage as Myst's daughter, I might be able to wrest control of it.

As my hand slid around the handle, I felt a shudder of joy run through me, a delight in the sharpness of the edge, the piercing point that could drive through bone and steel. This blade was magic, and it had an essence—a strength all its own. I clasped my fingers around the handle and a ripple of delight echoed through my breasts, my body . . . it was better than sex.

"I can mow them down with this," I said, looking up at Kaylin slyly.

And indeed, a swath of blood and destruction spread in front of me, and I knew that whatever might come, this blade would sever limb from bone, it would slice throats and pierce hearts and do anything I asked it to, sucking the pain right into itself as food, and with each kill, it would grow stronger, and so would I.

"I'm afraid." A thin river of regret ran through me and I glanced up at Kaylin. "I'm afraid this blade can change who I am."

"Only if you allow it to. Take charge. You have to be the one to rule. You cannot allow it to have its head—just like breaking a horse. You have to maintain control." He leaned over me. "We need every advantage we can get to stop them. You have to be strong, Cicely. You have to give a little of yourself—not all, not what Geoffrey and Lainule

were asking—but a little . . . in order to help win this war.
You can't remain the same and come through it unscathed.
None of us can."

I slowly inhaled, hefting the lightweight blade in my hand,
feeling the rushing waves of destructive joy run through me.
"I know. I know that we're not coming out of this without
some damage." Staring at the blade, I understood—it would
bring me in touch with who I used to be, who I was a lifetime
ago, as Myst's daughter. It would take me to the same place
Geoffrey wanted me to go, but without losing all of who I'd
become in the process.

"I'll do it. I will carry the blade."

A light knock on the door and my wolf whimpered,
excited. "Please, go. Give us just a moment and we'll be
down."

Grieve came in, his eyes glimmering with stars against
their blackened background. "We have little time. They're
approaching the house. Cicely, I'm not sure how you did it,
but I know you're responsible for Wrath freeing me. I hate
Lannan with a passion, but I will fight alongside him now,
and do my best to control my nature."

He swept me up in his arms and I melted against him,
pressing my head to his heart, shuddering in the warmth of
his embrace. I wanted him, then—there, without pretense.
Wanted to be with him forever, wanted to be his and only
his, to run away from the war and live in a quiet place
where we could settle in and just be happy.

"The enemy is storming our gates, my love," I whispered. "Myst has come to play and she's looking for you."

"I won't let her take me back." He pressed his lips to
mine and kissed me. I could have lived within his kiss forever, but there was no time.

"Let's go—we can't let the others down."

I took his hand, then stopped and turned. "I'm sorry—
I'm sorry I wasn't ready when you asked me so many years
ago. I'm sorry that . . . I needed time to know how I felt."

He shook his head. "I asked too soon. You were very
young. I should have known better. I just hoped you would

have remembered, but no matter now. We'll make it through, Cicely. We're survivors. We'll have our time."

And then we were headed down the stairs, racing to meet the oncoming storm.

✢

"Where are they?" I swung into the kitchen, where the rest of them were, but realized I'd just interrupted an argument. "What's going on?"

"Geoffrey just called me," Leo said. "He told me what happened. It appears I'm being forced to choose. He's given me an ultimatum."

"You have to pick sides." I knew it would come to this.

He nodded, staring at me with ill-disguised anger. "Yeah, thanks to you. I know where my strengths lie, and it's not with you and your war. Rhiannon, you're my fiancée. Kaylin—you were my friend first. Choose. Come with me and fight this war in a sane manner. Lainule and Geoffrey had a plan, and Cicely fucked it up."

"I chose not to hand my life over to Geoffrey—I chose not to let him turn me into a monster. That is hardly fucking things up, in my opinion. But choose—by all means. If you truly believe that I should have sacrificed myself on the altar for the vampires, then go with Leo—because you won't be of help here."

Rhiannon, bitter tears streaking her cheeks, shook her head. "No. I stand by Cicely—Myst took my mother. And I won't see her claim Cicely by default."

"I can't believe you're choosing your cousin over me. So be it, then. But don't come crawling back to me when you're alone and scared. Because I won't play second fiddle to some freak." He turned to Kaylin. "What about you?"

Kaylin's face clouded over. "Leo, dude, your ego's speaking. You'd rather be a little fish in a big frying pan than a little fish in a little frying pan . . . either way, you're going to get your fins burned."

"What the fuck are you talking about?"

"Just this: No matter how hard you try, Geoffrey's not

going to turn you. That's what you want, isn't it? I've been watching you for some time now. You crave power, and if it takes becoming one of the vamps, you thought why not? But Geoffrey won't turn you. And if he hasn't offered by now, he's not going to. With us, you aren't skilled enough to be one of the up-front fighters—and you aren't content with what you *can* do to help. You'll never be happy until you can accept who you are."

"Fuck that shit." Leo turned and, jamming his coat on, headed toward the front door. "I'll pick up my things later," he called over his shoulder. "If you are still alive to give them to me." Grabbing Bart's carrier, he slammed out the front door with the Maine Coon.

"Crap." I turned to the others. "We meet the Indigo Court outside. They'll tear down the house if we let them in here."

"We have another choice. We can make a run for it, move to a new location and plan out what we're going to do." Kaylin stopped my protest. "Before you say *no*, think about it: There are at least a dozen Shadow Hunters out there. They could have made a move earlier but were waiting—they were waiting for you to get home, Cicely."

He glanced out the window. "I can't see any of them now. But you can bet that they haven't faded back into the forest."

"Where would we go?" Rhiannon whispered.

But then, even as she spoke, the kitchen door slammed open and two of the Shadow Hunters broke through. At the same time, Lannan came racing through the front door, iron stakes in hand.

I was nearest the living room, and I reached out and grabbed one of the stakes from him as he passed by. He tossed the others to Kaylin, Peyton, and Rhiannon, keeping one for himself. Luna, looking horrified, grabbed up a flute, and my first thought was, *You aren't going to charm these savage beasts with music*, but the sound that came out of her instrument was low and sultry and quickened my blood. I stared at her, realizing she was casting a charm over all of us—a fighting charm.

And then there was no more time to stare because one of

the Shadow Hunters was staring me in the face. I swung, striking with the obsidian blade. The blade seemed to adjust my aim and I managed a clean swipe along the Shadow Hunter's arm. He let out a shriek, unlike any I'd heard when attacking with my switchblade, and a sudden fountain of blood sprung up and began to bubble over onto the floor.

The knife made the wound worse than it normally would have. I glanced at the blade and felt a rush of joy, powerful and strong, as the pain from the Shadow Hunter raced through me and I leaned my head back and laughed, undulating a horrible yipping cry through the kitchen.

The Shadow Hunter took a long look at me as I glared at him, the power of death flushing my cheeks. I held the power to destroy in my hands. I held the power of the night and the dark and the shimmering blades that ripped out hearts and tore apart the chest. Another swipe and his arm was hanging from a thread and he went down, frothing at the mouth, shivering as the blood spilled across the floor in an orgasm of ripples.

I turned to the second Shadow Hunter, who had engaged Kaylin. He saw me swing in his direction and yelped, racing for the door. I leaped over the dying Indigo Fae and gave chase.

"Cicely!"

"Where are you going?"

The voices were faint, behind me, mere annoyances. I had my enemy within range, and nothing would stop me from destroying him. I gasped as the cold hit my lungs but flew down the steps, keeping up with the creature that raced on ahead of me. He would not escape—no one did. No one ever escaped Myst's daughter when she chose her target.

Cicely—can you hear me? Cicely—slow down. Wait for the others!

But I didn't want to listen. Ulean howled along beside me as the yard went by in a blur and I raced directly into the forest. My blade sang, demanding blood, and I had to feed her. She was thirsty and so was I.

And then I saw him coming toward me, a bigger member of Myst's Court—one of her guards, no doubt. I let my body take over and instinct kicked in as I went sailing head over

heels and landed nose-to-nose with him. I swept the blade
across his chest before he could move, and he shrieked.

Laughing, I hoisted the iron spike in my other hand and
leaned back. My blade was feeding; let it feed well, the
spike would provide it with much blood. He tried to fight
back, tried to wave me off, but I plunged the tip through his
chest, ramming it into the bone, and blood spread across
the snow like a crimson rose.

As he fell, I went down by his side and pressed my face
to his wound, rubbing my cheeks in his blood. I dipped the
blade into the hollow next to the spike and—as he still
screamed, though much, much fainter—I let the blade feed
in the steaming pool.

"Cicely!"

The voice was not Ulean's, and harder to ignore.

"Cicely Waters, stand before your father!"

Wrath's voice broke through where Ulean's could not,
and I slowly raised my head, my surroundings coming into
focus. Oh fucking hell! I was over the border—but then
again, they'd broken through the wards, so did it matter?

"Get your ass off the ground and finish him off like an
honorable opponent. The Indigo Court may have no honor,
but *we do*." He reached out and snatched the blade from my
hand. "That should make it easier."

I forced myself to my feet, feeling the sticky mess on
my face. My breath was sour with his blood—I'd been
licking it up. Queasy, I turned back to my opponent and
realized he was still alive, and suffering terribly. I grabbed
the end of the stake and, feeling faint, shoved it through
him, ending his life.

Without a word, I turned to my father and, shaking,
allowed him to grab me around the waist. The next thing I
knew, the yard was a blur again as we raced faster than
even Chatter and Grieve could.

Back at the house, I saw Kaylin and Chatter fighting one
of the Shadow Hunters. Another was trying to get near Rhiannon, but she was holding him off with a firestorm. Luna
was treating a wound on Peyton's arm that was bleeding

profusely. Grieve was finishing off another one of the Vampiric Fae.

"We can't hold the house," I said roughly. "We can't hold it. We're vulnerable as long as we live here. Even if we take out this group, another will take its place. Until we can strike at the heart of their Court, we'll just keep getting eroded away by insurgent attacks. There is great power here, but we have no ability to tap into it. Yet."

"You're right." Lannan came up beside me. "You can't hold it. Best to fall back, regroup, and strategize."

"Where can we go? We can't go to Peyton's house—Anadey has linked herself to Geoffrey and Lainule."

Lannan let out a long breath. "For now, you may come to my place. All of you. You cannot stay there—that would not be wise, but you may come."

And then Rhiannon raced over to Luna and was shouting frantically to her. Luna nodded and ran into the house, as Rhia motioned to me.

"The house, the house is on fire. Do you have anything in there? Do you have your necklace and fan?"

I nodded. "Yes, I have them with me. But all your things—all of our memories—where's the fire?"

Just then, Luna came out leading a string of cats, following behind her, as she played a tune, leading them like the piper. Rhia jogged over and, together with Chatter and Grieve, grabbed up all seven of them.

I pulled out my keys. We sprinted around front and I opened the back door to Favonis, and we piled the cats in there. Luna crawled in with them, playing to charm them into a lulling sleep.

Turning to Rhia I said, "Where's the fire? I don't see the fire."

"I saw it—I know I saw it—"

As she gestured frantically, a sudden fireball appeared from the back and the roof lit up. The others raced around, Peyton and Kaylin and Wrath, and we watched as the flames engulfed the roof of the Veil House.

"Who set it on fire?"

"I did . . . " Rhiannon whispered, looking pale and terri-fied. "It was an accident. I caught a low-hanging branch and it smoldered. I was focusing on the Shadow Hunter, trying to stop him before he could get to me and then . . . by the time the flames chased him back, the branch burst and sent a flame to the shingles. It caught, but I thought it might go out there . . . the snow was coming down so thick."

"Magical fire burns hotter than regular fire." I glanced around. Myst's people hadn't come into the front yard. They were probably too busy watching the fire from the borders of the wood.

"Call nine-one-one?" Peyton asked.

I took out my phone and tried, but when the operator picked up and I told her what house it was, she cut me off and the line went dead.

"Either Geoffrey or Myst cut off our access to help. We are truly alone."

"Not so much. We have the Consortium—we can go to them. Bring in some of the powerful magic-born." Rhian-non shook her head. "Formalize our Society and then call on them for backing. If we're part of the Consortium, they'll have to help us."

I glanced at Rhiannon. "You might have something there. As of tonight, I form the Moon Spinners Society—and we who are here are the founders. Our initiation is by fire and ice—our powers of strength."

We joined hands, all but Luna, whom we mentally included in our circle, and with Ulean at my back, we made our pledges.

By life and death . . .
By sacred trust . . .
I pledge my honor . . .
I pledge my love . . .
I pledge my power . . .
I pledge my heart . . .
I pledge my magic . . .
I pledge my Art.

As we each repeated the charm, the power grew, and I stepped forward. I was High Priestess of the Moon Spinners, and it was up to me to take the lead. I pulled out my fan and, cheeks stained with the blood of our enemy, I whispered, *Hurricane Force*, and sent the wind speeding toward the house.

The wind whipped the flames into a fury, acting like a bomb, and exploded them high into the night sky. If we couldn't have the house, neither could Myst. She might try to harness the power of the land, but I had a feeling the ley lines ran far older than she, and my bets were they would refuse to be used by the Indigo Court. I hoped to hell I was right.

"Let all within earshot of slipstream and wind currents hear me: The Moon Spinners are coming for you, Myst. We will not rest until we grind you beneath our feet. And we are from all walks of life, and all paths, and all races. We will not bow before the Indigo Court. We will not rest until we've reclaimed and rebuilt our home. I, Cicely who was once Cherish, your daughter, lead the army."

As my words echoed through the yard, carrying on the wind to all quarters, carrying on the slipstream, I turned back to the others. "Lannan, your offer is a welcome one, but you're right—we can't stay there. Kaylin, can you find us a place to hide for now?"

He nodded. "All are pledged by death and honor to keep our new digs secret. You know that, don't you?" Looking specifically at Lannan, he waited for us. We each answered with a nod, even Lannan.

And so, as the Veil House roared in flames against the sky, we headed for our cars and passed off Vyne Street, a silent procession in the night. Wrath rode with me and Luna and the cats, who slept silently, engulfed in the depths of Luna's charm.

"My dear, you do realize what you have done?" My father glanced at me as we crept down the snowy streets, our engines muffled by the thick layer of snow Myst was wreaking upon the area.

"Yes, I do. I've created a force. I've created a power. And we will go to the Consortium and demand backing. They may not like the fact that we are Fae and magic-born, Were and magic-born, Fae and Indigo Court, yummanii, and vampire, but they will have to accept us. They gave me the challenge and I have risen to it. But I still want to learn to control my blade."

He shook his head. "The obsidian knife is a dangerous tool for one with Myst's soul blood—it's bad enough in the hands of one of her soldiers. Obsidian links with the energy of the Vampiric Fae; it's symbiotic."

"Then so much the better. I had no trouble killing off her warriors with it. Look at what the blade did for me—it turned me into a warrior—"

"No!" Wrath glowered. "It turned you into a killing machine. Look at your face—look at your hands. Think back to the joy in your heart over the devastation of your enemy. Though we must fight them, though we must destroy them, it is not our way to take great pleasure in the pain of others. Cambyra Fae are dark, yes; we walk on the edge of the Unseelie Court depending on our nature . . . but in my family, we do not align ourselves with monsters!"

I let out a slow cough, the memory of my sheer delight in the carnage tweaking me. "I know . . . but there may come a time, my father, when you will have to turn me loose against them. I may be the only weapon you have. And I will need every advantage I can garner. Put the blade away for now, if you will, but promise me you won't destroy it."

He sighed, then nodded. "I will do so. And in return, I will outfit you with a blade from my realm that will leave you joyful, but not a monster at heart. I have a silver dagger that I saved for you, when I knew Krystal was pregnant."

That was the first time he'd ever said her name, and I glanced at him. "Did you like her?" *Please, oh please, say you liked her. Please say you didn't just fuck her because Lainule ordered you to.*

As the streets glided by in a silent blur of snowflakes and flickering streetlights, Wrath let out a long sigh.

"She was a troubled young woman. I wanted to help, but it would have interfered with your future. I could have taken her to my realm, kept her among my consorts where she would have been happy—or at least, less troubled. But Lainule foresaw the future . . . she knew you would need the childhood you had in order to toughen you up. Your mother was . . . a sacrifice so that you might become the woman you are."

Tears streaming down my face, I pressed my lips shut and followed Kaylin and Rhiannon. He was driving her car, with Peyton and Grieve and Chatter inside. As we wove through the night, a strange inky cloak seemed to surround both vehicles and I knew it was coming from Kaylin.

His night-veil is awake, and it can create shadows to cloak movement. No one can see the cars or feel our presence.

Thank you. And Ulean, I'm sorry I didn't listen to you earlier. I was caught up in the rush of the blade, in the power of the hunt.

I understand. But Cicely, there are long, dark days ahead. Don't be so rash. Don't be so quick to lead the brigade. A good leader learns when to hang back and let someone more experienced take over.

It was Kaylin's idea for me to use the obsidian knife. Do you think he knew what would happen?

I don't know . . . but Kaylin runs clean energy, even now with his night-veil demon awake.

A peal of bells rang twelve times as we turned into the industrial district right outside town and crept into a maze of a parking lot. Old junkers filled the lot and we parked near the edge of a huge warehouse and climbed out.

"Welcome to your new home," Kaylin said. "Follow me."

And, under the veil of night, we followed the night-veil, carrying seven cats, into the heart of the darkness.

Chapter 23

Grieve and I stood in the middle of a makeshift bedroom, staring at one another. This was the first time we'd had a chance to be alone since our brief talk in the bedroom. I turned to him, still bloody from the fight.

"My love, what have we come to?"

He pulled me into his embrace. "We've come to a crossroads. We go into hiding and we fight from the dark. We become the monsters to fear, now. But not for the townsfolk . . . only for Myst and her people."

"Can you control yourself?" I whispered, hoping he wouldn't hear me but having to ask, having to take a chance.

"I'll try. We've come so far from when you were little and I first found you. Lainule knew you'd return—she promised me she'd help me find you again. And she did. I had no clue what she was grooming you for—what she and Geoffrey tried to pull. I wouldn't have asked for her help if I'd thought this would happen."

He slid onto a dilapidated sofa that was to be our bed and pulled me down on his lap. Kaylin was setting up operations in the other room, and everybody had graciously left us alone to get ourselves sorted out. Even my father, who didn't look all that thrilled when we slipped away out of the room.

I snuggled against him and rested my head on his shoulder and pushed the world away. The only thing I wanted to focus on right now was the fact that I had Grieve back, that we were together. Lannan would be a problem, I already knew that, and we had lost our home and all our memories, but we had each other and we had seven cats and soon enough, we'd have the Consortium behind us.

And Lainule and Geoffrey . . . we'd have to see how the shit hit the fan with them.

I wrapped my arms around Grieve and kissed him slowly, leisurely, my blood boiling. But as he began to nip at my shoulder, I realized—the bite wasn't enthralling me. He suckled the blood, one drop at a time, but as sensuous as it felt, his venom wasn't pulling me in. Anadey's spell had actually had an effect.

Deciding not to mention it to him—not just yet—I pulled away, slowly, and stared up at the towering ceilings of the warehouse. Rusty metal cans and stacks of boxes surrounded us, and the place felt dark and full of shadows. It was huge; when Kaylin had led us in, a shiver of fear had run through me because it reminded me of old graveyards and haunted warships. The place had once been a shipping warehouse, but now it was closed, standing empty on the outskirts of New Forest. We were nearer the mountains, away from the Golden Woods, at the base of the Cascade foothills. Here we could hide in the forest and not be immediately subject to Myst, although I wasn't sure how far she'd spread her poison.

And we had room here to spread out, to make plans and formalize our Society. Then I'd call Ysandra and talk to her. Or maybe take a day trip out to the local Consortium headquarters over in Seattle. Geoffrey was afraid the Consortium would take over, but he'd outed his own agenda. No more time to play favorites. We needed all the help we could get.

The warehouse was old and falling apart, but it was protected, and the suite of rooms Kaylin led us to had obviously been used as a home for a long time. His home. This was where he'd holed up. It was warm enough, with steam heat racing through the pipes, and he'd jury-rigged electricity. We had water and plumbing, and though Kaylin had warned us against using too much of anything lest we set off suspicion, we should be okay.

Yeah, it was creepy, but there were no Shadow Hunters here. I would have felt them on the slipstream.

Sometimes, the brightest light can be found amid the darkness. And sometimes, the best allies, as well. Ulean murmured an assent and passed by—I knew she was exploring the place.

I let out a long sigh and leaned back, staring at Grieve. "So, here we are. Together, on the run, with friends. I have an idea, you know—of how to win Lainule back to our side."

"How so, my love?" He nuzzled my neck. "You are so sweet, you taste so sweet."

"That may be, but control yourself while we talk business."

"As you will, my love." Grieve pulled back, listening.

"You thought of this before—and I think it's a good idea. Lainule's heartstone still lies within Myst's realm. If we can find it, we can use it as a bargaining chip. Lainule will be furious, but she'll have to deal with us—and it's better than waiting for Myst to find it and obliterate the Queen of Rivers and Rushes."

Grieve stared at me, long and hard, then inclined his head. "Cicely, my sweetness . . . you remind me so much of yourself when you were Cherish, sometimes. And that is not altogether a bad thing, so don't get upset for me saying so." He stopped me when I started to protest. "To fight a ruthless war machine, you need to become a little ruthless yourself. And you're doing so."

"Be good or my father will smack you down one."

"He could do so. Wrath is strong and powerful. And I'm not sure what he'll think of your plan, but there's no mistaking it's a viable one. But what of Geoffrey? What do we do about him?"

I shook my head. "I don't know yet . . . but there has to be some weakness. I am afraid that Lannan may give in because of his fear for his sister, and he knows too much now. But we can't afford to stake him—he could also prove a valuable ally."

A knock on the door interrupted us. It was Peyton.

She peeked in. "Not meaning to interrupt. I wondered—what about inviting my father here? He's definitely not on Anadey's must-welcome list. He might be able to help us with the Were community."

I considered the idea. "I think we should talk about it over dinner. Come on, let's ask Kaylin if there's any food in this joint."

Weary beyond belief, we stood and headed into the main room. I paused, turning Grieve to face me.

"Whatever comes, at least we have each other. Know that I love you, and I'll never leave you again."

"I know . . . and you know . . ." He didn't finish, just wrapped me in his arms and kissed me long and slow and deep. "When this is done . . . Cicely Waters—when we are triumphant, will you marry me and be princess to a prince with no kingdom?"

Kissing him back, I knew. I knew in my heart he would stay with us, would keep control. I knew that he couldn't entrance me with his venom. I knew that he loved me beyond life itself and would do everything he could to protect me—and the others.

"I will. If we can defeat Myst, I will be your wife, and we'll do our best to repair the damage." I took his hand and we joined the others. Luna was scrubbing down a make-shift stove—a pair of hot plates Kaylin had found for her. Rhiannon and Chatter were making up beds for everyone out of ragged blankets and seat cushions from old love seats. Peyton was helping Lannan test the locks on the windows and doors. My father was consulting a bag of bones he carried on his belt, divining our next move.

This was our new home, and would be until we could regroup and figure out our next step. Come good or ill, we were the Moon Spinners—standing against Myst alone, unaided. The vampires and Lainule were going to be a problem, but mostly, I thought about Myst. About the past and the future. We were facing a conflict that might take months to resolve.

But in the back of my mind, I wondered—how much time did we really have to carry out our private little war? I scooted closer to Grieve and took his hand, leaning my head on his shoulder as he wrapped his arm around my waist.

"For better or worse," I whispered. "This is as good as it's going to get. We can't count on anybody else."

"No," Grieve said, brushing the hair out of my face. "But we have each other."

I laughed then—just a little laugh, but it felt like a shock wave. "Yeah, and that is a priceless resource."

Character List

CICELY AND THE COURT OF THE MAGIC-BORN

Anadey: Friend of Heather's and mentor to Rhiannon. One of the magic-born, Anadey can work with all elements. She owns Anadey's Diner and is Peyton's mother.

Cicely Waters: A witch who can control the wind. One of the magic-born and half-Uwilahsidhe (the Owl people of the Cambyra Fae). Born on the Summer Solstice at midnight, a daughter of the Moon/Waning Year.

Heather Roland (*see* Indigo Court): Rhiannon's mother and Cicely's aunt. One of the magic-born, an herbalist, now turned into a vampire by the Indigo Court.

Kaylin Chen: Martial-arts sensei, a dreamwalker, has a night-veil demon merged into his soul.

Leo Bryne: Rhiannon's fiancé. A healer and one of the magic-born, Leo's a day-runner for Geoffrey.

Peyton MoonRunner: Half-werepuma, half–magic-born, she's Anadey's daughter.

Rhiannon Roland: Cicely's cousin, born on the same day as Cicely, only at daybreak, a daughter of the Sun/Waxing

Year. Rhiannon is also one of the magic-born, who controls the power of fire.

THE COURT OF RIVERS & RUSHES

Chatter: One of the Summer Court. Grieve's best friend. Has a crush on Rhiannon.

Grieve (see Indigo Court): Prince of the Court of Rivers and Rushes, one of the Cambyra Fae (shapeshifting Fae) now turned Vampiric Fae. Obsessed with and in love with Cicely.

Lainule: The Fae Queen of Rivers and Rushes, Grieve's aunt, the Queen of Summer.

Wrath: Cicely's father—one of the Uwilahsidhe (the Owl people of the Cambyra Fae).

THE INDIGO COURT

Myst: Queen of the Indigo Court, mother of the Vampiric Fae, the Mistress of Mayhem. Queen of Winter.

Grieve (see The Court of Rivers and Rushes)

Heather (see Cicely and the Court of the Magic-Born)

THE VEIN LORDS/TRUE VAMPIRES

Crawl: The Blood Oracle. One of the oldest Vein Lords, made by the Crimson Queen herself. Sire to Regina and Lannan.

Geoffrey: NW Regent of the Vampire Nation and one of the Elder Vein Lords. Two thousand years old, from Xiongnu.

Lannan Altos: Professor at the New Forest Conservatory, Elder vampire, brother and lover to Regina Altos, hedonistic golden boy.

Regina Altos: Emissary for the Crimson Court/Queen. Originally from Sumer with her brother and lover, Lannan. Was a priestess of Inanna. Turned by Crawl.

Playlist for *Night Veil*

I write to music a good share of the time and have been sharing my playlists on my website. I finally decided to add them to the backs of the books for my readers who aren't online.

—Yasmine Galenorn

Air:
"Napalm Love"
"Mike Mills"
"Surfing on a Rocket"
"Clouds Up"
"Playground Love"
Audioslave:
"Set It Off"
Beck:
"Scarecrow"
"Black Tambourine"
"Nausea"
Black Label Society:
"Rust"

Black Rebel Motorcycle Club:
    "Shuffle Your Feet"
    "Fault Line"
Blue Oyster Cult:
    "Godzilla"
Cake:
    "The Distance"
Cat Power:
    "I Don't Blame You"
    "Werewolf"
CC Adcock:
    "Bleed 2 Feed"
Chester Bennington:
    "System"
Chris Isaak:
    "Wicked Game"
Cobra Verde:
    "Play with Fire"
David Bowie:
    "Unwashed and Somewhat Slightly Dazed"
    "Sister Midnight"
    "Fame"
    "Without You"
Death Cab for Cutie:
    "I Will Possess Your Heart"
Depeche Mode:
    "Dream On"
    "Route 66"
Eddy Grant:
    "Electric Avenue"
Evans Blue:
    "Cold"
Faun:
    "Satyros"
    "Königin"
    "Rad"
    "Sieben"
    "Tinta"

Gary Numan:
   "Survival"
   "Noise, Noise"
   "Call Out the Dogs"
   "Dead Heaven"
   "Sleep By Windows"
   "Melt"
   "Hybrid"
   "Pure"
   "Cars (Hybrid Mix)"
   "Soul Protection"
Godsmack:
   "Voodoo"
Gorillaz:
   "Clint Eastwood"
Hives:
   "Tick Tick Boom"
Jace Everett:
   "Bad Things"
Jay Gordon:
   "Slept So Long"
King Black Acid:
   "Rolling Under"
   "Great Spaces"
Lady Gaga:
   "Paparazzi"
   "Poker Face"
Ladytron:
   "Mu-Tron"
   "Destroy Everything You Touch"
   "Ghosts"
   "Black Cat"
   "I'm Not Scared"
Lindstrom and Christabelle:
   "Lovesick"
Low:
   "Half Light"

Marilyn Manson:
    "Arma-Goddamn-Motherfuckin-Geddon"
    "Tainted Love"
    "Godeatgod"
Metallica:
    "Enter Sandman"
Nine Inch Nails:
    "Sin"
    "Get Down, Make Love"
    "Closer"
Nirvana:
    "You Know You're Right"
    "Come As You Are"
Oingo Boingo:
    "Elevator Man"
Orgy:
    "Blue Monday"
The Police:
    "King of Pain"
    "Don't Stand So Close to Me"
Puddle of Mudd:
    "Psycho"
Ricky Martin:
    "She Bangs"
Rob Zombie:
    "Living Dead Girl"
    "American Witch"
    "Never Gonna Stop"
Roison Murphy:
    "Ramalama Bang Bang"
Rolling Stones:
    "Gimme Shelter"
Saliva:
    "Ladies and Gentlemen"
Sarah McLachlan:
    "Possession"
Seether:
    "Remedy"

Shiny Toy Guns:
   "Major Tom"
Shriekback:
   "New Man"
   "Dust and a Shadow"
Simple Minds:
   "Don't You (Forget About Me)"
Soundgarden:
   "Spoonman"
Stealers Wheel:
   "Stuck in the Middle with You"
Susan Enan:
   "Bring on the Wonder"
Talking Heads:
   "Psycho Killer"
Tears for Fears:
   "Mad World"
Thompson Twins:
   "Love on Your Side"
   "The Gap"
Tina Turner:
   "One of the Living"
Toadies:
   "Possum Kingdom"
Tool:
   "Prison Sex"
Transplants:
   "Diamonds and Guns"
Warchild:
   "Ash"
Yoko Kanno:
   "Lithium Flower"
Zero Seven:
   "In the Waiting Line"

Dear Reader:

I hope that you enjoyed *Night Veil,* the second book in the Indigo Court series, and I hope you're looking forward to reading *Night Seeker,* the third book in the series, available summer 2012.

For those of you new to my books, I wanted to take this opportunity to welcome you into my worlds. For those of you who've been reading my books for a while, I wanted to thank you for revisiting Cicely's world. I loved writing *Night Veil,* and as I go deeper into the series, I hope you'll begin to see the scope of the Indigo Court world and the storylines that are evolving.

But don't fear—I am not done with the D'Artigo sisters and the Otherworld series (aka Sisters of the Moon)—and I want to assure my longtime readers that, yes, there are more books coming in that series. That's why we're including the first chapter of *Courting Darkness*—book ten of the Otherworld series—in the back of this book.

If you're a new reader, you'll get a taste of what my trio of half-Fae, half-human demon-hunting sisters are like. And if you've been reading the Otherworld series for a while, I wanted to give you a sneak peek at what lies in store for Camille. *Courting Darkness* will be available in November 2011.

So, without taking more of your time, I'd like to present the beginning of *Courting Darkness,* and I hope it whets your appetite for the next book!

Bright Blessings,
Yasmine Galenorn

Following is a special excerpt from

COURTING DARKNESS

the next book in the Otherworld series
by Yasmine Galenorn

Coming November 2011!

Home.

There it was—waiting for us. Home, with smoke drifting from the chimney, and clear sparkling lights surrounding the porch. From the driveway, the three-story Victorian shimmered like a beacon, both in the physical and in the astral realms. Flares of energy shot up like sunspots. I leaned back in the car, smiling. Our home, our haven against the demons.

A dragon built from snow guarded the lawn and driveway, rising stark and white out of the banks piled high around the yard. My herb garden hid under the creature, nestled under mulch until spring. Winter had claimed the land, full force, and we were getting hit hard. La Niña held sway and we were all her toys. At least it wasn't Loki this time. The Norse giant had brought the ice and snow with him a year back, until we'd dispatched his servant.

But as cold as it was, this was nothing compared to the Northlands, from where I'd just returned. There, in the high reaches, the winds had raged starkly through the winter woodland, shaking the timbers and sending avalanches down the mountainsides. There, life was harsh and often short, and fire a lifeline. As Smoky, Iris, Rozurial and I'd struggled through the woods, ranging higher and higher toward the lair of Howl, the Elemental Wolf Lord of the snow, more than once I'd thought we'd end up as Popsicles, frozen to the rocks.

But the trip had been worth it. We'd helped Iris come to terms with her past and forge a future for herself. Now, she stood clear and free, able to marry the man she loved. But she'd been through hell, and now she, like I, faced a future that promised to swallow her up, to force her into a position she wasn't sure she was ready to shoulder.

As the car slowed to a stop and Delilah turned off the engine, the weariness of the past few months welled up in my throat and I blinked away tears. So much had happened, and yet, so much still lay before us. We were a week from midwinter, and I was facing initiation into Aeval's Court, where I would willingly hand myself over to the Dark Queen.

As I let out a long breath and climbed out of the Jeep, a crisp wind swept through the night and I pulled the elfin cloak tighter around me. I was wearing the cloak of the Black Beast beneath that, but even with both, they couldn't fend off the chill that had lodged itself in my bones and I wondered if I'd ever manage to get warm again.

"You okay?" Delilah wrapped her arm around my shoulders. She'd picked us up at Grandmother Coyote's portal and now all I wanted was a hot bath, a soft bed, and a lot of sleep. As Smoky hopped out of her Jeep, then helped Iris to the ground, Roz slowly hoisted himself out the other side.

"You're a good sister," I said, leaning against her arm. "I'm just tired. The journey was harder than I thought it would be. And cold—so cold."

"How'd it go? Did Iris . . ."

I just shook my head. "It's her place to speak or not, as she will. She's with us, and Vikkommin is dead for good. She survived. But the Northlands are terrifying. I'd hate to be caught up there."

We headed toward the house just as Menolly came racing

out, the beads in her braids clicking in the chill night. She was carrying my purse.

"Finally! I've been waiting at the door for you. I just got a call from Derrick. We've got problems. Turn right around and head for the cars. Sorry to do this to you, Camille, but you need to be there."

"What's going on?" My heart sank. I was tired. I didn't want to fight goblins or ghosts.

"Demon in the bar, demanding to talk to you. He's already mowed down an elf and Derrick's got him in a standoff. Iris, you, Roz, and Vanzir stay with Morio and Maggie. Shade and Trillian are on their way out—there they are!"

Shade, Delilah's new love, and Trillian—my alpha husband—rushed out of the house and clambered down the steps. Shade was part dragon, part Stradolan—a shadow walker, and Trillian was Svartan—one of the dark and charming Fae. They both wore jeans and heavy jackets and Trillian was carrying a serrated edged sword he'd recently taken up training with.

"Demon? Asking for *me*? How delightful. *Not*." I didn't bother asking if they knew why he wanted me. I'd find out soon enough, and probably—knowing my luck—I'd find out the hard way.

Menolly whipped around, barking out orders. "Delilah—you and Shade take your Jeep." She tossed me my purse and keys. "Camille, here you go. You drive Smoky and Trillian. I'll go in alone."

And once again, we moved to our respective cars, off and running. There was no down time anymore. Everything had taken on immediacy. With that thought, I put the Lexus in gear and—as Smoky and Trillian jumped in—hit the gas and plowed out of the driveway.

✴

We pulled into a parking place that miraculously opened up as we neared the Wayfarer Bar & Grill. With a quick nod to the parking goddess, I forced myself out of the driver's seat. In the midst of the holiday season, a space along

Seattle's city streets was insanely hard to find. But I had luck with finding open spots, and embraced it. Hell, considering the rest of my track record when it came to serendipity, the smallest good fortune was cause for celebration.

As Trillian opened the door for me, I paused to give him a long kiss. "I missed you," I whispered. "I missed you a lot."

"Tonight, we'll see about wiping away those longings." He brushed my hair back from my face. "I never spend an hour without thinking about you."

Smoky grunted. "Come. We have a fight to take care of. I assure you, I took pains to make sure she didn't miss you or the fox too terribly." He arched his eyebrows in a knowing way and two tendrils of his hair rose to wrap themselves around my shoulders.

I bit back a retort. My three husbands were constantly zinging each other, each one striving for the top place in my heart, but I knew that, beneath all the bluster and insults, they'd developed a healthy respect for one another. None of them would ever admit it, but I suspected they even liked each other—at least a little. On more than one occasion I'd caught Smoky and Trillian playing chess, or Morio helping Smoky carry in firewood without being asked.

✦

The bar looked lively but I could hear the commotion from outside. We trailed behind Menolly as she slammed her way into the bar. She owned the Wayfarer Bar & Grill, and it was a hangout for Supes from all backgrounds, as well as the first stop on the journey for a number of Otherworld visitors. And now, the Wayfarer also sported seven rooms, a makeshift bed and breakfast.

As we hit the polished wood floors, I skidded to a halt, catching my breath. The bar patrons were crowded against the back wall, huddled together, terrified. Some were trying to edge toward a side exit, but for the most part, they stuck together in a little clump, afraid to move.

At the front of the bar, a demon watched them, his head bobbing back and forth like a snake. There was no passing for any generic Supe with this creature. He looked like the full-fledged demon of nightmares—with smoky skin and coiled horns rising high over his head. His skin, leathery and taut, shimmered across muscle hard enough to beat a sledgehammer against. He towered seven feet high on cloven hooves, and his hands bore long, razor-sharp nails.

And he was standing over one very dead body.

Derrick, the werebadger bartender, had wedged himself between the patrons and the demon, a sawed-off shotgun aimed at the creature, but the gun had a better chance of tickling the hell spawn than it did of hurting him.

Menolly let out a long sigh. "Yeah, that's one dead elf."

I nodded. "And one freaky-assed demon."

We were too late to help the elf, but with a little luck, we might be able to prevent wholesale carnage. We spread out, motioning for Derrick to move to one side. He waited for Menolly's okay, then nodded and stepped out of the way. As I turned toward the demon, I was clueless as to what we were dealing with—Vanzir could have told us, but it wasn't fully safe to have him and Smoky in the same room just yet. Smoky still didn't know what had happened between us, and I intended to keep it that way, at least until I could ensure he wouldn't go wholesale whoop-ass on Vanzir.

Menolly snarled. "What the fuck are you doing in my bar? Get your ass back to the Sub-Realms, and tell Shadow Wing we said hello." She strode forward, but the demon raised his head and his gaze caught her full on. She let out a squeak and dropped to the floor.

I rushed over to help her, but before I could get there, she sat up and shook her head, looking stunned. "What the hell . . ."

Damn, this was not the time for Morio to be laid up. Our death magic was far more powerful than my moon magic. Or at least, it tended not to backfire *so much*. But he still had a long ways to go before he was healed, and would be out of commission for quite some time. The hungry ghosts from our last skirmish had siphoned a dangerous amount of life force from him and left him bedridden for now.

"Stand your ground." The creature spoke. "I bring you a message from Trytian."

Trytian? Holy crap, this thing wasn't a demon—it was a *daemon*! No wonder we hadn't been able to tell what it was.

"What does he want?" I didn't trust Trytian. Not only was he a daemon, but he'd tried to blow us up when we were fighting the Bonecrusher. That didn't make for neighborly feelings, even if he was fighting against the same Demon Lord as we were.

"You are the one named Camille?"

I nodded.

"I speak with you. Alone."

Alone? No way in freaking hell was I cozying up with this creature alone.

"Um. Can I just say, *no*? Whatever you have to say, you can say it in front of the others." I backed up, motioning for Delilah to move. If he could knock a vampire off her feet with just a look, I didn't want to see what he could do with those claws and muscles against someone who was still alive.

"You wish me to speak freely in front of all of these patrons? You really want them to know about Shadow—"

"Stop!" I glanced back at Menolly. We couldn't let him talk about Shadow Wing. No one in the general public knew that Earth was on the verge of a demonic war. *Yet.* And we were inclined to keep it that way to stave off panic.

"You can't be serious. He's already killed one person." Menolly pointed toward the dead elf. We'd have hell explaining his death to Queen Asteria. She'd believe us, but she sure wouldn't be happy.

"I have to." I lowered my voice so nobody but the nearest Supes could hear me. "We can't have anything come out in public."

Smoky glowered. "Not *my* wife. Not alone with *you*. One other must join you and I claim the right."

The daemon looked at him and sniffed. "Dragon. Silver dragon—and a *mix* at that. The world is full of half-breeds tonight, it seems. Two halves of a dragon, a dragon-shadow mix. Three human and Fae girls. Interbreeding weakens the strains, you know. But you, dragon, you are a lord among your kind. I do not play toad to royalty. There are reasons you will not be present, my own skin being one of them." His voice was harsh, like the vocal cords had been burnt long ago, and he kept moving his head in a sinuous dance, as if he couldn't keep it still.

"Then my wife does not attend you."

"Actually, your wife will attend him." I glanced at Smoky. "I have to—we *can't* discuss these matters in public." Turning back to the daemon, I added, "We'll have our chat alone, but in a place of my choice."

It occurred to me that if we went to the safe room in the basement of the Wayfarer, the daemon wouldn't be able to (a) teleport out with me, (b) shoot magic at me, or (c) bathe me in fire. He could still break me in half; but if he'd wanted to do that, he already would have.

I pointed toward the floor. "Menolly, we need to use the room *downstairs.*"

She frowned, then her eyes lit up. "Oh, *that* room. All right. Come, follow me. Don't hurt anybody and don't destroy anything, either of you. Daemon, I hold you on pain of death that you won't hurt my sister."

The daemon grunted, looking suspicious, but followed Menolly, shaking the floor with each meaty step. I swung in behind. Smoky, Trillian, and Shade followed, leaving Delilah and the staff to take care of the dead elf and the frightened patrons.

Downstairs, we came to the safe room. No magic could enter here, nor creature teleport in or out. All natural abilities were muted. If a nuclear blast hit this bar, the safe room would stand.

I gazed at the door, swallowing my fear. Being shut in a room with the daemon—alone—was a daunting thought. Not so much fun. Not so much safe. But we didn't dare let him broadcast everything he knew.

None of the FBHs—the full-blooded humans—were aware that the demonic army led by Shadow Wing was trying to break through the portals to take over Earth and

Otherworld. Only a handful of our friends knew we were on the trail of the spirit seals, the pieces of a broken artifact that, alone, could seal off the Subterranean Realms from the rest of the worlds. We had to gather as many of them as we could before Shadow Wing did. Not such good news to have flying around as common knowledge.

As it was, we were in for a lot of damage control just from the daemon's appearance in the bar.

I motioned for him to enter the room and, with a scowl, he ducked his head so that his horns cleared the archway. As I followed behind him, Menolly touched me on the arm.

"One peep and we're coming in. Don't get near him. He can't work his magic but he could tear you apart."

"I know. Believe me, I know." And, reluctantly, I shut the door and turned to face the daemon, crossing my arms. The best defense was to show no fear. "Trytian has a message for me? Deliver it and then scram, hell spawn." I didn't bother asking for his name—chances were he wouldn't give it to me.

The daemon looked around. "A no-magic zone. Not stupid—not so stupid as some." A dark grimace crossed his face. "I would relish a fight with you, girl. And your friends. But this is not my battle to wage."

I decided to let that one pass. No need to press my luck. Letting out a long sigh, I asked, "What do you want? Why did you kill the elf upstairs?"

"He sought to interfere with me. He had to be eliminated." He said it nonchalantly. A given: *Dare to interfere with the daemon? Poof—you die.*

"Again, I ask: What do you want?"

"I bear a warning from Trytian."

Trytian was, like we were, attempting to stop the demon lord Shadow Wing, only he was going about it in a totally different manner. Unfortunately, since he *was* a daemon, he had no compunction about killing us if we happened to get in the way. And he was rude. Very rude. This warning—whatever it was—meant that he either anticipated needing our help, or he had suddenly sprouted wings and become a cute little cherub. And I sincerely doubted the latter.

"Okay, I'm listening. What is so important that Trytian sent you over here to stir the pot? And why you—why not someone who can pass out on the streets?"

I leaned against the small bistro table that was pushed against one wall. The room had signs of occupation—Erin, the daughter Menolly had sired into the vampiric life, was staying down here during the day, sleeping in safety. The bed was piled high with comfy blankets, there were cards and books on the table, and an empty bottle that had held blood.

"I was the only one available to send at the moment. Here is Trytian's message." He handed me a letter. "You will understand why I did not want to be alone with your husband when you read it."

Oh hell. Something to do with Smoky.

Gingerly, I took the paper and opened it. The writing was tight, neat, and precisely printed in red ink—at least I *hoped* it was ink, considering the color. As I began to read, I started to sink toward the floor, but one grunt from the daemon and I straightened back up again. No dropping my guard, not with a big, bad daemon in the room. Trytian had no scruples, and I didn't expect his cohorts to have any, either.

I glanced up at the creature. "Wait here, please." Before he could say a word, I slipped out of the room and slammed the door, locking it behind me. He could hammer all he wanted on it, he was locked in there till we let him out.

"What's going on? Are you all right?" Smoky leaned over me, and I could tell he was looking for signs the daemon had laid hands on me.

"I'm fine . . . at least physically. He gave me a letter from Trytian. If it's true, then you and I are fucked. Just plain and simple."

"Read it." Shade was staring at me, concern creasing his face.

I cleared my throat and held up the paper.

Rumors are running rife through the grapevine, but I assure you, this is no rumor. A white dragon was recently seen in the halls of the Demon Underground, hanging out with a snow monkey. He is not welcome there but no one dares tell a dragon to leave.

Camille: Scuttlebutt is that he'll be marching in your direction soon. He's made it known that you and your husband are on his shit list. And frankly, though you and I disagree on the method, all allies against Shadow Wing are valuable at this point, and I may need to call on your aid at some point. So be cautious and don't get yourself killed.

~Trytian

I let out a long breath. Hyto was in the area. Which meant death was sure to follow. And dying by dragon was so not my idea of fun.

Smoky's face drained of what color it had and his eyes began to swirl. Very softly, very slowly, he spoke. "My father has just signed his death warrant."

"Crap." Menolly leaned against the wall. "He's here, in Seattle, hanging out with demons and daemons? Not the news we needed right now."

I fingered the paper. "What's a snow monkey? Why would he have an ape with him?"

"Trytian's not talking about an animal," Shade said. "A snow monkey is slang for a powerful monk from one of the upper monasteries in the Northlands. Usually, snow monkeys are rogues—having been kicked out of their order. They're most often mad as a hornet, and they don't give a damn about anybody but themselves. If one's taken up with your father, Smoky, then he's bound to have been offered a great reward. They're dangerous." He gave me a sad smile. "I'd start watching my back if I were you."

"Like we don't already." Sighing, I leaned against the wall, letting them talk around me.

Mad monks were bad enough, but it was the thought of

Hyto being so close—the thought of him actually being in the city—that made me want to run home to Otherworld and hide. But I couldn't do that, either, having been exiled from Y'Elestrial by my father.

Smoky's father hated me. He hated my breath, my life, my existence. He had nothing to lose, he'd been cast out of the Dragon Reaches, denied by his wife, disowned by his children. And he blamed it all on *me*.

My cell phone rang and I flipped it open. Caller ID told me it was Chase Johnson. I punched Talk and answered.

"Camille—I was hoping you were back. I need you down here. We've got a problem in Tangleroot Park, and I am pretty sure it's magical in nature. In fact, so magical that I almost pissed my pants when I saw it. I've got my guys blocking it off for now, but I'm scared to try anything before you come have a look-see."

"*It?* What are you talking about? A monster or something?"

"I don't think so. Honestly? I'll bet you my paycheck it's a portal of some sort."

My blood ran cold. Hyto was my big worry right now, but he wasn't standing here in front of me. If Chase was right and there was a portal opening up in Tangleroot Park, we could be in for big trouble of a different sort. Because the random portals that had started showing themselves around the city were rogue, and could lead anywhere.

"We'll get our asses over there right now. Meanwhile, don't let anybody touch it or go near it." As I shut my phone, it occurred to me that my life was quickly coming to resemble a roller coaster, and right now, we felt at the peak, ready to take a long, dark ride down the tracks.

YASMINE GALENORN

Harvest Hunting

The D'Artigo sisters are sexy supernatural opera-
tives for the Otherworld Intelligence Agency. It's
Samhain, and the Autumn Lord calls Delilah to
begin her training with the Death Maidens. . . .
And she finds that she likes it. But the sisters have
problems: Werewolves are going missing and a new
magical drug, Wolf Briar, is being used as a weapon.
But most dangerous of all: Stacia Bonecrusher has
put a bounty on their heads. Now it's a race to take
out the demon general before she realizes the sixth
spirit seal is within her reach. . . .

Don't miss the new series from
New York Times bestselling author
YASMINE GALENORN

NIGHT MYST
An Indigo Court Novel

Eons ago, vampires tried to turn the Dark Fae in order to harness their magic, only to create a demonic enemy more powerful than they imagined. Now Myst, the queen of the Indigo Court, has enough power to begin a long-prophesied supernatural war.

Cicely Waters, a witch who can control the wind, may be the only one who can stop her—and save her beloved Fae prince from the queen's enslavement.

M714T0510

Don't miss a word from the "erotic and darkly
bewitching"* series featuring the D'Artigo sisters,
half-human, half-Fae supernatural agents.

By *New York Times* Bestselling Author

Yasmine Galenorn

WITCHLING

CHANGELING

DARKLING

DRAGON WYTCH

NIGHT HUNTRESS

DEMON MISTRESS

BONE MAGIC

HARVEST HUNTING

BLOOD WYNE

Praise for the Otherworld series:

"Pure delight."
—MaryJanice Davidson, *New York Times*
bestselling author

"Vivid, sexy, and mesmerizing."
—*Romantic Times*

penguin.com/projectparanormal

*Jeaniene Frost, *New York Times* bestselling author